A SLEIGH RIDE IN JULY

by
Margaret Tedford

Copyright © 2001 by Margaret Tedford
All rights reserved including the right of reproduction in whole or in part in any form
Published by **Mandrill** a division of Trident Media Company
801 N Pitt Street, Suite 123
Alexandria, VA 22314 USA

www.edenplaza.com

This work is purely fictional. Any similarity or correlation to persons living or dead, or to incidents described within is entirely coincidental.

Dedication

*This book is dedicated to my mother,
Vern Tedford*

-One-

Few people would attempt to understand why a fifty-nine year old woman by the name of Joan Enright Adelman would want to end her life. Fewer still would condone it. But most of all, they couldn't tolerate the anger that darted from her eyes and seeped through every pore of her body upon finding herself still alive and very much an unwanted burden in an understaffed and buzzing general emergency department.

While Joan was still unconscious, nurses and orderlies converged on her when she arrived via Urgences-sante, compliments of the City of Montreal. One nurse was putting down a nasogastic tube while another inserted an intravenous line. The lavaging process was started and that took time. Then the charcoal had to be given and repeated. It was a messy, tiresome procedure and when the patient gradually regained consciousness, it was a battle every inch of the way. Only this time the patient's first coherent words were, "I'm sorry it failed. I want to be dead."

The nurse who took the account from the ambulance driver passed it on to one of the doctors in E.R. and urged him to see the woman and clear her medically.

"How's she doing now?" the doctor asked. He wasn't too concerned. She had been breathing on her own when she arrived and her pressure was holding. At the moment he was busy with another patient who had come in with renal colic and was writhing in pain that was escalating by the minute.

"If you clear her medically, we can call psychiatry and get her out of here." Karen tilted her head and stepped closer to him. "We're running out of space."

"I know." Dr. Peter Simmons sighed. "Have they got a bed in

their emergency unit?"

"Yeah, just one. We're in luck."

"All right, I'll see her."

"Good." Karen nodded and handed him the progress notes. "Her vitals are fine. She's alert, fully oriented and madder than hell."

Peter groaned. "Will she cooperate?"

"Probably not. But she won't slug you either. Her husband's over there outside cubicle two. He looks worried."

"We'll call the psychiatry resident. Who is it anyway?"

"Pat Gainer."

"Fine. Let her handle it. I'll clear the woman medically." He started to walk away with the notes and chart in hand. Then he turned back. "Oh, and give this one fifty of Demerol and twenty-five of Gravol I.M." Karen nodded again. It was only 9:30. She had two more hours to go.

Dr. Simmons spent less than five minutes with the patient. Her long medical history was well documented, and since she wouldn't speak to him, but only glared at him with unblinking rage, he gave her a cursory examination and passed her on. Dr. Gainer got more details, not from the patient, but from her anxiously waiting husband.

When the call came through to Britt Erikson in the emergency psychiatry unit, her sole reply had been, "all right, but send her now."

"Well, we're busy right now."

"So are we." Britt shot back. "Never mind. Where have you got her?"

"The crash room and she obviously can't stay there."

"Obviously. Is she cleared?"

"Yes. Dr. Gainer's just finishing the psych consult and writing up some medication orders."

"I'll send our orderly over." Britt put down the receiver and turned to Bernard.

"Would you go over?"

"On my way, but that's the third this evening."

"I know," Britt smiled at him. "Two transfers and three admissions, but look on the bright side. It's our last bed. Now they'll just have to use the hallway."

Ten minutes later, Bernard dropped the chart and emergency notes and consults on her desk and went off to settle the patient in the last cubicle.

Britt glanced at the medical clearance and thumbed through the lengthy chart that had increased in size over the years. Then she carefully read the psychiatric consult. Twice she stopped and gazed straight ahead. The lights were dim in the dingy, tightly boxed-in unit and the tiny office area was equally subdued.

She had given out the ten o'clock medications, and now at nearly ten-thirty, there were no patients out in the tiny common room. Bernard was reading the newspaper. She bent her head once more and read the last few paragraphs. When she looked up again, a man was standing in the doorway to the office and looking over at her worriedly.

"You must be Mr. Adelman."

The elderly man inclined his head. "Yes, I'm Sam Adelman. Joan's my wife."

"Sit down Mr. Adelman." Britt waved him to a chair and stared back down at the consult. She had read many assessments, the histories of hundreds of patients, but for some reason this woman's story struck a resounding chord in her. It brought to mind that ballad about Molly Malone – the scummy streets of Dublin and the ghost of that woman wheeling the wheelbarrow. She shook her head and the image disintegrated, but the soft sad lilting of the melody remained in her mind. Then she glanced down at the medication orders and pursed her lips. "Do you think she'll take some medication, Mr. Adelman?"

"I don't know." The older man struggled out the words. "She's past caring, but I don't want to lose her."

Bernard appeared in the doorway again, and he'd heard the end of this exchange. "She's wide awake, not settling at all, Britt, and she's one mad lady--not violent, just mad...madder than anything, anyone, I've ever seen. It's not scary, but I'd just like to keep away from her, far away."

Bernard had a rather laid-back, lackadaisical manner of speaking and acting. He came from the Caribbean where the sun shined daily and there was always tomorrow.

Britt tried to suppress a smile, but it was an abortive attempt. Bernard grimaced.

"Nothing bothers you, Britt." He stepped closer to Mr. Adelman and mumbled while he watched her get the keys and go to the medicine cupboard. "It's true, mister. [And your wife nearly made it.] I know. I collected her from over there in the general E.R. and they were all annoyed with her."

Britt turned back with the medication in a small paper cup. She frowned at the easy-going orderly. "That crew is always bothered, Bernard. And sometimes I think if some of them survive through another shift, humanity will have been done a disservice. Besides, this woman has good reason to be angry. I'd be angry too. What the hell?" She shrugged, "I'm jaded already and nothing nearly so bad has happened to me." She clapped Bernard on the shoulder as she passed him on the way to Joan's cubicle. "You keep Mr. Adelman company until I get back."

On her way down the short corridor, Britt's thoughts clamped down on the life of Joan Enright Adelman as outlined in the one page consult. Joan was the only child of a Frank and Nellie Enright. They had a small stall at the Atwater market and sold fish. They were fishmongers and lived in a cold water flat on Grand Trunk Street in Pointe St. Charles. And they were poor. Joan helped out in the market stall after school and on Saturdays. When her mother died, she was fifteen, and there hadn't been much point in returning to school. She had missed most of the previous year taking care of her mother before she finally succumbed to cancer. She went to work with her father, and when he died several years later, she took over the stall selling fresh fish on her own. That's how she made a living, working ten hours a day six days a week. It was bearable, but difficult for a young woman and apparently no young man came along to expand her horizons. In fact, no one came along at all. It would be hard to know if handling the cold wet fish kept in ice set off the rheumatoid arthritis or just exacerbated it. In any case, since her late twenties, she had been under treatment and it had only become worse and the pain unmanageable. And then along came Sam Adelman who fell in love with her and married her. But by this time, she was forty-nine, long past her childbearing years. They had each other. Just that. Now this. Odd, Britt thought, a gentle and kind looking Jewish man in his mid-sixties and a worn-out Gentile woman with little to show for nearly half a century of living except a curious endurance and independence, a marriage, and the detour their lives took through friendship, warmth and belonging. But now that too was being threatened--so late in life found and prematurely ended. What did this woman look like? Britt wondered. She had only caught a glimpse of her being taken to her cubicle. The overhead light was on in the small curtained space and, drawing it aside, she found the small white haired woman sitting bolt upright in the bed and staring at her. Her eyes were round and blue and penetrating as she watched the nurse approach her. Britt put the medication on the side table just inside the curtained doorway and came toward the bed. She didn't say a word. Joan Adelman stared at her until she was right beside her and she would have had to turn her head. So she glared straight ahead at the sickly yellow wall and gaping mouth of the entrance. It was so silent in the closed-in space. So quiet and, yes, there was anger in the woman who looked to be seventy, and not fifty-nine. But it was a clean and unembittered anger. There was no hate and no contempt, nothing ugly about it at all. There was no nastiness or mean-mindedness in this woman. And there was no self pity. That was refreshing. Without realizing it, she was looking down at the old woman with the small finely featured face and sparse body and a soft look had come into her own yes. Unexpectedly, she found herself putting an arm around the woman's shoulders and mumbling, "a little I'm hurt, but not yet slain. I'll but lie down and bleed awhile, and then I'll rise and fight again."

What a dumb thing to say to her, Britt thought and wondered why the lines were just waiting to be spoken. They had simply come to her unbidden and they hung in the air. But now the woman was twisting her head around and staring up at her, still enraged and now also leery. But she was curious too and maybe even a little fearful as if someone had seen what lurked at the back of her thoughts that she'd kept well hidden and in the dark, even from herself.

Britt waited, returning her stare, and didn't remove her arm.

"You're very tired, Joan, but I don't think you'll be able to sleep." She reached back with her free arm and took the pills from the bedside table and held them out to her. "Will you take this medication? It'll help you sleep." When the woman continued staring at her, Britt moved the small cup closer. "Please, Joan. It's just a mild sedative and it will help."

Surprisingly, Joan's hand came out and Britt handed her the medication cup which she looked down at. She seemed to be wavering.

"Please. You do need it and must have it. It won't hurt you. Take it . . . please."

Joan took the pills and Britt handed her a glass of water which she sipped at, then gave it back to her.

"Now, lie back."

Joan lay back on the pillows, and Britt drew the covers up around her. She still hadn't uttered one word. She continued staring up at the ceiling, her body rigidly tense and remaining like that. The nurse turned and left the cubicle, hoping the medication would help relax her and she'd be able to sleep.

Mr. Adelman was still waiting when she got back to the office. He looked up as she entered. "Did she take it?" he asked.

Britt nodded. "Yes. Let's hope it works."

Bernard was getting ready to leave, and he put his head in the doorway. "I'm going, Britt. Nelson's here."

Britt looked out and sure enough there was Nelson, all six feet, four inches of him. He waved and she waved back.

"See you tomorrow, Bernard." She turned to Sam Adelman. "Your wife's had a hard time."

"Yes, she has."

"Was she still working at the market when you met her, handling the fish and all that?"

"Yes, did you notice her hands?"

"I noticed."

"After we got married she could have stopped all that. I wanted her to. There was no need. I haven't much, but a little, and I have my pension. You see, I've been married twice before. They died. But Joan had never had a man in her life. I was the first. Odd, isn't it?"

"Yes. Too bad you didn't meet earlier." Britt was watching him carefully. "But you had a few good years."

"Yes, we did. The arthritis started to settle down a bit. Then a couple of years ago it started up again. They've tried everything."

"Medication?"

"Yes, yes and the gold treatment and the hot wax treatment, or whatever, and nothing's worked. Sometimes she can't even get out of bed in the morning. It's so painful. And Joan's fought so long and so hard. So you see . . ."

"Yes, I see," Britt said and her voice was hardly audible. Sam Adelman had to lean closer to hear her. "So she's been feeling down lately?"

"Yes, a little depressed." He kept nodding. "But, it was all right until they told her about this other problem."

"What other problem?" The nurse looked down at the psych consult and then flipped over to her medical clearance. "I don't seen anything here . . . maybe in the old chart. I may not be up to date. They just keep adding things."

"They only just told her a week or so ago."

"What was it?"

"I don't know. Something about an ulcer or vari-something. Higher up."

"Esophageal Varices?"

"Yes, that might be it." He was pointing a finger at her. "Yes, maybe, but that just put her over the top."

"And she's never done anything like this before?"

"Overdose? My Joan?" He shook his head. "No, never. There's never been any trouble like that."

"No previous history of mental or emotional disturbances."

It was a statement more than a question, but Sam Adelman felt he had to drive home his point. "No, nothing at all. This isn't like Joan. She's never done anything like this before . . . never even thought about it. Will she be all right?" he asked abruptly.

"I think so. This time." Britt paused. "But she still wants to die, Mr. Adelman. She's highly suicidal, and it's true, I think, she's very angry."

"Yes, I know." He stood up. "I heard her and they told me. But her anger doesn't annoy you, does it?"

Britt twisted her pen thoughtfully for a few moments, then she looked up at him and slowly moved her head from side to side. "No, Mr. Adelman. It doesn't bother me. It's a good clean emotion . . .

anger, especially when there's reason for it. But you must know that most people find it very uncomfortable. It strikes head-on, you see. And they hate that, even when they're not the target. They think it's inappropriate."

"Inappropriate?" He mulled that over in his mind. "Well, flying off the handle at people is one thing, but this is different. Can I see her for a few minutes before I go?"

"Sure, I doubt if she's sleeping yet."

Britt got up and pointed down the short hallway. Then she came back inside the office and closed the door. She started to tape the evening report and didn't notice Adelman leaving. She gave a longer, more detailed profile on Joan.

-Two-

When she got home she showered and went to bed. By two in the morning, she was still unable to sleep, so, gathering up her pillow and a comforter, she went into the living room. Sometimes this worked, but it was early dawn before she finally fell into a heavy slumber full of dreams she couldn't remember upon awakening, and that was to the telephone jangling noisily.

She got up and stumbled across the room, collapsing into an armchair as she picked up the receiver.

"Hi, did I wake you?" It was Roderick. He sounded more cheerful than usual.

"No, Roddy. You didn't wake me."

"You worked last night, didn't you?"

He knew she worked last night. So why bother to ask? "Yes, I worked and again this evening. I'll be off the weekend."

"Well, maybe I could pick you up after work."

Britt hesitated. "All right."

"I'm having supper with Robert and his girlfriend. I was hoping you'd be able to come."

"Well, I can't."

"No, I guess not. Well, I'll wait for you outside the emergency, but if I'm not there, don't worry. I just wasn't able to make it."

"If you're not able to make it, call me at work. I'm not going to go hunting for your car if you're not going to be there."

"Okay, if I can't make it, I'll call. If you don't hear from me, I'll be there."

Britt put down the receiver and went into the kitchen to make some coffee. While it perked she went to wash her face and brush her teeth. Then she combed her hair. Someone was knocking at the door.

It was her mother. Mrs. Mary Erikson came into the kitchen and sat down.

"You're just getting up?"

Britt nodded. "It's difficult on shift work. It throws your sleeping pattern off."

"I know. I wish you could find something back in teaching."

"Well, there's nothing here in Montreal so why want what you can't have."

"No. There's nothing here in Montreal. Your father didn't want to come back here. I shouldn't have insisted."

Britt smiled. "What's he doing?"

"He's downstairs working on his carving. He takes it so seriously."

"Well, why shouldn't he? Actually he's pretty good at it. I like some of his work."

"But he hopes to strike it big in his own business with it. He's retired and spends more time doing this than he did teaching. Almost all day. Every day."

"Well, why should it upset you? You do look upset, Mother."

"It's all that machinery in our bedroom. I can't stand it anymore. It looks terrible!"

"Well, you need an extra room so he can have a sort of workshop space. There's no need to get so upset."

"We can't afford a higher rent right now. That's why we're here."

"In this apartment building?" Britt laughed. "That's why we're all here. Cheap rents and decent enough apartments."

"Yeah, but it is funny, isn't it?" Mary Erikson laughed with her.

"Nora is in Apartment five. You're in nine, and I'm in two. They're making a mint out of us. We rent and own nothing. All that money down the drain."

"Well, not exactly." Britt countered. "They're nice old apartments. High ceilings and hardwood floors. I don't know why people have to own their own places anyway."

"Oh, you're impossible. Always were. If you had any children you'd have to settle down." She stopped suddenly at the look on her daughter's face. "All right, never mind. But I doubt if Roderick can . . ."

"Mother, leave it . . . please."

Britt poured out some coffee and put the cups on the table. Then she went into the living room to get her cigarettes.

"Have you eaten yet?" Mary Erikson watched as she exhaled a cloud of smoke and sipped at her coffee.

"Not yet."

"That's why you're so thin. You don't eat enough. And it probably accounts for your headaches too."

"Doubtful and I eat plenty. Anyway, about this other matter . . . an extra room. Why don't you just take my apartment, and I'll take yours."

"Really? You wouldn't mind?"

"Not at all. I don't need the extra bedroom."

"Well, that would be perfect and your rent here is only slightly higher than mine."

"Good. That's what we'll do then." Britt grinned at her noticing that her mother's face had brightened considerably. "Now, Dad can have his workshop room, and you needn't look at all the ugly machinery in your bedroom."

"Yes, but it seems like all we do is move. I'll bet no other family has moved as much as we have."

"Oh well, we're descended from tinkers and Vikings. What did you expect?"

There was another knock at the door and finding it open her sister, Nora, came in with her daughter, two year old Ruth. The child made a run at Britt who scooped her up in her arms. "How's my girl!"

"Good. You got cookies?"

"If you can find one you can have it." She let the child go and looked up at her sister.

"Where's Aaron?"

"He's with Dad. Is that fresh coffee?"

"Yup. Help yourself. Oh, by the way, Mother's moving."

"Again!" Nora halted suddenly on her way to the kitchen counter and Mary looked at her.

"Yes, again."

"Where?"

"Right here," Britt put in. "We're switching apartments so Dad can have a workshop room."

"Oh, that's all right then." Nora went ahead and got her coffee. "I thought you meant out of Montreal."

"No, but that might happen yet." Britt twisted around to where her sister sat at the table. "Remember what I told you about answering the phone in English the other evening at the hospital?"

"About all the trouble afterwards?" Nora nodded and a look of disgust swept over her face. "Bloody idiots!"

"I could have lost my job, been fined, or worse!"

"They'll be satisfied when they've driven us all out."

Mary frowned. "Did you hear the news this morning?"

Both of her daughters looked at her.

"No, but it can't be good." Nora made a face. "It never is."

"The police shot some kid, a black boy, they'd already arrested for some petty thing. He wasn't armed, but he got scared and tried to run away."

"And they shot him?" Britt's forehead wrinkled, and she put her elbow on the table to hold her head up with one hand.

"Yes, in the back."

"Is he hurt badly?" Nora asked.

"He's dead."

"Damn them to hell." Britt looked over at her sister. "This is becoming a police state."

"As I see it . . . it already is. And racist, too." Nora added and then changed the subject.

"They won't take Aaron in school because he doesn't turn six until the end of October. So I'm going to call Greg tonight and see if I can get him in over in Toronto. Maybe I can start him in September and come back at Christmas. They'll have to take him then, won't they?"

Mary nodded slowly. "I suppose so. What do you think, Britt?"

"I think it might work."

Mary was wondering how Nora would get along living with her brother and his family, even for a short time. Nora's nature was anything but placid and her son was high-strung. There'd be fireworks. No doubt about that. Still it was a shame to hold the child back a whole year. He could already read and write. Britt was watching her niece. "Bring the box here, Ruth . . . I'll get one for you."

"Just one," Nora said. "I've got to go."

"Me too," Mary said and got up. "What are you going to do, Britt? Are you working again this evening?"

Britt nodded. "Yup. I think I'll go back to bed for an hour and take the phone out."

"Thanks a lot!" Nora snapped at her. "Why didn't you just say you wanted us to go?"

"I don't. But since you are leaving anyway, I thought I'd try to get a little more sleep."

"Well. I have to do some shopping." Nora was now beside her mother.

"Do you need anything?" she asked, and Britt shook her head.

Mary left with Nora and Ruth, and when they'd gone, Britt sat for a while thinking. Nora had a good heart. It was too bad she couldn't control her tongue. But she knew too, that she drove her sister crazy with her long and sometimes hostile silences. Still it beat yelling at people all the time, she concluded. It also scared them, just as that patient's silent rage did last evening. People, it seemed, got more annoyed at being frightened than anything else. They could stand screaming and shouting, but unvoiced anger really put them off.

She got up from the table and went back into the living room to stretch out on the chesterfield. With her eyes closed, images of Joan Enright Adelman flashed in her mind. I like that woman, she thought, and I understand her anger. Am I quietly enraged too? Is that it? But that seemed ridiculous because, in comparison, her life would appear charmed. Nobody ever really got what they wanted. So why should she? What do you really want right now? she asked herself. Never mind what's gone before. The failures and disappointments. But right now. That was easy to answer. . .a child. That's all. Never mind all the rest. Just a child. That's what she wanted most of all right now and had wanted for some time. The problem was that time was running out. And what about Roderick? It was hard to know just how she felt about Roddy. Did she love him? Probably not. Did he love her? She was almost sure he didn't. But he needed her to understand him and be there for him. He needed her loyalty and thoughtfulness. Her compassion. Not the best of foundations for a relationship. But Roddy was ill and had been most of his adult life. Any time now, he'd have to go back on dialysis. When one of the interns whom she had become friendly with at the hospital heard about it, she told her bluntly to give him up, that she didn't know what she was getting into, and there were lots of fish in the sea. She could remember Sylvia's exact words and the coolness in her voice which didn't match the concern in her face. "Let him go, Britt," she had said. "There can't be anything in it for you and you can't save him. Take my word for it. Get out of it. End it. It's an impossible situation." Then they had got on with the business of the day. But her words kept ringing in her ears.

The biggest problem, however, was not Roderick. No, the sad fact was that she didn't put much faith in relationships. She had seen too many fail--those that didn't seemed to have less to do with love, as contemporarily described or fabricated, as with commitment and making a life together. Companionship. As for herself, all she could truthfully say was that she had loved in that odd like of chemically successful way only twice and both times unwisely. Neither had been requited and had left her feeling sadly out of touch with the modern quality of reality. Love was not important. Playing the game was vitally necessary. Unfortunately she was a very poor player. On the other hand, she could have been married several times and to very respectable men. But she hadn't loved them. And to be painfully honest she didn't think they loved her either. But they had wanted her. And that was rather amusing because they didn't really know her, nor did they want to attempt to know her. All the same, she had always been respected and well treated, even admired. They just didn't seem to know what they desired. But most complex of all was that men liked her and she liked them. What's more, they trusted her. She was their confidante and counsel, and it was the same with women friends. Inadvertently, she just slipped into the role as one would an old worn-out pair of shoes, good for all kinds of weather. All in all, it wasn't such a bad way to be, and she wouldn't change things even if she could. It took a lot of years, starting in earliest childhood to build a persona, and she had been careful and demanding of herself in the process. The results were satisfactory, but what about the inner rage that might be building up within herself? Could she have identified it so unerringly in Joan Enright Adelman if there hadn't have been that resonance in herself. That was worth some deliberation.

As for having a child, well, it seemed that the harder she tried the more difficult it became. Even after almost a year of artificial insemination, there had been nothing. Perversely, her body, presumably directed by some intangible mechanism in the subconscious, rejected the idea and the repeated sporadic attempts were abortive. She became irregular and there had been no success. Twice she thought she might be pregnant, only to find weeks later that she needn't have bothered hoping.

So what now? She put her hands behind her head and stared up at the ceiling. She remained like that for so long that finally her eyelids began to droop, and she drifted into a light sleep. She was beginning to think that sleep was one of God's great concessions to man, as if He was patting that person on the back and saying "well done."

-Three-

Finding herself back in the same section of the Emergency Psychiatry Unit for the evening shift, Muriel raced out on the stroke of 3:30. The head nurse was just leaving too, and that left Virginia who was turning off the tape and swung around in her chair as Britt came in.

"That's a very angry lady," Virginia said mildly, looking up at her.

"You heard the tape?"

"Your report? Yes, I heard it. We all did."

"How was she this morning?"

"The same. She won't say anything."

Britt leaned against the doorway, frowning. "Did she sleep at all?"

"Hard to say for sure. Maybe." Virginia shrugged. "At least she was in bed all night. We transferred her over to the holding area."

"Oh."

"You're here with Helen."

"Who's over there?"

"Martha and Rolly . . . It's quiet. There's one free bed, and we're expecting a transfer from the General."

The head nurse came bustling back into the office. He swore profusely and then turned on Britt and Virginia. "Where's Helen?"

"She'll be here."

"Well damn," he stormed. "I'm in a real fix."

"What's the matter now?" Britt was taking off her raincoat. It was only early September, but there was a chill in the air. Autumn would be early this year.

"Can you two work tomorrow . . . days?"

Virginia groaned and looked at Britt. Neither said anything for a few minutes, but Tom Flynn could be very engaging when he wanted to be.

"Is that a yes?" he asked and smiled from one to the other.

"Can I leave early?"

"You do anyway, Britt, whenever possible. You all take turns, so why ask?"

"To avoid a shouting match, Tom."

"Don't start, Britt." He waved his hand holding the schedule. "So, you'll do it . . . ? Good, it would be better if you split up since you've both been on all week. Virginia, you'll stay here, and Britt you'll go to the other side tomorrow."

He left just as Helen was coming in, Virginia yawned and went for her coat behind the door.

"See you in the morning . . . Oh Britt," She turned back at the door. "Are you still taking those two weeks at the end of September?"

Britt nodded. "Yes, last week of September, first week of October."

"When are you going up to Labrador?"

"The second week. I think we'll move my parents the first week. It'll take one day."

"Where are they going?"

"Into my apartment."

"And you?" Virginia was frowning at her.

"Into theirs, of course. Where else?"

Helen burst out laughing. "Well, that's one way to get the spring cleaning done early . . . just move."

"I'll come over and help you." Virginia was shaking her head.

"Do you live near each other?" Helen was looking from one to the other.

"Across the street." Virginia told her. "But I pay almost double for my rent. The Erikson family has monopolized all the lower rent apartments and in a better building." She turned back to Britt. "Well, Nora's here to help too. Will your brother come down from Ottawa?"

"I'll call Rourke tomorrow evening and ask him."

Left alone in the office after Virginia went home, they got themselves some coffee and started the tape. Well so much for Roddy, Britt thought. If he didn't call she'd have to just send him home, and if he did, she needn't say anything at all.

Perhaps fortunately, Roddy called at nine that evening, and everyone was so busy that Helen took the message and relayed it to Britt who said nothing and turned away. Helen shook her head and went back to the office where she was trying to complete an admission. There had been transfers from the Annex, the first area of assessment, to the Holding Area, and from there to the Psychiatric Ward upstairs. Others had been discharged home. The general E.R. was full to overflowing. Well, so much for a quiet evening. And they had been hoping Britt would be able to get away by 10:30. Still it might calm down yet.

The new admission was an elderly woman, a survivor of the concentration camps. She was almost eighty and psychotically depressed. Apparently she had become gradually increasingly depressed in her latter years, over forty years after she had come to Canada, married, and raised a family. Now it seemed that the hard years were over, and she could sit back, relax, and admire her achievements. A deadly form of remembering set in, and all the horrors of the distant past came back with a vengeance. Apparently it had never really ended.

It struck at Helen's vulnerable spot. A large part of her family had been lost in the war; grandparents, aunts, uncles and cousins. All those that hadn't emigrated from the old country long before the war. Long before the mid-thirties when Canada put into place and acted on their anti-Semitic immigration laws, unwritten laws, but binding, under Mackenzie King. He was much more interested in the welfare of his dog and having séances to contact his dead mother than saving Jews. Of course, he disclaimed responsibility afterward and placed the blame on his minister of immigration who was a [sub rosa anti-Semite]--rabid, unrelenting, and not so surprisingly, effective in preventing those of the Hebrew faith from coming to Canada. They were sent back to certain death, and no country she could think of was blameless for the subsequent genocide, not even Israel. It was too bad, she brooded, that Menachem Begin hadn't had more influence at the time. Or better yet, Golda Meir. It was all so complicated. The Balfour Declaration and the infamous White Paper. But the bottom line was that nothing had been done – not even to save the Hungarian Jews.

But these thoughts were getting her nowhere. Now she had the old woman, hardly able to sit up, before her and not only was she staring at Helen intermittently through eyes terrified and then vacuous, but she appeared to be listening and not to the nurse because she had stopped talking, and it was dead quiet in the room. Finally Helen called the orderly and watched the patient shuffling off under his guidance in the direction of her cubicle. Then she sat down to write up her admission notes and assessment.

She had almost finished when Britt came back into the office and looked over her shoulder. She scanned the information and then looked off in the direction of the last empty cubicle, now filled. "How is she?"

"Not so good. She's delusional, but it's vague. She's not saying much. Paranoid, and I think she's having auditory hallucinations."

"Did she say she was hearing voices?"

"No, but she appears to be hearing things, and it's not the sound of my voice."

"Is there a language problem?"

"No. She speaks English, but I spoke to her in Yiddish."

"Wish I could speak Yiddish." Britt mumbled. "It's a very colorful language."

"And I wish I had your educational background." Helen finished writing her comments and looked up at her. "You're well informed. Too well informed I think sometimes."

"Can't be too well informed, Helen. Besides we're becoming a very racist society, here, in Quebec, and all over the country. You have to be vigilant."

"Look who's talking!"

"Well that's true," Britt laughed. "Thanks to you they never did find out who it was who answered the phone to that obnoxious social worker who reported 'some nurse from here' to the Consiel pour la Protection de la Langue francaise."

"Tom suspected it was you."

"I was going to tell him."

"I know. But it's a good thing you caught my signal." Helen paused. "You're a fool, Britt."

"Maybe, but you be careful, Helen. They'll go after the Jews first. You know that."

"They always do." Helen looked at her and appeared mildly irritated, but resigned. "Don't worry. It won't come to that."

"Don't count on it." Britt tilted her head to one side.

"Promise me you'll get out before it ever gets too bad here, Helen. I mean it."

"I know you do . . . Look, it's quiet now . . . at last. Why don't you go home? It's past 10:30."

"How are things on the other side?"

"Everything's fine. Martha or Rolly can come over if I need someone. I'm just going to finish up the charting and tape. So go home. It's hell having to come back here in the morning. But you'll be on with Eva."

Eva and Helen were close friends. Both were late middle-aged, with grown-up families, and both had children who had already left Quebec. Both had married highly successful men--one to a lawyer and current mayor of a municipality on the island of Montreal, the other to a doctor. It seemed sadly ironic that these people, like so many others, were having to leave Montreal, and that's just what they were having to do. Some were holding on longer than others. But not the younger generation. They had already left or were leaving by the droves. Britt had gone a number of times to other parts of Canada, the United States, and even to Australia for a year. But she'd always returned. And to what? she wondered. The question hung in her mind all the way home. Once there, she decided just to go to bed. Forget showering. It could wait until morning and hopefully wrench her into wakefulness.

Having showered and downing several cups of coffee in her apartment, Britt presented herself at the hospital awake and reasonably alert the following morning. While Eva was over in the Annex getting coffee for both of them, she relieved the night nurse and made a quick round of the patients in the P.H.A. while trying to avoid wakening them.

After all, it was Saturday morning. There were no psychiatric rounds on weekends. The resident on call answered pages. She had just come to Joan's bed when Eva returned and called her, but Britt was staring down at the woman and an alarm clicked on in her mind and quickened her senses.

"Joan?" She moved the woman's face toward her and the eyes meeting hers were glazed over with only the barest flicker of recognition or life of any kind in them. "Joan?" She called again, but the old woman was hardly responsive.

Britt checked for vital signs and the size and reaction of her pupils. The knuckles of her hands were red and swollen, but that was probably due to the rheumatoid arthritis. Her ankles and feet were slightly edematous, however, and that she had not noticed before. She was stable medically as far as Britt could detect, but something was happening or had happened. This was not the same woman she had admitted only two days earlier. The whole aspect of her was a distortion of what she had seen and intuitively known about her upon the first encounter. She turned and left the room quickly.

Eva was waiting in the office. She handed her a steaming hot cup of coffee and then looked at her face. "What's the matter?"

"Something's wrong with Joan."

"Joan Adelman?" Eva's brow wrinkled. "The night nurse didn't mention anything."

"What medication is she on?

"I don't know," Eva reached for the medication book, "check her chart Britt, and see what they've written up on her. What's going on with her anyway?"

"See for yourself," Britt mumbled.

"Well, she's not on much medication. Nothing heavy. They've started her on a mild antidepressant. She's still on low dosage."

"What is it, Ludiomil?"

Eva nodded. "Yeah, but only 50 mg, daily. That won't do much. She's also on a mild sedative and something for pain as required."

Britt was flipping through her chart and reading rapidly while listening to Eva. Then she realized the closet-like office was empty and looking round she saw Eva emerging from Joan's room and coming toward her.

"What do you think?"

Eva shrugged. "I don't know. I'm not familiar with the patient except what I've read and got on report . . . "

"Well there's nothing significant in here, except that she has trouble getting out of bed in the morning which isn't new. There's nothing new on her mental status either . . . nothing." Britt tapped the chart. Her thoughts were a jumble. There wasn't anything in the chart or on the report to corroborate her gut instincts. "There's something wrong with her, Eva. Something's wrong."

"What? She doesn't look too well, but . . . did you get her vitals?"

Britt nodded. "Yeah, they're all right. Well, not great but nothing to get worried about. There's some edema in the lower extremities . . . I don't know. I don't . . . but it's all wrong. The whole picture is wrong. That's not the woman I admitted. There's something, but I don't know what."

Eva bit her lip and thought for a moment.

"Well, we could try to get a medical consult."

"You know what they're like, and we haven't much to go on."

"We'll try. Who's on for psychiatry?"

Britt checked the schedule. "Krushner."

"He's good."

"It's not getting him to listen. It's the medical staff. And they'll have to get over from general E.R. You know what they're like."

"I know what some of the nurses over there are like . . . and some of the doctors too, but not all. Besides, we have duds in psychiatry too, and you know it."

"I know, so . . . "

"So we try," Eva picked up the receiver and dialed locating. "Would you get Dr. Krushner for P.H.A.?" She cradled the receiver and picked up her coffee cup.

Dr. Krushner rang through while Eva was preparing the morning medications and Britt was assessing the patients. When the orderly went to get Joan up, she asked him to wait.

"Hi, Eva. What's happening over there?" Krushner's voice was warm, but he sounded weary.

"You sound half dead already, Abe. The day's only beginning."

"I know. That's the problem. I'm swamped. There are no beds. Right?"

"Right."

"Well, two patients in the general E.R. can go home, but we'll have to keep one. He's in the psych room here. So, what's up?"

"We have a problem here, Abe."

Eva went on to tell him about Joan Adelman.

"That's pretty thin evidence to go on, Eva."

"Well, the nurse who admitted her is concerned."

"All right. Edith owes me a favour. She wants me to clear one of her medical patients. I'll ask her to come over."

Edith Hillier, one of the residents working in E.R., came into the holding area around mid-morning, and she brought with her an intern and a medical student. By this time Eva and Britt, with the help of the orderly, had managed to get Joan out of bed and into the common room. She turned away from the breakfast tray after only a few mouthfuls of cereal and Britt called the orderly.

"George, would you try to get her to take some fluid. At this rate she'll dehydrate, and we can't put an I.V. up in here."

"Sure thing." George smiled at her. "Poor old thing. I kind of like her and she hasn't said a word."

"She's only fifty-nine, George."

"Really?" George stared across the room at Joan. "Well, I'll be damned."

Britt watched Edith Hillier examine the patient and thought it a pretty poor show. She turned away and went back to the office to wait there with Eva. Within minutes Dr. Hillier was back in the office stating that she could find nothing significant.

"Well, I think there's something wrong." Britt stared at her. "Really, it's just too dramatic a change over such a short period."

Hillier shrugged. "Maybe it's the meds. What's she on?"

"Not enough of anything that would cause that reaction."

"Well, I can't find anything. If she gets worse call me back."

When she had gone, Eva looked at Britt.

"We tried."

"She didn't examine her very well. I could have done as much . . . and did. What about some blood work?"

Eva checked the basket. "Her CBC and SMAC are fairly normal. The toxic screen . . . well you know what that shows."

"That was two days ago. And they didn't do cardiac and liver enzymes."

"Well, we'll repeat them, but other than that there's not much more we can do, except watch her."

"And alert the evening staff," Britt added. "Who is she anyway? I haven't seen her around here before."

"She's new."

"God help her patients."

Eva laughed. "Yes, well what can I say to that?"

"To what?" Abe Krushner was standing in the doorway.

"They've medically cleared Joan again."

"I know. I met Edith in the hallway. She says it's nothing. False Alarm."

"Not so, Abe." Britt turned to him. "I'm sure of it. She's very ill."

"Well, there's nothing I can do about it. They won't take her into the general emergency. They're sticklers. You know that. Just wait and see . . . how are the other patients?"

"Fine. We'll call you if we need anything."

Joan became a little more alert as the day wore on, but she was placid and compliant. Too compliant, Britt thought, and she couldn't shake off her feeling of apprehension. By mid-afternoon Joan was so tired and in pain, they decided to put her back in bed. The evening staff didn't like the situation at all, and said so.

"Well just watch her carefully and alert the night nurse." Britt wrapped up the report. "That's all we can do."

The following day Eva and Britt were teamed up again in the

P.H.A., only this time they were both worried. Joan's condition had deteriorated overnight. Now there was pitting edema in her feet and ankles and moving up her legs. The woman looked dazed and had to be spoon-fed her breakfast. Britt had her hand at the back of the woman's neck, massaging it, as she stood beside her feeding her. Then she got her washed and into a fresh gown. Forty-five minutes later she was back in the office with Eva.

"She's worse. We've got to do something."

"I know. Murray Rosenweig's the chief resident in E.R. today. I saw him this morning."

"Is he good?"

"He's very good. I'm going to call him."

"Fine. I see Miriam Zelienski's on for psychiatry, but we'll call her later."

"Yes, I'll get Murray. He'll come if I call him."

He would too, Britt was thinking. Eva knew everybody worth knowing in the hospital. Murray came within a half-hour and went to work. Eva showed him the results of the blood work from the previous day. The values were unremarkable.

"Have they done an A.B.G.?"

"Blood gases?" Eva shook her head. "No, she didn't do one yesterday. You want to do one?"

"Yes, I'll do one, and we'll get a lung scan."

The orderly moved off to get the equipment from main E.R. as Murray bent to examine the woman.

Miriam Zelienski came by around noon and was in the office with Eva when Britt came out of Joan's room. The woman was so dazed and remote, they had put her back to bed and held all medication.

"Look, the woman's been cleared medically." Miriam looked from Eva to Britt.

But Erikson was worried and looked it. "And I don't want to

sound like an alarmist, but something's terribly wrong, and remember, Miriam, if anything happens in here we can't even get the crash cart through the door to the unit."

Miriam stared at her for a moment. "They were over again this morning. We'll have to wait and see. I can't just demand they take her in main E.R., and if I raise a stink over this and it turns out to be nothing, they'll have my head."

Britt looked away and pulled out a chart. She was both irritated and frustrated and it showed. Miriam got up and left the unit.

"Bloody hell." Britt muttered. "I think I'll go to lunch with Virginia."

"Yes, you go ahead. I'll go when you get back."

By three in the afternoon the tension had mounted. Now Joan's blood pressure was fluctuating within a narrow range and her pulse was thready. The A.B.G. results were back, and they were not normal, but could not be considered critical either. The most frightening thing was that she didn't seem to hear them when they spoke to her. Her eyes were glassed over, and there was no recognition in them, and more worrisome still, the edema in the lower extremities was much more pronounced. Her chest sounded clear, but there was no evidence of infection, so why wouldn't it, Britt thought.

In desperation, shortly after 3:00 p.m., she called through to nuclear medicine. The technician answered the phone and Britt asked abruptly.

"Has the radiologist read the scan on Adelman yet?"

"No, not yet."

"Well, we need the results . . . now."

"But he's not here right now."

"Page him."

"Is this an emergency?" The technician was frowning into the receiver. "Who's calling?"

"Britt Erikson in P.H.A. and yes, it's an emergency."

"Are you the nurse there?"

"Yes. Now, please get him and have him read the scan. He can reach me at 4563. Have you got that?"

"Yes, yes. I'll try to locate him."

Britt put down the receiver and started to write a quick note on a few of the patients. She had been charting on Joan all day and her file remained open on the counter. Eva was just finishing up and Britt was replacing her last chart with the exception of Joan's into its slot when the evening staff arrive at three-twenty. Eva gave report on her three patients first and then Britt launched hers. That took even less time until she came to Joan.

"Good God!" One of them cut in. "What'll we do if she arrests? This sounds serious."

"If she arrests, you resuscitate her. There's nothing else you can do . . . and get her out of the unit as quickly as possible . . . where she'll have access to a crash cart."

The two nurses look troubled. "Damn it, Britt, she shouldn't be in here."

"I know."

"Does the supervisor know?"

"Yes, she knows." Eva put in, and the telephone rang. Britt reached for the receiver.

"This is Dr. Finestein. Are you the nurse that called for the results on Adelman?"

"Yes."

"The scan shows she's positive for pulmonary emboli." Britt snapped to attention.

"Thank you."

"I'll send down the written results as soon as I have them ready, but I thought I'd call."

"Yes, thanks for ringing back." Britt pressed the dial tone button and called locating. "Get Dr. Zelienski for P.H.A., please."

"She's down there in the Annex. Someone just called for her."

Britt hung up and called the Annex.

Virginia answered. "Yes, she's here. Hang on."

Zelienski came on the line, and Britt didn't waste time. "Miriam, it's Britt. She's positive for pulmonary emoli."

"Jesus Christ!" Miriam swore. "All right, I'll call emergency immediately."

"I'll get her ready." And they did. It was all done so quickly one would think of it as a video set on fast forward. One of the nurses got a stretcher from the hallway and in a single concerted effort they jot Joan on it while trying to avoid jolting her body in any way and all the while Britt kept repeating to her, "you'll be all right, Joan. We know what it is now. You'll be all right. Can you hear me?"

Two orderlies showed up from the general E.R. just down the hall, and like lightning it had struck and was over. The patient Adelman was wheeled out of the unit and down the hall to the crash room in general E.R.

But it wasn't over for Joan. Not yet.

Her husband was standing back in the doorway and moved aside as they left with his wife, but he waited and caught Britt's arm as she followed them out of the room. "I heard you telling her you knew what it was. What is it?"

Britt looked at him. "They're taking her out front. One of the doctors will talk to you."

"But will she really be all right?"

"I hope so, Mr. Adelman. She's safer out there. They'll see to her."

He nodded and turned away. Britt looked around and everyone in the P.H.A. looked relieved.

"That was too close," one of them mumbled. "What a mess!"

"We've been trying all day, and yesterday. At least she's a little safer now." Britt's shoulders sagged. "I'm going home."

Joan wasn't in the General Emergency more than ten to fifteen minutes when she arrested. They called a code, revived her, and sent her immediately up to I.C.U. where they put down an arterial line with what they called an umbrella at the end so that an embolus could be caught before reaching the heart.

The following Wednesday, when Britt returned to work, again on evenings, she ducked out for a few minutes and went up to I.C.U. The nurse sitting near her bed looked over at the inert small framed body and appeared doubtful when Britt asked if she was going to make it.

"Maybe," she said finally. "She's arrested twice now. Once in the ER and once up here. But maybe."

The supervisor, Gertie Spalding, came by around eight o'clock and was sitting in the office talking with Rolly. Britt was with a patient, but when she returned to the office she found the supervisor waiting for her. Gertie looked up and hesitated.

"We heard about Mrs. Adelman and what happened here. The other nurses in the department have been talking about it and the slow response from the doctors in E.R. We're going to have an enquiry into it. It's high time doctors started listening to nurses. We'll need a written statement from you."

Britt looked at her for a moment and then shook her head. "Not a chance. I won't give you a written statement."

"Why not?" Gertie appeared confused and then annoyed. "They've got to start listening to nurses. Some do, but far too many don't."

"Why should they? Doctors will listen to nurses when nurses start listening to nurses. And as a general rule they don't. They're always back-biting and bickering. The staff here is different. For the most part we listen to one another. That's why I like it here. And, on the whole, the doctors listen too. Here, they listen. But those nurses in the General E.R. are an abominable lot. You know that's true. So we should clean up our own backyard first. What do you think?"

"Well, we're trying to make it better."

"But it's not getting better. It's getting worse. No statement, Gertie."

Several days later Joan Enright Adelman died, and there were few to mourn her except her husband. She had those ten years of marriage out of what seemed a lonely and loveless existence from girlhood. And she had burrowed into the memory of at least one other person. Britt Erikson knew she'd never forget her or what little she knew of this woman's life, all this without having heard a word from her to remember her by. Not one word. Only the look of her, her face, and the expression in her piercing blue eyes. Her silent rage and in the end, her solitary silence. Was death so bad after all, Britt wondered. Somehow she didn't think so.

-Four-

The next few weeks seemed to pass quickly with a series of domestic upheavals that the family found hard to put into proper sequence afterward. Nora decided to go to Toronto after all, and as Gregory pointed out to her when she telephoned him it would be wise for her to go the following week because the school-age children had already started back that very week. Labor Day weekend had gone almost unnoticed. Britt had other things on her mind, like what was going on at the hospital. She had forgotten to call Rourke on Saturday evening and only remembered on Monday, which was the first day she had off after seven straight shifts. And she only had that one day. She called her brother in Ottawa early in the evening and explored the situation.

Rourke laughed. "Well, what's another move after so many? Sure I'll come down. How about next weekend? That's a good time for me. How about you?"

Britt thought for a moment. "Next weekend's good. Mother will be delighted . . . to have it over with, I mean."

"How about Nora? Can she help?"

"No, Nora's leaving for Toronto to get Aaron into school there. He's too young to get into school here. It's the law."

Rourke found that very amusing too. He found everything about his home province ludicrous and told them all they should have got out long ago. Britt agreed with him, but circumstances always seemed to draw them back.

"So what's she going to do? Stay at Gregory's and put Aaron in school. Then what?"

"She plans to return at Christmas. They'll have to accept him when he's already started Grade I."

"Very clever." Rourke drawled. "Well, I'll bring along Reg and Lee. They can help and they're used to lifting."

Britt had forgotten about her teenage nephews. Reg was almost sixteen and Lee was fourteen. So, of course, they could help.

"That's great Rourke and Bernard, one of the orderlies at the hospital, has offered to help."

"Right, we'll see you Saturday morning. And if I'm not there on time, start without me."

"Not so funny, Rourke. We've got all Dad's tools and machinery, like his lathe machine . . ."

"Oh right! I was forgetting. Okay, expect me early."

When Britt hung up, she stared down at the phone and sighed. Nora had left that morning with the kids, and it seemed almost too quiet around the apartment building. She decided to go down and see her parents. They'd be happy to know that everything was settled for the move. That's where Virginia found her an hour later.

Over coffee she told the Eriksons that she had to go up to London. Her mother was very ill.

"Is she?" Mary Erikson looked concerned. "What's the trouble?"

"Everything, Mrs. Erikson. She hasn't been well for a long time."

"I see." Mary looked at Britt who turned to Virginia.

"When are you going?"

"Tomorrow, I'll take the train."

"What do the doctors say?"

"I don't know, but she's been bad before and come round. You know what it's like with diabetes, and my mother's not young."

"Well, neither am I." Mary put it.

"You're only sixty-one, Mother." Britt made a face, "and Dad's just sixty-four. How old is your mother, Gin?"

"Seventy-six."

Hugh Erikson came into the kitchen. He was a thin man of medium height, and Britt didn't think there was a child in the world who wasn't drawn to her father.

He had an odd quality about him, a calmness that made the world a safer place to be with him about. Her mother and father had always been able to talk together for hours and that amazed her. They could also go through a whole evening without saying more than a few words. The occasion of their union still caused everyone who knew them to break out in uproarious laughter. No one had given it more than six months and yet, here they were, almost forty years later, still married. Of course they had their disagreements, many of them, but they were still together. It had been a turbulent and troubled, warm and funny forty years. But life went on and so did they. Hugh still trying to make his fortune, and Mary trying to convince him it wasn't worth the bother.

Now he looked around the table. "Hello Virginia."

"Hi, Mr. Erikson."

Hugh pulled out a chair. "So, what's wrong?" Nobody bothered to question how he knew something was wrong.

"It's Virginia's mother, Dad. She's ill and Virginia has to go up to London."

"Oh, I'm sorry. Is it serious?"

"I don't know, Mr. Erikson. But I have to go up."

"Yes, of course you do. I hope she's all right." He turned to his wife. "Don't you think you should call Toronto and see if Nora and the kids got there all right?"

"Yes, I'll call now, but Aaron will only want to talk to you."

Hugh smiled. "I'll talk to him too . . . if he's still up."

Mary left the room, and a few minutes later she called Hugh to the phone. When she returned to the kitchen, she gave them a comical look. "What did I tell you?"

By Saturday evening the move was over and everything was in place in both apartments. Even the pictures were hung. Her parents had several good oil paintings and Mary was always very particular about getting them up in the right spots. That made it home again. It took no time at all, but then again they'd had lots of practice. It took one day. That's all.

"We should start our own moving company. A family business," Rourke commented before leaving to return to Ottawa. "We'd make megabucks."

"I doubt if any of the members in our family could stay together in one place long enough to start any sort of business," Mary replied. "Besides, I hate moving."

"No you don't." Britt laughed at her. "You thrive on it. It's something like we all hate the thing we love." Rourked looked at her. "No mind teasers. Not tonight. I've got to go."

Virginia returned the following Wednesday. Britt met her at the station.

"How did you know I'd be on this train?"

"Easy," Britt shrugged. "It's the only one connecting from London in Toronto and I didn't think you'd want to stay any time in Toronto."

"You were right."

"How's your mother?"

"Not too good. Most of the time she hardly knew I was there. I sat by her bed and knit."

"Didn't you talk to her?"

"Of course . . . whether she heard me or not."

"But her condition's not worse?"

"No. It's the same."

"Well, that's something anyway."

-Five-

By the end of September, Britt had a whole week off before she left for Labrador and a reunion with a friend she hadn't seen since before she left for Australia, and that was over three years before. It would be good to see Alice again. She was a care worker in a home for the severely disabled. Labrador, Britt thought as she lay in bed the first morning of her vacation. Her short stint in nursing up there at Northwest River just across from the Indian reservation seemed like a lifetime ago. Even longer. It was because of all the change and movement in her life she concluded and turned on her side, curled up and went back to sleep. When she woke up again, close to eleven o'clock, Roddy was gone and the bed was empty. She stretched out and yawned. Poor Roddy. It was a Monday and that meant dialysis from mid-afternoon until evening. They had stopped talking about marriage. Roddy would have none of it, although he clearly didn't want to leave her. There would be no chance of him fathering a child now--not since his kidney transplant had failed utterly and he'd had to go back on full-time dialysis. Three times a week. It was making him moody too, which was why Britt encouraged him to start his own business when he came up with the idea, and she lent him some money to get it started. Come to think of it, she should go over to the hospital and pick up her check today. There was nothing left in the bank.

    She got up, showered, and had the whole day ahead of her. That felt great. By early afternoon, she decided to go for a walk. Montreal was pretty in the autumn, and it was a bright day. Very nice to walk in after several days of rainy, damp or dark weather. This day had a crispness about it that assaulted her like a heady perfume. She walked for hours and didn't get back to her apartment until late afternoon, but she was reluctant to go in just yet. That's when she decided to head across the street to Virginia's. She had worked the night but she'd be up by now. It was almost five o'clock.

Virginia was indeed up and about. In fact, she didn't look like she had slept much at all. They sat at the kitchen table which looked something like a crudely hacked-down, wooden desk. Britt's friend liked the rustic look, Indian and natural foods, and herbal teas. All of which contrasted with her own penchant for cigarettes, coffee and ordinary tea. Things considered generally deleterious to the health and in keeping with the typically Erikson disregard for foods good or bad, popular trends and groups of any sort. Not acting individually or being one's own person was the worst sin an Erikson could commit and anyone breaking that one sacred unspoken rule felt himself or herself under the gun. Of course, the mirror was the gun and therefore unavoidable. No one had to say a word. Nobody exactly knew where these notions of self-determination and maybe even arrogance had sprung from, but Hugh Erikson had said to his wife once not long after their marriage when she complained to him that he was working himself too hard and driving himself unnecessarily, that he did it all because if that son-of-a-bitch whom he worked for at the time said one word to him, he'd quit the job on the spot. Mary knew by the look of him he'd do it too. So maybe that's how it all got started and was now bred right into their bone.

They were also, for the most part, empathetic and understood instinctively the way things were, especially if the channels were open and not clogged with imaginative fantasies. Britt knew almost immediately that something was wrong. So now she stared down into the strange concoction of herbal tea to which she'd added some honey and asked abruptly,

"What is it, Gin? What's the matter . . .? your mother?"

Virginia nodded. "Yes, my sister called and . . . "

She stopped suddenly, and her facial muscles worked.

"Is she worse? What did your sister say?"

"She's worse, but nobody knows when . . . or how long. . ."

"You'll have to go back up."

"I just got back."

"I know, but what if . . . I mean there's not much choice. You'll have to go."

"Well, I'll work tonight and then maybe . . . "

And all of a sudden, Virginia was crying and she looked like some lost child in a very black night who didn't know where to turn or how to find her way back home. But the tears stopped just as quickly as they had started.

"No. . .no." Britt shook her head. "You should go soon. I'll drive you up. My father will lend me the car."

"No, I can take the train . . . in a day or two. I'll wait . . . "

"You should go now, Gin. Something could happen. What then? Who's up there anyway?"

"My sisters. One of my brothers is out west . . . "

"And the other one?"

"My older brother. He's there in the same town too – Skipper. I haven't seen him in almost ten years . . . Oh God . . . Skip!" Virginia started to cry again and this time her whole body seemed to shake.

"What about him?" Britt sat back and gave her a worried, confused look. "What's wrong with him?"

"Nothing . . . everything . . . poor Skip." Virginia covered her eyes and all the dark and sealed closets of her past, now buried deep in her psyche, gaped open. She spoke little of her childhood and all the years she spent growing up in a small Ontario town just outside London. Britt had only been able to glean fragments of information and most of the memories were not pleasant ones although they were not overwhelmingly sad either. Maybe that was the problem. The past for Virginia was just gray as if largely obscured by fog. And fog could be deadly, she supposed.

"No listen Gin." Britt said, interrupting her own thoughts.

"Surely, you want to go up, and I'll take you."

"You've just started your vacation."

"Which is why I can take you, and it's no trouble at all. So, when do you want to leave, tomorrow morning?"

"Yes, all right, but won't your father mind?"

"Not in the least. Not at all." Britt waved a hand in dismissal.

"But you'd better ring the hospital. You can't work all night and then leave in the morning."

"Yes, I'll call them, and I'll speak to Tom in the morning before we go."

The trip up past Toronto to London seemed to take less time than they'd anticipated except for the last two hours. That seemed to take forever and in any case their best efforts had been defeated. Virginia's mother died two hours before they reached the hospital. The nurse told her just as she rounded the corner to the ward where the old woman had been during the last weeks of her life. Britt caught hold of her and motioned to the nurse who was regarding Virginia sympathetically and saying how sorry she was. Then she directed her back down the hall to the entrance waiting room. Virginia stopped at a pay phone.

"I'm going to call my sister."

Britt nodded and moved on. "I'll wait out here."

A short time later Virginia came out and Britt looked up. "Sit down for a few minutes. Just rest a minute and think what you want to do." There was a silence and then, "How is your sister?"

"She's all right. Shaken, of course, but okay."

"And the other one? The second sister?"

"Susan? She isn't going to take this well at all. I don't think she was any closer to my mother than Pam, but she needed her more."

"Your older brother?"

"They've finally reached him. He lives in the same town and they never see him." Virginia shook her head.

"They've called Russel in Vancouver. He's flying back

tomorrow."

"To Toronto?"

"Yes."

"And you, Gin?"

"I'm all right."

"What do you want to do? Go over to your sister's?"

"Not yet. I want to walk."

"Then we'll walk." Britt stood up.

They walked all over the small town. The autumn colors were splendid, but they were dying too and the mood of the town, with the light fading and evening drawing in to eventually be clamped down by night and the absence of light, locked Virginia's mind on every passing reminder of her youth: the factory where her father had worked until he died eighteen years before, the house where they had lived, still lived in by another family, but not looking abandoned, the school, the church, the old bridge over the almost dried up creek. All of it. She looked around and wondered where the years had gone and why coming home brought such a dull ache in her heart and always had. That's why she seldom came back.

Finally they ended up on Main Street and a restaurant taking up the whole of one corner. Virginia turned to her.

"Are you hungry?"

"Are you?"

"Yeah, we should eat something. Let's go in."

Death usually had drama attached to it and this one was not an exception. In this case no one was stunned by it. It hadn't been sudden or unexpected, but all were saddened by it. Some cried for what they had and lost. Some cried for what they thought they had and was no more, and others cried for what they never had at all. It wasn't true that you couldn't miss what you never had. That was a God-awful lie. Lies hurt and so did the truth. Virginia knew that and Britt suspected that she'd known it for a very long time.

-Six-

The following week Britt left for Labrador and Virginia returned to work. She requested nights and since very few wanted the graveyard shift, Tom Flynn was happy to oblige her. She also developed a passion for knitting. It was maddening to watch her sit and knit by the hour, but as one nurse commented, it was better than cracking up.

The trip to Labrador was restful and uneventful. Roderick drove her to the airport and promised to be there to pick her up on her return home. She was surprised therefore to find her father waiting for her. Looking at him standing there it occurred to her that he'd always done just that – patiently waited for her return home. A pattern had developed over the years and it seemed impossible to break. But when she came up to him now she looked a little anxious. "Where's Roddy?"

"He's in hospital, Britt. So I came."

"Hospital? What's wrong?"

"The shunt or whatever for his hemodialysis went on him. They had to do another."

"Oh God!" Britt closed her eyes. "That's a horrible procedure. Did they do it yet?"

Hugh Erikson nodded. "Yes, yesterday. I guess it was pretty bad. I saw him this afternoon."

Britt got her baggage and Hugh took the case from her.

"They put him out for it, didn't they?"

"No. Apparently not."

"Why not?"

"I don't know. There are reasons. He'll explain it all. Let's go home."

"But I should see him. It's not so late. Only eight-thirty."

"No, not tonight. He asked for you not to come. I've seen him. He's all right."

"But . . . "

"No, really Britt, he doesn't want you to go up there tonight. He's coming out tomorrow probably. You can call in the morning. It's what he wants."

Britt found some flowers on her coffee table at home. They were from Roddy and looked an oddly welcoming and thoughtful gesture, but probably her father had put them there.

"That was nice of him, wasn't it?" She turned to her father who nodded.

"He's a nice man, Roddy. I like him."

"I know you do," Britt took her father's arm. "You went to visit him every day in hospital when he had his splenectomy last summer."

"Yes, well he doesn't get many visitors. His own family doesn't go. So . . . "

"Well, he has us. Come on. Do you think Mother has tea ready?"

"I'm sure she does." He held the door for her. "By the way, how's Alice?"

"She's fine. Another fan of yours."

"I like Alice. Nice girl. Down to earth and kind." He smiled back at his daughter. They went upstairs to her old apartment which her parents were now occupying.

Scheduling at the hospital was erratic but Britt was happy to find herself on a string of evenings. The following morning, she rang the hospital and spoke with the charge nurse. Roddy was fine, and he was going to be discharged. She arrived at the hospital just as a nurse was changing the dressing on his left forearm. Roddy looked up at her and saw her lips compressing into a hard straight line. He shook his head and Britt kept silent. She had to bite her tongue because she was fuming and Roddy knew it.

"There you are, Mr. Coluzzi. I'll leave you some gauze and tape at the desk. Try to keep it dry. You're due for dialysis tomorrow?"

"Yes." Roddy's voice was barely above a whisper.

The nurse left the room and Britt sat down on the bed beside him. "How long did it take, Roddy?"

"Almost an hour. It wasn't supposed to take that long."

"And they didn't give you anything? No anesthetic?"

"No. They said they couldn't because they had to see how the nerves were working or something. Just a local . . . you know?" And when Britt nodded he concluded, "It didn't help much."

"Of course it didn't! They shouldn't have gone ahead. The bloody fools. Well, you won't go through it again. I won't let them."

"There you go again . . . always arguing with people."

"Well, you don't argue very well on your own behalf, Coluzzi." Britt sighed, "Never mind. It must be sore. I'll help you dress and take you home."

Nothing further was said between them concerning the whole matter. Roddy was strange. He wanted her help and her caring, but he kept pushing her away. It was as if he expected the ball would always bounce back to him and, so far, it always did. They had been seeing each other for almost two years. On a couple of occasions, as when she wanted to get into the recovery room after his splenectomy, she'd had to tell the staff she was his fiancée. Between lying to them about her relationship to Roderick Coluzzi and being a nurse herself and knowing all the right questions to ask, Britt got to where she had to be for Roddy's sake. She also had the answers for him when he didn't know them himself and was too shy to ask. But it was no thanks to the mulish Italian who was supposed to marry Italian if he ever got to marry at all. He had never introduced her to his family and seldom to friends. If nurses looked at her curiously during his bouts in hospital or when she came in to see him during dialysis which took hours, that was all right too. He never introduced her or explained her presence. If she felt awkward as well as obligated, that was too bad. And all things considered, Britt had to admit it was her own fault. But it seemed to her a damned if you do, damned if you don't situation. Breaking off with him would be like kicking someone when he was down. Was that fair? No, she didn't think so. But their relationship was going nowhere, and she knew it. She was beginning to realize too that it wasn't just his illness, although it did color matters considerably; it was Roddy. He didn't really want her. The problem was he didn't not want her either. It was a tangled web she'd got herself into.

Looking over at her as they drove west across Sherbrooke, Roddy said quietly. "Thanks for coming for me."

"You're welcome. I was going to come up last night but my father said you'd want to rest."

"Yes, I told him. He came yesterday."

"I know . . . Thank you for the flowers."

"Did you like them?" He smiled like a schoolboy.

"Very much."

"I'm glad. Do you think we could stop for coffee? I'm so happy to be out of that place."

"Sure, why not?" Britt laughed.

Over coffee Roddy told her that he had to go out to the airport to pick up his niece on Friday evening. Britt frowned at him.

"You won't be able to drive a standard by Friday. You can't move your arm now."

"It should be all right by Friday."

"I don't think so."

"Well, I told my sister I'd go for her."

"But you didn't know about this." Britt pointed to his arm resting in a sling. "That was unexpected."

"Still I have to go."

"Why can't your brother-in-law go?"

"He'd never drive that far . . . out to Mirabel? No way. You don't know Franco."

"I'm not sure I want to," Britt mumbled. "What do they have a car for? Idle curiosity?"

"He uses it sometimes and my niece uses it." Roddy added lamely. "Anyway I told her I'd do it."

"What time does her plane get in?"

"Around nine."

"All right." Britt nodded. "See how your arm is. I'm able to get Friday evening off if I work the weekend."

"My arm will be fine by then."

"I doubt it, Roddy. There'll be stiffness, and it'll be tender for some time."

And it was. He could do very little with his arm for days and Britt ended up driving him and his sister with her second daughter out to Mirabel. When he went to pick up his niece's baggage, Britt's eyes daggered him and his sister, catching the look that went between them finally got the drift. The women handled the luggage between them and once it was safely stacked in the trunk and his sister and nieces were in the car, Roddy asked for the keys.

Britt stared at him. "Are you out of your bloody mind?"

"I have to drive," he tried to explain.

"They'll understand, Roddy. You can't drive with your arm the way it is . . . and you're in pain. Don't bother to deny it."

"Please, Britt!"

"Not a chance." She walked away from him and around to the driver's side. He got in beside her and all the way back to town he showed no signs of being angry. But later that night he told her.

"You don't understand. You just don't understand the way it is."

"Oh, I think I do," Britt replied. "I'm beginning to understand only too well."

During the next few weeks, Roddy's mood was lighter than it had been in months. This could be attributed to having something meaningful to do with his time. He was working to get his store ready for opening after Christmas. He had gone into partnership with a friend of his, Gino. Roddy had told Britt that few people liked Gino because he couldn't be trusted. But he knew all his friend's faults, and so he didn't think there'd be any trouble between them. At the back of Britt's mind were a number of unanswered questions: why, for instance, would Roddy go into business with someone he couldn't trust; why did he keep and value friends who seldom came to see him, especially when he was very ill in a hospital; why did he always have to put on such a front for his own family – they didn't even know how seriously ill he was. Or maybe they did and that's why they kept away. She also wondered why he hadn't gone to his father for the money he said he needed to get the business started instead of coming to her. Five thousand dollars wasn't much, but it was all she had at the time and her parents had no money. Old Mr. Coluzzi owned the duplex where he lived in the lower flat and Roddy in the upper. He had two pensions coming in. So, why?

Britt couldn't plumb the mystery and she stopped trying. She didn't like any of the answers she was coming up with. She was fond of Roddy and so was all her family. Not everybody could be wrong.

By the end of October, autumn came to an abrupt end. There was an early frost and the leaves, all colored and still changing, suddenly browned and then withered and died. The trees were left prematurely naked and their branches interlaced and reached starkly against a cheerless, steel sky. The days were darker and duller than usual, and people started to welcome the hard bright light of winter. But an early snow didn't come and the grayness continued day after day.

Virginia was talking about making a change. She was restless and felt she had been working in Psychiatry too long. "Over fifteen years," she said to Britt when they were working together one Saturday at the hospital.

"So why now?" Britt wanted to know. "And where would you go?"

"The Palliative Care Unit at the Vic."

"Oncology? Where you get only the terminally ill? It's too soon Gin. Don't you think?"

"Maybe," Virginia shrugged. "It's a difficult ward. No doubt about that. But it's just basic care. I don't want anything high-tech, I can't go back into all that now."

"Why not?"

"Because I've been out of it too long. I don't remember my medical or surgical nursing all that well. It's been years, and I haven't any interest in I.C.U. or general E.R. I'm not like you, Britt."

"I still think it's too soon for you, Gin."

"Yes, well, I'll give it to spring. Then I'm definitely making a change."

"Spring would be better," Britt agreed.

Virginia left for lunch, and she decided to call Roddy. They had increased his medication for high blood pressure, and he had been feeling more tired than usual. After a few minutes on the phone with him, her brow clouded as she detected an undercurrent of fear in his voice.

"You don't sound well, Roddy. What's wrong?"

"Nothing. I'm just a bit dizzy when I get up."

"You went to dialysis yesterday?"

"Of course. I think it's just the extra medication, and it takes time readjusting to dialysis."

"Sure, I know. What's your blood pressure now?"

"It's coming down, but still high."

"Okay. I'll call you back."

Britt put down the receiver and motioned to a patient standing in the doorway that she wouldn't be long. Then she called her parents and her mother answered the phone. Mary Erikson sounded concerned. "No, he shouldn't be there alone. Where's his father?"

"I don't know. Is Dad there?" Hugh Erikson came on the line and the conversation was brief and to the point. ". . .so will you go and get him, Dad, and bring him up to my place? It's too dangerous for him to be there alone. I'm afraid he might pass out."

"Sure I'll go and get him."

"Thanks. You kept a key to the apartment, didn't you?"

"Of course."

"Good. I'll call you back a little later, and Dad . . . ?"

"Yes?"

"Don't take no for an answer. He won't want to come with you."

"Don't worry. I'll get him."

When she called her parents back an hour later, Roddy was in her apartment. Britt knew her father too well not to realize that there would be very little chance of him not succeeding.

Roddy stayed at her place for three days. When she was at work, one or the other of her parents was usually around the building and her father, in particular, often dropped in just to make sure he was all right. But his blood pressure wasn't fluctuating so erratically, and he was rapidly stabilizing.

If Roddy's one remaining parent was a mystery to Britt, he had even less understanding of Britt's unreasonably negative reaction to her father's occasional breaches of moderation in drinking.

"He simply can't drink!" Britt stormed at him when they were alone again. Her parent had come to supper one evening and Britt noticed that her father had been drinking.

"But everyone drinks a little." Roddy shook his head.

"You make it sound like a crime. I think you hurt his feelings. You were very cool toward him."

"I'm mad at him! And I was cool because I care. I hate seeing him like that."

"But what's the big deal?"

"He can't drink. He never could and he knows it. That's the big deal!"

The following morning, Britt went up to see her mother and her father was out.

"He won't be long" Mary Erikson explained. "He had to go down to the hardware shop. He decided to walk. I should get out too. I'm beginning to feel like a troll."

"It's just the weather . . . not very inviting." Britt paused and gave her mother a speculative look. "Maybe Dad's not too happy. What do you think?"

"Who is?" Mary glanced at her. "You're annoyed over last night. You shouldn't be too upset, but I understand."

"You understand? I should hope so. You've always hated it and made no secret of it."

"Don't blame me for how you feel."

"But you did hate it."

"Yes, but you're an adult and have been for a long time. Make up your own mind."

"That's just the problem. I do blame him and then feel bad because I've made him feel bad . . . but do you think he's unhappy? Maybe that's why he's drinking."

"He not drinking that much, Britt. Last night was just unfortunate, embarrassing."

"I wasn't embarrassed. I was angry, but now I'm worried. I don't think he's happy."

Mary signed. "Well, he hasn't been the success he thought he'd be. Able to retire at forty and all that. It's also been a fight every inch of the way to get his pension. They've put us through hell. It takes its toll, and you know how he hates systems. All of you balk at systems. He's at their mercy. He finds that hard to tolerate."

"So do I . . ."

"I know. That's why you're unhappy, one of the reasons, anyway. But with your father . . . well, they've given him no peace for over three years. Mental anguish is as bad as physical, you know. But it should ease up when he turns sixty-five, and it's his birthday in two weeks."

"I know . . . do you think maybe he's missing the kids, especially Aaron? I'll bet he misses Aaron."

"I'm sure of it, and the boy adores him. Of course, so does Jeremy, but then he has Gregory. Just like Reg and Lee have Rourke. But Aaron's never known his father and if ever a boy wanted a father, he did. So, your father took his place. You know that and I know that."

Britt stared at her mother. Aaron was also her favorite grandchild. There had never been any doubt in her mind about that. But Mary conceded readily that Aaron would rather be with his grandfather than anyone else with the exception of his mother which didn't count because she was his mother.

"Well, maybe he should go up for a visit. They've been gone for almost two months. Maybe a week away would cheer him up. It would give him a chance to see Aaron, and he hasn't seen Gregory in a while."

"Yes, he might like that."

They heard the front door of the apartment opening and Hugh Erikson came in. Probably one of the nicest things about her father was his ability to let bad or hurt feelings go, and he never seemed to expect an apology. Her mother often complained that the Eriksons could never admit they were wrong about anything. But then they weren't such a bad lot, a bit stiff-necked maybe, but never mean-minded and never petty. So now Hugh just smiled at his wife and daughter and rubbed his hands to warm them over the burner. When Mary suggested that he take a trip up to Toronto, he jumped at the idea.

"Why don't you call and make the reservation now, Dad. When do you want to go?"

"Next week, I think. Yes, next week."

When he left the room to call for a train reservation, Mary looked at Britt and smiled. "Well, that did cheer him up."

"I thought it might." Britt mused.

Down in her own apartment, Britt soaked in a hot tub before changing and going to work for the evening shift. She thought about her family, but especially about her father. He really was unhappy although he plied himself with improving the techniques of carving and he was an avid reader. He was always busy doing something, and he was never bored. But happy? No. Still, as her mother pointed out – who ever is? Certainly she wasn't. Although many things made her happy, there was something at the core of her being that was eroding and there didn't seem to be anything she could do to stop it. If she sensed her father's unhappiness, he sensed hers and the knowledge of it was driving them apart instead of bringing them closer together. As a child, if anyone had asked her, she would have freely admitted that he was the sun in her life. But something had happened over the years. The love was not less but it seemed like she was always reaching for him across a great distance. They understood each other too well. Maybe that was the problem. That's what frightened Britt, and she wasn't even aware of it.

At the hospital, the pace was steady and sometimes harried. Tempers were short, but then it seemed that something humorous would happen to relieve the tension. Administration was applying the thumbscrews, and it appeared that Tom Flynn was a primary target. As head nurse without a degree, his position was precarious at best. It didn't seem to matter that he had experience and knowledge. They wanted degreed personnel, preferably from McGill. The new director of Nursing was a McGill graduate. Her knowledge was minimal, but textbook perfect. Her lack of experience in nursing or understanding people could only be surpassed by her abysmal lack of experience in management. That meant chaos, and Tom naturally took out his frustrations on his staff. Some days he was able to shrug off his worries, but not often enough to suit the staff.

Britt had worked the weekend and was back at work Tuesday

morning. Dr. Ave Lavin was filling in for Jon Greiser and that was fine with her. When Greiser took a holiday everyone else on staff felt like they were having a holiday too. Rounds would be starting shortly, and Lavin was reading over some charts while Britt prepared the morning medications when the telephone rang.

It was Mr. Rosenfeld inquiring about his son. Britt answered his opening questions calmly and politely, but the man continued to gabble on about all the reasons he hadn't been into the hospital to see his son more often and why he couldn't bring him home for a visit. He hoped she understood. He was still very concerned over his son.

"Well, frankly I don't understand, Mr. Rosenfeld, "Britt launched her counterattack. "I do know that your son needs your support and approval. He will not have much chance of getting well without it. I had a long talk with Richard the other evening. Remaining at the Yeshiva and taking Rabbinical studies only was making him ill. Leaving without your approval and being shunned has made matters worse. He might always have to deal with manic-depressive illness, but keeping him outside the pale, excluding him will only make matters worse . . ."

"Yes, but my wife . . ." The man tried to explain, but Britt cut him off.

"Yes, he told me about that too. She's not Richard's mother. You remarried when he was eight, and she's a very religious woman. And you changed your lifestyle. You, yourself, are an accountant, but Richard has to be a rabbi. Isn't that right? He tells me he's not allowed home for Shabbas or any of the holidays. Is that true?"

"It does upset my wife, yes. She adheres to all the rules and Richard had broken away. But I still want to help him," the father added emphatically. "He's my son and I love him. I haven't abandoned him."

"He thinks you have, Mr. Rosenfeld. He thinks he's alone and going to remain that way. But I must tell you that he's been badly hurt by it all. There's been damage done, but if he's ever going to regain some kind of mental and emotional balance, you'll have to love and accept him as he is, not as you want him to be. Leaving the Rabbinate is not so terrible. He's still a good man, and a Jew. I would have thought you'd be proud of him."

"Well, I . . . what's your name?"

"Erikson. Britt Erikson."

"Thank you, Miss Erikson. Will you tell Richard I'll be in?"

"If I tell him that and you don't come, he'll only be disappointed. But he'll be here or upstairs on the ward. He's not going anywhere."

When she put down the receiver, Lavin gave her a speculative look.

"What was all that about?"

"Richard Rosenfeld's father. Do you know the background?"

Lavin shook his head and Britt explained. Then she added. "I should have passed him on to you."

"No. You did just fine. It wouldn't have been any easier for him to hear it coming from me."

Maybe not, Britt thought, but it would have carried more weight coming from another Jew. Richard really was such a nice man. Even when he was so manic he couldn't sit still and managed to get in everyone's way. Some of the nurses thought he was manipulative. But them some nurses found all patients either threatening, manipulative, or acting out. Suddenly she started to laugh and Ave Lavin glanced at her with a curious expression on his face.

"You know one of the funniest things that ever happened to me, in Psychiatry, I mean?"

"No, what?"

"Well, I was working at the Vic in the general E.R., and we usually had nothing to do with psych patients. They have their own nurse, and she was there all day, but not around when one of her patients was having a small crisis. Well, small . . . that's relative. Right? Anyway, I was coming down the corridor when I noticed that this particular patient was banging his head on the wall. Well, I looked around for her, but she was nowhere in sight. Another nurse came along just behind me and said she'd go and find her. In the meantime I went into the room and gradually got him away from the wall. He sat down on his bed and started to cry, so I sat down beside him and put an arm around his shoulders. He was so upset I could hardly understand him, but he was mumbling something about things not being fair and people were judged by their size and he was a freak, deformed, etc. Of course, I knew he was sexually preoccupied, but what did that matter under the circumstances?"

Ave Lavin shrugged. "It doesn't matter. So what happened?"

"Well, I was getting him quieted down, but he was still sobbing. Mind you, he never touched me. That had little bearing on the judgment of the psych nurse whom they'd finally located. She stood in the doorway and called me out of the room . . . told me I was sexually arousing him and that that was no way to handle a psych patient . . . that I should know better."

Ave burst out laughing. "He wasn't the only one sexually preoccupied. What did you tell her?"

"I asked her if she'd have preferred I let him knock himself senseless and where the hell was she when she was needed."

"Well, never mind. I've seen and heard worse. Sometimes I have to wonder who are the patients."

Britt nodded. "I often wonder about that."

At the end of the following week, Britt picked up her father at the train station. Either the train was early or she was a bit late because he was standing outside waiting for her. The moment he got in the car, she noticed he'd been drinking.

"I only had two glasses of beer on the train. That's all," he said, watching her closed expression.

"Dad, you could have ransacked a brewery. I don't know why

you do it. You just can't drink."

They fell silent and not another word was spoken between them until they were at his home and around the table. Then Britt started to talk more easily and the tension was released. The atmosphere started to warm up. By the time she left, things were back to normal. At least a truce had been declared.

Left alone together Mary looked at her husband. "How are things going up there?"

"Well, you know Gregory and Nora. They always did go at it tooth and nail, but they're all right."

"And the children?"

"Ah. Jeremy's still having trouble in school. Gregory's going to have to think of something soon. But Aaron's doing fine. Marsha's out at work full time. So Nora keeps the house for them. It's her way of paying them back."

"It's only until Christmas."

Hugh looked doubtful. "I hope her plan works. It's not easy for her being up there. Ruth is comical. That little monkey can outwit them all. She'll give them a good run for their money."

"She'll have to. Girls have to be twice as smart as boys."

Hugh didn't challenge his wife. He thought she was probably right. But he'd known women in positions of authority, and it seemed to him that they didn't fare any better than men. Sometimes they were downright overbearing and that irked him. He did not, of course, apply that rather narrow old-fashioned view to his own daughters. He had wanted Britt to become an architect, which is what he'd wanted to be. Failing that, he pushed for law. He was never really satisfied with her success in the teaching profession and he knew her excellence in that line didn't fulfill her either. It wasn't challenging enough. It came too easily for her. He was the same way. He needed a challenge. Always did. But he did not like the idea of her going into the health sciences because he hated doctors and considered most of them charlatans. Mary had been very sick episodically for many years and look how they'd bungled her case. No, he had no faith in them. They called themselves healers, but he'd found precious little evidence of it. No, indeed, they were money grubbers. So he was sorry when Britt wanted to study medicine and got turned down, but he never really wanted her to be a doctor at all. He was only sorry that she didn't get what she wanted. However, he was sorrier still that she wanted it at all.

On the other hand, Mary wanted very much for her daughter to be a doctor and encouraged it all the way. In her estimation all lawyers were shysters and justice was important, but had absolutely nothing to do with practicing law. No, the only worthwhile thing to be was a doctor or, failing that, a nurse. She also recommended teaching as a career. It was a solid, honorable profession and much in demand. But nothing ever worked out as you planned. Rourke wanted to be a priest, and he was married and selling life insurance. Gregory was in quality control and sales. That wasn't what Mary had hoped for him. And neither did Gregory for that matter. He wanted something different, more personally rewarding. And Nora. Well, she had always hated school and there didn't seem to be much anyone could do about that. You could only push so hard and for so long. People eventually went the way they were meant to go, according to Mary Erikson. But whatever the power working behind the scenes, it seemed to be running adverse to the natural undercurrent of human desires. Nevertheless they were better off than most. That was undeniably true and, besides, self-pity was loathsome and led to self-hate. The gospel according to Mary and brought to life by Hugh Erikson. He never gave up and neither did his wife. Their offspring, therefore, were an oddly mangled combination of character traits that they didn't seem to notice, but outsiders certainly did.

-Seven-

By the first week in December, the days continued drizzly and were darker than ever. They were also noticeably shorter and the nights longer. Nobody seemed to mind. For the first time in a long while, people were more than ready to abandon autumn, the best-loved season for most Montrealers, and they welcomed the outset of winter. But winter stubbornly refused its cue, and the city and its inhabitants were caught in a seasonal limbo.

Hugh and Mary Erikson had gone up to see Rourke in Ottawa on the Wednesday morning that Britt went down for what was to be her last attempt at artificial insemination. Only her mother knew of this desperate attempt to have a child. Her periods had become so erratic that management of the process was difficult, but a few times she had indeed been ovulating and with any luck at all she should have conceived, but didn't. It was frustrating, and she hated the whole process. However, one thing was certain: Roddy couldn't give her a child, not now that he was back on dialysis. And she couldn't just give him up. She didn't want to. That seemed callous. At the same time, she didn't think she owed him any explanations either, so she didn't tell him. She didn't tell anyone, only her mother. But it just wasn't working, and so she had started once again inquiring into adoption while still trying to have one of her own. Either way, it didn't matter.

Returning home after spending most of the morning at the clinic downtown, Britt made some tea and lit a cigarette. Her chances of adopting a child in Canada were just about nil. Even for an older child, the doors were closed to her and everyone else too. The children were being kept in foster homes and not released for adoption. It was a racket, and big money was involved. Between bureaucratic bungling and a good deal of cash passing through greedy hands, the child's welfare was the last thing to be considered. Bonding with natural parents was promoted even when the parents weren't visible or actively involved. It was all a great charade and again a classic example of textbook mind twisting. Social workers had been educated to believe in the almighty system for the common good. Professionals were convinced of its merits, and that's what counted. Now people were starting to look elsewhere for children who needed a home, and a lot of countries were finding the whole sordid affair highly profitable.

Britt had finally written to Mother Theresa in Calcutta and was surprised that she actually answered her. But the response itself didn't come as a shock. Her order had given up trying to deal with Canadian red tape and governmental demands. They dealt with France, Belgium, Holland, Germany and many other countries, but not Canada.

Then Virginia told her about a program called Outreach headed up by an American living in Maryland, Don Willet. They didn't exactly get involved with adoptions, but several couples had found children open for adoption through them. Don willet traveled to Nepal twice a year, and he had connections there. She had written to the man several times and spoken with him on the phone. He was in Nepal now and promised to look into the matter for her. She allowed her hopes to surface once again. Sometimes people got lucky. Sometimes.

That night she had a disturbing dream. She dreamt she was being hanged for some crime she'd committed, but she didn't know what the crime was, and no one would tell her. There was no guilt involved, just some crime against society and the penalty was execution. So they hanged her in a sterile looking room without any personality to it. Certainly no one lived there, and there was nothing anyone could do, not even her mother. The problem was they bungled it, and so she felt the sharp relentless pain throughout her body, especially down her spinal cord and went unconscious. She was supposed to be dead, but found herself alive. When she came to, she was till hanging and the pain was agonizing. And she remembered her first waking thought in the dream was, "Oh Christ! I'm still alive. They missed." But then her mind flipped into the safe space of logic and reason. She was thinking, and quite rightly, that she couldn't be hanged twice for the same crime--whatever it was. That was against the law.

She shuddered upon awakening and lay very still thinking about it. Then she started to smile and laughed at herself. Logic and the use of reasoning were lost in the turbulent living of day to day. But it was a fine human achievement. In a world where little made sense, trying to make sense of random happenings had to be a worthy challenge. No harm in that. Of course, expecting answers was useless and bothersome. But there had to be some value in trying. That's how societies evolved, she supposed. And that's why the lack of trying brought about their disintegration. If we don't try, what are we here for? And if there's no reason for us being here, then why were we here at all? There were lots of cliche answers to that, and she didn't find any of them acceptable.

* * *

Exactly one week later tragedy struck, and the Erikson family reeled under its impact, but to all outward appearance, they were as stoic as ever. Inside, however, each one sought the eye of the storm where he or she could find a calm and quiet place while the storm raged all around them.

Around 1:30 in the morning during the second week in December, Britt heard someone knocking at her door. She stumbled out of bed, still half asleep, and started down the hallway.

Unfastening the lock, the door swung open revealing her mother, standing in the dimly lit corridor. She blinked and rubbed the sleep from her eyes.

"What's wrong? How long have you been knocking?"

"Quite a while."

"I must have been in a heavy sleep."

"Can you come up?"

"Yes, sure. What is it?"

"Your father . . . I don't know. I can't. . ."

"Just a minute."

Britt went back to her bedroom and grabbed her robe. She was pulling it on and tying it as she kept in step with her mother who was heading back down the hall and up the stairs to her apartment.

"What's wrong with him?"

"I don't know." Mary shook her head. "He's taken that horrible sleeping pill that I've asked him to get changed. It has such a bad effect on him."

"What . . . the Halcion?"

"Yes, but it's never been like this before. I can't wake him up."

They were in the apartment now, and Britt followed her mother into the bedroom.

"How many did he take?"

"Just one."

Britt frowned and went over to her father who was lying in bed and seemed to be sleeping, and very peacefully. But then he'd always been a quiet sleeper. She felt his hands and face. His body was warm, but not fevered. His fingers were pliant and loosely interlaced over the covers, but when she called him repeatedly and shook him gently, there was no response.

"Could the sleeping pill do that?" Mary asked.

"I don't know," Britt muttered and felt for a radial pulse. She couldn't get one there, so she tried for a carotid. Still nothing. But then he'd always had low blood pressure and a slow light pulse. She did too. So maybe her fingers, usually sensitive enough to find anyone's pulse, where deceiving her. My stethoscope, she thought, but there was no time for that now. Suddenly she pulled one of the pillows from under his head, slightly hyper-extending the neck, and pinched off his nasal cavity. Then using the other hand to position his jaw, she put her mouth over his and exhaled a long breath, watching to see if his chest would rise. And it did. "Oh Christ!" she thought, "He's out." She glanced at her mother who was standing back and watching her. On the verge of telling her to call 911, Britt rejected the idea. That might cause panic, and her mother was every bit as terrified of what was happening as Britt was. So she gave him two more quick breaths and hurried from the room to get to the phone at the end of the hall. The ambulance dispatcher wanted details and Britt's voice rose irritably.

"Listen, damn it, I'm a nurse, and I can't get a pulse. I think he's had a coronary. Get someone here. Now!"

The woman took the address and apartment number and Britt waited a few seconds before turning to see that her mother had heard everything. But there was no time for all that now.

"Wait here for the ambulance, Mother." And Mary was left in the living room while Britt headed back down the hall to the bedroom. She continued breathing for him. He was still warm, but had no pulse that she could detect. Compressions, her thoughts raced in. But how? On a soft surface, they'd have little or no effect and trying to get him on the floor might do more damage.

She was still working on him and considering what more she could do when the ambulance arrived only minutes after she'd put the call in. The team was fully equipped with a portable defibrillator and injectable medications. A doctor was in attendance. They put Mary Erikson and Britt out of the room and went to work. Not a word passed between the two women as Mary seemed to be rooted to the spot where she stood, and Britt prowled back and forth across the length of the living room. They were only in there with the door closed a short time when Britt marched back down the hall and into the bedroom. They had her father on the floor and a full code for cardiac arrest was underway. One of the attendants came quickly toward her.

"You must leave the room."

"It's all right. I know what's happening."

The doctor looked up at her. "I know, but you can't stay. Get out . . . please!"

The attendant was moving her toward the door, but not before she had a chance to glance at the monitor. He was in ventricular tachycardia and, by the look of that rhythm, it was small wonder she couldn't get a pulse. But he wasn't in ventricular fibrillation. Not yet. Still, his chances weren't good, and she knew it. The attendant pushed her through the door and closed it behind her. Mary Erikson was waiting, and all she could think to say to the poor woman was, "prepare yourself. He mightn't make it."

They waited in the kitchen until the team emerged from the room and both of them looked at the doctor. He shook his head and then sat down at the table to write out the death certificate.

"What was it?" Britt asked. "A massive coronary?"

The doctor looked up and nodded. "I think so."

"A heart attack?" Mary looked from Britt to the doctor.

"But there wasn't anything wrong with his heart. Nothing. And he's been checked thoroughly."

"It happens, Mrs. Erikson."

"But with no warning? No. . . ." She was shaking her head. "We have to know for sure. I've got to know."

"Well, we could do an autopsy."

"Yes. We should have one."

"No autopsy." Britt's voice cut in.

"But Britt, we've got to know for sure. I've got two sons. If there's anything . . . He was a healthy man!"

"No autopsy." Her daughter stared at her. "No one's touching him. Leave him be."

Mary looked away from her and back at the doctor. She didn't press it further, and he went ahead and completed the form.

"Will you be taking him to hospital . . . until morning, I mean?"

"No. If you call a funeral parlor, they'll come. There's twenty-four hour service." The doctor stood up. He looked from one to the other. It had all happened so quickly and quietly.

"I'm sorry," he said. "Very sorry."

Mary saw him to the door, and when she got back to the kitchen found, Britt leaning with her head against the fridge. The harsh, racking sounds coming from her daughter brought her back to reality and what had actually happened.

"Don't, darling. Don't do that."

Britt wrenched herself away from the cold surface and out of the brief paroxysm of grief. She never cried again in front of her mother or anyone else, for that matter.

"No, all right," she mumbled, "We need a number to call. A funeral home."

"Yes, we'll find one."

Britt called them and they were coming.

"We should call the others."

"I'll call them," Mary said. "I should do that. You go and stay with your father. He shouldn't be left alone."

"No, he shouldn't."

Britt walked away from her and down the hall to the bedroom. They had left him on the floor, covered up. Even his face was shrouded. That shouldn't be, she thought. They shouldn't cover his face. She drew the sheet back and knelt down beside him. Then she scanned his face. He looked so calm now and surprisingly young again, as if all the care and worry had been lifted from him. To her he seemed beautiful. Angelic. Yes, like an angel, miraculously released and free again after a long bondage. Without her realizing it, her hand came out, and she laid it against his cheek, still warm and not in the least drained of color. She bent and kissed him on the forehead and, keeping her hand on his face, she remembered how the Irish blessed those who were departing from them. Without any conscious effort on her part, the words assembled themselves in her mind. Yes, she thought, I hope the road rises up before you and that the wind will always be at your back, that the sun shines warm upon your face and the rains fall soft upon your fields and that until we meet again, God holds you in the palm of His hand. I wish all that for you and believe you have it now.

Then an emotion close to envy assailed her and obliterated the deep sense of loss. But there'd be plenty of time for that later, maybe even years. Right now, time and pain were suspended, and in their place came a sense of awe and wonder at the look of him. His face was luminous in the soft lighting of the room, and she knew that very soon faces all around her would be contorted with pain and shock. She too would be putting up her guard behind a closed and impenetrable expression. There was no other way.

By the time the men from the funeral home arrived, Mary Erikson had called Rourke in Ottawa and Gregory and Nora in Toronto. As if by preternatural awareness that something was wrong, none of them had been able to get to sleep that night. And now they knew why. They'd be leaving at first light for Montreal and home.

Mary and Britt, once again, went into the living room to wait. As they were taking him out, Britt turned away, but she did follow her mother to the window. The street was dark and empty, and the bright orange shroud covering the body of Hugh Erikson stood out like a neon sign marking the end of a life. Then he was placed in the waiting van, and the door slammed shut. No one noticed except the two silent women looking down from the apartment window. They waited until the vehicle was lost to their view. It was 3:30 in the morning. Britt turned to her mother. "You can't stay here tonight. Come down to my place."

Mary nodded. "Yes, first I should go through his personal papers before everyone arrives."

"All right. I'll fix up the room and strip the bed. What do you want me to do with . . ."

Mary shivered. "Get rid of it all."

It took them less than an hour to finish up in the apartment. Then they locked the door and went down to Britt's flat to wait until the others arrived. They made coffee and smoked quietly. There didn't seem to be much to say.

Rourke arrived first with his wife, Claire, and sons Reginald and Lee. They all appeared stunned, and Rourke looked like he'd stepped outside himself, and the cost of re-entry at this time was beyond his means. The others wouldn't be down until sometime in the afternoon. They were driving down from Toronto and that would take at least six hours. So Rourke went out with Britt to make the funeral arrangements. She had already called Father Kiley, a very old man and now formally retired, but Britt wanted him to do the service, and she knew he wouldn't refuse her. They were due at the rectory between ten and eleven in the morning and so they went to the funeral home first. When the usual information was required, Rourke couldn't get the words out, so his sister answered and made the stipulation.

"The coffin is to be closed and opened only at the request of immediate family." She looked at her brother and he nodded. "Remember," Britt stressed the point. "Keep it closed."

"I understand." The director looked at her and then at Rourke. "Exception only for immediate family and then closed again. I understand. That's how it will be." They finished wording the brief and unadorned notice for the newspaper. The director would take care of all that too. "Now, about the coffin. Would you like me to take care of that?"

Britt looked at Rourke and he shook his head. "We'll choose one." The director led the way. There were a number of them. Britt looked around. "Which one, Rourke? He valued wood . . . worked in it all his life. Which one?"

"This one," Rourke moved his hand over the glossed surface. "It's oak. That's best."

The interview with Father Francis Kiley was equally strained, but Britt was very fond of the gentle, old priest, old-fashioned in his views, but soft-spoken and understanding. Rourke liked him too and that was clearly written all over his face. The mass was arranged for Friday morning, and when they came to the music Father Kiley tilted his head to one side and thought about Britt's request.

"The Faure Requiem," he paused. "I guess she could manage that, but I'd better call her today so she'll have at least a day to practice. It's a difficult piece . . . and you should select a hymn. Ave Maria? She has a beautiful voice."

"I know." Britt nodded. "Do you know what her fee is, Father, because I want her. No one else. And yes, Ave Maria."

"She'll do it, of course . . . And she usually doesn't charge anything, but the Faure Requiem." He rubbed his chin.

"There'll be something for her, Father." Britt managed a smile. "And for the service?"

"A donation. That's all." He looked at the pair of them. "About the reading, would someone in the family . . ."

Britt looked at her brother, "Rourke?"

"No." He shook his head. "I don't think so."

Britt glanced at the priest. "I guess not, Father."

"No, all right."

They all got up, and Father Kiley went with them to the door. "If you need me, just call. I have your number in case I have to reach you." When they had gone the old priest sat and thought for a short time. He was fifteen years older than Hugh Erikson who had died so suddenly having just turned sixty-five. All of his own brothers and sisters were dead, and he'd buried all of them. He had only nephews and nieces left and all of them were out of Quebec. It felt strange to have come from such a large family and now to be left so alone in his last years. He thought about the two younger people who had just left, both stricken and yet so contained. Neither had had more than an hour's sleep. That was obvious.

Nora was sitting beside Aaron's bed very early in the morning. He still slept unaware of her presence but soon, she knew, she'd have to wake him and tell him that his grandfather, the man whom he'd thought of as his father, was dead. Her father.

My father, she thought, and remained so still she could have been in a trance.

Hearing the words from their mother, neither Gregory nor his sister had been able to say anything. They stared at each other across the kitchen and didn't move. All at once both felt as if a great weight had taken up residence in their hearts and indicted them to a silence which they willingly accepted. Marsha glanced from one to the other and found the absence of any sound whatsoever even more frightening than death itself. She started to jabber, moved jerkily around the room and finally clutched at her chest.

"Stop it, Marsha." Gregory finally snapped at her, breaking the spell. "You're hysterical."

"I'm not," Marsha gasped. "I'm having palpitations. They're terrible . . . terrible. He can't die just like that!"

Nora turned away, "I'll make some coffee."

"Yes, yes do that." Gregory nodded to her. "Will we let the children sleep a few more hours?"

"Yes, it's the middle of the night. We'll wait until dawn."

"Jeremy's going to take this hard, and so will Aaron, especially Aaron."

"I know." Nora's face was flushed, and she couldn't trust her voice to say anything more.

"My God, how could this happen!" Marsha started up again, "It's just not fair. Not right. He's too young. There was nothing wrong . . ."

"Will you shut up!" Gregory turned on her savagely. "Shut up!"

"But my heart . . . the palpitations. They're worse. I'm having pain."

Gregory shook his head and sighed. He felt like letting go right then and there. It took all the will power he could compel to sit down in a chair and remain quiet.

"I have to go to the Emergency..." Marsha jumped up. "I have to! Something's wrong with me."

Gregory glared at his wife and came very close to striking her.

"I'll take you." Nora looked from Marsha to her brother and back again. "Go and get dressed."

Gregory looked disgusted. He got up and went into the living room. It was dark in there, and he stretched out on the couch and stared up at the ceiling. As he heard the front door closing behind his wife and sister, he allowed the tears he'd kept dammed up to flow freely and gradually. The tightness in his chest subsided, and his head no longer felt like it was ready to burst.

At the Emergency, the doctor examined Marsha. He even went so far as to order a cardiogram which he studied carefully and then shrugged. "There's nothing wrong with you, Mrs. Erikson. Your heart's fine."

"No, well we've just received terrible news. My father-in-law died. That's what caused all this. So my sister-in-law brought me here."

"Your sister-in-law?" The doctor glanced at Nora.

"You mean it's your father?"

"Yes, my father."

"And she . . ." The doctor stopped and looked confounded.

"Well, Mrs. Erikson, I'll give you some serax. It'll help calm you down."

"But I don't like taking . . . "

The doctor didn't listen further. He called a nurse and asked her for a half dozen tablets. Then he wrote out a prescription. "Here," he handed the small envelope containing the tablets and the prescription to Marsha. "For your own sake and everyone else's, take them, Mrs. Erikson." Then he looked again at Nora as they were preparing to leave. "Are you all right?"

"Yes, I'm okay."

"I'm very sorry," he said and walked away.

Marsha went up to bed when they got home. It was four o'clock in the morning. In two hours they'd have to wake the children and prepare to leave. Nora went into the living room and Gregory sat up. "She's all right, I suppose?"

"Of course." Nora looked over and could see him quite clearly. Her eyes had adjusted to the darkness in the room. "She's fine . . . just fine." Gregory reached over to switch on a lamp and Nora added, "Why not leave it off."

"Yes, all right. There's some brandy left."

"That would be good."

"Yes, yes it would. I'll get it."

At six in the morning they went upstairs. Gregory into Jeremy's room and Nora into Aaron's room where Ruth was sleeping in a bed against the far wall.

Aaron was slow in waking. It was still dark outside and Nora switched on the bedside lamp. Finally he was fully awake and looking at her. Then she told him. Aaron stared at her, wide-eyed and unblinking. He knew what dead meant. But that God should take him, the man he loved best in all the world . . . take him away from him now. The small boy, just turned six, shook his head. No there was some mistake.

"Why would God do that?" he asked.

"I don't know, Aaron. Nobody knows."

As the child's eyes filled up and the tears started to splash onto his face, Nora reached for him and hugged him tightly in the now unbearably quiet room. Then she woke Ruth up and she too seemed to understand that something had gone terribly wrong in the night and that she too had lost someone she was going to miss.

Britt met them in the hallway around three in the afternoon. Nora stared at her sister and said nothing. She didn't need to. There was a volume of words in the look that went between them. But Gregory came forward and hugged her tightly. He didn't seem to want to let go. She didn't know if she wanted him to.

Now everyone knew except Roddy. Virginia had just left. She was taking the evening shift at the hospital, and she'd explain everything to the head nurse. Britt didn't need to call him. Virginia had only found out because Britt had to call and cancel some plans they'd made for the morning. She had wanted to come over as soon as she heard, but her enigmatic friend put her off, reminding her that she'd only recently lost her own mother, and she needed to take the trip she'd planned to Central America. Britt's cousin was going to sign the documents for her passport renewal and the arrangements were already made for that day.

Roddy called around 5:30, and Britt told him.

"Why didn't you call me?" he asked.

"I don't know." Britt shook her head. "I didn't have the words. I still don't."

"When's he being waked?"

"Tonight."

"So soon?" Roddy's eyebrow shot up.

"Yes, tonight and tomorrow. The funeral's on Friday."

"Tonight," Roddy paused. "I'm supposed to lay the tile in the store. I've arranged to meet Gino there well, never mind. I'll come. What time?"

"Around seven." Britt had caught the hesitation in his voice and knew that although merely noted, she would never forget it.

"I'll come around seven then."

"That would be nice of you, Roddy."

She put down the receiver and banished the doubts from her mind. It would be weeks later before she thought again of that conversation.

That period of time; the days and weeks that followed became a blur in the memories of those closest to Hugh Erikson. But if the progression of time as such was lost, the impact, certain flashes of things happening, the expressions on individual faces, what was seen and what was kept hidden, were to remain forever. They were all at least partly in shock, but every one of them madly attempted to bury whatever feelings that rose to the surface along with the man.

Father Kiley called Britt on the Thursday evening before she left for the funeral home. He wavered and then plunged on. "About the reading, Britt . . . If not someone from the immediate family, perhaps an uncle or a cousin."

"No, no." Britt closed her eyes for a moment. "He's my father. I'll do it."

"Fine, I've picked out a few to choose from. Can you come by the rectory?"

"Yes, I'll come soon . . . on my way to the funeral home."

Later that evening, Rourke came over to her. "You're going to do the reading?"

Britt nodded and Rourke went on, "then I'll do the eulogy. One of us has to do it. Nora and Greg have their hands full."

"I know. Aaron's very upset. . .so is Jeremy."

"Yes, my boys are older. They can handle it better."

When it was all over and Rourke was preparing to leave, Britt took him aside and they went into the bedroom of her apartment. "We go back a long way, Rourke. You and I."

"Yes, we do."

"You don't want anything to break that, do you?"

He was sitting on her bed, and now he looked up at her and moved his head from side to side.

"No, I don't."

"Then leave all Dad's tools and the lathe machine here."

"But why? Mother doesn't want them around in her apartment."

"I know. She can't stand the sight of them. But you and Greg could put them in Nora's apartment. Leave them for Aaron, Rourke."

"But what would a little boy do with them?"

"I don't know." Britt shrugged. "But right now he feels better with them around. He lies on the floor by the lathe machine and stares by the hour."

"Well, Mother said . . ."

"Mother said to remove it." Britt walked away from him and went to the window. "So remove it and all his tools, but not to your place. Not yet. Right now and for the next little while Nora needs them for Aaron. Try to understand, Rourke. Reg and Lee have you and Jeremy's got Gregory, but Aaron . . .? He thinks that Dad is his father and now compare his loss to the others. We had our father for a long time. Aaron only had his for six years."

Rourke finally nodded. "All right." I'll have Greg and the boys to help me. We'll put it in Nora's apartment. She'll be back again in two weeks for Christmas?"

"Yes, they're coming back. And Rourke," she added, "It's not forever. Just for a short time. You'll get all the tools and equipment, but not yet."

"Right. I understand. I'll lock the machine so he can't get hurt."

After he left, Britt lied down on the bed and closed her eyes. She didn't want to go upstairs where most of the family was. They were re-arranging the apartment, and there'd be no vestige left to signify that her father had lived there. It annoyed her, but she understood. It was the only way for her mother to go on. Her impulse would be to lock the door and walk away for a while. Time healed, or did it? And as for the squabbling, well, that happened in most families. It wasn't always motivated by greed but a desperate need to have something belonging to or was a part of what was lost to them.

She got up and decided to go for a drive. There'd be no one at the cemetery now. No onlookers.

Rourke undertook to settle his father's estate for his mother. What there was of it which didn't look like much. Mary gave him all the papers. "There's not much you can do, Rourke. He had term insurance with the school board. It's all cancelled when you turn sixty-five, but I can apply for the widow's pension."

"Well, we'll see," Rourke replied. "We'll just see about it. I'll look through the policy and all this correspondence that you've kept. I'll call you Monday or Tuesday."

He kissed his mother goodbye and was gone.

On the way out of the city, he had an accident. No one was hurt, but his car was wrecked. He turned to his wife.

"You were right, Claire. I should have let you drive."

"Well, no one's hurt." Claire replied. "That's the main thing."

-Eight-

The important thing now was to get through Christmas. The family was still in shock and the numbness actually helped. Yes, it did. Britt for one kept waiting for her father to walk through the door, and he'd smile and remove his hat. She saw him everywhere.

It came as a relief to return to work on Tuesday morning and an even greater relief when she realized that Virginia must have explained the way things were. Some people felt better talking about personal loss and some didn't. So they were concerned and kind, but they didn't ask any questions, and they noted too that she never mentioned her father. When Dr. Brian Yeung, the Chief of Psychiatry, came in around ten o'clock to do rounds, he came up to Britt first.

"It was very sudden, wasn't it?"

"Yes, it was."

Yeung said nothing. He took up the list of patients, "Let's see, what have we got?"

"Full house." Britt looked at him sideways as he stood beside her and pointed to the first patient on the list. "He can probably go and there's a bed in P.H.A."

"Good, I've got two out in the hall. They've got to be admitted. So let's start, shall we?"

"Right. Helen's with a patient. I'll call her. Who do you want first?"

"Kaminsky. Is Tom around?"

"Yes, he's been here. I think he's in his office."

"Good. I'll be right back . . . Oh," he stopped and turned back. "Have you got a cigarette?"

"Sure." She tossed him her pack of cigarettes. "The lighter's inside."

"Thanks." He smiled at her. "I'll bring them right back."

They're a fine people, the Orientals, Britt thought as she left the office to find Helen. They could say just enough without uttering one word. I like that.

Mary Erikson, left alone in the apartment, now found the time long and she too said very little. It would be better when Nora returned with the kids at Christmas. It surprised and pleased her that Virginia visited, and when she came for an hour or so in the evenings or during the afternoons, the time passed more quickly. She was good company. Better than some of her long-standing friends who telephoned almost every day, but seldom came around. She wondered about it and thought that maybe her daughter was right-- her husband's death reminded them of their own mortality.

Rourke called her Tuesday evening and said he'd be coming down the following day. Britt was at work, and she was alone when he arrived around noon. Rourke was as mild-mannered and quiet as ever until she asked him about the insurance policy and all the correspondence with the company and the school board.

"Yes, I read through everything." He replied in an undertone. "I had no idea. Those sons-of-bitches put him through a wringer for the past three years." He was angry and quiet. A deadly combination. Mary knew her offspring better than most mothers. They were all basically good and descent people. Strong individuals all of them, but they had their faults. Gregory could be selfish and self-centered. He could also be unreasonable. Nora had to be right, even when she was clearly wrong and knew it. She seldom bothered to hold in and lashed out at people. She could also be vicious and was often unreasonable. However, Britt and Rourke were very alike in many ways. They usually presented themselves as calm and easy-going, and as a general rule they were, but God help anyone who crossed their path. Always watch the quiet ones was a very wise and true old saying.

Their rage wasn't easily sparked, but once ignited it became an explosion and there was no thought given to the consequences for others or themselves. So now she looked at her eldest son who was almost forty and tried to diffuse some of that rage because what he was saying was not news to her.

"Well you're an insurance agent yourself so you know how it is."

"Yes I know all about it," Rourke nodded, "but those bastards had no right to do what they did. They badgered him. Repeated medical exams, statements, X-rays . . . even a psychiatric exam? What the hell did they think they were doing?"

Mary shrugged. "Following the usual procedure I guess. Everyone goes through it."

"General procedure? Running a man in circles. Making him squirm? That's rich! Well, they'll pay for what they did."

"It's over now, Rourke. Everything cancels out at sixty-five."

"Maybe . . . yes maybe." Rourke gave her a baleful look. "But there's a clause. A very small clause, hidden away, but it's there."

"What clause?"

"The clause that says that if the insured person dies within thirty days of turning sixty-five the policy is not null and void and the claim is payable in full."

"They'll never pay anything. They'll fight it."

"You think so? Well, I'll fight them every inch of the way. I'll nail them right to the wall. But first I have to know if you want me to go ahead because it might get dirty . . . and we may still lose."

"I told you to go ahead. Do what you think best."

"I'll have to make a few calls." Rourke sifted through the bundle of papers and found the name he was looking for and the number. Once on the phone, he directed all the rage that he'd carefully avoided releasing up to that point on what he considered the morons on the other end of the line. When the receptionist told him that the director was in a conference for claims' adjustment policies, he shouted at her. "No. I don't want his assistant! I want Stuart Clarke."

"Who's calling, please?"

"Rourke Erikson from Great Eastern Life."

The secretary noted the name and sighed. "Just a minute, Mr. Erikson. They should be breaking for lunch. I'll see if I can locate him."

A few minutes later, Stuart Clarke came on the line. "Mr. Erikson? Do I know you?"

"No, but you will."

Clarke frowned. There was a threatening undertone in the voice coming at him.

"What's the problem, Mr. Erikson?"

"The problem is you insured my father under the Windsor Board of Education. The problem's you've used every dirty device you could conjure up to renege on your obligations. You've twisted this policy I have before me every which way to suit your means. You've used every filthy trick in the book."

"Now wait a minute, Mr. Erikson!"

"No, you wait! You better take down the name. Hugh Erikson. Policy number 9 0 7 8 4 7 9. Got that? Well, he's dead."

"Just a minute." Clarke buzzed his secretary and asked for the file on Hugh Erikson. Once he had it before him, he looked it over. Finally he spoke again into the receiver. "Yes, Mr. Erikson, I have it here."

"You've probably also noted he just turned sixty-five."

"Yes . . . Yes, I see that."

"Well, he's dead. He died on December the seventh."

"I'm sorry to hear that, Mr. Erikson."

"You should be!" Rourke's voice rose. "You killed him! If it hadn't been for your colossal greed and chicanery, he might well be alive today. My father's dead, and it's your fault! You killed him.

You're responsible. You jerked him around."

"That's absurd!" Clarke's face was apoplectic.

"Is it? He died of a coronary. That could easily translate into a stress related occurrence and you sure as hell provided that."

"Well, that might be hard to determine, legally or otherwise, and I don't like your accusations."

"And I don't like anything about you or your way of doing business. Listen carefully, Clarke. My father turned sixty-five on November 17th. He died December 7th. That's within the thirty day time frame so generously extended by your company. The policy extends to cover 30 days following the date of birth. So the claim is legal and payable."

"Well, I don't know." Clarke wavered. "No claim can be put in after the insured turns sixty-five."

"Read your policy. Find the clause. It's there. Even you avaricious bastards can find it. Use a magnifying glass if you have to."

"I'll need the original or notarized copies of the required documents to proceed . . . if, in fact, we do proceed."

"You had better, Clarke. I'll sue you bastards. Count on it . . . and the company I'm associated with has a battery of very competent lawyers that would consider your company's questionable business ethics excellent fodder for the legal grind. But you first, Clarke. You're number one on the list."

"If that's a threat . . . "

"That's a fact. So . . . expect to hear from me, Clarke. I'm Rourke Erikson, Great Eastern Life, and I'll have the documents in the mail to you. Forty working days, Clarke. I suggest you expedite settlement." He hung up before Stuart Clarke had time to reply.

Mary had overheard everything, and she looked up at him as he came back into the room. He was still furious, but a small, short smile relaxed the muscles around his mouth. He glanced at the woman he knew so well and was so seldom speechless. "Come on,

Mother. We'll go out for lunch. What do you say?"

"Sure, Rourke, why not?" She paused. "That was some conversation."

"A siege is a siege, Mother. And I intend to hound them. Right now, that bastard is probably running a check on me."

"Is that a problem?"

"No, it's not. I'm clean. That'll make them sweat even more." Then he shook his head. "I can't believe what those sons-of-bitches did."

Mary looked at him. "I can't believe you didn't realize how bad it was."

"Nobody every really knows much about another person. We just don't know and then it's too late . . . but I'll try to get this for you. I can at least do that much. It's a long shot, but win or lose, we'll put up a fight."

Rourke was right. As soon as he put down the receiver, Clarke called his assistant and asked him to run a check on Rourke Erikson from Great Eastern Life in Ottawa. Then he leaned back in his chair in the very spacious office he occupied and read over very carefully the complete file on Hugh Erikson.

Christmas finally came and it brought with it a curious respite because its approach had seemed relentless and trailed fear in its wake. Fear, because this was a holiday of hope and no one was feeling very hopeful and they worried that the children would suffer from what they lacked in themselves. But everyone pulled together in one concerted effort for the sake of the young ones. Britt opted to work Christmas Day, but she kept Christmas Eve open and that's when the family gathered. Nora came down with Aaron and Ruth. Gregory followed with Marsha and Jeremy. Friends dropped in, and they had eggnog laced with brandy. They gathered around the piano and sang carols. Jeremy sang one song alone, and that surprised everyone because no one had guessed that the boy, only eleven years old, had such a fine and mellow voice. But no one, not even the children, found it easy, and there was an undercurrent of sadness that was almost tangible. Nonetheless, nobody wanted to banish the ghost that pulled their minds into past Christmases and, at the same time, they fought for control and reached for something better that could be passed on to the children. Mary was finding it most difficult of all, and there seemed little that anyone could do.

Rourke came down Christmas Day, and he waited around after the dinner up at Nora's flat for Britt to return from work. It all turned out better than most expected, and it had been decided that there'd be no celebration for New Year's.

For the second time since Britt had known him, Roderick was annoyed with her, and this time he simply brooded over it and didn't tell her until several weeks later when Britt asked him over and told him outright that she didn't think they should see one another anymore. When he didn't say anything, she looked over at him sitting beside her on the sofa. "The relationship's just not working, Roddy. You're not happy, and I'm tired of trying."

"You're not happy either, are you?" he said quietly.

"No, I'm not," Britt admitted.

"Well, I would have thought you'd at least have talked to me about New Year's before deciding to work. You might have asked me first."

"Did you have plans, Roddy?"

"It doesn't matter now, does it?"

"No, I suppose not."

"But it was New Years and you might have considered that we do something together."

"New Year's . . . ? It never crossed my mind to celebrate it. You went to your family? Your sister's place, I suppose, or friends maybe?"

"Maybe." Roddy fell silent.

"Well, you should go now," Britt resumed after a few minutes. "I'm working tomorrow."

"You're working more than usual. Extra shifts."

"It helps," Britt said, and she turned away from him thinking . . . yes work helps. It takes my mind off things. And you do nothing for me. There's no comfort in you, and I see now that you've done very little to let me be something to you . . . no comfort to you really, as a woman or even, just as a friend.

"Yes, I'd better go." Roderick got up and Britt went to get his coat. At the door he turned back. "But we can keep in touch, can't we? I'll call you."

"Sure. Keep in touch. You'll be opening your store soon."

"Yes, next week." Roddy smiled briefly, and then it faded.

"Well, good luck." Britt opened the door. "You deserve a little mazel in your life."

"Mazel . . . . what does that mean?"

"Yiddish. It means luck."

He bent and kissed her on the cheek. "I'll see you, Britt." Then he closed the door and was gone. It was an odd thing not to feel anything at all. But that's how Britt felt. As for Roderick, his thoughts quickly left the long relationship he'd had with Britt Erikson. But she was a good woman and strong. All the same he didn't miss her, although clearly there was no animosity between them. And he'd be in contact. Of course, he would. However, uppermost in his mind was the opening of his new clothing store. Even having to be on dialysis again wasn't so bad. At least it was bearable now that he had this small enterprise going for himself. It made all the difference.

It was around the middle of January when Britt received the letter from Don Willet. It was dated December 22nd. The Christmas mail rush must have delayed delivery. But then delays and confusion had been the norm over the past weeks.

Finally a good Catholic grade school was found that would admit Aaron. Nora was constantly in contact with her lawyer who was wrangling for s settlement from Ruth's father. He was wealthy, and it seemed he intended taking it all with him. The hearing date had been set. At long last, it had been decided they wouldn't come to court before January twenty-sixth. It would be a relief when that was finally all over. Certainly it had been straining her sister's nerves. The real impact of their father's sudden death hadn't set in yet, and they all knew it. Britt thought her mother was doing quite well, but she knew too that this interval of time was just a smoke screen. When the smoke cleared the reality would remain, and then what? Gregory and Marsha decided that they wanted another child. That should be interesting. Their marriage always seemed to be in turmoil, riddled with separations and passionate reunions. One never knew with those two. They had been married more or less for a dozen years, and few had given the union more than a year. Mary thought her son should be canonized for his efforts and, on principle, the family generally agreed. Gregory could be difficult at times, but Marsha irritated everyone much of the time with the possible exception of Britt and Rourke. Neither of them actively liked or disliked her. Both of them felt she couldn't help the way she was, so why all the fuss? It was senseless for Greg to be driven into an emotional frenzy over her time and time again, especially since everyone knew that he could have Jeremy. There was never any question about that. As for Rourke, well nobody ever really knew anything for sure. The family might speculate, but nobody was certain because Rourke never discussed his very personal and private affairs with anyone. Mary often felt sorry for Rourke. He might act strangely at times and distance himself from the family, but he never complained, and you had to admire him for that. Nobody ever really suspected how very lonely he was much of the time and had been for a long time.

And no one was even remotely aware of the desperation growing in Britt, and that she knew she was fighting a losing battle and felt compelled to fight on anyway. After her father died she gave up entirely on artificial insemination. Her body simply wouldn't comply, and it crossed her mind that she was going against the laws of nature and that's why everything was going wrong. She was losing weight and had little appetite. Her whole menstrual cycle was off balance and that, combined with tension, brought on headaches. That's why, as Roderick pointed out, she was taking more shifts. At work she didn't have time to think about herself or worry about what was missing in her life. Other people had greater problems, and hers were dwarfed in comparison. She had a lot to be thankful for and knew it. A lot of people had much less.

But this letter from Don Willet brought new hope. One of his contacts in Nepal had found a small boy, seven years old, who wanted to be adopted. Don wanted to know why she hadn't gone to Nepal in early September as he thought she had planned. The family of the child had been expecting her. He wanted to know if she was going over within the next few months or did she want to wait until spring when he was scheduled to go over himself and he'd look into it for her. Apparently there were no complications.

Britt rang up Virginia who had the day off like herself. "What do you think, Gin?" she asked when her friend had finished reading the letter.

Virginia was sceptical. "I don't know, Britt. What would Don or his contacts know about it anyway?"

"I don't know." Britt threw up her hands. "You're the one who has known him longer . . . and you've been over there yourself. Do you think it's true and if so how difficult can it be?"

"I think it's probably true there's a child, but it can be very difficult. This child's Tibetan."

"So?"

"They're a very tight and proud community in Kathmandu, and I can't imagine any family there wanting to have one of their children adopted. You should call Don and get some more information."

"I will, but it looks promising, don't you think?"

"I guess so." Virginia frowned. "Are you thinking of going over now?"

"No, not yet. I haven't got the money . . . well, not enough anyway. But I will within a few months."

Virginia thought about it. As far as she knew, Britt had saved some money. Still it would be wiser for her to wait awhile and confirm that there really was a child and that he was adoptable. "I'd call Don," she said finally. "International adoption isn't easy and as for the Nepalese authorities, well, they're as corrupt as hell. Everything's done over there using baksheesh."

"What's baksheesh?"

"A pay-off. Everyone you have to see and everyone you'll have to contact to get to see the person or persons you have to see will expect it. You can depend on that."

"But can I get it through, do you think?"

"I honestly don't know."

Mary was delighted with the whole idea. "Well, this might be your chance," she said to Britt that evening. "I wouldn't wait on it. He's open for adoption now. Who knows what will happen in a few months?"

"I can't leave right now, Mother. I have to work, and I need more money."

"Oh, we'll find the money somehow." Mary gave it some serious thought. "For this, we'll find the money. I know you've had setbacks, but this looks good and you have to try."

"Yes, but I'll have enough money soon. I've been taking extra shifts. They're short of staff at the hospital."

"I know, but don't overdo it. You're always tired. I wish you could get back into teaching, especially if you get a child. Besides, it pays better."

"I know." Britt nodded. "There was an ad in the paper. They want a teacher who's also a nurse."

"Well, that's hard to find." Her mother smiled. "And you've got both."

"The position's in Alberta, Mother."

Mary sighed. "Quebec hasn't much to offer, dear. Not with a name like Erikson. We'll all have to get out sometime in the not too distant future. Even Nora. At least you have some French. Nora hasn't a chance here. She's just waiting for the settlement and that won't be long now."

"I hope she gets it."

"So do I. She could certainly use it."

The following week Britt called out west to a Mrs. Janice Leonard, the Director of Personnel for a school board just north of Edmonton. When Britt expressed an interest in their advertisement in the *Toronto Globe and Mail*, the older woman's interest picked up. She asked a number of pertinent questions and was very satisfied with the answers.

"Well, you sound perfect for the job. It's difficult to find someone with experience in both professions and it's a bonus that you can teach senior English, Biology and Chemistry as well. Your background in psychiatric nursing is a great help, too. Part of your duties will be to act as a part-time school counsellor as well, and as our high school is large, so we have a number of crises, emotional and otherwise."

"Well, having worked in emergency psychiatry for over two years, that shouldn't be too difficult to handle."

"Yes, but you'll be teaching full-time as well, Miss Erikson, and acting as school nurse. It's not an easy assignment. You should be aware of that."

"I understand. If you're interested in my application . . ."

"Oh, we are. Most interested. Why don't you send me all the documents I need to process your application? You already have an Alberta teaching certificate, so that's not a problem. Yes, get it to me as soon as possible and a phone number where we can reach you."

"Yes, of course, Miss Leonard. I'll get everything in the mail to you."

"Fine, I look forward to hearing from you."

Britt put down the receiver and sat thinking about it. Alberta. She had taught in Calgary for one year, and it hadn't been too bad at all. That was the year she started putting on drama and musical productions. Quite a lot of fun, really. Alberta had been strange territory to her. Every bit as distinct as a native Albertan would have found Quebec, or even Newfoundland. Widely considered to be redneck country which to a large extent it was, they were also refreshingly straightforward in their dealings with people. They also had big dreams and a big open sky which compensated, at least in part, for the flatness of the terrain. On a more practical note, the job would pay twice as much as she was making now with half the labor. And her mother was right. Their days in Quebec were numbered. The government was on a false high, protecting and promoting their distinct society, even overriding a Supreme Court ruling using their constitutionally unfounded right of veto. It boggled the mind and their language vice squads were both laughable and an ugly reminder that oppression and racism were very much alive and indeed thriving. The Anglo-Montreal community was divided and ineffective. Few entertained the idea of fighting back. No wonder the German people kow-towed to Hitler and others kept silent, including most of the Jews. No one liked a bully, but few were prepared to fight him or his thugs. Fear took over and governing became nothing more than a reign of terror. That's what was happening in Quebec, and it could only get worse. It seemed that people had to fight for their rights or they ended up having no rights at all. She knew too that fighting back meant fighting alone, and that meant sure defeat. Nothing had changed really. The Second World War might never have happened at all, or the civil rights movement of the 1960s in the United States. People merely felt there was nothing worth fighting for. The "just society" had died at its inception. People found it difficult enough protecting their own backs and getting their lives together. And who could blame them? But the fear around everywhere was disturbing. Fear and love were the two most crippling emotions.

Britt sat brooding about it all. Finally she shook her head and set about collating all the documents required for the teaching/nursing/counsellor position out west. A small town called Westlock, just north of Edmonton, didn't sound very exciting, but she was in a rut. So maybe a change of venue would help. In any case, it wouldn't hurt to submit her application. She could decide on it later if, indeed, they offered her the position.

A number of things happened around the end of January which had a sort of domino effect. Nora's lawyer called to inform her that the hearing was finally set for January twenty-fifth. There'd be no further changes. She also told her that Ibrahim's lawyer, a Mr. Marvin Katz, one of the finest in Toronto, had put in his final settlement offer. Nora made a face.

"What is it, Anna?"

"Thirty thousand. And he's adamant about it, Nora. Not a penny more."

"Not a chance. Fifty thousand and he's getting off easy."

Anna Waldmann sighed. "Nora, be reasonable. He'll never go for that, and you know it."

"Then I'll see him in court."

"You don't want that. Cases like this are messy and can drag on for years."

"He'll have to appear too and that means coming down to Montreal each time."

"That's not the point, Nora," Anna argued. "He hasn't played his trump card. You know it and I know it."

"Well, he hasn't played it, Anna. So?"

"He still might. Ibrahim probably hasn't thought of it. But you can be damn sure Katz has. He doesn't miss a beat. He's sharp. Believe me."

"I believe you. So why hasn't he?"

"I'm not sure. He knows that all he has to do is ask for visiting rights for his client . . . which you have to give him if he agrees to continuing support, and you'll drop all the proceedings against him."

"I would Anna. Immediately. So why?"

Anna shook her head and smiled cynically. "I think he likes you."

"Then I have to wonder what he's like with people he doesn't like."

"He's only doing his job, Nora. It's nothing personal. But he being soft. Take my word for it. He probably knows that his client's the father and, besides, he can afford it. I don't think he wants to go into court, either. He wants an out-of-court settlement, and that'll be handled at the best possible moment, just before we're ready to be called at eleven o'clock, January twenty-fifth."

"They're cutting it very close."

"So are we. But give me something to go on. Fifty thousand is just too high."

"Forty-five then, but . . ."

"Forty thousand." Anna cut in. "If you go with that I think I can settle with him."

Nora hesitated, then she said crisply. "All right, Anna. Forty thousand and not a cent less." Then she added, "And he relinquishes rights. That's definite and he must sign off."

"Agreed. " Anna nodded. "That's what we'll ask for and probably get."

"If not, we go to court, Anna."

"All right." Anna sighed, half in relief, half in exhaustion. "But let's hope this works. You don't want it dragged into court. Believe me."

"He doesn't want that either. Take my word for it. I know him. Going to court scares the hell out of him."

"Let's hope so. I'll see you on Friday. Half past ten in the morning. The courthouse."

Britt was on evenings throughout most of the week. On Tuesday afternoon she arrived at the hospital and walked into mayhem. Nicole Gautier was in the annex, and she looked not only tired, but frustrated and harried. There was no one in the office, and Britt looked around. "What's the matter? You look beat."

"I am. I've been alone here all day, and it's been hell."

"Alone? How come?"

"Martha called in sick, and Tom couldn't find a replacement."

"Why didn't he pull someone from P.H.A.? It's not as busy over there."

"Don't ask me. I haven't had time to tape and didn't get through all the orders." Nicole let her arms drop by her side and appeared on the verge of tears. "It's been sheer hell! Rounds ended late. There have been transfers and admissions. I've almost finished one admission, but the other one I haven't even seen yet. So. . ."

"You'd better just go home."

"But I haven't taped."

"I'll read the charts and Amanda will be along soon. Late, but reliable. That's Amanda." Britt laughed. "Go on. Get out of here. You've had enough for one day."

"Thanks, I'm sorry about the mess. I tried, but . . ."

"Don't worry about it."

After Nicole left, Britt rapidly started reading through her charts and doing the orders at the same time. There was a multitude of things left over from days, and she was trying to get things sorted out. In the middle of all this turmoil, the intern reappeared, and the triage nurse followed on his heels. Diane possibly thought him a good catch, and that's why he could do no wrong in her eyes. Opinions about him varied, but a number of people, including Britt, thought him a prick. Privileged rich boy to petulant, demanding man, and now a doctor--God's gift to patients and women, Solomon Cooper.

He interrupted Britt, slapping a chart on the desk and tapping it with his fingers. "I want this man transferred. He has to go to the General. They accepted him."

"I'll see to it when I get a minute," she continued signing off an order and making up a medication card.

"No, now." Cooper's eyes squinted and his face reddened.

"When I have the time." Britt looked over at him, and the room was rife with open hostility.

"This has priority. Do whatever else you have to do later."

Britt turned on him and almost shouted. "No. I'll do it later when I have time! Right now I'm busy."

"I'll go and get the chart copied and call transport." Diane cut in.

"Oh, all right." Britt glanced at her. "If you could get that done, I'll be able to take care of the rest. Right now I can't leave here. As you can see, I'm swamped." Solomon Cooper marched out, tossing his head and muttering to himself.

Britt didn't see him again. By four o'clock, Amanda arrived and Britt explained what was going on.

"What a mess!" Amanda said and took the new admission that Nicole didn't have time to assess. Eventually things quieted down.

The following evening, just after Britt arrived at 3:30, Tom stormed into the office and motioned the day nurses out. He slammed the door after them. Amanda hadn't arrived yet. He looked down at

Britt sitting at the desk and went on a rampage.

"I'm told you refused to carry out an order, a doctor's order."

"What order?" Britt's eyes were fixed on him. "What are you talking about?"

"I heard about what happened here last evening with Dr. Cooper. I won't stand for that kind of behavior."

"He was demanding and unreasonable."

"I don't care. That's not for you to decide."

"No? Well, I do. I was busy at the time. His request or order, as you put it, didn't take priority."

"That's not your decision to make!" Tom shouted. "You do what you're told when you're told!"

Britt's anger was rising, and she came back at him with equal force. "When I have the time, and I'll use my judgement."

"He's a doctor and . . ."

"He's a schmuck! An arrogant, ill-mannered prick! And you know it!"

"It doesn't matter what he is." Tom argued and his irritability obscured his ability to analyze the situation. He was going too far. "The patient had to be transferred, you transfer him."

"Yes, when I have the time. I was very busy."

"It gets busy in here. If you can't handle things maybe you shouldn't be here."

"What did you say?" Britt almost came out of her chair. "Are you saying I'm incompetent . . . ? That I can't do the job here?"

"I didn't say that, but if you can't . . ."

"That's exactly what you're saying." Britt stood up and her eyes flashed. Amanda had come into the annex and was staring at them. So were all the patients.

"You have to be able to cope and if . . ."

"I always cope and I always do a good job!" Britt raised her voice. She was enraged. "I'm one of the best nurses on your staff and I'm fast. And you know it! I do assessments quickly and they're accurate. You know that too. Don't ever say that to me again! Never!"

She should have stopped but she went on. It was as if much of the emotion she'd kept safely under lock and key suddenly exploded inside her, and she didn't care what she said. Tom looked at her uneasily and stepped backward. She stormed at him. "How dare you accuse me! It's your fault this place was such a bedlam when I got here yesterday. It was all work left over from days. The orders weren't done. There was no tape and so no report on any of the patients. And an admission to finish and another one to start. And that wasn't Nicole's fault either! You left her alone in here all day. She had everything to do. That's impossible and you know it! But it was your responsibility to keep this place staffed and you didn't. So when I came, it was a mess, and I can't very well get much done if I don't know anything about the patients . . . So I was busy! Don't ever say what you did to me again!"

Tom started to say something, then he changed his mind. He turned on his heel, flung open the door, and stomped out of the annex.

Britt sat down again. All at once she felt tired, so tired. Now that her anger had subsided, the sadness was back and it was plain for everyone to see. Amanda came in and stood quietly for a few minutes, then she sat down. "I shouldn't have said all that to him." Britt mumbled. "I was so angry."

"He had no right to say what he did to you. He goes on rampages. Only this time someone yelled back."

"Yeah, but I lost my temper."

"You should have ignored him. He's done it to everyone. We ignore him."

Britt flicked the pen she was holding on the desk. "Maybe I should take some time off."

"Yes, you should. Why don't you call Grace Peters?"

"You think I should see her?"

Amanda nodded. "Yes. Talk to her about it."

Britt reached for the telephone. "I doubt she'll still be in her office. It's after four."

But Grace Peters was in and when Britt asked to see her, she said to come right up. It was a very curious interview.

Seated across from the assistant director of nursing, Britt was at a loss about how or where to begin. Grace Peters waited as the minutes ticked by and then said quietly, "you wanted to see me?"

"Yes."

"What's it all about?"

Britt didn't want to mention anything about Tom Flynn's rampage and her outburst.

"I think I'd like some time off."

"You mean take your holiday now or . . ."

"No . . . no, just time off."

"Without pay?"

"Yes."

"So you want a leave of absence?"

"Yes."

Grace Peters was studying her carefully and Britt could feel her eyes on her even as she fixed her gaze on a single point across the room.

"You must have a reason. What is it?"

Britt started to tell her, but the words wouldn't come. She simply couldn't say the words. It didn't take a very perceptive person to know that something was wrong. Peters did the only thing she could think of to penetrate the wall of silence and get the information she needed. She reached for the handbook of employee guidelines and regulations, checked the index, and then turned to the list of circumstances under which a nurse could get a leave of absence. She started to read slowly and glanced up after each possible cause: pregnancy, illness, special training leave, and finally she came to, a death in the immediate family. At this, Britt nodded and bit down on her lower lip. Grace snapped the book closed.

"Who?" she asked.

"My father."

Grace thought for a moment and then nodded. "Did you return to work right away?"

"Yes." Britt started to relax, but she was still so tense she had to will herself to remain seated and at least appear calm, however Grace Peters wasn't fooled.

"But surely you realize you must have time to grieve. You must take that time."

When Britt didn't answer her, she continued. "Would two months be sufficient?"

"Yes. That would be fine. Thank you."

"You're very welcome. I'll advise personnel, you'll get a notification from them within the next few days."

"Thank you."

Grace Peters nodded and Britt stood up. It had been a very short meeting. On the way back to the annex, she stopped to have a cigarette in the lounge. By the time she got back to work she was composed again, but still angry with Tom Flynn. His timing was bad and she hated that.

Amanda was delighted with the news of her leave of absence.

Within two days she received her notification from personnel relations that her leave was granted. Presumably Tom Flynn received the information too, also through the Director of Human Relations. But he'd made no changes on the current schedule or the new rotation that had recently been posted. At the same time, he was avoiding her and that wasn't hard to do. He just made himself invisible, and she remained on evenings when the only possible time they could encounter each other was at change of shift. She didn't want to see or talk to him either. In all fairness, even if Tom wanted a reconciliation which he probably did, he knew instinctively that any advances he might be prepared to make would be rebuffed. And he was right. Britt's anger might be under control, but it hadn't dissipated.

Most of the staff knew what happened. Britt told only one person on staff, and she was also a personal friend--Virginia, but Amanda had told several of the other nurses, and news always spread quickly in a hospital. All the same, Britt didn't go to the union. It went against her principles. So the stand-off continued for days until finally she did consult Linda McCleary, the union representative who probably knew all the facts, but not from Britt. What the latter needed to know was why the schedule hadn't been altered. Linda shrugged. "You have to put your request in writing to the head nurse."

"But why?" Britt was confused. "I have permission to take leave from the Assistant Director of Nursing, and Human Relations has already approved it."

"Doesn't matter. It has to go through Tom. He has to grant it, but you have to make a formal request."

"That's absurd," Britt remained rigidly impassive. "I don't see the need for it. He's just being obstinate."

"So are you," Linda glanced at her. "He was out of line and in the wrong. He could be brought up by the union, but you didn't approach them."

"I don't want to." Britt scowled at her. "People should fight their own battles."

"You never win fighting alone. Anyway, if that's how you feel just write him a note. He'll have to respond."

Left alone in the lounge, Britt tapped her fingers on the arm of the chair and thought about it, but so many other things were going on that her mind quickly jumped to other concerns.

Nora had to go to court in the morning. The day had finally

come. Her lawyer thought it best to bring Ruth just to have her there. That's how it had to be. Anna Waldmann had orchestrated this legal showdown, bringing to an end, one way or another, the long and often harrowing suit against Tony Ibrahim for refusal of child support. At the same time, Nora never really had any intentions of allowing Ibrahim anywhere near her daughter. She had loved him, and probably still did if she'd allow herself to think about it, but things hadn't turned out as she hoped. She was hurt and disappointed and that translated emotionally into anger and resentment.

Britt sat thinking about going down to the new Palais de Justice the following morning. She had told her sister she'd accompany her and keep the baby with her. Ruth was Britt's favourite child and everyone in the family and even friends knew it, including her sister. She loved Aaron too, of course, and all the others, but Ruth was special. She looked different from the others too. She had aquiline Semitic features and an aggressive, tenacious nature. Oddly enough, the child, still just a baby really, loved Britt too. The little girl had come to her naturally almost from birth and there was no justifiable reason for that either. Her aunt certainly wasn't the emotionally effusive type. She liked children and had always wanted them badly, but she usually ended up talking to children, even babies, in a normal adult tone, and it seldom occurred to her that they mightn't understand a word she was saying to them. They seemed to be listening, and that was enough. Little Ruth, Britt mused, I wonder what kind of woman she'll become. Would she be loyal and true? Aaron was softhearted and kind. He was a dreamer and yet wanted to be a doctor. Could a child really know what he wanted to be at six years old? Well, maybe. But getting there was something else. Ruth, on the other hand, was a discerning realist. She was also very canny and determined. A different type altogether from her brother. But then families were very interesting microcosms. There was love and enmity, resentment and bitterness and all the many variations in between. Certainly she and her sister were poles apart and yet . . . yet what? She wondered.

"A penny for your thoughts." Britt twisted round. The voice was coming from behind.

"I didn't hear you come. Hi, Nicole."

"Hello, yourself. You were lost in thought."

"Not worth a plugged nickel."

"I don't believe it." Nicole lit a cigarette and offered one to Britt.

"Thanks, I left mine in the unit . . . which reminds me, I should be getting back."

"Don't worry. I stopped in the annex on my way over from P.H.A. You're on with Helen. It's quiet. She says to take your time."

"Who's with you?"

"Rolly." Nicole exhaled a cloud of smoke. "I heard about what happened with Tom."

"Hasn't everyone?" Britt looked amused. "Flynn's tirade and Erikson's outburst. Quid pro quo."

"He can be very understanding at times and then he just goes off." Nicole waved a hand in the air. "It's been worse lately."

"He has a paternalistic attitude, and he's under a lot of pressure. That's not a good combination."

"Well, I just say nothing and let him rant on."

"Yeah, well I'm not very good at keeping my mouth shut."

Nicole looked at her, "You know you seldom complain."

"No, I explode." Britt laughed. "Not often. Rarely, in fact, but it still happens."

"Are you still angry?"

"Furious." Britt got up and stubbed out her cigarette. "But I still like him. Weird, isn't it?"

Once back in the unit, Helen went to supper and Britt set about talking to some of the patients. Then a call came through from General E.R. They were getting another admission. "Well, so much for leisure fantasies." Britt said to the orderly.

Bernard grinned. "Who is it?"

"Young male, 30 years old. Psychotic. Homicidal tendencies. Paranoid schiz, long standing. He's been medicated, but still in restraints. Can you keep an eye on things here? I'll just go and check him out."

"Sure, go ahead."

Britt was back in a few minutes. "I think he'll be all right, Bernard. Do you want to go and get him?"

"Sure." The orderly nodded.

"But we'd better keep him in restraints. He's due to be re-medicated. Then maybe we can remove them. Apparently he was swinging at everyone when he came in." Bernard left and Britt sat down to read through the initial E.R. notes and the old chart. By the time Helen, returned the man was admitted and everything done.

Once home, Britt went to bed. She was bone tired, and she wasn't looking forward to tomorrow. But then, she supposed, Nora must be even more anxious about having to appear and watch Anna wrangle a deal. She also must be worried about the outcome.

Everything went with surprising speed the following morning. But to Britt waiting with the small child the time seemed interminable. She kept her at the far end of the long corridor, away from the office where the lawyers were haggling and the clients were glancing at each other with intermittent hostility and the sadness of something once sweet gone sour. Finally it was over. Nora got her settlement and went off with her lawyer to settle accounts. Britt took Ruth home.

By Monday afternoon, Tom still gave no indication that he acknowledged Britt's leave of absence, so she decided to put the request in writing. If it was formality he wanted, she'd give it to him. The letter was scathingly polite, impersonal and to the point and she addressed him as "Dear Sir." It was just a mockery, and Tom was more frustrated than ever. He didn't reply to it. A few days later, she wrote another request, not a letter this time, just a note but there was no ridicule or contempt in it. Flynn's reply was equally cool and impersonal. She would be replaced for the months of February and March. Leave of absence granted.

-Nine-

Having coffee with her mother and sister the first morning of her leave, Mary commented, "wouldn't this be a good time to see about that child in Nepal?"

Britt looked at her and then glanced away. "Like I said. I haven't enough money right now."

"Well, how much do you have?"

"I'm not sure. I still have to pick up my last check at the hospital, around two thousand dollars."

"That's not bad. Did you save that in the last few months?"

"Yup. But I'm on a leave of absence now so I have to go easy."

"I know, but your rent's low. How much would it cost anyhow?"

"Oh, I don't know," Britt paused. "Gin says the rates are low in February. It's off season, around seventeen hundred. But I'll need some money once there. It'll cost."

"Well, I can help you out a little," Mary hurried on as if she was about to be interrupted. "The boy's up for adoption now. He's the perfect age because you'll have to work. You were going to go over earlier. Remember? In early September before you even received this letter from Don what's his name."

"Yes, I was going to go with Dad. That's a male dominated society over there, but that was before . . . well, before everything else happened."

"And before you lent what you had to Roderick."

"That's all over too. Why even talk about it?"

"Well, she's right," Nora cut in. "You give things away and then something like this comes up. And I don't think that store has much of a chance. Things aren't very good in Quebec. It'll probably go bankrupt. Poor Roddy. He doesn't have much luck."

"No, he doesn't," Britt agreed. "And what luck he gets doesn't count for much." She got up and her mother looked up at her.

"Where are you going?"

"Downstairs. I've got things to do . . . write a letter of application and get all the papers ready to be sent out west."

"Oh yes. Get them in. That's a good job. So they're interested?"

"Very interested. I called last week . . . spoke to a Janice Leonard."

"Good. That would be just the job, especially if you got a child."

"You're the eternal optimist, Mother."

"You say you want something, Britt, but you don't go after it hard enough."

Britt stared at her for a moment and then turned away. "I'll see you later."

When the apartment door closed behind her elder daughter, Mary turned to Nora.

"You know, she comes up, stays for a few minutes, and leaves. She's so distant." Nora didn't think so. She and Gregory both thought that her sister was her mother's favorite. She didn't know what Rourke thought and couldn't have cared less. "You know it's almost as if she can't stand being here."

"Maybe it bothers her. Does it bother you?"

"Sometimes. I've changed things around. But, yes, it does at times. I'll probably get another apartment when the lease is up here."

"It'll cost you a lot more." Nora was practical. "But if you start looking early you might find something."

"Yes. What plans have you made, Nora?"

"You mean with the settlement?"

Mary nodded.

"Well, it's safe and sound in a bank in Ontario. But my days in Quebec are numbered. I know that. The problem is where to go."

"There's some property up around where Rourke is. Maybe you

can get into a small business there."

"I know. He mentioned it to me. But you know Rourke. He gets big ideas."

"So for the time being you'll stay here?"

"Yes. I'd like Aaron to get through this year and probably next year. It'll give him a good foundation. This is a good school he's in and believe me, they're hard to find."

"I know. Britt looked all over for that one. The principal's name was familiar to her and when she checked it out, it looked suitable."

"He's doing good work. Aaron needs a structured environment to work."

"Yes, I know." Mary was silent for a few moments. "If you're not going to use the money right away, why don't you lend her a few thousand dollars?"

"Of course, she can have the money." Nora looked surprised. "Whatever she wants. She doesn't need to ask."

"Well, tell her. She'll go if she gets the money."

"No, you talk to her. If I try she'll only say no."

"Why do you think that?" Mary frowned at her.

"Because she will. Take my word for it. You talk to her. I want her to have it. She should go over. You have to go after the things you want."

When Nora left to give Ruth some lunch and put her down for a nap, Mary thought it all out. That evening she went down to see Britt. She could hear her playing the piano as she came down the hallway. For someone only playing by ear, it didn't sound too bad at all. All her children had some kind of musical talent which surprised her because both she and Hugh had none at all.

"Hi there." Britt opened the door to her. "What brings you down?"

"I was wondering what you were up to," Mary paused. "It's almost seven o'clock. Have you eaten?"

"Not yet."

Mary grimaced. "Well, eat something! No wonder you're so thin."

"Gin's coming over a little later. So what's new with you?"

"I was talking to Nora. You can borrow a few thousand dollars from her. She wants you to have it."

"Oh, I don't know. She needs her money. That's her stake."

"You'll pay it back. You always do. In fact, you're seldom on the receiving end. You have to be able to accept gracefully too. It's only fair. Otherwise people are always in debt to you."

Britt lifted her shoulders in resignation. "I suppose so. But I'll have to call Don Willet first. There's no point going off on a wild goose chase."

"Well, call him." Mary was exasperated. "Ask some questions and get the information you need. Call him now."

"I'll call him. He should know about it. He has contacts."

While Britt was on the phone, the doorbell went and Mary let Virginia in. They chatted in the kitchen while waiting for her to join them. When Britt finally came into the kitchen she appeared cautiously hopeful, and as she expanded on what she'd been told by the man who headed up the Outreach programme, her spirits visibly rose. Her mother was heartened by it all and even Virginia had to admit that the plan sounded viable.

"Are these the contacts he gave you?" She reached out and took the paper from her hand.

"Yes. A Mr. Shestra is the man who can put me in touch with his Tibetan contact."

"And who's that?"

Britt pointed to another name hastily scribbled and hardly legible. "Tashi Phintso. His father is Kunchowk. He owns a shop in the Tibetan section of the town."

"Buddha 'Nath?"

"Yeah, that's it. You see I wrote it here."

"And he suggests you stay at the Tibetan Guest House?"

"Yes." Britt nodded. "It's on the other side of town from the Tibetan community, but he knows it. It's fairly cheap and it's clean. Also, the desk clerk there, Tsuten, is Tashi's cousin."

Virginia shook her head. "So Kunchowk's brother owns the hotel. How convenient."

Britt laughed but Mary Erikson was frowning.

"Well, you've lost me. The names are confusing and so are all the contacts."

"Connections." Virginia corrected her. "You have no idea of what goes on over there, Mrs. Erikson. Our bureaucracy's a bother. Theirs is a nightmare. And the black market doesn't just flourish like they say it does here. Over there it's a way of life."

"I thought you loved it over there, Virginia."

"Oh, I do, Mrs. Erikson. India has a soul. That's what I love, its spirit."

"All countries have souls." Britt said impatiently. "What's so alluring about theirs?"

"I don't know. But let's not get into it again. You've never agreed with me about it and you've never even been there."

"I've read about it. But, you're right, I should see it first before making a judgement."

"You should see all of it before deciding."

"I disagree. I can find out more about a place in two weeks than some people can in two years. And I'll prove it to you."

"You don't have to prove anything to me. I've been there three times and for long periods. We just don't see things the same way, Britt. You're a cynic."

"Maybe. But has it ever occurred to you that a cynic's just an idealist turned inside out?"

"Or one gone sour."

"Never mind all that," Mary interrupted again. "What about the child?"

"Yes. His name is Lobsang. He's one child in a large family. He's the second son."

Mary looked skeptical. "But he is an orphan, isn't he?"

"No. The parents are alive. They have a small eating place. Don didn't quite know how to describe it."

"Those aren't the best circumstances. It's risky."

"Your mother's right," Virginia put in. "It's not the Tibetan way even if he was just an orphan, but with parents . . ." She shook her head.

"I know," Britt said gloomily. "I pointed that out to Don, but he didn't think it a problem at all. You see, the father has T.B. He was sick for a number of months last year. They're quite poor, so they want to have one of their sons adopted. Don's friend Kunchowk and his son Tashi know the family quite well. It's what they want to do. The older son, Karma, is being sponsored by an American family . . . to go to school, I mean. But they want the seven year old adopted. I don't know. It sounded odd to me too."

"What about the younger children?" Mary asked.

"There's a smaller boy, four or five years old, and a baby."

"What about them?"

"I asked Don about that. He didn't know. All he said he knew for a fact was that they wanted Lobsang adopted."

"Maybe they're hoping to find sponsors for the others when they have to go to school." Virginia looked at her doubtfully. "Maybe it's really a sponsor they want for Lobsang, and not an adoptive parent."

"I asked him that too, Gin. He said they wanted him adopted, not sponsored for an education."

"Did he know anything about adoption in Nepal?"

"He didn't know much about that, but he said Tashi, who gets around quite a bit I gather, thought it could be done. It might take some finagling and that's his specialty."

"Well, in that case," Mary pursed her lips. "You should try for it. You've tried here in Canada and so have thousands of others. It's impossible. People are going all over the world today to adopt. Why not you?"

Britt looked at her friend. "What do you think, Gin? I can tell by your expression you're not too enthused."

"You're taking a chance. It sounds straightforward, but there are snags like the parents, and more importantly--getting the kid out of Nepal."

"Maybe I could put him on my passport. It can, or at least, used to be done that way. I'll have to go to the British Embassy. We have no Canadian Embassy in Nepal."

"No. I know." Virginia thought for a moment. "At least you'll get to see the country."

"Oh Christ, that's not why I'm going! This isn't a sight-seeing trip. I want a child. That's the only reason I'd go over right now."

"I know and I hope you succeed. I really do."

"But it's dicey. I know, Gin. Then again, what am I supposed to do? Just let it go without even trying?"

-Ten-

Britt flew Kuwait Airlines because it was the cheapest way to go. It was a circuitous route, from Dorval Airport to Laguardia, then over to Kennedy International in New York. From New York they flew to Heathrow and from London down to Kuwait City where there was a several hour wait through the early hours of the morning. After this came the long flight down to New Delhi. The traveller beside her on the plane was a Sikh from the Punjab. He was living in Toronto and hadn't been home in ten years. There was trouble there and going home, even on a visit, put him in danger of being nabbed by the Sikh militia or becoming a target for Hindu reprisals. But his father was ill and he had to chance it. They talked for a long time. Britt broke her natural reticence and told him why she was going to Nepal. His reply heartened her. He thought the only way to do it was to go over herself as she was doing and then fight like hell to get what she wanted. It wouldn't be easy, but she'd find a way, he assured her.

They dozed off for a while and then chatted sleepily for another hour or more before arriving in New Delhi. At the international arrivals section, he tried to be helpful, but despite the fact that she'd obtained a visa for India, she was directed over to another very quiet area where several other passengers were waiting. Apparently travellers in transit were confined to a separate area of the airport. They collected all her luggage and brought it to the lounge where they directed her. It was comfortable enough, but obviously security tight. There were long synthetic leather couches where people were trying to sleep and a bar just up a flight of stairs. The change in time zones landed them once again in the middle of the night, but it had been well over twenty hours since leaving Montreal and it wasn't over yet.

Already exhausted, but unable to sleep, Britt looked around and thought about what lay ahead of her. Even the atmosphere of the airport was foreign to her. And she had done some travelling. It would come as somewhat of a shock to anyone who had never left Canada or North America. She found herself idly curious over the extensive measures airport personnel were taking to keep passengers who were meant to be in transit separate from all others.

She signalled a security guard, and he came toward her as she approached him.

"Are these people going up to Nepal too?"

The guard nodded, "Yes, madam."

"And what about people taking domestic flights to other areas of India."

The young man looked confused for a few moments and then smiled at her as he caught the gist of the question.

"Oh, they are in another section, madam."

"And I can't go in there even though I have a visa for India?"

"No, madam, you must remain here, please." Then he added helpfully, "but there is a bar and restaurant just up the stairs here. It's nice up there. Quiet. If you cannot sleep, you could go up. I could bring your bags for you."

"You're very kind, but no thanks. I'll just leave them here. There's nothing worth stealing."

The guard looked doubtful. "I'll watch them for you, madam."

"Thank you." Britt paused. "Will the flight for Kathmandu be on time . . . at nine in the morning?"

"It should be here, madam." He nodded. "We think it will be here. Yes."

It was difficult to know what to make of this exchange. They were so impeccably polite and yet why did she get the feeling that there was nothing very definite about anything here. She looked up the stairs as the guard pointed the way and started walking away from him when she turned back.

"Will there be an announcement to let me know when the flight is ready?"

"Oh yes, madam. You will know. We will call you."

Once upstairs in the bar, she looked around and found it almost deserted. There was one middle-aged man sitting at a table nearby reading a play by David Mamet. He glanced up as she came in and Britt approached the table.

"Would I be disturbing you?"

"Not at all," he smiled and started to get up. "Sit down. Would you like something to drink? I'm having gin tonic."

"No, I don't think I'll chance it."

He grinned. "Come a long way?"

"Montreal via New York. And you?"

"Chicago, also through New York. Where are you going?"

"Nepal, Kathmandu."

"Me too. Are you taking the Nepalese airline flight?"

"Yeah. It leaves at nine. That's three hours from now. Why do I get the feeling that's a very doubtful departure time?"

"I have the same feeling." He started to chuckle. "I don't know why but all this is very strange. Not a bit like Europe."

"It's my first time over here too. And you're right, it's another world."

"I'm Gary McFadden."

"I'm sorry." She held out her hand. "Britt Erikson."

"Wouldn't you like something to drink? Maybe just tonic water?"

"Thanks. I'd like that."

He signalled the waitress and ordered sandwiches and tonic water. For himself he ordered coffee. Looking at him, Britt found this man, probably, in his late forties, handsome and appealing. His face looked young, and he had a soft smile. Looking her over, Gary McFadden didn't know quite what to make of this woman somewhere in her thirties, travelling alone, and yet so conservatively dressed--somewhat like a business woman, but with the remote air of an academic. But it was her quiet voice and calm demeanor that interested him most. There was nothing boisterous or bouncy about her. He had the oddest feeling she would be just as at ease talking with the Pope as with some homeless indigent and would probably give them the same time and attention. She looked kind.

"Are you vacationing in Kathmandu, Mr. McFadden?"

"Gary, please, and yes, I'm going trekking. It's something I've been promising myself to do for a very long time. They say there's nothing like it. I hope I'm in shape enough to get somewhere. I'm not tackling Everest but, any part of the Himalayas is a challenge, don't you think?"

"Yes, I do. Are you joining a group?"

"No, I've hired my own guide and parties. It's expensive, but I got a good deal for a private arrangement like this. And I've only got five days. Then I have to leave."

Very curious, Britt thought, and asked, "where are you going after you leave Nepal, Gary?"

"Brussels. But, before I ramble further, why are you going to Kathmandu? Vacationing too?"

"No. Personal business. I'm not here for the sights. Not this time anyway."

"I see." Gary mulled it over and decided he very much wanted to explain himself to this stranger who so obviously would rather listen than talk. "Well, I'm a businessman, a financial consultant. I just sold my firm a few months ago and I owned most of the stock, not just the controlling interest. I made a bundle. Bailed out just in time. There was a dramatic drop in stock values shortly after the purchase. Look at this." He opened his briefcase and handed her a newspaper clipping. It showed the man sitting across from her, and she read the caption which described him as a millionaire. She read the article carefully. He was praised for his business acumen. He made a lot of money, and the buyers were already in financial difficulty.

She looked up at him. "You've done very well. It seems your timing was perfect."

"In business, yes. But I guess I'd like to take another look at my life. That's why I dropped everything, and I'm taking this trip and reading David Mamet." He laughed but there was something else behind the laughter and it wasn't humour.

"Of course, I still have some business to transact by phone from my hotel. A three-way conversation and it can't wait."

Britt smiled at him. "Well, while you're trekking you'll have time to think. Just be careful of elevation sickness."

"I heard about that. I've been doing some reading in advance. Now what about you?"

"Oh, I'm not a millionaire or even rich . . . not even well off really. I just work and get along."

"What do you do?"

"Dabble in two professions, Teaching and Nursing. Right now I'm on a leave of absence from a hospital in Montreal, the Emergency Department, Psychiatry, to be exact. But I've done other jobs as well."

"You're versatile."

"That's a nice way of putting it. Others might call it scattered. I like change, but employers are suspicious of that and they seldom approve."

"But they still hire you."

"So far, yes. I can do the job and my educational background is, as you say, versatile."

"They like tenacity. Sticking to the same job for ten, twenty years."

"Yes. That's an absurd idea . . . like marrying someone and asking them to promise they'll bloom forever."

Gary burst out laughing and this time there was pure enjoyment in the sound. "Are you married, Britt?"

"No. I'm not. Are you?"

"I got divorced about a year ago."

"I'm sorry."

"Don't be. It was an amicable parting of ways. My wife likes horses, you see."

"And you don't?"

"Oh sure, but that's her sole interest, horses. I have two sons and they're both in college now. They're grown up and there was nothing left of the marriage. So she still has her horses and a very select social circle and I have . . ." He glanced down at the book laying face down on the table.

"David Mamet?"

"Yes, well something to read. I thought I'd start with him. Read any of his stuff?"

"One or two of his plays. He's not one of my favorites."

"He poses some interesting questions."

"He does that." Britt agreed. "But to be honest with you, I find more drama and real life going on in an emergency room or even a classroom. He writes a lot about finding meaning in life, and I guess we all take that journey, but I'll take Eugene O'Neill or Tennessee Williams or Brian Friel or Sean O'Casey over Mamet anytime . . . but everyone's tastes are different."

"Yes, a friend of mine suggested Mamet."

"He's interesting. I should read more of his work. I just haven't got around to it."

They talked on for a long time and finally Gary McFadden suggested they go downstairs and see what was going on. There was absolutely nothing going on. The day had come up, but it was overcast and there were more people in the waiting room. All of them apparently waiting for the same flight. By nine o clock everyone had headed down to the departure area where they all sat cramped up with their luggage. They were still waiting at 12:30, and at one point everyone got up thinking they'd heard the announcement for departure. Several security guards blocked the wide area and they had machine guns. Everyone sat down again.

Gary looked over at Britt. "Why argue?"

"My sentiments precisely." She frowned at him. "I wonder why they haven't given any reason for the long delay."

"They don't have to. They're armed. This is like in a movie."

They didn't board the smaller aircraft until 1:00 p.m., and by this time everyone looked exhausted, even the Indian passengers who had arrived in the morning to catch the flight. They sat together on the ancient aircraft which was packed without a seat to spare. It seemed few people were able to sleep. Arriving at the small airport outside Kathmandu, everyone deplaned and there was noise and confusion everywhere.

"Would you like a lift into town? I'm getting a taxi."

"That would be great. Thank you. But I'm staying at the Tibetan Guest House. Is that out of your way?"

"I don't know," he shrugged. "I'm at the Yak Yak. That's on one of the main streets."

"I know. I'm a ways from there, I think."

"No matter. Come on. Let's get out of here."

It seemed like people were coming at them from all sides. Gary picked the first cab driver. They loaded all the baggage in the beat-up looking taxi and were on their way. Fortunately the driver knew where the Tibetan Guest House was. Only the main streets had names. In areas of town off the central road, the streets weren't marked, became narrow and often unpaved. It was like a giant, busy beehive maze, complete with rickshaws, bicycles, carts of every kind, buses, cars, and people everywhere. The taxi weaved through the thronging mixture of moving objects. The driver honked the horn repetitively, but it made little difference. Every other car was honking too, and voices were raised in all directions. Britt's eyes darted around trying to take it all in, but Gary appeared to have shut down his senses.

"Quite a place, wouldn't you say?"

"I'd say so," he replied. "I'm not going to even try to take it in."

When they were nearing her hotel, he turned to her.

"Would you like to have dinner at my hotel? It's back there on the main drag. Kanti Path Road. You remember?"

Britt nodded. "I'd like to very much. But aren't you tired?"

"I'm beat, but maybe I can get some sleep. A few hours anyway."

"All right, but I'll call you. We're probably both more tired than we think. It hasn't set in yet."

"I know, so we'll see. But you'll call?"

"Of course."

Tsuten was not at the main desk when she got inside, but she had her room reserved, and the staff was helpful. They also spoke some English. One boy grabbed her bags and before she knew it, she was installed in her room. Bone tired, she stared around her and then walked to the window. The courtyard was below, and the street choked with bodies and vehicles beyond that. She decided she'd call Mr. Shestra. He was the only contact Don Willet had given her who had a phone. He would connect her with certain members of the Tibetan community.

B.W. Shestra was not only in, he sounded delighted to hear from her and declared he'd "run right over."

"Just let me freshen up, Mr. Shestra. I just got here."

"Of course, of course," he replied hurriedly. "In about an hour and a half then. It will take me a little time to get there."

"Have you a car?"

"No, I don't. In an hour and a half, then. We can talk."

Britt put the receiver down and sighed. She certainly wouldn't be having dinner with Gary McFadden, but this was much more important. It just surprised her that Shestra wanted to "run right over," as he put it, the moment she contacted him. She put off calling Gary. If he was as tired as she was he was probably trying to sleep. Instead she ran a bath and was delighted that the water came out hot because she had been warned about the temperamental water heater by the head clerk when she first arrived. Soaking in a bath was heavenly, truly a luxury after the long journey. In her mind, it seemed she had left Montreal long ago and far behind her.

Afterwards, she changed her clothes, dressing carefully, but conservatively in skirt, blouse, and jacket. The professional or business look. Being alone and a woman in Nepal or India, it was the only way to get things done. And she did not, after all, come here to have a good time.

She was lying down on the bed with her eyes closed and letting her mind drift when the telephone started ringing. It was concerning a Mr. Shestra. The front desk clerk wanted to know if he could come up. "Thank you. Yes. Please send him up and would you have the number of the Yak Yak Hotel?"

"Yes, certainly." The clerk gave her the number. "Would you like some tea sent up to your room for yourself and your guest?"

"Yes. That would be fine. Thank you."

Mr. Shestra arrived first, smiling, cheerful and very willing to be of assistance. Apparently he had received a letter from Don Willet and had been expecting her. They talked for a while about random things and smoked a few cigarettes. But this was going to take some time, Britt concluded, and it wasn't going to be easy. Intricate maneuvering meant looking at every angle. So before going into particulars, she called Gary McFadden and apologized for having to cancel their dinner engagement.

"Oh, don't worry about it," he replied. "I'm not in the greatest shape myself."

"Were you unable to sleep or did I wake you? You sound tired."

"No, I couldn't get to sleep at all. I think I'll just have something sent up and try to sleep. My business call is scheduled for midnight, and I'll be leaving for those five days of trekking at dawn."

"Well, have a good time," Britt smiled.

"I have one evening and night here when I get back before flying out. Maybe we could meet for dinner then."

"Sure. Call when you get back. Just leave a message if I'm not in."

She put down the receiver. Mr. Shestra was waiting. They had to make some arrangements, and to be honest with herself, Britt had to admit she wasn't even sure where to begin or how. She was hoping this suave looking man in the light tan suit could help her understand how things worked in Nepal.

She continued for a while longer trying to find out how Shestra figured into the scheme of affairs. As far as she could gather from the man's oblique answers, he was working on a part-time basis for Don Willet who conducted tours of Americans over to Nepal twice annually, and he found sponsors in the States and Canada for Nepalese children in order that they might go to school.

"And are you paid for the work you do?" Britt asked him.

"A small sum monthly, Miss Erikson, but I do other work as well." It seemed Mr. Shestra did a little bit of everything.

"And what about adoption? Is it possible here?"

"I would think so, but it may be difficult. Nothing's easy here."

"Why difficult?" Britt prodded on. "Are there many orphans in Nepal?"

"Oh yes." Shestra nodded. "But I'm not sure if it's possible to adopt one."

"But you just said it was possible." However frustrated she might be, it was important not to show it. "Is it just a matter of getting a few officials to stamp a few documents? A service for instance, that might not be exactly according to government regulation?"

Shestra appeared visibly more relaxed. "That's it. You understand?"

"Yes, I think so."

"But I do have some connections in immigration and other ministries."

"Is there an orphanage here, Mr. Shestra?"

"Yes. There's one right near where I live, however, I don't think it would be the right place for you to go, but maybe . . ." He shrugged.

"Well, I was just asking. I'd like to meet with one of the administrators there merely to learn their attitude toward foreign adoption. It would be helpful to know if we should avoid government offices. Don't you think?"

"Yes, it would be good to know that." Shestra bobbed his head. "Things are very different here, Miss Erikson. It's very hard to explain."

"Not so different as you might imagine," Britt smiled at him. "Actually, there is a child in the Tibetan community that I'm specifically interested in. He's the one Don Willet wrote me about."

"Is he a Nepalese citizen?"

"I don't know." Britt frowned. "Isn't everyone who has been born here a citizen?"

"Oh no! Not at all. Only a very few Tibetans get citizenship. It's much worse now. The price is very high."

"Buy citizenship! But most of them don't have much money. So what are they?"

"Refugees."

"Then that's another matter altogether. Isn't it?"

"I'm afraid so. You can't put their documents through government offices here."

"Are they allowed to leave?"

Shestra tilted his head and frowned. "I'm not sure about that. People in the Tibetan community would know more about that than I do."

"I see." Britt paused. "Well, I'd very much like to meet the family. Are you able to spare me any time, Mr. Shestra?"

"Yes, of course. As much as I can. You will need an interpreter here. Do you know how to find the family?"

"Yes, I think so. There's a man, Kunchowk. He owns the first shop on the right as you go through the main gate. His son is Tashi Phintso."

"The stupa at Buddha' Nath?"

"Yes, and if he can't direct us we can go to the school where the oldest boy attends. A man by the name of Nirala is the principal. Don knows him well. Do you know Kunchowk or his son?"

"No, but I know the school. I help Don in matters like that."

"Well, I should go over tomorrow," Britt hesitated. Are you very busy tomorrow?"

"No. I can help you."

"Thank you. Once I locate Tashi Phintso, I should be able to navigate. His cousin is the chief desk clerk here. I didn't talk to him when I arrived. Now he's probably gone, but I'll talk to him in the morning."

Shestra got up. "I should go. You're very tired. I see that."

"Yes, I am really. It was a very long flight, and we were delayed in New Delhi. So will we meet in the morning?"

"Yes, what time is good for you?"

"How about between half past nine and ten? And I'd like to go to the orphanage first just to check it out."

Shestra looked doubtful, but he complied. "If you wish to go, I'll take you."

"Thank you. Perhaps I could meet you some place nearby it so you won't have to come all the way over here first? Just write down the meeting spot, and I'll be there."

Shestra drew her a sketchy map showing her how to find her way out of the maze of unmarked streets and onto the main road through the city. Then he marked with a cross the place where they were to meet. When he was ready to go, Britt handed him a package.

"I hope you like it. They told me you couldn't get it here."

It was a large bottle of scotch, an expensive malt whiskey, that she had bought in the duty free shop at Kennedy International Airport. Virginia had been right. He was more than pleased to get it. When he left, Britt went straight to bed. She couldn't remember when she'd last eaten, but she was too tired to care. By this time the dining room would be closed and, in any case, she had to be up early in the morning.

The following morning came up crystal bright and clear, but cold. So chilled, in fact, that Britt wondered if she shouldn't have brought along a winter coat. The staff in the guest house was mostly Tibetan and not all of them spoke English well, but they certainly wanted to learn, and most of them, she was to discover in the next few days, wanted very much to get out of Nepal altogether. The young waiter who approached her had an open friendly face, and he smiled as he saw her rubbing her hands together.

"You are cold?" He asked and looked suddenly concerned.

"Yes, I'm freezing." Britt laughed. "And my wool suit and sweater don't help much."

"You look very nice." He gave her a speculative glance and then added. "Are you here visiting? We do get many visitors."

"You mean tourists?"

"Yes, tourists from all over the world."

"I heard that. Yes, I know, some of my friends have been here. And many people return, but no, I'm not here on vacation."

"You don't like it?" The Tibetan had a boyish smile. "It's very beautiful. Many think so."

"Oh, I just arrived and haven't seen much yet. But if I have time, I'll look around."

"Good. I will show you if you like." The young boy who looked already to be a seasoned waiter smiled happily.

"Thank you, I'd like that." Britt pulled the paper out of her jacket pocket and spread it out on the table. "I have to get here this morning."

The waiter looked down at the crudely drawn map and nodded. "Yes, I will show you, but first you must have some hot tea and then something to eat."

"Yes, a large pot of tea first. That would be perfect."

The young fellow went off grinning and shaking his head. There were a few other guests in the dining room which was clean and sunny and all the tables were set for the breakfast crowd, but few guests materialized. Those who were there and the others who came in had very little to say to the waiters. They were tourists and what could they have to say to the people who lived and worked in these beautiful mountain surroundings? Then again, they were mostly in pairs or groups and tended to talk among themselves. Britt found herself wondering how her father would handle all this. He'd enjoy it. She was sure of that. And Hugh Erikson talked to everyone. By the time his stay was over he'd know all the staff, and he'd know their names and how they came to be there and what their hopes for the future were. And they'd know him. She'd get to know them too and what was going on with them as far as it was possible to try and understand the ways of a totally different and diverse culture. A culture within a culture really, because that seemed to be the situation of the Tibetans in Nepal. It was important to attempt to know how people felt, even if that knowledge could only be wrapped in a fog and was full of shadows.

The waiter had explained the map sketch to her in greater detail, starting at the gate to guest house, what direction to start out in and just where to turn and then turn again. It was a twisted, tortured route out to the main thoroughfare, but not long. Shops lined the muddied streets that looked more like a series of alley ways. The vendors were out peddling their wares, and any foreigner looked to be a likely target. Britt managed to dodge all of them, but she stopped at a tiny pharmacy or medicine shop druggist as they were labelled. Virginia told her that all medications could be bought over the counter. Prescriptions weren't necessary. She also warned her that most visitors became ill some time or other. The water was contaminated and foreigners knew better than to drink it. Even brushing one's teeth and accidentally swallowing a small amount could bring on illness that debilitated a person for days. Besides, diseases such as T.B., typhoid, typhus, amoebic dysentery and all kinds of chest and intestinal infections were rampant. She wasn't going to take any chances, but the shop that she found herself in was like something out of the middle ages, a mere rough wooden counter and a dirt floor. The back and side walls were lined with boxes and packaged goods haphazardly opened and with no recognizable system of organization. All the same, when she asked for penicillin and the dosage per capsule she wanted, the vendor, certainly not a licensed pharmacist, produced it without any delay whatsoever. No frantic searching, no bungling, and this amazed her. How could anyone find anything in this confusion? But it was no problem. The Canadian medical community wouldn't approve of her methods, but Britt didn't care. She was a great believer in prophylactic medicating, and that was especially applicable just now. She couldn't afford to get sick. There was too much to do, and too little time or money to delay her actions in getting it done. So she had every intention of taking antibiotics for the duration of her stay. Considering what looked to be like an open sewage system and the extent of poverty she encountered on every side, it was no wonder that preventable diseases claimed so many lives and left so many others in despair.

She tucked the antibiotics into her bag and kept walking until she finally got up to the main road where there was again some semblance of order and ordinary looking shops and buildings. There were fewer vendors in the streets promoting their goods and haggling. And there were sidewalks. She also didn't notice any more open sewers and the crowds of people, natives and tourists alike, thinned out.

Mr. Shestra was waiting for her.

"I'm sorry I'm late," she greeted him. "I've kept you waiting."

"I thought perhaps you lost your way." He smiled agreeably. "It can be hard to find your way out of that section of town."

"It wasn't too bad. Is the orphanage far?"

"No, no. A ten, fifteen minute walk. And not so difficult to find. I'll come with you and wait."

They were walking along, and Britt didn't notice the direction they were taking, but soon they were cutting across a park-like area with tall trees and walkways.

"That's it over there." He pointed to a large building on the far side of the park."

"It looks like a nice building. How many children do they have?"

"I don't know, but over a hundred."

At the main front doors he stepped back.

"Aren't you coming in, Mr. Shestra?"

"No, I'll wait for you here. One of the administrators should be there. Just ask anyone."

Britt went inside. She didn't mind going alone, but it crossed her mind that this might well be one of the government agencies where Shestra didn't have connections and clearly didn't anticipate having any. When she met the administrator, she could well understand the reason for her new guide's reserve. The man didn't get up and he hardly looked at her. And when he did, his eyes shifted quickly away as if he held her in contempt.

"Yes, we have children, Miss Erikson. What is the reason for your inquiry?"

"Are they adoptable, sir?"

"Some, but not all."

Britt hesitated. "Do you have any special regulations about adoption? Foreign adoptions. I'm Canadian."

He looked up at her. He hadn't asked her to sit down, and in that look she read his thoughts. Yes, you're from North America and worse still, you're a woman and here alone without your husband. Women act that way in North America. And you want to adopt one of our children?

"We have very strict regulations, Madam. Very few meet our requirements."

He didn't want to know anything about her, and as she looked around his drab office that opened off the equally drab corridor which in no way reflected the building's outer appearance of respectability, she understood that there'd be no child for her to adopt here. No indeed, the children unwanted and uncared for could live or die in this limbo of squalor before they'd allow one of them to be adopted. It was resentment and something else she couldn't identify in this man's eyes. There was indifference too. And she had seen the same look in the faces of officials back home. Not all, but some. And children in Canada, as elsewhere, weren't uppermost in the minds of welfare agents and the governments that made it all possible.

Once again Shestra was waiting for her. She told him what happened, and he didn't appear in the least surprised. He wasn't disconcerted either. One learned to accept things the way they were in Nepal. One became resigned and became practiced in the art of the inevitable, but it was a sad and ugly art form, small and mean and devoid of resistance. To a large extent it was the same back home. It was useless trying to fool herself. Canada was systems heavy and there were few channels left for independent thinking and no chance at all for solitary action. Freedom was just a word. Her own country was only comparatively free. It was a long way from the dream of a promise that came with the words "New World."

Britt checked the time. "It's almost noon, Mr. Shestra. I'd like to go to the Tibetan Community now."

"Buddha 'Nath?"

"Yes. The main entrance or stupa, is it? Is it far?"

"The other side of town. It's quite far."

"Then, we'll take a cab."

The taxi weaved its way across town, and all the way over Britt was thinking that this was her best, probably her only chance to adopt a child in Nepal. Shestra's expression was closed. He appeared lost in thought and at the same time frustrated at his own entangled defeats. Life had to be easier elsewhere. Maybe where this lady came from life was simpler. Yes, life was easier in North America. People got a chance there. He turned to her. "You have a profession, Miss Erikson?"

"Yes, I do . . . and perhaps you could call me, Britt."

"All right, Britt," he smiled. "It is not so difficult to get an education and get ahead in Canada, is it?"

"It's difficult, but not impossible, Shestra. It's very different from here. But it has its problems too, like loneliness and high-tech despair." She smiled at him. "Why do you ask?"

"I have three children. Two sons."

"You seem to be doing well enough. Your children can get a higher education here, can't they?"

"I'm not so sure of that." He shook his head worriedly. "I'd like them to go to college. There's not much hope here."

"And you were hoping they could come to Canada?"

"I hope. Maybe one of them. If I could get just one through."

"Maybe you will, Shestra. Maybe here or out of the country. I'll help you if I can."

He nodded. "Thank you. We're here. The stupa's just over there."

He leaned forward and gave instructions to the driver. Britt got the fare ready and handed it to him. Shestra started to explain what they were seeing around them. He didn't speak Tibetan, but most Tibetans spoke fluent Nepalese. They had no choice in the matter. It meant their survival.

They finally located Kunchowk's shop and found it closed. Shestra asked around. Everybody seemed to know him, and one man in an adjacent shop said that he'd be back later in the afternoon, possibly very soon. He had just gone back to his house for lunch.

"How about the school, Shestra?" Britt asked. "Couldn't we go over there first?"

"It's over here." Shestra led the way to a larger building off on one of the side streets. Part of it was in view from where they were standing. Once there, a student pointed the way to the principal's office.

Mr. Nirala stood up as he ushered them into the room. He was a large man and looking at him, Britt was undecided. But then they shook hands and she told herself it was irrational but there was something about this man that unsettled her. He was friendly but brusque. Shestra explained the reason for their presence. Then he switched into English.

"Yes, one son is in a school here."

Britt nodded. "Yes, Karma, the oldest boy. Don Willet told me. But it's the second son, Lobsang, that I believe the family wants adopted."

Nirala gave her an odd look. "Yes, well I have nothing to do with that."

"Could you tell us where the family lives?" Shestra asked him.

Nirala wasn't sure of the exact address, but he knew the general area--the main street outside the stupa.

"Don't you keep records?" Britt frowned.

"It's not so easy to keep records of addresses here, Miss Erikson." He spoke perfect English, and it seemed he'd been educated abroad. But there was something wrong. He was on the defensive, protecting his turf.

In the face of his unnecessary guardedness, Britt remarked coolly. "You needn't worry, Mr. Nirala. It isn't Karma I've come to see. He attends your school with the help of American sponsorship. I know that. So you don't need to worry about any interference from me. It's Lobsang I'm interested in. Or were you expecting him to become a student in your school too? Don Willet didn't tell me that."

"No, no. I didn't think that." Nirala started to backstroke. "And I wish you every success."

This was the man Don Willet said he had spoken to and would probably be of assistance. His school, after all, was largely financed through an outreach program. Britt didn't find him much help at all.

Once outside again she turned to Shestra.

"I don't think I like that man, and I don't trust him." Shestra didn't say anything. He worked for Don too.

"Let's see if Kunchowk's back yet," he suggested. "If not, I know the vicinity to look in. Many people here have the same last name, but we should be able to find them. They operate a small eating place. Problem is government regulations make their livelihood illegal. So . . ."

"I don't understand."

"I'll explain later."

They were once again approaching Kunchowk's shop, and as luck would have it, he was standing just outside it and seemed to be waiting for them. He looked friendly enough and his oriental features were more pronounced. Perhaps Nirala wasn't Tibetan, Britt thought and stood aside as Shestra lapsed once again into his rapid Nepalese. She heard her name mentioned and then Don Willet's name.

Kunchowk was nodding. Then he turned to her.

"Hello, Miss Erikson. I don't know anything about all this and my son, Tashi, is away until the end of the week. He's in Northern India with the parents of his new wife. But, of course, I know the family you are here to see. We know most of the people in our community, at least around here. Come. I'll take you." Kunchowk led the way out the main gate and a short way down the street. Then he crossed over dodging the traffic and they followed him.

"Here, this is the place." Britt looked at the narrow building which seemed to be made of mud and clay. "The eating place is in the front. The family lives at the back. Tenzing and his wife should be here."

He brought them inside and a handsome looking middle-aged man came forward. He was tall, and he too looked more Oriental than Indian. Kunchowk made the introductions. It was dark inside the room compared with the bright afternoon light they'd come from, but the father was beaming at her and holding his two hands together, he bowed and greeted her in Tibetan. Then he urged her and Shestra into a booth, and Kunchowk sat just opposite them. He called his wife and explained. She too looked happy to see them, but she was also nervous and fearful, or perhaps worried. But wouldn't any woman be anxious, Britt thought. Any woman would be. And giving up a child must be the most difficult thing on earth even under dire circumstances. So she studied her face carefully and found that she couldn't come to any decision about the woman at all. Shestra was talking to Kunchowk and the father and the wife disappeared from the room for a few minutes. When she reappeared she had a small boy with her. She pushed him into the booth beside Kunchowk and the old man put his arm around the boy and smiled at Britt. "This is Lobsang."

Britt wondered if it was possible to love a child on first sight because that's how she felt toward him. But he had such a sadness about him that it would melt anyone's heart. "Lobsang." She repeated his name softly and Kunchowk, and the parents were watching her. Then they all started talking again in Nepalese because Shestra had asked them a question. Then he turned to Britt.

"He's wearing the woolen hat because he fell and cut his head. It's almost healed now."

Everything had to be said through translators and that made it difficult. She turned to Kunchowk. "Would you ask the boy if he really wants to be adopted? I'm Canadian and that's far away from here."

"Here, children do what their parents want, Miss."

"Yes, but please ask him anyway." Kunchowk put the question to the child who looked over at her suddenly and nodded. "Did you explain to him that he could change his mind?"

Kunchowk spoke once again to the child who nodded and mumbled something in Tibetan. "He says he wants to go with you."

"Ask him why, Kunchowk."

"I imagine the parents here have talked to him about it, Miss Erikson."

"Yes, I should think so, but what does he say?"

Once again, Kunchowk addressed the child who seemed to be more relaxed now.

"He says because it's better. He wants a better life. A future. There's not much future here." The father brought some tea to the table. It was strong and tasted sweet. Kunchowk smiled. "That is not real Tibetan tea. You will have to try it sometime."

"This tastes very good." Britt smiled back at him. She looked from him back to Shestra. "Now could you ask how the parents feel about this?"

The talk went on in Nepalese and Britt looked from one parent to the other, and then back at the child. She wondered how he felt having his future so freely discussed in front of him. Oddly he didn't seem to mind, but he was taking it all in. The mother spoke rapidly and forcefully. The father was a quiet man. He looked to be gentle and kind which he probably was. It was hard to know about the mother except that she appeared eager for things to go ahead.

Shestra finally turned back to Britt and shrugged. "They want you to adopt their son. Apparently they had a very bad time last year. The father was sick for months. He has T.B. It could come back any time. They think it's best to have at least one son adopted."

"And they're sure, Shestra?"

"They are very sure. I asked them. Besides, they know you've come halfway round the world."

"Well, right now, that doesn't matter, but they have to be absolutely sure. It's not too late for them to change their minds. I wouldn't be angry. It's understandable. But once the child's adopted . . ."

Shestra nodded to her. "Yes, I see what you mean. I'll ask them." And he did. He put it to them in a straightforward manner and Britt saw both parents nodding and looking at her. "That's what they want," Shestra said finally and Kunchowk smiled at her again.

"They feel it's best for the child, Miss. You must understand we do things very differently over here."

By the end of all the translations going on back and forth, Britt was satisfied that the parents' decision was firm, and more importantly, the child wanted to come with her.

"So what's the best way to go about it?" she asked.

"I don't know." Shestra said and looked at Kunchowk who spoke to the parents. Again the conversation lapsed into Nepalese which everyone in the room could speak except the woman who was going to adopt the child. After what seemed an interminable time, Shestra turned to her again. "They think the Tibetan Refugee Center might be able to help. Tashi will be back in a few days. In the meantime another man, a friend of the father's, will help you. He can translate."

"Good," Britt nodded. "I'll come back tomorrow then to make some arrangements. What's the function of the Tibetan Refugee Center?"

"I'm not sure." Shestra looked around. "But we should go now, Kunchowk has to get back to his shop."

"Yes, I must go." Tashi Phintso's father stood up.

Lobsang got out of the booth and the old man followed. When he was gone Shestra and Britt stood up. Now as if out of nowhere the other two sons appeared. Karma, who was nine, was quite tall and handsome. He looked like his father, and he also spoke some English. Lingwan, who was five, darted around the room and then hung onto his mother's long skirts when he was introduced and then Tenzing's wife brought in the baby. The only girl in the family. She was a beautiful baby, but Britt's eyes returned to Lobsang. There was something about the boy that drew her attention. She wondered what he'd look like happy. The others looked vibrant and happy enough. But not Lobsang.

Shestra left with Britt and instead of taking a cab they walked. "Tomorrow I can't come with you. I'm very busy all day. I'm sorry. But there will be someone there to translate."

"Oh, that's all right, Shestra." Britt walked along beside him. "You've been a great help already."

"Thank you. I'm afraid I don't know much about how things work for refugees, but you may want to contact the Home Industry for visas, and I know someone there. Also there's a Canadian Cooperation Office here. A man by the name of Tempa runs it, but your closest Consulate is New Delhi."

"Oh, I see." Britt pulled her lower lip between her teeth. "What does the cooperation do?"

"Not much. They're just starting, but the man in charge there might have some information or he may be able to direct you."

"Do they have private adoption here, Mr. Shestra?"

"I'm not sure. I think so. I've heard of people doing it that way. But the government will probably be involved in some way. You have to get the child out of the country."

"Yes, but once the adoption is done, he's legally my son and therefore, de facto, a Canadian citizen or on his way to becoming one. The actual citizenship might take a few years, but he'd no longer be a Nepalese citizen."

"But he's a refugee," Shestra reminded her.

"That might make things easier," Britt reasoned. "I gather your government can put up obstacles."

Shestra seldom really laughed and even now he only chuckled, and there was more grimness in the sound than merriment. "The government is really a kingdom. A small one, but still a kingdom. I should have pointed the palace out to you. But come, I want to show you something. Are you tired?"

Yes, she was tired. Jet lag probably, but she shook her head. "No, I'm not tired. Where are we going?"

"You'll see. I'll explain when we get there."

Britt had no idea where they were going except that it was back toward the center of town, but out of the way.

"What river is this?" she asked as they crossed a short bridge.

"The Bagmati River. It's quite long really."

"It looks shallow."

"It is at times. See over there." He pointed across the bridge to a hill on the other side. It looked layered with progressive elevations like indentations filled with stone embankments. There were steps leading up from several directions and a massive looking temple crowned the top.

"That's PashupatiNath. A Hindu temple. One of the oldest and the largest here in Nepal. There are many temples. Some are Buddhist temples. There's a very big one, here, in Kathmandu."

"Are you Hindu, Mr. Shestra?"

"Yes. A holy holiday, Shiverati, is coming up at the end of the week. All government buildings will be closed on Friday."

Britt had followed him up the long climb to the temple, and then they wound their way halfway down the hill and sat for a short time on a stone bench. She could see a wild looking naked man with long hair a distance down the incline. He was lurking behind one of the stone huts that dotted the hillside.

"Sadhus." Shestra commented. "A holy man. They come up here for the holy holiday. It's very rare for you to see one."

"Mustn't he get very cold at night?"

Shestra smiled. "They keep apart. Live like hermits. Usually they stay further south where it's warmer. But they travel up for Shiverat."

"I see." Britt lit a cigarette and offered him one.

"This is a very old civilization, Miss Erikson. Very old."

"What's that smoke over there?" Britt pointed to an entrance to the bridge across the river.

"That's a funeral. They're burning the body."

The faintest amount of smoke drifted toward them and the slightest suggestion of a sweet scent. She would have missed it altogether had the wind shifted or she hadn't noticed the smoke billowing and asked about it. Burning flesh, Britt thought, and switched her thoughts off. She couldn't see any mourners. Maybe it was all over and they had gone home.

Shestra left her back at the hotel and promised to call her the morning after the following day. Shestra was nice, and he was trying very hard to be helpful, but as he had candidly pointed out to her, he knew very little about adoption, and in Nepal it seemed everyone had to be careful. She asked for some tea to be sent up to her room and found out the clerk at the reception desk was Tsuten. He was just getting ready to go off duty. He mentioned that his cousin would be back in a few days, and he'd let her know when he got in. He said nothing in favor of or against his uncle Kunchowk in whose home he was presently obliged to live or of his other uncle, Kunchowk's brother, who owned the Guest House. He too lived at Kunchowk's home. The family was obviously very enterprising, and not all its members, at least those of younger generations, were happy campers.

Britt went up to her room and washed her face. It had become quite warm during the afternoon hours, and she felt gritty from the dust in the air and the dirt of the town. She brushed her teeth and combed her hair. Then she felt almost human again. She was on her third cup of tea and smoking a cigarette when she noticed someone at the door which she'd left open. There was a knocking and she said quietly. "Just come in. The door's open."

A woman in her early or middle fifties stood in the doorway. It was hard to tell what age she was, but she had light brown hair to her shoulders and was small and slight in build. "I'm Donna Newland from the United States. I noticed you coming in and you left your door open."

Britt introduced herself and waved her to a chair. "You don't like smoking?"

"Do I look that disapproving?"

"Yes. If it bothers you I'll put it out."

"No, no. I just don't like it, but you go ahead. I'm not going to start choking or anything like that."

"Oh good. I've been out all day, and I'm just sitting here collecting my thoughts."

"You look tired."

"I am."

"Have you eaten yet?"

"No. Not since breakfast."

"No lunch?"

Britt shook her head.

"Well, I know a nice restaurant. It's not far, and the food's good.

You have to be careful about salads and such, but this place is all right and it's reasonable. Do you want to come?"

"Sure, thanks. What time?"

"In about half an hour, six o'clock. I want to make it an early night."

"So do I. What room are you in?"

"Room five. Just down the hall."

Dinner was pleasant, and Donna was good company. She also made frequent visits to Nepal and knew the country well. At least about Tibetan tradition which was her special interest.

"I'm based in Houston, Texas, and I give a series of lectures using slides and research studies." She told Britt. "I also write papers on the subject. I'll be here a few weeks and hopefully get some coverage on the Tibetan New Year."

"You take your own photographs?"

"Yes, and make them into slides. A personal experience is worth much more than the usual tourist information. The university picks up part of the costs. They're very curious about the environmental problems here."

"You mean about the open sewage system, or I should say the lack of a system altogether, and all the preventable diseases that are endemic here?"

"Well, yes, that too. It's a given, isn't it? But I'm more interested in the long-term environmental problems. The deforestation of the mountains is much more important."

Britt lifted an eyebrow. "More important than the social problems? The poverty? The diseases around? I haven't the numbers yet, but I'll bet they're high."

"They're probably staggering," Donna agreed. "But populations have always suffered. Some more than others and it's sad, but if we don't preserve the environment and curtail the damage there'll be nothing here to come back to. Their civilization will die."

"People are more important than any civilization to which they might belong. And the same goes for tradition. It's important but not more than human lives."

"There's a lot going on here, Britt. I'm not denying that." Donna pursed her lips and thought for a few moments. "But it's a matter of priority."

"I guess we have different priorities."

"Maybe, and then again it might just be a question of semantics or different ways of tackling a problem. We're coming from different directions. But people and their futures . . . that's the common denominator. And we're not doing all that well back home, are we?"

"No, we're not." Britt made a face. "And all we ever hear about is the growing deficit. It's a sham. Everyone's in debt to everyone else. The debts cancel each other out. Who are they trying to kid?"

"The people, of course." Donna tried to suppress a smile. "And so, what are you doing over here? Are you going to go trekking after you see Kathmandu?"

"No, I'm here on what you might call personal business." Britt went on to tell her the reason for her trip and the progress she'd made so far.

"I see. That's quite a story. Very different." Donna nodded. "I hope you succeed. The government here is horribly corrupt, but, as it's a Tibetan child, that might make a difference. They don't much care what happens to them. They don't care about their own either, but, well, they have their regulations. No one else can have them either."

"Well, it's their collateral, wouldn't you say?"

"Possibly. Yes, that could well be their reasoning."

"It's mangled thinking and inexcusable." Britt said hotly.

"I agree."

"Do you have children, Donna?"

"Yes, one son. He's over thirty now, and I never see him. I've been divorced from my husband for a long time. Now, I don't see my son either. He goes his own way." She said it flatly and without a shred of emotion. For some reason or other she'd put thoughts of her son aside and buried them. If it had hurt her, she wasn't going to allow the pain to continue.

Once outside, Donna suggested that they take a rickshaw back to the hotel, and Britt stalled, balking at the idea. There was a driver waiting who came forward hopefully as they emerged from the restaurant.

"It's his livelihood," Donna reasoned. "I know you don't approve. Neither do I really, but who are you hurting besides this man trying to earn enough to feed his family?"

Britt looked at her and let her shoulders sag. "All right. What the hell! But I don't much like it."

"Neither do I," Donna retorted. "So just this once treat yourself and do him a favor at the same time. Come on."

Back at the Guest House, they went to their separate rooms. Before closing her door, Donna called after her. "Keep me posted on how you're getting along. Tomorrow evening I'm going out to a friend's house for dinner, but I'll be around, and you know where to find me."

"I will." Britt promised. "Tomorrow will be hectic, but it's very nice having someone to talk to, and I enjoyed our dinner."

-Eleven-

The next few days brought on a flurry of activity that drove Britt to the point of exhaustion. She spent most of the next morning telephoning various agencies. Any information she could glean would come in useful, and it seemed that most of the data had to be wrangled obliquely from international organizations that had been in Nepal for some time and had dealt with Nepalese authorities. It was useless to call up the officials at the various ministries directly. One needed connections, and finding the right government employees in the right ministries was important. She made appointments to see Tom Atkinson, the Director of Save the Children Agency and Keith Fitzgibbon who headed up World Neighbors. She also rang up the Canadian Cooperation and arranged to meet with Baja Tempa, a native born Indian from Bombay. He had been educated in Edmonton, Alberta and then returned to India and recently to Nepal at the request of the Canadian government. He told her frankly that he had very little real official capacity here in Nepal. They were just starting up and everything still went through New Delhi, but he was in frequent contact with them. And that was fine with Britt. At least it would have to do. She made all the appointments for the following week. Just before leaving for Buddha'Nath and Lobsang's family, she decided to make one more call and that was to the Ministry of Justice. They put her through to a legal advisor and his advice was to contact one of the professors at the university's faculty of law, a professor Ram Persad Shestra. Shestra? She wondered. A relation to the B.W. Shestra, Don's employee? She checked the directory and got her answer. There were hundreds of Shestra's and those were only the ones with phones. The professor listened and then tied the customary legal knot in proceedings. Yes, private adoptions were done in Nepal, but most lawyers refused to do them because the government had not made the transactions official. But no, it wasn't actually illegal. Not at all, but again very few lawyers undertook such cases. And no, he couldn't reveal the name of any attorney who would handle an adoption. Britt put down the receiver and stared at the phone. Circles within circles. Couldn't give her a name, she thought. Why the hell not? And was it legal or wasn't it? Yes and no. More bloody idiocy. Well, there had to be a way to get a lawyer's name if absolutely necessary, and considering Nepalese officialdom, that may well be the only way to go.

The day had warmed up considerably through the morning. By evening it would be cool again, and the night would be cold. At the moment, however, the sun was shining, and it was time to head over to the Tibetan community. The narrow streets were once again clogged, so much so in fact it made walking difficult and the incessant honking of horns and the screeching of breaks bringing cars to sudden stops wracked the nerves. She stopped at a vendor's stall to buy a candy bar. It would serve for lunch, and she could eat it on the way. Chocolate was expensive, surprisingly so, by Nepalese standards. On a whim she bought four more and stuffed them into her handbag. Most kids liked chocolate. As she kept walking up toward the main thoroughfare, it occurred to her that she hadn't seen one toy shop. And there were no department stores in Kathmandu. There were a lot of unusual items around, from Buddha's of every description, to any number of Hindu deities, tankers, scarves, musical instruments, jewelry, but no toys. When she finally got to Kanti Path Road she hailed a cab. It seemed useless to take one through the labyrinth of narrow back streets she'd just emerged from. It was faster to walk.

The driver stopped just opposite the main entrance and Britt continued on foot down the street thinking she'd have little difficulty finding the narrow shop attached to many others in a long row, but she kept passing it and doubling back until on her third try, the mother emerged and signaled to her. Once in the tiny bar-type eating place, the father smiled at her and bowed. Then he hurried off and returned with his friend. That's how she came to meet Norbu Tsewang who proved to be just as tenacious and resourceful as she was. Britt liked this tall and ranging, rugged-faced Tibetan on sight. He could also write and speak English perfectly. He translated for the family. The children came in after they'd been talking for over an hour. And there was Lobsang again . . . watching her.

"I've known the father for many years," Norbu told her. "We were in the Indian Army together. Much later we came back up here to settle down. He's a good man." He smiled up at Tenzing. "He was so sick last year we thought we were going to lose him."

"I hope it's what they really want," Britt searched his face. "It's a hard thing to do."

"I have two sons, and I couldn't do it. But I hope to get them into a Tibetan school down near Madras. It's a much better school. There's another school in Northern India, closer and also very good, but I don't think there's a place for them."

"What's wrong with the schools here?"

"They're not as good . . . most of them. And besides, Tibetans aren't allowed to go to university here. Most of us aren't citizens, you see, and even if we could there's no money. That's why Tenzing wants to do this. Our children have no future here."

"I see," Britt paused. "So you're not a citizen either?"

"No. And any kind of work I do is illegal. For instance, when I take groups trekking, I do it illegally. If the government finds out they'll stop me. It's a criminal offense. It could bring me a lot of trouble. Also, Tenzing runs this place without a license. Usually we get warned in advance. If government officials come around, it's closed. There's nothing here. They haven't been around in a while, and he has some fake papers just in case."

"What a nightmare!" Britt mumbled.

"We're refugees. That's what it means."

"So it would be easier if you were a Nepalese citizen?"

"Oh yes, but most of them have it hard too. They have nothing really. Only a very few. That's why they need sponsors too in order to educate their children. An education is very important." Tenzing asked him a question and he nodded. "He wants to know if you have a profession."

"Tell him yes. I'm a teacher and I'm also a nurse."

"Both?" Norbu looked surprised. "That's very good."

"It's handy."

Norbu turned to his friend and explained. Tenzing clapped him on the shoulders. "He's happy." Norbu nodded to her.

"So you'll be coming with us to the Tibetan Refugee Center tomorrow?" Britt changed the subject.

"Yes, they've asked me to go. The mother will be coming too."

"Do you think this center will be able to help?"

Norbu looked doubtful. "The man in charge there isn't very good. He might not want to do anything. He's been arrested a few times. Now he does nothing. He's afraid."

"Is it worth our time going?"

"Yes. He might be able and willing to help or knows where we can get help."

"So it's worth a try?"

"Yes, but there are other ways too. They told me Tashi Phintso is supposed to have connections." Norbu shrugged.

"His family is quite well off. So maybe . . ."

"Is Tashi a citizen?"

"I don't know him well, but Kunchowk is, so Tashi must be too."

Just before leaving, Britt handed the chocolate bars to the mother.

"Would you ask her if I can take the children out, Norbu . . . next week, perhaps?"

After he translated the request, the mother nodded to her, and spoke again to Norbu. "She agrees and says that someone will come along with you. Someone who can speak English because the children can't. Also you should come and visit whenever you wish."

That evening Britt went out and had supper alone. The restaurant, Narayan's, just down the street was reputed to have good European food that non-natives were able to eat. The rumor was right. Looking around her, she found that almost all the clientele were foreigners like herself. She felt conspicuous eating alone. All the others were in pairs or groups. To counteract this she studied their faces, quite a number of them, and wondered what their reason was for being here. Tourists probably. Many of them looked like university students or older people travelling for pleasure.

The following day she went back over Buddha 'Nath and waited around until Tenzing could find Norbu. To save time they took another cab over to the Refugee Center. The mother sat in the middle. Along the route, the taxi got snarled in a traffic jam and a large crowd of people swept by carrying a long, white banner.

"What's that?" Britt asked.

Norbu leaned forward and sideways. "It's a funeral, I think." And the mother nodded her head in a single jerk. "Yes. Dead body."

Those were the first English words Britt had heard her utter. The Tibetans had a different way of burying their dead. Finally at the center which looked badly in need of repair, the mother sat rigidly upright with a determined expression on her face and Norbu spoke with one of the officials at the counter. Britt walked around and noticed a small group of people in a drab office off to one side. There was a Tibetan and some foreigners discussing intently a matter they couldn't seem to agree on. She recognized one of the women and the man with her from Narayan's restaurant on the previous evening. It seemed odd to find them in the Refugee Center. Norbu turned away from the counter and joined her as she started back across the room toward the mother.

"We'll have to wait. He'll be free in a little while. But you don't need to stay in here. Why don't you go outside?"

Britt nodded. "All right. You might do better without me."

"Yes, maybe, but don't be too hopeful. As I've said, he's reluctant to do anything just now. He was just released from prison a few weeks ago. But he's never been much good for us. I wish they'd replace him. Of course he knows the right people. Still there are other ways. Don't be worried yet."

"I've no intention of giving up, Norbu." She gave him a brief smile. "I'll find a way if there's any way at all." Nevertheless, once outside Britt sat down on the top step, and her thoughts were dark. So dark in fact, she was still sitting there when the woman whom she'd remembered and had been in the small office came out on the porch. She was alone and as Britt looked up at her there was a flicker of recognition in her eyes.

"I've seen you before, haven't I?" The woman began hesitantly.

"Yes, at Narayan's, last evening."

"Oh." She frowned and then shrugged. "Why are you here?"

"I'm waiting for some people inside. They're Tibetan. What are you doing here?"

"I'm with the Swedish delegation. I usually make it up two or three times a year. Our main office is in New Delhi. I've been there ten years."

"Do you like it?"

"New Delhi?"

"Yes."

"I did at the beginning, but not now, and here!" She waved a hand in dismissal. "I hate coming up here now. And you? Do you like it? Most do."

"I don't." Britt didn't even have to think about her answer. It was out before she even realized what she was saying. "I mean . . ."

"I know what you mean." The Swedish woman about her own

age nodded. "This place is even worse than New Delhi, and it's bad there. I'm involved with funding and social advancement projects. We, and a number of other countries, have put hundreds of millions of dollars into this place. Nepal is terribly corrupt, even more so than India, and it's bad there. They've always wasted . . . insisted on handling the funds and managing the distribution themselves. Well, we complied. So did the other countries and what have they done with the funds? Nothing ever gets better here."

"They haven't even put in a sewage system" Britt muttered. "No wonder disease is everywhere."

"Well, more funds have come into Nepal than anywhere I can think of and what are they doing with all that money? It all goes into the hands of the ruling class. It's almost as bad in India. I'm sorry to have to say it, but I wish the British hadn't left. I never used to think that way before coming here."

"I would never have thought I'd come to think that either," Britt said quietly. "I'm no colonialist, but I'm even sorrier the British left."

"And it's going to get worse," the Swedish woman shook her head. "We are going to advise our government to stop funding. The money's being wasted. There's no point in keeping it up. It's useless."

The door swung open and the man and another woman joined her. They talked together a few moments and then started down the steps. The woman turned back. "Good bye. We're going back to Delhi on the weekend. Good luck with whatever . . ." She waved her hand, indicating the Refugee Center and then went off with the rest of the Swedish delegation.

It was almost a half hour later when Lobsang's mother and Norbu emerged from the center. The mother's face showed a tightly controlled angry expression which might curiously be translated into a mask of frustration combined with desperation. Norbu looked downhearted, but not especially perturbed, as if the outcome was no more than he had expected.

The mother marched right past her, but Norbu stopped and lit up a cigarette. He offered one to Britt.

"No go?" she asked.

"No. They can't or won't do anything." He shrugged. "I have to be careful too. Some of them know me in there."

"They wouldn't do anything, Norbu."

"You can't trust them." He looked around. "You can't trust many people."

Britt smiled at him. "We're alike, Norbu. We're not really distrustful people at all. It's just that we've found too few people that can handle trust. It's a burden, after all, isn't it?"

Norbu laughed. "Yes, but that's not usually why it's broken. There are different reasons. Not worry or strain. Other reasons."

"Not so noble ones. I understand."

"Dolma's waiting. She didn't take it so well. She doesn't know what to do."

"Is that her name . . . Dolma? I've just known her as Tenzing's wife or Lobsang's mother."

"Yes, Dolma. Same name as my wife." They started walking toward the curb where the mother was waiting.

"I'd like to meet your wife, Norbu. Does she speak English?"

"Oh yes. She's a teacher for young children, but not for a long time now."

They found another cab and went back to Tenzing Lama's eating house. Britt spent what remained of the afternoon with the family and Lobsang, in particular. She was getting used to having whatever she needed said translated. The boy understood more English than she had supposed, particularly if one spoke slowly and directly to him. Simple things, but it was enough.

Friday was a holiday, a holy day for the Nepalese people, and that morning at breakfast in the Guest House, the same friendly Tibetan waiter who served at the same table she always sat at greeted her with cheerful familiarity. "How are you, Miss? Not busy today like other days."

"It's a holiday for you too, Kaisang?"

"No, I'm Tibetan. You know that. I told you."

"So, you're Buddhist?"

"Yes, but it's a big Hindu holiday. Everything's closed. So you can't do any work today." He grinned at her and went off to bring back a pot of hot tea. Britt never thought of herself as a person of habit but in eating she was as predictable as time passing.

"What will you have this morning, Miss? The same?"

"Yes Kaisang, the same," she laughed back at him. "How old are you?"

"Seventeen."

"How long have you worked here?"

"Three . . . almost four years now. That's when I left my village."

"And your family . . . are they still there?"

"Yes. My parents, brothers, sisters. I go back when I can . . . once a year maybe."

"So you've been working since you were around thirteen . . . fourteen."

"Yes. Always here. It's not so bad here."

"You like it?"

"Yes. I meet many people, learn English, maybe someday something better." He paused. "What will you do today?"

"I'm going out to JawelKiel to see a Fr. John Chemparathy."

"Father?"

"He's a priest, Kaisang. A Jesuit. There's a school there. St. Ignatius Loyola School . . . but that's this afternoon. This morning I'm free. Maybe I'll look around. Where do you recommend?"

"I can take my time off this morning. I could take you where you want to go. Have you seen Swayambhu?"

"No, what is it?"

Kaisang tilted his head. "The big Buddhist pagoda. Like a temple. It's very big, very beautiful."

"I've seen the large Hindu temple, but not the Buddhist one. I'd like to go. Yes." Britt nodded. "How about around ten o'clock?"

"Sure. Ten o'clock." Kaisang reached for the tea pot to have it refilled. "I'll wait for you outside in the courtyard."

Kaisang proved to be good company. He pointed things out and took the roundabout route up to the Swayambhu Temple or Pagoda. Britt wasn't sure what term they used, but once there it was a long climb to the top. It was indeed very beautiful, very impressive.

After a while they started down again and didn't get back to the hotel until nearly one-thirty. Kaisang wasn't expecting anything, but he beamed at her with unexpected warmth and shyness when she handed him some rupees. It was more than he earned in two full weeks working twelve hours a day at the hotel.

"You don't have to, Miss," he mumbled, embarrassed and pleased at the same time.

"Take it, Kaisang. You earned it, and I enjoyed every minute of it. It was nice of you to take me."

A number of the other young fellows and women staff of the hotel were looking on. It seemed they had materialized as if out of nowhere. They all needed something and they worked for very little. A place to sleep, something to eat, and maybe help keep some of their families. But Britt was on a tight budget and this wasn't a pleasure trip after all.

The visit to Father John Champarathy whom she'd called the previous evening proved to be both informative and helpful. It also confirmed her increasing misgivings about the tiny kingdom of Nepal.

"We keep a very low profile here." The priest sat in his chair after placing tea on the table between them in his clean, but modestly furnished study. "You noticed there's no cross outside. On the whole, we're not very well received here."

"I noticed." Britt looked at the soft-spoken and gentle man across from her. "You're suspect, I take it. This is Hindu and Buddhist country."

"Yes, but they've nothing to fear from us. We're through with proselytizing pretty well. We run the school and have this small church. Most of the students are Hindu. Some are Buddhist and that's what they'll remain. Instruction is in English."

"Are there fees, Father?"

"Yes, we have to charge. We're not government funded. But it's not a large amount."

"I see."

"It's difficult here. Quite often they reject help. Even Mother Theresa couldn't set up much here. They weren't going to let her in at all. The government officials didn't want her here."

"They didn't want Sister Theresa? But why?"

"No interference," the priest lifted his shoulders and let them drop. He looked sad and resigned. "Finally they let in four of the sisters of her order. That's it. Just four. They have a center for the homeless here near the town square. They can't do much, but it helps."

Britt shook her head. All of this and everything she'd heard so far didn't argue well for her chances to adopt, not through an official government agency in any case.

She said quietly, almost dreamily, "She's so well known, not just in India, but everywhere."

"Yes. I think there was some outside pressure, and it wouldn't look very good if they rejected her entirely and it was found out."

No it wouldn't. Britt thought. What would happen to their international funding then? There was a silence between them until finally the priest shattered it.

"When you called, you said you were having some difficulty . . . about an adoption?"

"Yes," she went on to explain the situation and Chemparathy nodded and thought for a few moments.

"I really don't know how I can help you, Miss Erikson. Maybe Father Dexter will be able to help. He's Canadian too, and he's been here ten years. He's fluent in Nepalese, and he knows about visas because they're always revoking his or setting expiry dates and he has to go down and have it renewed. He knows a few people in immigration." The priest telephoned the school that was in the same small compound. He spoke briefly with the secretary then turned back to Britt. "Yes. He's in class." The mild-mannered man rubbed his chin. "That's a special class he takes when he has time. The students aren't here today. But I could speak with him later, and if you call me next week I'll arrange for you to meet him. Maybe he'll be able to help you."

"Yes, I'd appreciate that," Britt got up. "Getting a visa for the child will be necessary because I think it's going to be a private adoption."

"Yes, that would be best. I don't think government officials will be much help."

"No, I don't think so either." She shook hands with him. "I'll call you next week then. And thank you. I hope this didn't take up too much of your time."

"Not at all. Come anytime." He held the door for her. "And call next week. I'll talk to Peter . . . Father Dexter."

Now the weekend lay ahead of her, and it should have loomed as a welcome respite from the week's entanglements with Tibetan and Nepalese officials. But her mind kept conjuring up the small boy's face and, trailing in the wake of the image, were all the hopes and aspirations that had brought her on this long journey.

For diversion she dined out with Donna again on Saturday

evening, and they sat at a long table in Narayan's restaurant and conversed with two young men from Holland. Britt had seen them there before, but they'd never spoken. One of them smoked and when he found that his habit was annoying Donna he came and sat beside Britt. It was cheerful and warm and interesting. It also took her mind off the vital reason for her being in Nepal. Unlike the others she felt riveted to a purpose that was starting to drain her emotional reserve and tax her resources.

Still, there had to be a way, some way to do this thing. Sunday was uneventful except for the sudden appearance of Tashi Phintso, and initially Britt thought her problem was closer than ever to a resolution. After all, Tashi and Shestra were the contacts Don Willet had given her. Tashi would know what to do and how to go about it. He was fairly well dressed, bearing out his status in the Tibetan community and purportedly he had contacts. He spoke of them and the family that was anxious to have the child adopted. When she mentioned Nirala, the principal of the school which Karma, the older boy, was attending, he shook his head.

"I don't like him either, Miss Erikson . . . Britt. Many in our community don't trust him."

"Why not? I thought it might just be my own false impression."

"No. It's not just you." Tashi's eyes shifted. "You see it's suspected he has transactions with the Chinese, the Communists, and we won't have anything to do with them. Not after what happened in Tibet."

"I see." Britt nodded. "Well, I just concluded he wasn't going to be very helpful. But Don likes him. What about that?"

Tashi twisted uneasily in his chair. He sipped at his tea and lit a cigarette. Finally, he shrugged. "Some trust him. Don does. That's why he likes to get sponsors in the United States so that more students can attend his school. My father likes him also . . . but me, well, I've nothing to say."

Britt lifted an eyebrow. "Does Don know you feel this way?"

"I tried to tell him. He listens to my father."

"To Kunchowk?"

"Yes. We all do . . . have to, more or less. He wanted me to marry. So I finally gave in. Now I'd like to get enough money to have my own place and not live at home."

It seemed to Britt that everyone lived at Kunchowk's house, including his brother who owned the guest house where she was staying and the clerk, Tsuten, Tashi's cousin. They were in her hotel room now.

"Are you comfortable here?" Tashi asked, changing the subject.

"Yes, it's fine . . . fine. Now about how we're going to proceed . . ."

"Yes, I'll come for you in the morning, and I'll introduce you to some people in Buddha 'Nath. Another principal of a school that's just opened there."

"Sure, but have you any notion how to go about all this? The adoption?"

"Meet people," Tashi shrugged again. "This man is very good. Not like Nirala."

"Yes, but do you know any Nepalese authorities?"

"No, but I could help you go where you want to go."

"But where?" Britt threw up her hands. "It's the Nepalese government we've got to deal with eventually. We'll need a visa for the child."

"Yes, but there are ways."

"I've heard that before," Britt eyed him carefully.

"What are these ways?"

"I'll work on it," Tashi stood up. "Don't worry. There are things we can do. Come with me tomorrow to Buddha 'Nath. Meet the other school principal and one other person."

"Yes, I'll be over in the morning."

"Good, I'll come and get you. That would be better."

"But there's no need," Britt protested. "I can get there."

"It's no trouble."

"I'm taking the boys out this week too. Probably mid-week."

"I know," Tashi smiled at her. "I stopped into the family's place before coming here. I'll come with you on the outing. They don't speak very good English."

When he had gone, Britt sat thinking, and concluded that she'd have to handle what had to be done. Both Tashi and Shestra were willing but helpless, and possibly hopeless, in handling the finagling that inevitably had to be done in this corrupt little kingdom.

Tashi turned up again the following morning just as she was having breakfast in the dining room of the guest house. When they were ready to leave, Britt told him she was going to the Canadian Cooperation first and Tashi thought that a good idea. The small office run by one secretary and Baja Tempa was on the other side of town. It was a crude and hastily built little building on a separate plot of land and had only bare office essentials: a telephone, a typewriter, and a wooden counter with two or three wooden chairs against one wall.

Baja was courteous and patient. He listened carefully and then without actually saying anything, his eyes indicated just how hopeless it was to proceed with an adoption through Nepalese authorities. Finally Britt changed her tactic.

"If I do adopt him legally--"

"But you can't," Baja interrupted.

"Well, if I can get it done . . . hypothetically Baja, then he'd legally be a Canadian citizen, wouldn't he?"

"No, you know it takes time for citizenship."

"Yes, of course." Britt expelled a long breath. "But I'm Canadian born and as my son legally, he would have a right to enter Canada, wouldn't he?"

Baja covered his mouth with one hand and looked down for a few moments and thought about it. "I guess so, but I'm not sure."

"Well could you put him on my passport . . . as a minor?"

"Oh no. Don't handle passports or even visas. That goes through the Canadian Embassy in New Delhi."

"That's India. This is Nepal. Since we have no embassy here to handle such matters, it should go through the British Embassy. We're part of The Commonwealth. It's standard practice."

"Not anymore. I don't think so." Baja shook his head.

"But you can try."

"I will." Britt nodded and looked annoyed. "In any case if that fails you are in frequent contact with Delhi, aren't you?"

"Yes, the diplomatic mail pouch goes out several times a week and it gets there without delay."

"I'll be in touch."

Once again in another taxi, Britt looked over at Tashi. "All I seem to be doing is taking cabs, but driving here looks lethal and public transport is impossible. Why are the buses so packed? They've got people hanging out their doors and windows. Even on the roof."

Tashi smiled. "You're better to avoid it. They are always packed. Too . . . too many people and the cabs are all owned by the government. There are people with cars who drive people, but it's not legal. The cars aren't marked."

"Really?" Britt frowned.

"Yes. And all the rickshaws too. The government gets a big percentage. The drivers just work for government agencies. All the big hotels here too. All government owned."

Britt stared out the window at the busy noisy tumult of people, moving vehicles, even animals, all of which seemed to be converging and scurrying in different directions. Downtown New York might be buzzing maddeningly, but it was nothing like this.

Once in Buddha 'Nath, she paid off the cab driver, and they continued on foot over to the Shanti Milarepa School where Tashi introduced her to a very nice man, Shukia Tsering, the principal. They walked around the buildings which were as yet unfinished.

"You have a nice school, Tsering," Britt commented when they were back in his office.

"Thank you. Some English teachers are going to come and teach here for a while too. At least I hope I can get a few."

"You went to school in England, Tsering?"

"Yes. I know some people there, so I'm hoping. Also hoping to lure some students who have sponsors here. So far the enrollment is down, but by the time we open for the new term, there should be more."

"Well, good luck." Britt smiled at him. "You've heard I'm trying to adopt a child here?"

"Yes, Tashi told me. That's hard to do."

"That's an understatement." Britt pursed her lips. "What about a private adoption? Do you know any lawyers who do adoptions?"

"No." He glanced again at Tashi. "What about Chandra Shastri and his wife. Haven't they had something to do with adoptions?"

"Who are they?" Britt asked.

"People over near the Teragoon Hotel. Not far from here." Tashi answered her. "Tenzing and his wife know about them, but they don't actually know them. Neither do I."

"It's worth a try." Britt shrugged.

Dolma Lama thought it worth attempting too. She had inquired from people in the community about where to get help or direction. As Britt and Tashi sat drinking tea in Tenzing's dreary little eating place, the mother disappeared into the back room to see to the baby. Behind a waist-high counter Tenzing was cooking. There were no other customers in the shop and that's how it usually was. Tashi told her it livened up in the evenings. People came in then to eat and drink, but mostly to drink. It wasn't legal, but it was better than starving, Britt reasoned. People did that sort of thing in Canada during the twenties and the days of prohibition. It made some people very rich, but the Lama family looked to be able to eke only a living from it.

"Yes, that's true," Tashi nodded when Britt commented that things were indeed bad, but the family wasn't starving and many families were. "But if he gets sick again, they'll starve."

"During the last episode did he have medication?"

"Yes, some. But not enough and it was a very long illness."

The mother came hurrying back into the room. She was ready to go. It was a short walk to the Sastri dwelling near the Teragoon Hotel. In fact, the wife worked there. Tenzing's wife moved swiftly along the street and only Tashi, trying to explain where they had been and who they'd seen, slowed her quick pace. Then they started to mount three flights of stairs. It was narrow. The mother started to climb first, followed by Tashi and Britt followed behind them. When they'd reached the second landing, the mother halted suddenly and turned back, whispering fiercely and rapidly to Tashi. Her face looked troubled, and the hard lines about her mouth seemed to be put there by impending threat and fear. But then it passed, and she pushed on ahead up the last long flight of stairs. Britt pulled at Tashi's arm.

"What did she say to you?"

Tashi looked at her in dismay and his eyes wouldn't meet hers. She said, "Why don't you just have your own child."

"What!"

"I don't know." He shook his head. "I don't understand." Britt felt suddenly very tired and then alarmed.

"Listen, I've asked her repeatedly if she wants this. Is she changing her mind? I've got to know."

"Yes. We'll see about it. I'll talk to her. Now we must go up."

They could hear voices at the top of the stairs. A door had opened and another woman was speaking. Once in the room, Britt remained off to one side listening and not understanding a word. But her mind was working furiously. What the hell was going on? The letter stated unequivocally that Lobsang was up for adoption and the family wanted to know why she hadn't been over earlier. Don Willet's confirmation of the family's intent and the ability to adopt in Nepal seemed encouraging. Friends of his had adopted in Nepal and Thailand. Could it really all be a hoax? But then Tashi had mentioned another woman, a single mother, who wanted someone to adopt her five year old daughter. She rubbed a hand across her eyes, and the pressure seemed to relieve some of the tension in them. Why didn't she have one of her own? That was a good question. It was laughable really. Wasn't it laughable? And how many other women-- attractive, educated, and married or in relationships were in exactly the same position? Childless. How many? And how many couldn't find any good reason for their inability to conceive?

Britt stood watching the people in the room, detached from them as if they were characters in a movie. The gods might be watching too. Would they think this a tragedy or comedy, she wondered. There was a curiously unique point in the affairs of man when the tragic became comic and the comic was tragic. So you didn't know whether to laugh or cry. Rare, but true in every time and in every place. It defied reason, ridiculed it. It occurred to Britt, and not for the first time, that all the poor bastards who sought reason were seeking it in vain. But she couldn't help herself. She had always looked for it. And understanding was always somewhere just beyond her reach. Smart people stopped asking why. Smarter people found a medium to make their lives worthwhile. That made sense. Good sense.

Finally the conversation came to an end and they found themselves trooping down the stairs. Once out on the street, Tashi was explaining that their visit with the Shastri family had not proved very useful. In fact, they were not one whit wiser. The mother had caught sight of her eldest son playing with some boys on the street, and she was eyeing him closely. Britt looked Tashi in the eye and held up a hand to arrest his flow of words.

"It's all pointless, Tashi. That woman doesn't know what she wants."

"No, I think she knows. It's just . . ." He lifted his shoulders and let them drop. The mother had turned her attention back to them and was looking from one to the other.

"It's hard. It's a very hard thing to do. And she knows I can't bring him back to visit every year, not from Canada. It's too costly. Now, if she wants me to help finance Lobsang's schooling here, in Nepal, I'll do it. I'll try. But adoption's different."

"I know," Tashi frowned and darted a glance at the mother. "She told me she wanted him adopted."

"Well, I think she's changed her mind."

"I'll talk to her."

"Yes. You talk to her. Find out. Make sure, because once it's done, it's done. It's final. You understand?"

"Yes, I'll go and see her and the father this evening, and you'll know for sure."

"Yes. Find out. Make sure. Make very damn sure."

Tashi nodded. "I'll find out. Then I'll contact you."

Britt turned and walked away. Her thoughts were in a whirl. Direction didn't seem to matter much. Finally she hailed a cab and headed back to the Guest House. Once there she went directly to her room and ordered tea. She sipped at it and lit a cigarette. Then she tried to think, but all that came to mind was her father's face, and there were no words for the way she felt or the reasons for it. The tears slipped her lids and rolled unheeded down her cheeks. She was perfectly motionless and still. The convulsions of grief had come to this. A ringing silence at the center of tempestuous living. Laughing, crying, singing, sobbing. The tumult was out there. In her, there was a quickening silence, and she had never felt quite so alone before.

The following morning broke with a hard bright light that penetrated the blinds at the windows and danced crazily across the ceiling and along the upper edges of the walls. There was no need to hurry and dress, get down to breakfast, and make plans for the day. She could take her time. Today she was supposed to take the children out. The three boys: Karma, Lobsang, and Lingwan. To the zoo probably. Yes, Britt nodded to herself, still lying in bed; kids liked going to the zoo. But she'd put everything on hold. Noises drifted up from the street below. Kathmandu woke up early, and there was no way to insulate yourself against its urgent clamor that had a riotous rhythm, unsettling and jarring to the senses. Every bit as bad, if not worse, than the ugliest of city sounds back home.

Britt threw back the covers and got out of bed. First a hot bath. Why not? There should be lots of hot water this time of day. She was wrong again, naturally. The water was only tepid, and she reckoned it must take them most of the day to heat up enough water for the required evening supply. Still, most people in the city had no indoor water supply at all. What had she to complain of? Nothing really.

She didn't get down to the dining room until 9:30, and all but an elderly couple had been to breakfast and departed already for their new day's adventure. She dawdled over her tea and even more so over her breakfast, pushing the food around on the plate and occasionally taking a mouthful. Kaisang, cheerful and obliging as ever, was eyeing her curiously and then worriedly. He brought over a fresh pot of tea, newly brewed.

"Something wrong, Miss?" he asked haltingly.

"No, Kaisang. Nothing at all." She looked up at him and read the knowledge he had of her in his eyes.

"I think maybe something. Yes." He smiled tentatively and his face was full of compassion. A sensitive boy, Britt thought. And what kind of man would the boy become? But then this boy had been living and assumedly been taking on the responsibilities of an adult for some years now. Not like some of the kids back home whose childhood had extended well into their forties and beyond. Not very mature. Then again, perhaps her expectations didn't reflect a very mature attitude toward life either. Maybe. At the other end of the spectrum was resignation. And somewhere in the middle, she supposed, was recognition of the way things were and getting on with one's life. All very well so long as one didn't become complacent. That seemed to Britt the greatest contemporary threat. Socially and even personally. Unconsciously, she tossed her head at the circus movement of her thoughts.

Kaisang was still standing at her table. "Why don't you sit outside, Miss? In the courtyard. It's sunny warm now. There are a few people out there. One of the guests . . . you know the student from Japan? Yes. Well, he's trying to play one of our flutes. Not too bad." He nodded and grinned at her. "Take your tea with you."

And that's where Tashi found Britt about an hour later. The young Japanese fellow was doing very well, and the light and happy, and sometimes haunting tunes filled the air. The staff, on their successive breaks, stood around, listened and smiled. It was like a little bit of magic and looking from one face to the next Britt felt that it helped. Yes, it did. People needed a little bit of magic in their lives.

Tashi moved around the small gathering, catlike fashion, and stood for a few moments staring down at her before speaking.

"Miss Erikson . . . Britt?"

Her head jerked up and around. "Oh Tashi! You startled me."

"I'm sorry. Startled? Does that mean you are surprised?"

"It does," Britt nodded. "Sit down."

As she moved over on the step, Tashi sat down beside her. "I went over to speak with Tenzing last night, and I spoke with the mother, too. They do want the boy to be adopted."

Britt clenched her lower lip between her teeth and tried to think, but her thoughts were scuttled. That's because her heart was telling her one thing and her mind another. That always happened when she let her feelings get in the way. She wanted to believe him. That was the problem.

"I'm not convinced," she said crisply. "The father . . . maybe. He's been ill. He's worried. So is the mother, but not enough to give up one of her sons."

"But it's better for him," Tashi argued. "There's nothing for him here."

"I'll sponsor him in school here. I told her that. You did tell her again, didn't you?"

"Yes, I told her, but she has decided it would be better for him to go. She is sure. She wants this very much."

Britt turned toward him and searched his face. He couldn't escape her eyes.

"I'm skeptical, Tashi. I saw the look on her face, and you told me what she said."

"She is very sure now. Very sure. We spoke for a long time."

"And the boy?"

"Oh Lobsang is very happy to go." Tashi started to relax.

"I spoke to him too."

"It's difficult, Tashi. If she changes her mind . . ."

"She won't," he assured her and went on emphatically as he saw the expression of suspicion on Britt's face. "She won't change her mind. At least come over and speak with them again. They want you to come."

Finally Britt nodded. "All right, Tashi. I'll come with you."

When they entered the shop, the father came forward looking very pleased to see her. He put his hands together and bowed. Britt returned his smile. Then he spoke to Tashi.

"He wants you to come in back where they live." Tenzing led

them through the make-shift cooking area and into the single room with a hard dirt floor that had an old rug spread in the middle of it. There were bench like seats around the room and several small tables stacked with some of the necessities of living. The center was kept clear. There was no bathroom or a sink with running water. Apparently the whole family slept in this one room, including the grandmother, Dolma's mother and her brother who had left the monastery and the life of a monk sometime previously. But now there was only the immediate family about. The boys were coming in and out from a door on the side, and the mother was trying to quiet the baby who appeared heavy-eyed and miserable.

"The little one has a cold." Tashi said as he saw Britt's attention pulled toward the child. The mother nodded and smiled briefly. Then the smile just as quickly disappeared and the habitual expression of anxiety and determination returned and remained planted in her face. But she'd seen the look of distance and disbelief on Britt's face. Nothing escaped the perceptive wife of Tenzing Lama. In comparison, the husband was forthright and disarmingly guileless. Now he was bringing some hot tea, heavily sugared and strong.

As Britt sat for a few minutes with Tenzing and Tashi translated, the mother was tending to the baby who was fussing, and covertly watching the youngish looking Canadian woman in the tailored suit, and she noted with increasing concern the legion of emotions that crawled almost imperceptibly under the calm demeanor. This woman was not easily fooled, Dolma concluded, but she could make a difficult decision. And she wasn't deceitful by nature. She probably never had to be. Not like her. She couldn't live a day without worry. If this woman withdrew now, as she very well might, her chances were lost, and helping out financially with Lobsang's education in Nepal didn't come anywhere near her aspirations. She needed more than that for her family . . . her children. Now the woman was saying something to her husband and Tashi interpreted rapidly.

"You might say you want your son adopted, Tenzing," Britt paused. "But it's too hard on your wife. It's the most difficult thing for a mother to do. I want him, yes. That's why I'm here, but it's just too hard on your wife."

Tashi listened to Tenzing answer and then turned to her again. "He says it's his wife who wanted their son to go in the first place. She wanted it and he agreed."

"Well, tell him that I'll put the boy in school here and try to keep up the annual payments so she doesn't have to worry."

Tashi spoke to Tenzing again and then sighed. "He says that's no good. His wife knows it's better for the boy to go with you . . . so, he can get an education . . . and college. He wants to know if he can go to college."

"Yes . . . yes, of course, if he wants to go onto college, he can go, but he doesn't seem to understand that it's my concern that she doesn't really want to let him go. She'll only change her mind and this will all have been for nothing. Adoption is final. I don't think he understands that and what it means."

Tenzing nodded and then shook his head as Tashi told him what was said.

The father started to reply, but the mother intervened and spoke forcefully to Tashi while glancing intermittently at her husband. Then Tenzing was looking at his wife and nodding thoughtfully. Finally, he agreed and appeared even more relieved. He motioned to Tashi to explain to Britt what was being said. And Tashi obliged.

"The mother now thinks it best that you take the smaller son too. Tenzing agrees. It would be better if they went together. They don't have much hope of finding a sponsor for the little one."

"Lingwan?" Britt frowned and appeared more confused than ever. "She wants me to take him too?"

"Yes, if you want to . . . if you can manage it."

"I can manage it . . . and it would be good for the brothers to have each other, but why? He's only five, and they might find a sponsor for him. There's still time. If she's having trouble giving up one son, two will be doubly hard. One is agony for her, but two!"

Tashi once again spoke to the parents, and the conversation bounced back and forth until finally Tashi glanced again at this foreign woman who couldn't understand a word of what was being said. "They want you to take both boys. They feel better having them go together. And as we've all said before--there's absolutely nothing for them here. Nothing. At least in Canada they'll have some kind of future, but not here."

"All right." Britt stood up. "Tell them I'll adopt both. I'd be very happy to do that. And they'll have love and a good home . . . but I hope they know what the hell they're doing." She studied the mother's face, but could find no undercurrent of emotion that was tugging her away from this drastic decision.

Tashi told Tenzing and his wife and they both looked back at her and smiled happily.

"They are very sure they know what they're doing. Very certain. And they are very happy about this chance their sons are getting."

Just before leaving, Britt thought of one last thing. "Tell them I'll take all three boys out to the zoo the day after tomorrow, around two in the afternoon."

"Oh, I can't come with you that day," Tashi said, "I'm busy. There are some people I must see."

"I'll bring someone with me."

"Who, Mr. Shestra?"

"No. There's no need to take him from his work. I'll bring someone from the hotel."

"Who?"

"I don't know yet," Britt shrugged. "But someone who can speak Tibetan and English."

It wasn't until she got back to her hotel room that she felt a wave of relief sweeping over her. It was too good to be true. Britt figured it must take an awful lot of love to give up two children, even if it did give them some kind of chance at a better life than what they had. She had been wrong. The mother must indeed want the adoption very much for her not only to agree to give up two sons, but to do everything possible to see that it went through. And that's apparently what she was doing because before they left Buddha 'Nath, Tenzing's wife told Tashi that her brother still had friends in the Tibetan monasteries in their community, and she thought perhaps one of the head monks might know what to do. They had influence and might be willing to help. No doubt Buddhist monks in such a religious community might have some pull, Britt thought, but she had plans of her own.

That evening she called Mr. Shestra. He sounded doubtful about her plan, but agreed it might work.

". . . but, no, I don't know of any lawyers who might do a private adoption. I don't even know how to go about finding one."

"Well, the Ministry of Justice referred me to the Faculty of Law at the University, but they won't release any names."

"I didn't think they would. I didn't think there were any or even that it could actually be done privately."

"Oh yes, it can be done," Britt thought for a moment. "Maybe the man in charge of the Canadian Cooperation here knows a few names."

"He might, but you'll still need two visas. That has to go through Nepalese officials."

"Maybe, but once they are legally adopted, they'll be technically Canadian and Nepalese law mightn't apply to them."

"Well, I don't know about that," Shestra hesitated. "You still have to get them out of Nepal."

"If I can get them adopted here, I'll be more worried about my own government. They might not recognize the adoption. I may have trouble getting them into Canada."

"Why is that? Canada's a big country."

"Yup, second largest in the world. Still I'm worried. Our immigration laws are strict . . . but I know a few people who know a few people. I'll see about it."

Shestra laughed. He couldn't help it. "You're very resourceful, Miss Erikson. You'll find a way . . . if there is a way."

Oh yes, Britt thought, when she'd hung up the receiver. I'm resourceful. She had initiative. That's what everyone told her, and it was true. But her plans, well laid and executed, were often abortive. That was also true.

The following morning, she called the Canadian Consulate in New Delhi and spoke with a Karen McLeod. She was in charge of immigration. Britt didn't mention any particulars. That would be premature and might endanger her position. But she did want to know about general procedures. That's what she asked about, and McLeod came back at her sounding frustrated and harassed.

"What exactly are you trying to do, Miss Erikson?" Britt deflected the brusque question and asked about the immigration situation in general. "It's a mess," Karen sounded irritated. "I've literally thousands of requests on my desk, and all I have to do is look out my window to find thousands more. Everybody here wants to come to Canada. There are files that have been sitting here on my desk for months. And that's where they'll stay until I get to them. This is India, Miss Erikson. And I'm sure you know the regulations set up in Ottawa. Now, just what is it you want?"

"I think you need a vacation, Miss McLeod."

"I certainly do. But right now nothing gets by my desk without ministerial clearance."

"Ministerial clearance?" The words clicked in Erikson's brain.

"Yes. That's top priority, and right now I've enough of those to handle."

"Well, you will be hearing from me again," Britt said vaguely.

"You'll be contacted through the Canadian Cooperation up here."

"They can't do anything. It has to go through our consulate here."

"I know," Britt said and got quickly off the line, leaving Karen McLeod grimacing and staring grumpily around her stuffy office.

So that is it! Britt prowled around the room and ended up at the window staring down at the courtyard and the street beyond. She could also try the British Embassy and see if they'd put adopted children, as minors, on her passport. A friend of hers had used that method taking children out of Guatemala. It was worth attempting. Right now, however, she had to get over to Buddha 'Nath.

Tenzing and his wife were pleased but surprised to see her. There was no interpreter but they understood her mangled way of telling them that she wanted to see Norbu Tsewang. Tenzing nodded and went off to find his old friend. In the meantime, the boys came in, and Karma smiled and mumbled a few words in English. He wanted to show her his copybooks and the work he had been doing in school. The handsome older son, only nine years old, seemed assured and at ease, but Lobsang came and stood beside her as she sat down in the last booth. Britt smiled at him, and he gave her a shy smile in return. She moved over in the booth, and he slipped in beside her. There was something about the small boy that melted a reserve she'd maintained for her own protection. He looked vulnerable and kind of lost, not like the other two sons at all. It occurred to her that it would be very easy to love this child who was small for his age. Maybe there were the beginnings of love already, and she just didn't realize it. It was too early, and nothing was for certain. It would be dangerous and damaging for either of them to become too attached. And that's what seemed to be happening. Lingwan, on the other hand, was running around, coming in and out, but keeping his distance. He was staying very close to his mother and seemed very attached to her.

Tenzing came back and Norbu Tsewang was following him. He

smiled good-naturedly and dropped into the booth opposite her.

"So, what's going on?" he asked. "Tenzing told me a little." Britt looked at him and felt he was the one person here she could probably trust. Still he was the father's best friend, and he couldn't be expected to understand the deep sense of loss and the hidden and unaccepted fears of what might never be that had driven her to embark on this venture. He wouldn't understand the narrow thread of hope it represented either. Besides, it was personal, and everyone needed a private place. A secret place that ensured their island nature and, at the same time, let them know they were human and could find part of themselves reflected in other human beings. It was a mystery, a curse and a blessing.

"What's the matter?" Norbu asked.

"Nothing."

"Well, what can I do? You need an interpreter?"

"Yes, but no, I need a phone. I wanted to call from around here so I could have access to the family if necessary."

"We could try across the street. I have a friend there. He has a small office."

"What does he do?"

"That is a difficult question." Norbu started to smile. "Everybody does a little bit of everything around here."

"Will he let me use his phone?"

"Maybe, if he's not using it. There might be a small charge."

"Even the use of a phone was problematic for most of the people here, all built up and teeming with humanity, yet still not into the twentieth century. But Norbu's friend let her use the phone for a price. Britt handed him some rupees and got out the number."

"Who are you calling?" Norbu wanted to know.

"The Canadian Cooperation."

Norbu lifted a shoulder and let it drop as he glanced from Britt and back to his friend as she tried again and again to get through to the party at the other end.

"The connection's not always good." The man behind the desk explained to Norbu. "You know it's difficult sometimes."

"There's a lot of static," Britt mumbled. "And then the line goes dead."

She tried again and again redialing the same number. When she saw the anxious look on the man's face, she reassured him. "Don't worry. I'll pay you. It's costing you and taking up your time." She glanced at Norbu. "Tell him it's important, will you? I'll pay him."

After repeated attempts, she finally got through, and then she had to explain to the secretary that she had to speak to Baja Tempa. It was important and no, it couldn't wait. As Britt's voice raised, Norbu shifted his weight from one foot to the other and folded his arms. This was getting interesting. What was this foreign woman, who was usually so soft-spoken, going to do now?

Baja Tempa came on the line and listened while Britt explained why she was calling and what she wanted from him. Then he answered haltingly and wavered. "I'm not sure private adoption is legal here ... according to official Nepalese policy."

"The policy is cloudy at best, Baja." Britt turned her head and saw Norbu watching her intently. "Now, you know there are lawyers in Kathmandu who do adoptions. I know it, so you must also."

"How do you know? Who told you?"

"The Faculty of Law at the University."

"Well, then they must know a lawyer you can contact."

"They won't release names." Britt paused. "Now, you must know a good lawyer who handles such cases."

"I can't say, Miss Erikson."

"Why not, Baja? What's the big deal?"

"I'm not allowed to release a name. You must know that."

"I know no such thing!" The irritation came over in her voice. "That's ridiculous."

"Try to understand my position." Baja came back at her. "I could be in serious trouble if it is ever traced back to me."

"It won't be traced back to you. For God's sake, Baja, what are you afraid of?" When the vacillating representative remained silent, Britt plunged on. "You're supposed to be representing me here. You should remember that first. Now what do I have to do? Call every lawyer in Kathmandu because that's what I'm going to do."

"Miss Erikson, I'm not even sure it can be done. Private adoption here doesn't extend to foreigners. It's for Nepalese children by Nepalese citizens staying in Nepal. And it's very rare. That's not the way it's done."

"Baja, neither you nor I know that for sure." Britt continued patiently. "What possible harm is there in giving me a lawyer's name? I won't tell anyone who referred me, so no one's going to know you were in any way involved. And, in any case, how can it possibly be illegal to consult a lawyer. That's ludicrous."

Finally Baja Tempa capitulated. "All right. Try Madhu Sharma. He's involved with adoptions, but I must warn you . . ."

"Yes, yes. Everything strictly legal. I understand. Where is he?"

"At the Annapurna Hotel. He has offices there. He's a very expensive lawyer," Baja said dryly. "His fees are very high."

"Aren't they all?"

It wasn't a question and there was no need for him to answer it. She thanked the reluctant informant and hung up. Then she glanced at her watch and fumed.

"I don't believe this. Ten minutes just to wheedle the name of an attorney. What progress!"

The men looked at each other and grinned. Then Norbu shook his head, still smiling.

"Well, you got it. Now what?"

"Call him, of course. What else? I've got to get an appointment with him." She glanced at Norbu's friend. "Do you mind? I'm sorry for the delay . . . holding up your phone."

"No, it's all right, go ahead. But I will have to charge you."

"Yes, of course," Britt nodded. "Have you got a phone book?" The man turned in his seat and produced one from a wall shelf.

The lawyer's secretary was cautious too, but she finally put her through to Madhu Sharma. "What do you want to see me about?" he asked.

Fair enough question, Britt thought, but stalled. It was so easy to be put off over the phone. "It's a personal matter, Mr. Sharma. And naturally I realize your time is precious."

Since she was so obviously willing to pay for an initial interview, Madhu Sharma had fewer qualms about giving her an appointment. He checked his calendar. "Would Monday morning, ten o'clock suit you?"

"Yes, fine."

"You know where I am?"

"Oh yes. The Annapurna Hotel."

"Yes, come right through the lobby. My offices are on the second floor."

Britt put down the receiver and got out her change purse to find some more rupees for the man with the tiny office and telephone. Then she asked Norbu to let Tenzing and his wife know about the appointment.

"Should they go with you?"

"No, not this time, but they should start digging up whatever documents they have. Birth certificates . . . that sort of thing, and I'll be over tomorrow to take the boys out. Right now, I've got to find a taxi."

"Oh, that's no trouble. Come." He walked with her up the street and flagged down a cab. It was mid-afternoon by the time Britt was sitting opposite Keith Fitzgibbon of the World Neighbors

Organization. He knew Tom Atkinson who headed up Save the Children. Apparently both were involved in the same kind of work and both were considered international agencies.

Fitzgibbon laughed and wagged his head when she told him her reason for coming to Nepal. "Well, I wish you luck," he said and handed her a cup of tea. "Nothing's easy here. I hope you won't be disappointed."

"I hope not too."

"So you say you're a nurse?"

"Yes. Why? Do you need help?"

"No . . . no, we've only one medical unit going now. It's mobile. We try to cover as much territory as possible."

"Only one unit?"

"Right now, yes. I've a few nurses working part-time."

"What do they do?" Britt looked at him curiously. "There must be a lot of people needing medical attention."

"There are. At least a third of the babies under two die every year."

"So you're trying to get around to inoculate as many as you can, I suppose."

"No." Keith Fitzgibbon shook his head. "No, we'd like to, but don't."

Britt found herself staring at him and looked away. "Why not? It would be the logical thing to do."

"Well, for one thing we don't have a fridge to keep the serums and . . ." but now Britt had locked her eyes on him unbelievingly, so he added hastily, "besides, the government won't let us."

"Won't let you! Why not?"

Keith shrugged. "That's a hard question to answer. They have their reasons."

"So what do you do?"

"We get a supply of Depo-Provera and give it to the women who will take it."

"Depo-Provera is a dangerous drug."

"It's better than having a baby every year," Keith countered. "And it's a legal drug in most countries."

That's true, Britt thought. They used it in some northern parts of Canada. Mostly for Inuit and Indian women. She'd had to give it once while working in Labrador. The doctor had ordered it, and when she warned the patient of potentially serious side effects, the woman had wanted the injections anyway. It was easier than having to remember to take a birth control pill on a daily basis. Easier, but dangerous. She closed her eyes for a moment.

"So that's it?" She looked at Keith. "Many children die and you dole out injections of Depo-Provera."

"Sounds terrible, I know. But it's what's allowed. Few children here get vaccinated."

"You must be very frustrated. Of course, we have our own problems back home, but . . ."

"Yes, so . . . ? We're doing the best we can. It's better than nothing."

I'm not so sure of that anymore, Britt thought, but said nothing. Instead she asked,

"Have you been here long?"

"Oh yes. You could say that. Almost ten years."

"So you like it?"

"Very much." Keith nodded. "I love it here. I've no desire to return home. It's a good life here."

"Yes, I can see that." She could hear the irony in her voice and stood up. "I've taken up enough of your time. Thank you for seeing me."

"I've enjoyed meeting you. You're welcome anytime."

He saw her to the door. Once outside, Britt looked around. The building was situated in a quiet back lane in the section of town near where most of the embassies were located. She'd had trouble finding her way in. No doubt it would be doubly hard to find her way out. But she'd heard enough. Quite enough. All the way back to the hotel she thought about the idiocy of it all. There was idiocy at the root of societal problems in Canada too. Only very callous and clever, but twisted minds allowed social pathologies to perpetuate themselves. Many individuals tried. They really did. But the vicious cycling went on and on, changing its face every so often to provide the perfect anodyne for people everywhere--massive confusion coupled with fear.

The trip to the zoo the following afternoon turned out to be quite an adventure for the children and an opportunity for better insight into the different natures of these brothers for Britt. It also accentuated the difference in cultural norms. Without a doubt coming to live in Canada would be a cultural shock for them, but she knew too that children were often noted to readjust more readily than adults. Social mores and living patterns weren't so deeply ingrained. But it would be difficult for them, and it would take time. Time. Well, she'd have to find more of that while even working full-time, and her family was very supportive and good with children.

She had brought another young fellow, Yutang, a Tibetan and a friend of Kaisang's, with her from the hotel. Having explained the situation to him, the young man nodded and seemed to know exactly what was expected of him. He also anticipated the snags and knew better than Britt how to handle matters. The boys got into the back seat with her, and he slipped in beside the driver and slung his arm over the back of the front seat, turning slightly so he could keep an eye on the boys. They were in a state of high excitement. It seemed they'd never been in a car before. Lingwan, in particular, was quick, and his eyes darted in every direction. Britt didn't want him so near the door on the opposite end of the seat from her. Already he was half hanging out the window. "I'm afraid he'll get hurt," she said to

Yutang, "He's leaning on the door."

When she tried to pull him back, he resisted, keeping as far away from her as possible. Karma and Lobsang were immediately beside her, and her presence didn't seem to bother them in the least. Finally Yutang said something in Tibetan to Lingwan and he pulled his head in and sat down, still crouched against the door and peering avidly out the open window. Yutang told Karma who was sitting in the middle to hang onto his arm.

Once at the zoo, they all poured out of the cab, and as Britt paid the driver, she asked Yutang to warn the boys to stay close. "I don't want to lose one of them." She smiled at him, and he nodded understandingly. He was explaining to the boys in Tibetan when Britt joined them at the gate after paying the entrance fees. Karma and Lobsang complied and remained close to her or in sight, but Lingwan was another matter altogether. His main concern was keeping as far a distance from her as possible. Eventually Yutang couldn't help but notice the child's behavior which seemed to be premised on fear, and he took the small boy's hand. That satisfied Lingwan. He settled down and didn't run away from this fellow male Tibetan.

Yutang tried to explain. "Tibetan boys don't usually allow a woman to take their hands. They don't stay close to their mother."

"These two don't seem to mind," Britt looked down at Karma who was just walking a little ahead of her and Lobsang who had slipped his hand into hers and seemed comfortable beside her.

"No, but this one is different." Yutang looked down at the five year old. "It's because I'm male and Tibetan too." Part of that was most likely true, Britt thought, but she knew instinctively that there was something else bothering the little boy, and it had nothing to do with taking the hand of a male rather than a female or being Tibetan.

Toward the end of the afternoon, they stopped at a stand selling soft drinks and candy bars. She bought some cold drinks for everyone, herself included, and chocolate bars for the boys. They drank the cool beverages because it was hot and they were thirsty, but they eyed the candy bars eagerly and still refused to open them.

"Don't you want them?" Britt asked. "You said you did." They stared up at her from the step where all three of them were sitting in a row. Even Karma couldn't find the right words to explain with his limited English. Finally he looked over at Yutang hoping he'd be able to tell her for them.

"They're saving them," Yutang smiled and shook his head. "They don't get chocolate to eat. It's too expensive."

"Oh."

Britt looked down at them without a hint of sympathy in her eyes. These children didn't need her pity. And offering to buy them more chocolate today would be clearly insulting. Even children, who were usually innately greedy, could be sensitive about such a thoughtless overture. No, that would never do. Instead she shrugged and nodded.

"That's a very good idea. Save them for tonight as a treat before bed, but in that case, maybe I should get one for your baby sister too. She'd probably like one also, don't you think?"

Yutang translated and the children's faces lit up as they nodded back at her. She bought an extra bar and handed it to Karma. "For your little sister. All right?"

The boys enjoyed the ride back to Buddha'Nath too, but it was a more normal pleasure. Not a frenzied excitement like the one they'd demonstrated on their departure. Back at the family's eating place, Tenzing understood immediately that the Erikson woman had something to discuss with them, and an interpreter was needed again. Yutang had to return to the guest house. He was serving in the dining room and couldn't afford to be late. Britt paid him handsomely and made sure he had enough extra to take a cab back. Tenzing went off to find his friend, and the boys disappeared into the back. All but Lobsang who hung around her until his mother shooed him out to play. Tenzing returned. He couldn't get Norbu, so he brought his wife, Dolma Tsewang. She was a thin, good looking, and dignified woman whom Britt responded to immediately. Mild-mannered and a certain discriminating gentleness from hard earned wisdom rested in her eyes. No wonder Norbu had married her. He was a smart man. She sat down in the booth beside Britt.

"Norbu told me about you. I'm happy to meet you."

"I've been looking forward to meeting you too."

"Well, I'm Dolma. Maybe I can help. My husband won't be back until Sunday."

"Yes, I'd appreciate it . . . and please call me Britt."

Tenzing brought some tea and sat down opposite them, but his wife remained standing close by, watching.

Britt turned to Dolma and explained as quickly and concisely as she could what the problem was. Norbu's wife nodded thoughtfully. "I see." she said.

"Yes. I could be wrong, Dolma, but I don't think so. Lobsang is fine, and I do believe he really wants to come with me. In fact, he's a very odd and loveable little boy, and it seems to me he's wanted to be adopted from the beginning. Karma acted very well too today. He seemed to enjoy it and didn't seem to mind being around me. But Lingwan, well, I'd love to have him, but I think the boy is terrified of leaving here. He wouldn't come near me, and I think he still very much wants his mother. He's just a little boy, only five, and he doesn't understand. To take him away from her now would be very damaging to him. I believe that. It would be the wrong thing to do. What do you think?"

Dolma looked at her pensively for a few moments. "I think you are right . . . you are also a very nice person and very understanding."

"Well, the youngest boy is obviously very attached to his mother and now, I think he's very frightened. Taking him away would be terrible for him. Would you explain to the parents?"

"Yes, of course." Dolma turned to look at Tenzing and his wife.

She explained the situation and listened to the mother's reply. The conversation went back and forth. It seemed Tenzing had little to say. Finally Dolma turned back to Britt. "The boy's mother says that it's true that Lingwan is very close to her. He was sick as a baby, and she spent much of her time with him. That's why he's so attached to her." Dolma paused, glancing back up at the parents. "They'll speak to Lingwan this evening and see how he feels about it. But she wants to know if Lingwan doesn't go, would you take Karma instead?"

"Karma?" Britt stared up at Dolma Lama and then at Tenzing. She was trying to understand this most unusual woman who spoke for both herself and her husband. Finally she turned to Dolma Tsewang who would translate for her. "Karma is a lovely boy, and I'd love to have him if he's certain he wants to come with me. But I don't understand. He has an American family sponsoring him in school here. He's their eldest son. Why do they want him adopted?" Dolma sighed. "It's difficult to understand, I know. But you must realize that their future here in Nepal is not good. My husband and I are trying to send our boys to school in India. It's a little better there. But wait, I'll ask them."

Again, Norbu's wife launched into a long dialogue with the boys' parents. Finally she shrugged and turned calmly back to Britt. "It's as I've said. They are worried. But tonight they will speak to Lingwan and to Karma. They want to know will you be back tomorrow?"

"Tell them I'll come, and thank you for coming, Dolma."

"It's no trouble, and when my husband returns perhaps you will come to our home for tea. We are just down the street."

"I'd like that. Thank you."

Britt returned the following day to learn that her suspicions about the fears of the smallest boy were entirely true. When his parents spoke with him and asked him if he'd be willing to go, apparently he'd become very upset and started to cry. By the end of it, he was almost hysterical, and the parents decided against it. Karma, on the other hand, was thrilled about the prospect of being adopted and going to live in Canada. She got all this from Tashi Phintso who had appeared on the scene shortly after she arrived. But Britt wasn't taking any chances. She was sure about Lobsang and had been from the beginning, but she wanted to hear from the handsome and engaging older son directly. So they sent for Karma. When he came in, Britt got up, and putting her hands on his shoulders, she turned him away from his parents and faced her. She spoke slowly and used limited vocabulary.

"Karma, you want to come with me to Canada?" The boy looked up at her and nodded solemnly. "Are you sure, Karma? Really sure?" The boy nodded again. Britt bit her lip and then started to smile. She put her arm around his shoulders and asked playfully. "What would you like to be when you grow up?"

"A teacher."

"A teacher?" Britt glanced down at him, and her interest quickened. Most kids didn't know what they wanted to be, except maybe a fireman or astronaut. "You think you might like that, Karma?"

The boy had been straining to understand her, but he caught the gist of the question and nodded again. "Yes."

Tashi said something in Tibetan to the boy, and he answered him and moved away to the back where the family lived. "He is learning some English in school."

"He's doing very well," Britt paused. "By the way, have they told you I have an appointment with a lawyer Monday morning?"

"Yes. Tenzing told me. I'll come with you."

"There's no need, Tashi. I'll go alone. I don't need anyone with me."

"No, I'd like to come."

Britt looked back at him just as she was preparing to leave the Lamas' dwelling. She shrugged. "All right, if you want to. The appointment's at 10:00 a.m. I'll meet you in the lobby of the hotel."

Then she was gone, heading back to the Guest House and wondering idly why Tashi had so badly wanted to accompany her. He didn't seem to know what to do himself and yet was interested in sitting in on the interview. Well, there was no harm in him being there, Britt concluded, and he was a Tibetan after all. The lawyer was Nepalese.

It was in the very early hours of Sunday morning when Britt was awakened from a deep sleep by someone pounding on her door. It was one of the hotel clerks, and having stumbled across the room in the frigid darkness, she could see even in the dimmed lighting of the corridor that the young clerk had been sleeping too.

"Telephone, Miss. Can you come down to the desk?"

"Of course, I'll come. Is it long distance?"

"Yes, Miss. I think so."

Britt snapped on a light in the room and grabbed her robe. Then she followed the clerk downstairs. It was her mother, but the static was so heavy that she could hardly hear her. Britt raised her voice and a few staff members sleeping in nooks off the lobby were aroused as well as the groggy clerk who had awakened her.

"Mother? I can hardly hear you!"

"Britt? Speak into the receiver and louder."

"If I speak any louder I'll wake the whole hotel. It's 2:00 a.m. here."

"Oh, I'm sorry, dear," Mary Erikson shouted back. "Are you all right?"

"I'm fine, Mother. Everything okay back home?"

"Yes, yes, but what's happening there?" Britt told her about the double adoption. She didn't go into all the difficulties she had been having and those that loomed ahead. "You mean they want you to take the older boy too. He's nine, you say? But that's marvellous, darling."

"He's a lovely boy, but Lobsang . . ."

"Yes, I know," Mary interjected and laughed. "But you can't have favorites, Britt."

"I don't! It's just that . . . well, Lobsang's different. Anyway I'm seeing a lawyer Monday. I don't know how it'll go, and it still might be difficult getting them out of Nepal and into Canada."

"Well, I've good news for you. The insurance money came through. I've put ten thousand dollars in your account. You can draw on it. So, whatever it takes, Britt . . ."

"Really? You actually got it?"

"Yes, thanks to Rourke. I guess they got nervous. Anyway, they decided to settle it and quickly."

"Well, you know Rourke."

"Yes, but I was surprised. I didn't think it possible. Insurance companies . . . ach, never mind. I thought you'd be relieved. You don't need to worry now . . . well, it's not a great amount, but it'll help."

"Yes, it will . . . immensely" Britt paused. "Are you all right?"

"I'm fine, dear. Everyone's fine."

By the time Britt got off the phone, she was fully awake and now she realized just how worried she had been. She could make more money, but that would take time, and besides, she owed her sister three thousand dollars. Now she could pay her back right away. And maybe that teaching position out west would come through. It paid very well, and it would be ideal if she got the boys. If . . . Britt wondered if all human equations had so many "ifs." In her experience that had usually been the case. Tonight, however, she felt lucky, and the future looked brighter. She rubbed a hand into one of her eyes and headed back upstairs to her room. Maybe God would do this one thing for her. If she got Lobsang, she'd give him her father's name. He'd be Hugh Lobsang Erikson. It wouldn't matter then that she couldn't seem to have any of her own. Everybody had disappointments. They got over them. In the present and the future, there was hope. That's what really mattered.

She was being ushered into the rather plush offices of Madhu Sharma, Attorney at Law. Mr. Sharma was cordial, cagey and very relaxed. Britt explained what she wanted to do, and he listened politely. Then he bunched up his mouth, and there was regret registering in his eyes as he shook his head.

"I can't do it, Miss Erikson. I handle adoptions, yes. Private adoptions too, of course. But for Nepalese citizens. And that applies to adoptive parents as well as the child or children to be adopted. You are a Canadian."

"Yes." Britt nodded.

"It's against Nepalese law for you to adopt a child here. Foreign adoptions . . . It wouldn't be legal."

"But the children are Tibetan."

"So?" The lawyer shrugged. "It's still against our laws."

"They're refugees. The children are not citizens of Nepal, so Nepalese law shouldn't apply to them."

The lawyer stopped toying with his pen, thought for a moment, and then darted her a quick glance. He started to laugh. "You should have been a lawyer, Miss Erikson. Yes, that might work." He sat back, nodding to himself. "Yes, Nepalese law mightn't apply here."

"Well, it shouldn't," Britt went on. "They're not citizens, nor are their parents. It's a straightforward adoption, pure and simple."

"And their parents are willing to relinquish all rights?"

"Yes."

"And is there documented proof that they are indeed refugees?"

Britt turned to Tashi. "What kind of documents do they have?"

Tashi looked from the lawyer to Britt. "They must have a registration of their birth. I do."

"You'll need proof of their refugee status."

"Would a sworn statement from Tibetan officials be sufficient?"

"Yes, that would do." Mr. Sharma nodded. "I'll also need passport size photographs of the two boys. I must have all the documentation. My law clerk here will take care of it." He indicated a young lawyer sitting off to one side of his desk. "I'll draw up the papers. Once the original documents are cited, we can make copies and notarize them."

"Fine, it shouldn't take more than a day or two to get all the official papers," Britt turned to Tashi,

"Will you get their documents and bring them here to the law clerk?"

"Yes, I'll see Tenzing this evening."

"Thank you." She turned back to Mr. Sharma.

"Now about the actual adoption? Where will it take place?"

"At the family's dwelling in Buddha 'Nath. Once I have the papers of identification for both children and also those of the parents, including proof of refugee status, the rest is very simple. There should be witnesses. We should try to make it as official and binding as possible. Your country must recognize the adoption too, remember. You must get them into Canada."

"To be completely safe, how many witnesses, Mr. Sharma?"

"To be safe--three representing you, and three for the parents. The father and mother must sign first. Then you, as the adoptive parent. After that the witnesses, for both sides. All prominent people, all accountable."

"When would be the best time?"

The lawyer looked at his calendar and spoke briefly with his clerk assistant, "If we have all the documents by Wednesday, I think Friday afternoon at three o'clock."

"Fine." Britt stood up and shook hands with Sharma and his clerk. Tashi followed suit, and then a secretary was ushering them from the office. Once outside, they went to a coffee shop adjacent to the large center city hotel. "Witnesses," Britt said as she sipped at her coffee and lit a cigarette. "Well, I'll ask Mr. Shestra and Donna Newland."

"Who is she?" Tashi asked.

"A friend I've made here. An American. She's a university lecturer. And I'll ask Shukla Tsering. He's the principal of a school. He'll do it, I think. I'm going over to see him tomorrow and give him a year's tuition for Lingwan, including boarding."

"Oh, I didn't know. You didn't tell me," Tashi looked interested but not surprised.

"I thought Tenzing might have. He's coming with me." Britt gave him a calculating look. "Now who will Tenzing and Dolma Lama get as witnesses?"

"Oh, I'll take care of that. To make it very official we should get the head monk at the main monastery. I can sign. I'm a citizen and Shastri can sign. He is well respected in our community and he is also a citizen, and we could ask Mr. Shestra, just in case."

"That's perfect. Now I've got to get back to the Guest House and call Mr. Shestra. Then I'll have to talk to Donna. I hope she doesn't mind doing this."

"She shouldn't mind. I'll go back to Buddha 'Nath and tell Tenzing and his wife. And then, I'll see about the head monk. I know him. We all do really. The Tibetan New Year is coming up. I have to see him anyway. Will you be over later this afternoon?"

"Oh yes. We'll have to work fast, Tashi. We need those papers and some passport photos."

"I'll get them and the proof of their refugee status. The head monk handles official matters like that."

"Good . . . which reminds me. I have to call Father Chemparathy and meet with Father Dexter."

"Why?" Tashi looked confused.

"Because I've got to get them out of Nepal. Once the adoption is done, I can work on getting ministerial clearance in New Delhi, but I have to do that from Canada and the Department of Immigration must contact our consulate there. Even if that is done, with Canada recognizing the adoption, I still have to get them out of Nepal and down into India."

Tashi didn't have anything to say to all these additional plans. He was wondering how he could manage a trip to America himself. Maybe he'd even be able to find a way to remain there. Britt guessed what was going through his mind, and she thought that if she couldn't simply put the boys on her passport as adopted children and minors and had to get ministerial clearance, which would probably be the case, perhaps having Tashi escort the boys over to Canada might be worth considering. Again she had to rein in her thoughts which were leaping ahead of her again. One thing at a time, she told herself. Outside the coffee shop, she and Tashi separated--each to go his or her own way. There was much to do.

Donna Newland told her that she wouldn't mind in the least witnessing the adoption. She was very enthusiastic about it. "Would it be all right if I video it?"

"Video it?"

Donna watched the younger woman's brow wrinkling, and she rushed to explain. "For my lecture series, Britt. This is something different, and you know I'm gathering material on cultural norms, religious ceremonies, the way of life here. Something like this will be interesting for people back home. But if you feel it an invasion of your privacy . . ."

"No, no. That's not an invasion," Britt started to smile reluctantly. "You know, Donna, I don't think it's possible to invade another person's privacy--not unless they want it . . . and maybe unconsciously that's what they want. Then they get annoyed for allowing or rather wanting it."

"Well, I'm not sure I agree with you there, Britt. We usually end up having to evade prying eyes and ears. Just ask anyone about the

IRS and all the profiles they have on you in every institution you've ever attended."

"Ah, what do they know? I mean really know," Britt laughed. "They're pesky. That's all, like flies buzzing around your head."

"But harder to catch and squash," Donna retorted wryly. "Anyway, we're off track. So it's all right? I can bring my equipment?"

"Sure, I'm just so happy . . . this is the closest I've ever come . . . you don't know . . ."

"No, I don't. Maybe you're right. No one could invade your privacy even if you wanted them to. And that's probably true of everyone."

"Yeah, understanding is accidental at best. And accidents scare the hell out of people, don't they?"

"I don't know. You're losing me." Donna expelled a long breath. "Hang on to the happy feeling. Who else have you got?"

Britt told her about the calls she'd made to Mr. Shestra and Father Chemparathy, and meeting with Father Peter Dexter during the week. At Donna's inquiring look, Britt started to pace the room. "I've got to get them out of Nepal. I was hoping to be able to take them with me. That would be best rather than going home and trying to get ministerial clearance."

"Can you get that?"

"I think so. Pull a few strings, you know? There's an election coming up."

"That helps." Donna was cynical. "You know a few people in the right places?"

"Yes, or people that know people. But I'd really just like to take them with me. So I tried the British Consulate. I thought maybe they could just put them on my passport."

Donna nodded. "That's how you usually travel with children."

"Yeah, and the British Embassy should represent me here, but I spoke with the Commissioner . . ."

"Humm, the head man . . . so what did he say?"

"An unequivocal no. The fellow's name was Wither, and the bloody place was packed. He's a busy man, but it didn't take him any time at all to settle my inquiry. They just don't take care of such matters for Canadians anymore. It all goes through Delhi." Britt sank into a chair and, resting her elbow on the armrest, brought a hand up to support her head. "It was a long shot anyway."

"Right, so you think this priest--Peter Dexter might be able to help?"

"Well, he knows the ropes," Britt made a face. "They keep revoking his visa or whatever, so he knows people in the immigration department. Maybe . . . it's weird, you know. They won't let most Tibetans be citizens, and yet you can have a hell of a time getting them out."

"So get ministerial clearance if you can. Clear them at your consulate in New Delhi and as for the rest--well, just get any Tibetan or Nepalese to travel with them down to India. They never check people going back and forth from here to India. For all they know, the kids could be going to school down there. Test the waters for visas from the government here, but just inquire, don't tell them what you're planning. Don't you go in to see them. Don't mention anything about adoption at all. Your name shouldn't be used either."

"I was worried about that which is why Dexter might be the perfect intermediary."

"As long as he's discrete," Donna cautioned her.

"Jesuits are always canny. It goes with the training."

"They're shrewd, or so I've heard. I'm not Catholic. I'm not much of anything really."

"You're a very clever lady who is worried about the environment. I hope there are humans around to enjoy it."

"Let's not get into that again. I'm not oblivious to the misery here or back in the States either. I just look beyond it."

"I wish I could," Britt's face was troubled. "But I don't think that's possible."

"Neither do I." Donna got up. "Well, you've got a busy week ahead. Meet me for dinner--around seven?"

Britt nodded. "I'll be back by then."

It was a hectic week. All the required documents were delivered to the lawyer's office. Lingwan's tuition at the private school was paid in full. It came to over six hundred dollars, U.S. The legal expenses were seen to, and Britt found her funds dwindling rapidly. She thought again how fortunate she was to have enough to see to everything. Father Peter Dexter did his best. He drove her across town to the Ministry of Immigration, and she waited while he went in to speak to a few officials. When he finally did come out, he told her quietly to drop it. The boys could be taken down to New Delhi by anyone--preferably not her, and she could meet them there. That is, of course, after she returned home to get priority clearance. If she could get that, she or anyone travelling to India could get them out of the country and into Canada. And naturally the adoption had to be recognized in Canada.

By Friday, Britt was both tired and worried, but excited too. Everyone met in the small, single room dwelling where the family lived. The head monk from the monastery came in his robes and sat silently looking on. The dingy room was decorated for the Tibetan New Year and with so many people dressed in suits and dresses, including Donna who had discarded her tourist garb for the occasion, it appeared almost festive. The atmosphere was certainly solemn enough. The mother looked tense and Britt kept watching her across the room. She appeared more resolute than sad. Britt thought she must be feeling very badly, but was mastering her emotions remarkably well. The father's expression was serious, but softer. He knew that most Tibetans tried to get their children away to school if they could and often didn't see them more than once a year. Even that wasn't always possible. It was hard, but at least they could have a better life than he did. They could have citizenship and an education. And he liked this Canadian woman. She would take good care of his boys, and if he got sick again for a long period or if he died, his wife could manage. He looked over at Britt and smiled. There was a gentleness in him that made her heart lurch. An unspoken understanding went between them. If he lived, he would, without a doubt, see his sons again and their roots would not be forgotten. When it was over, drinks were served, and then the gathering dispersed. Britt remained to talk with the children. And finally, she too returned to the Guest House.

Over the weekend, she spent the afternoon with the family and going for a long walk up to the famous Kopan monastery with the boys. The following week, she made arrangements to return home. Shestra was trying to secure her on a flight out of Kathmandu. The seats were booked solidly, but he finally managed to get her a place for Thursday morning.

On Wednesday afternoon, she arranged to meet Tashi in the same coffee shop on Kanti Path Road where they'd gone after leaving the lawyer's office. He knew the predicament she was in. They had tried everything possible, so he merely nodded when Britt explained. "I'll have to return home and get the adoption recognized and what we call ministerial clearance. It shouldn't take too long. Now take this." She passed him an envelope containing four hundred U.S. dollars. "I'll write you and let you know what progress is being made. When the clearance comes through, will you bring the boys down to New Delhi? You go down to India often, don't you?"

Tashi nodded, "Yes, often, for business . . . and my wife is from northern India."

"Good," Britt nodded. "Don't say anything to the airport officials here. If they ask you, just tell them the children are going to school in southern India. You're flying to Delhi and then taking a train. There's a big Tibetan school in Madras."

Tashi nodded again. "I understand."

"I'm leaving some money for the boys and the father . . . in case he gets sick again. Now I'll have to go over and talk to them. Will you come?"

"Yes, of course."

In the family's single room Britt motioned to Tashi to explain everything to Tenzing and his wife. Then she handed Tenzing an envelope with over three hundred dollars--a sizable sum by Nepalese standards. "Tell him it's in case he gets sick again. There's enough there for him to get the medical attention he needs."

Tashi translated and Tenzing looked at her gratefully. In a separate envelope she left ample funds for both boys until she could bring them to Canada. Lingwan had already been taken care of. By this time both Karma and Lobsang were standing nearby, and they had heard everything. Karma looked disappointed that he wasn't going to be flying off with her, but he was not too upset. He understood that it was only a matter of time. Lobsang, however, looked at her as if she'd betrayed him. His face started to crinkle, and he was on the verge of tears. Britt sat down and pulled the boy toward her. Looking at the boy intently, she said quietly but earnestly. "I promise, I'll come back for you, Lobsang. It won't be long. I promise, I'll come back for you and take you with me." She looked up at Tashi in desperation. "Tell him, Tashi. Tell him it's impossible for him to come with me now, but I'll come back for him. It's a promise."

For the first time since they'd met Tashi's face was full of compassion as he explained what Britt said to the small boy. But after she hugged him and then looked into his face, she saw only fear struggling against desire in his eyes. After a few moments he broke away from her and ran out the door. Tibetan children didn't cry openly and not in front of people. She was learning, but the fear she'd seen in his eyes disturbed her. Disappointed she could understand. But fear? Didn't he trust her at all? He had legally been adopted her son. Surely he must understand what that meant and that she could never abandon him now. She got up and quickly left the room that she found was beginning to suffocate her. The following morning she left Kathmandu and started the long journey home.

-Twelve-

Mary Erikson awaited her daughter's return home with the kind of anticipation that worked like a healing balm over an open wound. The full impact of her husband's sudden death had not set in. The realization was there, and the weight of sadness that came over her at times brought tears welling in her eyes and a vivid memory of that night less than three months ago. But still, it seemed impossible that he was actually gone, and she was left to face alone the remaining years left to her. She wasn't really old, only sixty-one, but there would be no one else for her and she knew it. Their marriage had had its troubled times, but what she and Hugh had was rare, so unique, in fact, that she couldn't find the words to explain it even to herself.

When Britt received the unexpected letter and then decided to go to Nepal and try to adopt the child, her mind remained largely focused on her daughter's happiness, and she tried to visualize what the little boy looked like. When she heard about the second child, the nine year old boy, she was overjoyed. But it was the sound of Britt's voice and the new look of something lost being found at last that she hoped and expected to see in her daughter's eyes that thrilled her most. It had been a long time since she'd heard or seen that quality of joy in the woman she'd raised, and her father's death seemed to have had a curious effect on her. It was more than just loss or grief. Mary couldn't understand it, and what she couldn't explain she tended to dismiss, at least on the surface. Nevertheless, it frightened and worried her, more so than she could admit. That there had been a distance growing between them she couldn't deny either. It had nothing to do with love. She was sure of that. It seemed to Mary that Britt was in a limbo of mangled thoughts and emotions. But nobody knew for sure. They had facts, not all, but some, and that was all they had. It simply wasn't enough. Maybe now things would be different. She certainly hoped so.

Britt arrived in New York during the evening and caught the last flight up to Montreal. Her family wasn't sure just when to expect her, and she didn't bother to call. Instead, she took a cab from the airport. She dug in her bag for her keys and deposited her cases in the living room, and then she glanced at the time. It was almost 10:00 p.m., but she'd noticed that the lights were still on in her mother's apartment when she got out of the cab.

Her mother was up and Nora was with her. The apartment doors were open so that they'd hear the children if they awoke. They were more than just a little surprised to see her standing in the doorway. She was like an apparition. Mary got up and came to her. "I thought you were going to call from New York."

"There was no time. I got the last seat on the last flight. It was a rush, and I didn't want to stay in New York overnight."

"How was the flight?"

Britt told them all about the flight back which was almost as harrowing as the flight over. But it was amusing in the telling of it.

"You mean they used the same plane with a fire in one of the engines to fly you out of Kathmandu?" Mary looked aghast.

"Yes, they just put the fire out and took off anyway."

"That's crazy, and you're crazy to have got back on the same plane."

"Well, I got a very good aerial view of the Himalayas."

Nora laughed. "I'll bet. I'd love to go and see it. It must be beautiful."

"A lot of people think so."

"But you don't?"

"No, I don't."

Nora went back to her apartment to check on Aaron and Ruth. Mary turned to Britt. "You should call Virginia."

"It's after ten."

"She's not working tomorrow, and she asked for you to call her when you got in. I'll make some tea."

They sat around the kitchen table and drank tea. Britt was doing most of the talking. Mary looked at the adoption papers. Finally she nodded. "Well, these look official enough. You certainly have enough witnesses." She passed them to Virginia.

"The lawyer didn't want to take any chances. It's a legal adoption. I hope Canada recognizes it."

"Why wouldn't they?" Nora asked.

"Because it's a foreign adoption." Virginia answered her. "But it should be all right. People are adopting children from all over the world, refugees too."

"Have you got pictures of them?" Nora's eyes danced.

"Oh yes, and copies of all the documents." She handed her sister an envelope containing pictures and documents.

"Here, let me see." Mary looked over Nora's shoulders. She studied their faces intently. "The older boy is certainly handsome."

"But the little one looks kind of sad," Nora murmured.

"I can see why he's so appealing. So that's Lobsang?"

"Yes, and the older one is Karma. But they'll have Canadian names too."

They talked on for more than an hour. It was almost midnight. Britt looked drained, but not sleepy. Mary suggested that they all go home to bed, but no one moved from the table. Virginia grinned at her. "You're on a high, Britt."

"I've been up over thirty-six hours. Well over that. I stopped counting, but I don't know if I can sleep just now." Nevertheless, she got up and collected all the papers. "Oh, I almost forgot. I brought you back something." She reached into her purse and brought out three sets of earrings. "They're supposed to be good ones."

"They are." Virginia confirmed it. "Where did you get them?"

"A special jewelry shop. Tashi knew the owner. So choose. You first, Mother."

Mary chose the pair of opal earrings set in finely filigreed silver. "I like these ones."

Nora and Virginia liked their sets.

When they had gone, Britt said to her mother just before going down to her own apartment. "I've still an awful lot to do. And I must get priority clearance for them, or it'll be tied up in New Delhi indefinitely."

"You'll get it. Don't worry." Mary reassured her. "The hardest part is over. The adoption is done. That's the main thing. The rest is just red tape. Try to get some sleep."

"Yes, I'll start tomorrow."

Mary smiled. "Well, I didn't think you'd waste much time. By the way, they called you back about that job out west. The superintendent wants you to call him. I've got his name and number."

"I'll call him soon . . . I've got so much to do."

"I know . . . I know. But you did it, Britt." Mary's eyes locked on to her daughter's. "They're lovely children."

"They are, aren't they?"

"Yes . . . you'd better get some sleep."

Britt went downstairs and drew a bath. She soaked in the hot water and started to sort out what she had to do. Finally, she went to bed and slept a long, deep, and peaceful rest full of anticipation.

Mary was more than satisfied. Her daughter was happier than she'd seen her in years. There was that light in her eye that she'd hoped to see . . . thinner than ever. Too thin, she thought. Probably not eating properly, as usual, and letting herself get run down, but that was going to change now. A lot of things were going to change, and they were going to change for the better, at least for Britt. She hadn't voiced her own plans yet, nor the new arrangements Nora was making. But trying new things had never bothered her family. Or maybe it did unnerve them and they just couldn't help themselves. The dread of stagnating was in every one of them. Hence the outward chaos of their lives that cloaked an ingrained stability.

The following morning Britt set about the arduous task of finding the best and shortest route of getting ministerial clearance. First, she called a friend of hers whom she'd dated a few times after she broke off with Roddy. The man didn't stand a chance. Britt had stonewalled him. She didn't need or want anyone new in her life. Edward Barrett didn't mind. His timing was bad and he knew it, but he was delighted to hear from her. Edward didn't like his mother. In fact, he'd had a miserable childhood, but she worked for the liberal party and a number of politicians owed her favors. He gave her his mother's number at work and, in return, asked if she'd have dinner with him Saturday evening. Britt agreed.

Mrs. Barrett sounded very pleasant over the phone, which belied her true nature. But then she was in politics. So what could you expect? She told Britt that the most effective Member of Parliament that she could think of to help her get what she wanted was Gilles Belanger, the M.P. for Verdun. He worked closely with Francois Martineau, the Minister of Immigration in Ottawa. Failing that, she might try Irving Burgher who was the Assistant Minister of Immigration. He was a crusty, seasoned politician, but he had his riding in Montreal. Of course, Belanger and Martineau were Conservatives, but the Conservatives were in power and wanted to stay there, so they might be inclined to be more helpful, considering the upcoming election.

Britt called the M.P.'s office expecting to be put off and have to start a siege; but no, Belanger was miraculously accessible. He listened and agreed to see her on Friday morning. Then he added cautiously. "But the adoption must be legal and recognized in Canada."

"Well, it should be recognized," Britt sounded confident. "It's a legal adoption."

"Good. Then just file the papers. There are forms to fill out."

Britt frowned. "Where do I go for that?"

"The Department of Manpower and Immigration. The head office is downtown, but I wouldn't try here."

"Why not?"

Belanger hesitated. "Because it's harder here. Go to Cornwall. Have you got an Ontario address you can use?"

"Yes, my brother lives near Ottawa. Well, outside really. Not too far from Cornwall."

"Well, go there. It's much easier. Call ahead for an appointment."

"All right." Britt's face had set into lines of determination.

"But I'll still need ministerial clearance. This can't go through regular channels."

"Well, if there are no complications, I see no reason . . ." Belanger began and Britt interrupted him.

"But there is very good reason, Mr. Belanger. I was in contact with the consulate in New Delhi and, as you can imagine, they're swamped."

"I see," Belanger was wagging his head tiredly. "Well, get the adoption filed at least and bring me a copy of the form. If it's approved, I'll see what I can do. I'll be at my office in Ottawa next week. Ministerial clearance has to come from Ottawa."

"And you know Mr. Martineau quite well, don't you?"

"Yes, quite well." Belanger sighed. "I'll try."

When Britt got off the phone with the M.P., she called the Cornwall office and set up an appointment with Gary Whelan, the Immigration Officer.

Having done all that, she decided to called her brother in Ottawa. Fortunately he was in his office and the main secretary put her through to him.

"Britt!" Rourke's voice, usually so quiet, boomed over the wire. "When did you get back?"

"Last night," she smiled. "You make it sound like I've been away for a year."

"Well, it seems like it. How did it go?"

"Fine, I have the adoption papers, but there are a few snags."

Britt went on to explain. At the end of the convoluted saga, Rourke's gravelly voice came back to her. "So what do you want me to do?"

"Who's you're M.P. up there?"

"Warner. I think that's his name. I haven't met him personally but I've heard he's good. He's on the up and up . . . gets things done. Not like some of the other assholes in office."

"What is he? Conservative?"

"Yeah, but don't hold that against him. He's not a party favorite."

"Well, could you contact him? I have an appointment with an immigration officer in Cornwall on Wednesday afternoon."

"Oh? You're coming up here to do it?"

"Yeah, it's easier, or so Belanger tells me."

"He's probably right." Rourke paused, "All right, I'll try to get through to his office. But you're not giving me much time. You want to talk to him Wednesday afternoon after seeing the Immigration Officer?"

"Yes, if possible. Check around and see if he knows Irving Burgher?"

"Who the hell is that?"

"The assistant Minister of Immigration. If Belanger backs out, I don't have access to Martineau. But I've heard that Burgher is very influential. Maybe even more so than Martineau."

Rourke laughed. "Playing every angle, aren't you?"

"What choice do I have?"

"Not much. They're scum. All of them, but sometimes it's worth their while to make their constituents happy . . . better give my address."

"Of course, what did you think I was going to do?"

"God help the poor bastards if you ever got elected," Rourke teased her. "They wouldn't know whether they're coming or going."

"You wouldn't notice much change in them. They're terminally disoriented as they are."

"Oh, that's rich!" The sound of Rourke's low gurgling mirth made her smile.

"You're not half bad yourself, old boy. Tangling with that insurance company and winning is no small feat."

There was a silence at the other end of the line. Finally Rourke's quiet voice came back to her, carrying with it an undercurrent of lethal anger. "I work for one, remember? Those sons-of-bitches were going to pay. One thing's certain. They weren't going to walk away. Not this time."

"I guess not," Britt replied softly. "The course of some people's lives reminds me of a ticker-tape parade. Don't let it get to you, Rourke."

"I'm not. Watch out for yourself. So when am I going to see you?"

"Soon. Very soon."

"Great. I'll get back to you about Warner. And Britt . . . I'm tickled as hell about you getting the kids."

"Thanks, Rourke. I'm very happy too."

She put down the receiver just as Nora and her mother came in with Ruth. The little girl crawled up on her knee and refused to budge. Britt folded her arms around the child and gazed fixedly down at her. Nora ran upstairs to bring down some tea. Neither she nor their mother had seen the look that had come into Britt's eyes. "I wonder if it's wise to love so much a child not your own," she muttered in an undertone.

"What? What did you say?" Mary asked.

"Nothing. Nothing at all." Britt looked up at her mother. Her expression had changed again. She became remote.

"So what have you been up to?"

"All kinds of things, Mother. I'm driving up to Cornwall on Wednesday. Want to come along?"

"Okay. What are you going to do?" Britt launched into yet another lengthy account of the morning's endeavors.

The Department of Manpower and Immigration was a moderately sized modern building. After driving for over nearly an hour and a half through a drizzly gray late morning mist with vapor rising from the fields spread out on either side of the highway and shrouding the trees, the town was a welcome sight. Britt parked the car and turned to her mother. "We're a little early. How about a cup of coffee?"

"We should have some lunch."

"Right. There's a coffee shop over there."

Mary ordered a sandwich and another one for Britt. "You've got to eat," She urged her. "No wonder you're losing weight."

Britt didn't answer her. She bit into the sandwich, got through half of it, started sipping at her coffee and ordered another cup. She lit a cigarette and checked the time. "We've got ten minutes."

Mary nodded. "I know." She glanced at her daughter who appeared so calm. Calm, be damned, she thought. All that tension and for what? "I'm sure everything will go fine. I have a good feeling about this."

"Well, good. Let's go then. It's almost time."

The immigration offices were empty. Britt looked around and then approached a woman behind the glassed-in office area. She slid open the window aperture above her desk. At Britt's enquiry the woman answered pleasantly. "Oh yes. He's here now. He's only in part time. It's lucky you called for an interview. Come this way." She came out of her enclosed space and led them down the hall.

Gary Whelan was a young looking man around forty. He didn't scowl, and he was polite. Britt told him only the essentials. He smiled and appeared intrigued. "That was a long way to go, Miss Erikson. Have you got the adoption papers?"

"Yes," Britt handed him the documents. "A sworn statement as to their refugee status is there also, as well as the children's identification and that of the parents'."

Whelan read over the papers carefully. It took him some time, but finally he looked up. "Well, everything's in order here. It's a legal adoption. And you are a Canadian citizen, born in Canada?"

"Yes, in Montreal. Here's my passport and social security number." Britt handed them over to him, but he waved them away.

"You're Canadian, and this adoption is recognized under Canadian law, you now have two sons. Very nice looking boys. Tibetan . . . interesting. Congratulations, Miss Erikson."

"Thank you."

"Now you must fill out a form. You can put both boys down on the form as your sons."

Britt nodded and filled out the document. She handed it back to him, adding, "They're refugees. That should help processing in New Delhi, shouldn't it?"

"It should. Here too. I'll get things underway and fax the document over to our consulate there."

"Our consulate representative in such matters is Karen McLeod."

"All right," he made a note of the name. "You're anxious to get them over here. I understand."

"Yes. I'm working on ministerial clearance."

Whelan laughed. "That should speed things up." He stood up. "I'll register it immediately and get it faxed over. Good luck."

"Thank you, Mr. Whelan." Britt shook hands with him and left the office. It felt like she was walking in a dream. A lovely dream that was becoming reality.

"What about that?" She glanced sideways at her mother and beamed her a smile.

"Sounds good. There was no trouble at all."

"No, it's hard to believe. But there could still be trouble with the consulate in New Delhi. They don't want any hassles with the Nepalese authorities."

"But like you said, the kids are refugees," Mary reasoned.

"Exactly," her daughter's jaw was set in determination.

"That's what we're going on. But we need clearance, or they'll notify the Nepalese government, and they'll balk at the underhanded methods used. You can't imagine how corrupt they are. Problem is, I couldn't even find anyone to pay off. Baksheesh be damned. You'd have to pay off at least half a dozen low-life officials to get the right one to put his official stamp on what I already paid a high price in legal fees to have done. They won't even take their own rupees. They prefer American or Canadian money. Preferably American, and they detest Americans. They just like the money."

"Really?"

"Absolutely." Britt scowled. "I haven't told you everything."

"So tell me."

"Later. Let's get over to Warner's office. We've just enough time to make it."

Randall Warner was a strikingly handsome man. He had pure white hair and a young face. In addition, he was engaging and suave. The interview went well. Toward the end of it, Britt asked him outright if he knew Irving Burgher.

"Irving? Oh yes, we're good friends. And I see where you're headed." He smiled at her and Britt gave him a smile in return.

"I need all the help I can get."

"Well, let's see what Martineau will do. He's the minister after all. But failing that, it might put you at ease to know that Burgher handles most of the immigration. The petitions all go by him. Martineau takes on the other duties like changing policy . . . legislation."

"So you'll help?"

"Yes, of course. I have a lot of admiration for people who do what you did. A friend of mine and his wife have gone through it. Call me after you hear what Belanger can do. It might take a week or two."

Britt left the office and sighed in relief. "It's working," she said to her mother. "On Friday I see Belanger, and next week he'll be at his office in the parliament buildings. He'll get to see Martineau. After that, we'll see . . ."

That evening, Virginia came over, and they talked at length about her trip. Naturally, their opinions were at opposite ends of the spectrum. Neither of them seemed to mind the other's opposing view. But Virginia did not agree that aid should be cut off. "What you're saying is probably true," she argued. "But the people really do need help."

"Not this way," Britt stubbornly disagreed. "If their governments are going to handle the funds, I wouldn't contribute another cent."

"You've already spent a wad of money over there."

"That's different. The family needed it. And there were families worse off. Such abject poverty is appalling. How could you find the place beautiful?"

"Nepal is beautiful and if you want to see real poverty, you should see Calcutta."

"I'd probably need a sedative just to walk through it."

"You probably would," Virginia agreed. "But Don's program is different. That's why I agreed to sponsor a kid over there."

"Don's program might do some good, but it's largely ineffective. Besides, you know that principal, Nirala, who runs the school that costs four to six hundred dollars to sponsor a kid?"

"Yes."

"Well, I met him and didn't like him. More importantly, the Tibetan community doesn't care for his ways either. There's talk about him, and Don has trouble in his ranks over there."

Britt told her what she'd heard was going on and ended with, "it's true, Gin. That's what I was told, and having met the man, I believe it."

"You should tell Don. At least call and tell him you got the adoption through."

"All right, I'll phone him." Britt called Don Willet and told him about her trip. He was delighted until she continued to inform him about what she'd heard was going on. After that he became irritated and said little. He asked to speak to Virginia. They were on the phone for a long time, and it sounded to Britt like her friend was trying to placate him. She left the room and went into the kitchen to make tea. Almost twenty minutes later, Virginia came into the kitchen.

Britt looked over at her. "Well, what was all that about?"

"He's as mad as hell. He said he expected more than ingratitude from you after all the people he asked to help you and put at your disposal . . . using his contacts."

"They didn't do that much. They didn't know what to do and besides I paid Tashi . . . . over three hundred dollars U.S."

"What!"

"Oh yes, I did. And he didn't do much at all. And I was very generous with Shestra."

"Did you tell him that? Three hundred dollars over there is a lot of money. You didn't tell him?"

"No, why should I?"

"He thinks you just used his contacts and had nothing but criticism to give in return. He's also angry about what you said about

Nirala. Don has found sponsors for a lot of the students he has in his school. And he's mad about you putting the smallest boy in the other school."

"Don's a fool, and he's so in love with Nepal . . . just like you . . . that he can't even see what's going on. He goes over at least twice a year, and he still can't see."

"Now wait a minute!" Virginia balked. "Don might be blind, but I'm not!"

"All right, you're not. So what did you say to him?"

"Well, I didn't know you paid those people. I just tried to calm him down."

Britt didn't say anything. They talked of other things, and Virginia left shortly afterwards.

On Friday morning she went to her appointment and enlisted Belanger's help. All she could do then was wait. Saturday evening, she dined out with Edward Barrett, but she was so distracted that she had to apologize. "I'm very poor company. I'm sorry, Edward."

He covered her hand with his. "That's okay. You've had a rough week."

"But a rather successful one, don't you think?"

"Yes, I do." He smiled at her. "I'd help you, but I don't know what a music teacher could do for you right now."

"Music's very soothing."

"And what would you like to hear?"

"I like Chopin, and I'm rather fond of Wagner, believe it or not."

"I believe it. It's very early. Why don't you come back to my place?"

Britt looked at him. "I'm not ready for anything, Edward. Not now and I don't know when or if I will be."

"I understand," he shrugged easily. "I don't want anything either. Not unless you do. I've already been through one bad marriage, so I've learned patience, and I'm in no hurry either. It's too dangerous and damaging."

"Yes, women certainly have a way of getting their hooks into a man."

"You're as bitter as hell, Britt, and you're well named too." To his astonishment, she burst out laughing and Edward frowned. "Come on, you're crazy or overtired. I'm taking you home. We can listen to music another time."

The following week, a letter arrived from Don Willet. Britt opened it and scanned the typed paragraphs, all very skillfully structured. Then she began again reading it carefully and slowly, her brow drew together into deep furrows and her lips whitened. She was clenching her teeth. The words assembled before her were full of accusations and invective. Aside from maligning her character, he alleged that she might well have ruined or in some way jeopardized all the good he was doing and wanted to continue doing in Nepal. He insinuated that she was either misinformed or lying, or both. In any case, she was certainly uninformed and ignorant about a country she'd only visited once, and she couldn't possibly have got anywhere without his help . . . his contacts. It went on and on.

By the end of it, she was more sickened than angry. She threw the letter on the kitchen table and decided to take a shower. But then the phone was ringing. It was her mother. "I've made coffee." Mary paused and then added. "Have you had breakfast?"

"No, not yet." Britt felt a great lassitude coming over her. "I slept late."

"Well, come up."

"I'll be up soon. Did you sleep well?"

"Yes. Well no. It's hard some nights, you know?"

"I know." Britt closed her eyes. "It's very hard." She could hear Ruth in the background. "Is Nora there?"

"Yes, she came in a few minutes ago. We've been talking over a few things."

"What things?"

"Come up."

"All right." This family was crazy, Britt thought. Always hatching new plans. But this time a change was well overdue. Yes, her father's death required that. Demanded it. "I'll be up. It won't be long," she added.

A half an hour later she was showered and dressed, her damp hair was clinging to her head and falling into her eyes. She combed it back from her forehead. On her way out of the apartment, she spotted the letter on the table and brought it along with her. Somewhere out there, there was a sense of outrage lying in wait for her; but right now she was merely contemptuous of its contents and the author of such venom. No doubt, her mother would most likely find it interesting reading. Ludicrous.

Opening the door of her parents' apartment, Ruth came scurrying down the hall toward her, and she could hear Nora and her mother deep in conversation. With the baby in her arms, she came down the hall and into the kitchen. "So what's new?" Methodically she stirred the coffee placed before her, her thoughts miles apart. "Is something new with Gregory? You know, I haven't heard from him since I got back from Nepal."

"No, nothing new." Mary answered her. "He called on the weekend. I forgot to tell you."

"So, what is it?"

"He wants me to go up there."

"For a visit?"

"No, move up there," Nora replied, glancing at her sister. "He suggested I go too."

"Oh? Do you want to go to Toronto?"

"No," Mary frowned, "not Toronto."

"It's too expensive," Nora explained. "There's work, but I could never afford to make enough to live there."

"No, it would be difficult," Britt agreed.

"So, I was thinking of looking around Ottawa . . . or maybe London."

"Ottawa would be better, Nora," Mary put in. "It's not far, and Rourke's there too."

"Maybe," Nora considered it. She turned to her sister. "Mother's thinking of coming with me to Ontario."

"Oh, I see." Britt mulled it over. "Well, you'll have to get out of Quebec anyway, Nora. Now that you've got the settlement and can do something. Why delay it?"

"Yes, but I want Aaron to finish his year in school here. So it won't be until June. Still, that only gives me three, four months to look for a place and find a job."

"It's a good idea, and you'll go back to working in the bank?"

"If I can. It's been a while . . ." Nora looked doubtful and then brightened up. "But Phyllis, you remember Phyllis? Well, she's assistant manager now in Brockville. She's still with the Toronto-Dominion."

"So try there. That's promising." Britt turned to her mother. "And how about you, Ma? How do you feel about it?"

"Well, Nora can't work here. Not now. It's impossible for her, and I'd like to be near the kids."

"Yes, that would be good." Britt was careful not to mention all the things purposely left unsaid. "Maybe a change would be best, all things considered."

"I'll be moving from the apartment anyway," Mary declared. "The rooms are all changed around, but I don't want to be here."

"I'm amazed you stayed at all," Britt said suddenly. "I don't think I could."

Well, that explains a lot, Mary thought. Like the brief, if frequent visits. You'd rather just close the door and walk away. Just like you become all stonily walled off from those around you when everything's going wrong. You go into yourself.

"Have you called that superintendent out west yet?"

"No, but I will. Today."

"Yes, you should," Mary nodded. "I hate to see you go so far away, but it would be the ideal job for you, especially since you have the boys now. They should be here by next fall. Don't you think?"

"I hope so. This has to move fast. They've already got the adoption forms registered here and at the consulate in New Delhi. If they start digging . . ."

"What if they do?" Nora asked.

"They'll contact the Nepalese government first thing, and that means trouble. They'll find some dumb regulation and apply it to refugees."

"They can't do anything!"

"They can do anything they want, Nora. I suspect they make up the laws as they go along. No, the only way is to clear it quickly and get Tashi, maybe, or Norbu to bring the kids out of Nepal and down to India."

Mary was thinking. "By the way, have you heard from him yet? You wrote him, didn't you?"

"Yup . . . told him the adoption was recognized here . . . everything, including getting priority clearance."

"I thought you would have heard from him by now."

"So did I. He's supposed to be working on it."

"And you haven't heard a word? That's odd."

"Yes, I thought so too, but well . . ." Britt shrugged, and then she remembered the letter and pulled it out of her pocket.

"Here, read this. It came in the mail this morning."

Mary took up the letter. "I've got to get my glasses."

"Who's it from?" Nora asked.

"Don Willet."

"With all the long distance calls you've made to him since last summer you should buy shares in Bell Telephone. Gin said you called him again last week. What's it about anyway?"

"Read it." Britt looked away from her and Nora flared.

"Damn it, can't you even answer a person. I asked a simple question. That's all. Oh, forget it!"

"Just a minute, Nora" Mary said in an undertone. She was halfway through the letter and still reading . . .

Finally she looked up. "What's the matter with the man? He's attacking you! What did you say to him anyway?"

"What? What's in it?" Nora got up, moved around the table, and took up the letter her mother had put down.

"I didn't say very much to him really." Britt's eyes were troubled, but she was otherwise ominously composed. "He likes the principal of that school. I don't. Many of the people he gets to sponsor children go to that school. The Tibetan kids anyway. I don't think they're getting their money's worth, not in my opinion, but I didn't mention all that to him. Maybe that's what he concluded when I told him I put the youngest boy in the other school . . . I really don't know what I could have said to cause this kind of reaction."

"Well, I don't know, Britt," Mary looked concerned. "He's really angry, but there's no cause for him to write a letter like that."

"There sure as hell isn't!" Nora stormed. "Who the hell does he think he is anyway? The son-of-a-bitch! He's got no right . . ."

"No, he doesn't," Mary agreed. "Write him back and . . ."

"Respond to that?" Britt glanced from the letter to her mother. "Not bloody likely."

"You mean you're not going to respond?" Nora looked at her, incredulous, and then angry. "That letter's disgusting, and he's smearing your character!"

"He's a pompous fool," Britt replied tersely, but she appeared despondent. "Only fools try to justify themselves to fools. Consider the source."

"Source be damned." Nora spat out the words. "So you're not going to do anything?"

"There's no point, Nora. I'm not even going to acknowledge it. The only thing he'll get from me is silence."

"I don't understand you," Nora said glumly.

"No, well, maybe I don't either, but it would just be a waste of energy." Britt rose from the table. "I'll see you later."

"What are you going to do this afternoon?"

"I don't know . . . I'm not used to having time on my hands. Read, maybe . . . go for a walk."

"And call that superintendent," Mary reminded her.

"Yes, that too. And I'll let you know what he says."

When her sister had left, Nora shook her head and addressed her mother. "You know she's crazy not to answer that jerk. I would."

"I know you would, but you two are very different people. Not that I understand either of you, but . . . well, it seems that whereas you flare and have an outburst, Britt just lets it seethe and annihilates even more effectively with the looks she gives you and her deadly silences. But you have to admit," Mary smiled at her youngest daughter, "it's a rare occurrence with Britt. She's usually easy to get along with, and when she does get angry, it's usually with good reason."

"You mean not like me!" Nora shot back. "I'm always in the wrong . . . never in the right."

"You see what I mean?" Mary threw out her hands. "You're warm and kind, and often very thoughtful and perceptive. You'd feel better if you stop comparing yourself to your sister. She doesn't compare herself to you."

"She wouldn't be caught dead comparing herself to me. She's too good for that!"

"I don't think so" Mary said. "You have much, and I think you know it. Britt knows it too."

"So does she," Nora argued. "Her life's been exciting. Everyone thinks so. Two professions. Travel. Good friends. As for children, well, she's got two now. But I don't think she tried hard enough to have her own."

"Well, we don't know, do we? We don't really know."

Mary could keep a confidence. She didn't mention anything about what she knew of her daughter's affairs which she realized wasn't complete. Maybe Nora was right. Britt could have tried harder, she supposed. But she didn't know. Who ever really knows?

"I still think she should write him back."

"So, we're back to that, are we?" Mary propped her chin in her hand and couldn't resist smiling, but the smile never reached her eyes. "Well, so do I. She'll only brood over it." Her daughter's methods might be very effective, Mary decided, but they also took a heavy toll.

Britt called the head of the school board, a Mr. Ashcroft, who spoke with her for some time and then offered her the job.

"I've looked over your credentials. They are excellent," he told her. "My only concern is that you come to stay for a while. Your resume indicates that you move around quite a bit."

"I've always honored a teaching contract," Britt answered him. "Besides, I've just adopted two young children, so I'll have to settle down."

"Oh, I see. Yes, that will make a difference," Ashcroft laughed. "Well, this is a good place to raise children." Then his voice became serious. "All right, Miss Erikson. I'll send a telegram off today. A formal offer of the position. If you want to accept, send me back a telegram within twenty-four hours. When you get here we can sign the contract."

Britt responded immediately, accepting the position. She felt better already . . . until she thought about the letter she'd left up at her mother's asking her to trash it. That's where it belonged. In the garbage. Now it felt as if the anger she'd buried was being exhumed and monopolizing her thoughts. A quiet but relentless wrath which she seldom allowed to surface took possession of her body and spirit. She bitterly resented the unfounded accusations; but that only entrenched her resolve not to reply. She seldom considered or cared if people thought she was right or wrong. Now, for some reason, she felt herself caring very much, and that's what bothered her most of all. Not the letter, but her visceral reaction to it, made her feel foolish. Ruminating over it brought on self-contempt. It was like swimming in sewage; futile, degrading, and corruptive. Finally she put aside the book she was trying to read, went into the bedroom for a pillow and blanket, and returned to the living room to curl up on the chesterfield. It took some time to achieve sleep, but it did come finally, and with it came a world of wonders full of colors, shapes, and sounds; a kind of Valhalla for the restless and bruised.

She awoke to the jangling of the telephone, and answering it she must have sounded still half asleep because Edward asked immediately, "did I wake you, Britt?"

"No," she lied, "I was just sitting here by the phone waiting for your call."

"I don't believe it," Edward sounded jovial. "But I'd like to so what the hell . . . now, why don't you stroll down to Sherbrooke and . . ."

"Stroll down to Sherbrooke? Why?"

"You didn't let me finish, dear heart. I'm asking you out to dinner."

"Oh, that's nice of you, considering our last dinner together."

"I thought about that . . . actually I enjoyed It. You have a weird sense of humor, Britt."

"So they tell me."

"You'll come, then?"

"I'll have to change. Why don't you just pick me up?"

"My motor died, but they're repairing it now . . . should be ready by the time we're finished eating. So you'll come?"

"All right. Where'll I meet you?"

"I'm at Murray's, near Victoria."

"Okay. It's four now. I'll try not to be too long."

Britt put down the receiver and yawned. She had slept for over two hours. Now fully awake, she changed hurriedly, dabbed on some make-up and was into her coat and winter boots when she remembered that her mother would probably wonder where she'd gone. Instead of phoning, she walked upstairs, knocked, and entered the apartment. Her mother was in the kitchen standing near the sink, and Virginia was at the table with the letter in her hands. Britt took in the whole scene within seconds--her mother watching her apprehensively and her friend glancing up at her from the letter which she'd obviously read and was still holding in her hands. The look that went between them seemed suspended in time.

"What are you doing here, Gin?" Britt's voice was low, but cold. And then she tried to manage her thoughts . . . be reasonable and fair. This wasn't her friend's fault. She wasn't responsible for the kind of railing coming from Don Willet. "I mean, I wasn't expecting to see you here."

"She's visiting me, Britt . . . are you going out?"

"Yes. I'm having dinner with Edward."

"Who's Edward?"

"Edward Barrett. Just a friend. His car broke down. I'd better go. He's waiting."

"Just a minute," Virginia indicated the letter. "You're really not going to answer this?"

"No, I'm not, Gin."

"Then would you mind if I do?"

"Don't do it on my account." Britt stared at her "I want nothing more to do with him, but there's no need for you to get involved in all this."

"So you don't object?"

"I don't care, Gin. Do what you want." She turned to her mother. "I'm not sure what time I'll get back. If it's early enough I'll drop in, if not, try to get a good night's sleep, and I'll see you in the morning."

Then she was gone.

Virginia turned to Mary Erikson. "She's so angry."

"I know, but how would you feel?"

"Annoyed, but anger like that's not good, Mrs. Erikson."

"I know that too, Virginia."

"Well, I'll write to him. He's supposed to be going over there in May if he gets enough people."

"How do you mean?"

"Well, when he gets enough people for a tour, his trip is paid for."

"That doesn't sound right" Mary frowned. "I don't understand."

"I'm not sure I do either, Mrs. Erikson," Virginia stared down at the letter again. "But I'll write him and see how he responds."

Britt had a great time with Edward Barrett. She decided to relax and put everything clamoring for attention out of her mind--hopes, worries, disappointments, death. This medium height, slender, nondescript looking man was funny and good company.

After an early supper, she walked back with him to the garage to get his car, and he drove her unprotesting to his apartment in N.D.G. Once there, he poured some drinks.

"So you like cognac?" He commented as he placed the glass before her on the coffee table.

"Yes, scotch too, but I don't drink much now."

"Why not?"

"Too many headaches."

Edward laughed and Britt thought, what a pun! She had been prescribed medication for intractable migraine for years now. Nothing helped much. Sometimes she was lucky, and the pain subsided after eight to twelve hours. Other times it lasted for two or three days. She lit a cigarette. Another taboo. But Edward was just as fatalistic. He smoked too.

"So what would you like to hear?"

"Ah, music . . ." Britt smiled. "You choose. You're the expert."

"All right." Edward crossed the room to his stereo and the selection of tapes.

"No, no." Britt interrupted his search. "You play."

"Me?"

"Yes, you. I want to hear you."

Edward taught violin, but now he went to the piano. "So what'll it be?"

"I don't know." Britt teased him. "Play something you think I'd like. That should be interesting."

He gave her a calculating look and then worked his fingers over the instrument for a few minutes, warming up. Finally he thumbed through a book and found the composition he was looking for. As he started out the piece, focusing solely on the music and his interpretation of the composer's intent, the whole aspect of the man changed. At that moment Britt thought she could possibly love him. She put her head back and closed her eyes. It was totally silent in the room when he finished playing. Then he was standing over her, and she looked up at him. "That was different. Sounding opposite to undercurrents . . ."

"Chopin's second prelude. Yes it is. It's like you."

"What will you play now?"

"Edward Grieg's piano concerto." He winked at her. "I've got the tape. You'll like it."

Edward was right. She did like it. Very much in fact. There was also a feeling of warmth and comfort when he put his arms around her and a stirring of passion when he kissed her. When she did pull her head back, however, it was only to remark lightly and with laughter in her eyes, "You're very good, you know, as a musician, I mean."

"You're not so bad yourself, for someone playing by ear. Of course, your chording and coordination is off, but that can be improved with practice."

"Lesson's over for today, professor."

"Nonsense." He grinned at her. "Come here."

Once again in his arms, she could feel his strength, surprisingly firm and secure, in so slight a man. But this can't be happening, she thought. I haven't the time, and the children are coming. The responsibilities I've wanted and went after for so long. There was also the contract she had virtually accepted and couldn't renege on that would be effective in six months. And then, of course, there was the extended relationship with Roddy and finally its termination. That was a good word for it -- termination, and the impact of it jolted her, causing her to draw back. Edward leaned back and glanced at her sideways.

"What's the matter, Britt?."

"Nothing's the matter. I can just see where this is going, and I don't think that's where I want to be."

"Why not?" Edward asked casually. His calm demeanor unnerved her, his cloaking device so like her own was every bit as disarming. "Why not?" he repeated softly when she didn't answer him.

"Because you don't love me. You don't even know me."

"Well, that's a silly statement, isn't it?" He reached for the packet of cigarettes, lit one and handed it to Britt, then lit one for himself. After a few moments he continued, selecting his words carefully. "I think I know as much about you as it's personally safe for me to know. And that goes for you too in your knowledge of me. Sometimes nature's very kind in its limitations."

"Most people would rather just not know."

"Of course, but people are usually pretty stupid about it. They don't trust the wisdom of nature. They really needn't worry at all about ever getting closer than they can handle to the truth about anyone or anything. Don't you agree?"

"Yes and no." Britt thought about it. "Yes, one can never really know another individual. And no, some people quite often trip over more truth than they can possibly handle."

"So you think we shouldn't bother trying. Right? Just what I was leading up to."

"Wrong. Not to bother trying is cowardly."

"Oh, don't be self-righteous, Britt."

"I'm not. Don't be an ass! You know, we have a whole new set of obscene words in our vocabulary these days, some so foul, in fact, we never hear them at all--like honor and integrity. And forget courage. That has to be a given, never something we're meant to strive for."

"All right, never mind all that. I hadn't planned on an argumentative debate over abstracts. What about love?" He put an arm around her shoulders. "You said I didn't love you. But fair is fair, you don't love me either, do you?"

Britt twisted around and grinned at him. "It would probably scare the hell out of you if I said I did, wouldn't it? You'd be in full retreat."

"Probably," Edward nodded at her and laughed. "You're horrible . . . putting a guy on the spot like that. What if I said I loved you?"

"Oh, that's easy. I wouldn't believe you."

"You wouldn't?"

"No, I would not."

"Not only are you a cynic, but skeptical too. I'd call that first degree skepticism."

"Call it anything you like. But you know something?"

"What?"

She leaned back against him, and he could feel the tension in her released as if she were sleeping and narrating a dream. "When you were over there playing the piano and so intent on what you were doing, it seemed like you were trying to capture something beyond your reach, something outside yourself; I thought I loved you then. I mean really loved you, and it had nothing to do with being my friend or bringing me physical, or even emotional satisfaction."

"Really?" He gazed down at her and turned her face toward him. "Why is that?"

"I don't know," she murmured, and then his mouth was over hers stopping the flow of words. After a few moments he stopped caressing her, and as she withdrew her arms from around his neck, he stood up and pulled her to her feet.

"I told you you'd run a mile," she laughed at him.

"I heard you, and I'm not running anywhere." He gave her a speculative look. "But I am taking you home."

"Why?"

"Because you're not ready, Britt. Too many irons in the fire. You know what I mean?" And when she nodded, he added, "but it's not over for us, Erikson. It hasn't even begun."

"Quite right, Barrett, I've a lot on my mind."

"And, unfortunately, I'm not part of it. Not yet, anyway. But patience is my long suit."

"Is it? Well, good. I've so little of it myself."

"You'd better acquire some." Edward advised her.

"With two freshly adopted kids you're going to need it."

"Think so?"

"Absolutely. I know you teach, but not violin. Believe me. That takes patience."

He clumped down the stairs behind her and out to the car. Britt glanced at her watch. It was almost midnight.

Late that night as she lay in bed her thoughts turned to Edward Barrett. He was forty years old and had a teenage daughter living with her mother up in Windsor. He kept a picture of her in his living room. All she knew about the girl was that she loved her father, but hated music. Edward could never understand it because he had started teaching her violin when she was four, and she had adapted to it very well. She was six when her parents separated and the lessons ended there.

Tossing around in bed, her mind raced on, and she conjured up the faces of Lobsang and Karma, especially Lobsang who had broken away from her and run out of the room when she tried to explain why she had to leave without him. Promising to return hadn't seemed to help. Adults often broke their promises. Kids learned that from an early age. Eventually she fell asleep. It was almost 3:00 a.m.

The following day she called through to Belanger's office at the parliament buildings, and this time he came on the line to reassure her once again that he would talk with the Minister of Immigration before returning to Montreal on the weekend. Things would be done as quickly as possible.

It was all true, but nevertheless, time seemed to dig in its heels and refused to advance. She was restless. There were over two weeks remaining of her leave of absence, and she thought about returning to work, but that presented too many problems, and she didn't relish the prospect of having to talk it over with Tom Flynn. The Canadian Heart Foundation was offering a course in advanced cardiac life support, but that would take a lot of prior study culminating in a harrowing weekend that everyone, doctors and nurses alike, came away from feeling drained and convinced they'd never put themselves through it again. They did of course, because the certification once obtained, had to be renewed every two years. It was the same for the advanced trauma course which was offered in the States and other Canadian provinces. She decided against it.

There didn't seem much point in it. In the fall, she'd be teaching health sciences and have to review much of the theory anyway, and in the meantime her efforts would be best spent getting the boys into Canada. On Monday, she'd call Belanger again when he was back in Montreal. If he wasn't sure about Martineau, she decided she'd call Warner and have him call Irving Burgher who had a reputation for expediting matters. But Monday was still five days away.

Friday morning, she went upstairs to see if her mother was ready. Mary wanted to make a small grocery order, and Britt was taking her. Leaving the building, she stopped to check her mailbox. There were several bills and a letter from Nepal.

"It's a letter from Tashi," Britt said, turning it over.

"Well, open it. What does it say?" Mary was curious and pleased. "He's written at last. That's good. I was beginning to wonder."

"So was I." Britt admitted. "Come on, I'll open it in the car."

"It's cold in the car."

"No, it's not. I've had it running for the last ten minutes."

"Oh, good. Well, let's go then."

Once in the car, Britt opened the envelope and glanced over the single paged correspondence.

"What's he say?"

Britt was frowning, and then her face became completely expression-less. She was rereading the single page. "He says they're not coming. Neither of the boys is coming. Their mother won't let them go."

"What! What are you saying?" Mary turned in a sudden movement. "It was done legally and before witnesses. She signed the adoption papers!"

"She isn't going to let them go." Britt's voice carried an undercurrent of dazed anguish bordering on a curiously contained angry frustration, but her face remained rigid. She dropped the letter beside her, put the car into gear, and pulled away from the curb. Mary picked up the letter and glanced at her daughter.

"I haven't got my glasses with me. Doesn't he give any reason at all?"

"No, he just says that the mother changed her mind. That's all."

"What are you going to do?"

"There's nothing I can do. She is their mother" Britt replied tonelessly. "I can deal with politicians, finagle a way through with officials, cut through bureaucracy and all the rest of it, but I can't fight her. Not the mother. The one area where I have no recourse. She knows that, too. She knows I won't do anything. Even if I could, I wouldn't. She knows."

"She never intended to let them go at all." A look of disgust carved new lines into the older woman's face. "All she wanted . . ."

"I know what she wanted." Britt interrupted her and then fell silent. But Mary was worried. She wanted to discuss it . . . above all she wanted to hear her daughter talking. Talking helped. It could help diffuse the elemental savagery of inner turmoil that might well cause irrevocable damage.

So she continued analyzing it from various angles and talking about it, but she might as well have been pitting her voice against the wind. Nothing came back to her. Britt had nothing further to say. Finally she too subsided into silence. She too was angry and could find no quarter for her turbulent thoughts. That woman, Dolma, Lobsang's mother, was no fool. She was a conniver, and she was cruel. Mary knew about women like her, but she hadn't met many. She realized that she too could be easily duped, just like her daughter had most certainly been. And for what? Money. This whole elaborate undertaking had been a scam--a bloody deception premised on a lie with no thought given to the emotional cost which by far outweighed the large amount of money already spent. She felt like choking the deceitful, scheming woman, and if she had her before her at this moment, that's probably exactly what she would do.

They were at the supermarket, and as they traveled up one aisle and down the next, the conversation turned to small, inconsequential things, and for Britt this was easier by far. Mary was hopeful. At least she was speaking again, if only in monosyllables, and she was not so distant from her and remote in her silence. For Mary it was much harder. It was very hard to comfort people when they were really so near you physically and yet completely out of your reach. She walked ahead picking items off shelves, and Britt trailed behind her at a short distance, wheeling the basket. They were just about finished, and Mary turned to her. "I just need macaroni. It's up this aisle, I think. I'm going to make that goulash."

"Oh, that'll be good."

"I thought you'd approve."

"Well, it lasts for a week, Mother."

"I know." Mary sighed.

"Leftovers are always welcome." Britt thought it amusing, and her mother's expression of boredom at eating the same thing day after day heightened the humor. "Don't worry. It won't go to waste."

"I didn't think so." Mary grimaced. "Okay, so you'll wait here? I'll go and find it."

"Yes, I'll be here."

Mary went off, and it took longer than she expected. She came back with a few extra items and by a different route only to find her daughter leaning slightly over the basket with an expression on her face that made her heart contract sharply as if someone had jabbed at it abruptly with a sharp instrument. The younger woman's eyes were like two deep hollows staring emptily into space, beyond torment and the far reaches of sadness. Mary was horrified and moved instinctively toward her. "Oh God, Britt, don't look like that."

"Like what?" Britt caught herself, righted her stance, and the expression dissolved, changing radically into something more within the bounds of normal disappointment.

"Like that . . ." Mary stared at her, suddenly inarticulate. "I know you feel bad, but . . ."

"I'm fine, Mother. Really. It's all right." Mary was still clutching the articles in her arms.

"Here, let me have that stuff. Need anything else?"

"No. No, that's all."

They got through the lines at the cash registers, and Mary suggested going out for coffee. And so there they were a half an hour later seated opposite each other in a cozy restaurant on Sherbrooke Street just as they had so many times before. But things were different; changed utterly for Mary Erikson because she'd had Hugh for so long, and now she was alone. Looking at her mother, Britt thought her vulnerable. And this was only the beginning. What about the years ahead? In herself, she felt numb. Her father's death had, for some reason, eclipsed the sun of her inner life. And that was odd because he'd been less in her thoughts than usual during the months before he died. He was always going to be there. She needn't worry about losing him. But her own life had become a dry well, and that's what had been uppermost in her mind, preoccupying her thoughts when the light she didn't know she possessed suddenly went out, leaving her in a dark void. And then a hidden door had opened. An opportunity she couldn't turn away. A little boy in a remote corner of the world wanted to be adopted. His parents wanted him adopted. And now this. A steel door clanged shut, but not before she glimpsed the last image she had of Lobsang and the look of disappointment and betrayal on his face. Perhaps the boy had sensed it all along. Her doubts had been quenched, but not the child's. Her promise had been broken. Quite possibly he had never believed it at all.

Her mother was looking at her with concern, and finally Britt locked onto what she was saying and had to admit that her mother was right. She should be feeling all those things--rage, frustration, loss. At the moment, however, she couldn't manage to feel anything at all. But she did unclench her lower lip and dredge up a smile, unaware that it was full of unrecognized pain.

"I'm fine, Mother. It's all right. Really." She lit a cigarette and watched its tip burn red. "Think how the children must feel, especially Lobsang. Why would parents want to do that to their own kids?"

"I don't know." Mary gave her a long look. "Mankind doesn't have a very good record."

"No, that's true. I wonder if anyone's keeping score." Britt didn't bother to add that to her this was yet another failure, one too many. There was nothing to say, nothing she wanted to say.

Once home, after helping her mother put away the groceries, she disappeared into her own apartment. Mary was left to tell Nora, who was both furious and combative, but said little. Once again Virginia appeared. She came knocking at Britt's door shortly after seven in the evening. "I heard," she said without preamble. "Your mother told me."

"News travels fast." Britt pointed to her satchel. "What have you got there?"

"My knitting."

"Do you want some tea? I was just going to make some."

"Sure. What are you doing?" Virginia looked around.

"Watching television . . . reading." Britt shrugged. "Ruth is watching some kids' show."

"Oh, is she here? Must be a good show, or she's into something. She's too quiet."

"She's sleeping here tonight. I was just going to give her a bath."

"Go ahead. I'll make the tea."

By the time she got Ruth bathed and into her nightdress, it was close to eight o'clock. She sent the toddler scrambling down the hall to watch the end of her show and took a bath herself. Gin didn't mind. She'd made the tea and left it to steep in the kitchen. When Britt came out, she caught the baby up in her arms and the child giggled. It felt so good to have her close. It made things seem right when everything else was going wrong.

"Bed time, my love." When the child started to protest, Britt glanced over at her friend who continued knitting and was absorbed in her own thoughts which were causing her to scowl. She carried the child from the room, tucked her into bed, and told her that she'd soon be along to bed herself because she was very tired.

"Soon?" the child asked, reaching up and putting her arms around her aunt's neck.

"Very soon." Britt whispered back. "I'll leave the light on."

Back in the living room the weekly show *Beauty and the Beast* was just beginning. Britt stood in the middle of the room. "I like this show."

"So do I."

"Hang on, I'll get the tea."

Britt watched the show and saw very little of it against the background circus of her thoughts. Gin had one eye on the television and the other on her knitting. Halfway through the program, Britt found her gut being wrenched and twisted deep inside, and she was shaking uncontrollably . . . all inside and beyond her power to arrest it.

"I can't seem to stop shaking," she blurted out and then regretted having uttered the words. But Gin sat imperturbably and went on knitting.

"Of course, you've had a shock."

A shock. Was that it? Just a shock. The shaking continued. Attempts at making it subside were abortive. It seemed as if she'd caught a chill, and it would have to run its course. Finally, it ended and only the memory of it disturbed her.

Virginia went home, and Britt was left alone. She was relieved in a way because she was entangled in her own dark labyrinth of thoughts that teetered precariously on visions of shattered hopes, and she could sense a different sort of quandary in her friend. The friend who loved India, or what she called the soul of India, and especially Nepal. Almost everyone loved Nepal, and now she found herself not only disliking it, but hating it. And that, she had to admit, was completely irrational. She had always used logic as her trump card, and now it seemed the only deck of cards she held was stacked with jokers; all with contorted faces of emotion. The truth was she felt like hell and hated the feeling. Feeling bad about what happened equated in her mind with feeling sorry for herself and that was unacceptable. All of it went round and round in her head, and the future had no face at all. It was a lonely, featureless landscape.

-Thirteen-

During the next few days Britt made a number of rapid decisions. Some were bold and blaringly conspicuous, like an artist streaking a canvas with colors no longer muted, but falsely vibrant and alive, and others that were much less obvious and, at this juncture, necessary. She needed to regain her lost sense of balance, and she needed answers.

On Monday morning she called Belanger's office and left a message with his secretary requesting that he discontinue any action on her behalf. That was no problem. He'd be only too pleased to oblige her. She needn't worry about anything going anywhere. Then she called a friend in Philadelphia who was married to a lawyer. Walter Tynan could be tiresome and clownish, as her friend had so often depicted her unpredictable husband, but he was an excellent attorney, and Britt decided she needed some sound legal advice. Terry knew about the adoption and the sudden reversal of its outcome came as no shock to her. Furthermore, she'd speak to Walter and he'd get back to her.

That done, she rang up the director of nursing personnel at the hospital and made an appointment to see her the following day. That same afternoon, she decided to walk up to the hospital and try to find Tom Flynn, preferably alone. She avoided the main work areas of the Emergency Psychiatry Department and went directly to the office section. Fortunately, she found him holed-up in his tiny office that looked very much like a closet at the end of the hall. When he looked up and saw her standing in the doorway, there were a few charged moments of fleeting hostility that gave way quickly to a reluctant smile and she sat down. He had papers all over his desk.

"What are you doing, Tom?"

"The schedule, of course. What else? Look at these requests!" He threw down his pencil and ran a nervous hand through his rapidly graying hair. "What are you doing here? Your leave's not up until . . ."

"The end of the month. I know." She nodded, "But I wanted to speak to you."

"What about?" Tom was on the defensive, and Britt shook her head.

"No, not that. Nothing like that, but what would you think about me switching to General E.R.?"

"General E.R.?" Tom's eyes widened. "But why? I thought you liked it here."

"I do. To be honest with you, this is the best nursing position I've had. I've enjoyed working here."

"So . . . why?"

"I need a change, Tom. Do you understand? I need a change."

The head nurse leaned back and studied her for a few moments. She looked thinner. Apparently taking time off hadn't done much good.

"I understand. But have you ever worked General E.R.?"

"No, but what if I took the advanced trauma course and the advanced cardiac? Wouldn't that help?"

"Sure." Tom shrugged. "It's a lot of study. Have you started?"

"Not yet, but I will."

"Well, they don't require it. They'll train you, but I don't know, Britt. I've heard things about their staff over there. Well, you know how they are. You've dealt with them."

"I know. They're vultures . . . certainly not like the staff here."

"No, not at all. So why walk into that? You'll hate it."

"Maybe, but I think I'd better do it."

Tom sighed. "You're a glutton for punishment . . . Do you want me to make a call for you?"

"To whom?"

"Heather Donovan. The head nurse over there."

"Do you know her . . . ? I mean, well enough to . . ."

"Oh yes. She's always over here complaining. The administration is driving her crazy too. She's acting head nurse. They've offered her the position twice and backed down twice."

"You mean they withdrew the offer? What reason did they give?"

"None. They can't find any fault with her. I tell you, Britt, this place is a madhouse."

"Why doesn't she just leave?"

"I told her that. She can go anywhere. Not like me with only a diploma. I'm stuck here, and I've got a family to support. You too. You're single. Get out of here and out of Quebec."

"I'm going to, but not yet."

"So you want me to call?"

"Yes. Call and see what she says."

"I know what she'll say" Tom grumbled. "They're so short staffed it's ridiculous." He broke off speaking as he dialed the main E.R. and asked for Heather Donovan. Before she came on the line, he had time to add, "I hope you won't be sorry."

After that, she sat back and listened while Tom spoke with the harried head of the main E.R., acting head, officially. When he put down the receiver, he turned to her, "she wants to see you."

"Oh, should I call her for an appointment then?"

"No, she'll see you now. Come on. Knowing you, you'll never find it even though it's in our area."

"I know where Main E.R. is. We're back and forth all the time."

"Yes, but not to her office . It's hidden away like mine. Come on, unless, of course, you've changed your mind. I think you should change your mind, Britt."

"No, Tom. After your glowing report I couldn't do that." Flynn left her outside Heather Donovan's door and disappeared back down the hall and around the corner. The interview with Heather didn't take very long. She called in the clinical instructor, Sylvie Allard. Before Britt realized what was happening they were discussing her starting date.

"Ah, well, I'm due back from leave at the end of the month, and then I have to give Tom two weeks notice." She was thinking of things she had to get done and started.

"No, you don't," Heather frowned. "Tom's much better staffed than I am. He won't mind. Just a minute, I'll ask him."

She got Tom on the line and put the question to him in such a way that he'd find it hard to refuse her. He was about to say he'd waive the obligatory notice when he changed his mind and asked to speak to Britt. Heather handed her the receiver and, in one of his rare flashes of insight, Tom asked, "Need a little more time back here to rest up from your leave?"

"Yes."

"I thought you might." Tom laughed. "All right, put Heather back on line."

A few minutes later, it was settled. "All right," Heather gnawed at her lower lip. She checked the calendar. "You start on Monday, April seventeenth. That okay?"

"Yes, fine. I'll try to get these courses in between now and the time I start."

"Good. But they don't offer the Advanced Trauma course here."

"No. But they do in the States. I'm certified in Pennsylvania."

Heather stood up. "Well, no matter. On the job training . . . I'll see you on the seventeenth then."

And that was that. She kept her appointment with personnel to sign the necessary transfer papers. That evening around supper time, she called Ronit, another friend of hers, who worked on the gynecology ward at the Queen Elizabeth Hospital. Ronit was Israeli born, semi—religious, and traditional in her living style, and she'd been pestering her husband, Rueben, who operated a small kosher bakery shop to return to Israel with their four children. She wanted to be with her family again. The troubles in the Middle East didn't bother her. She'd grown up in all that turmoil. Rueben flatly refused. His sons would be required to do military duty, and he'd seen quite enough of what went on to dissuade him from ever taking his family there. They bickered over it constantly, and Britt often wondered how they managed to have four children together, and another on the way, with all the wrangling that went on. By the tone of Rueben's voice when he answered the phone, she reckoned they'd been at it again. But Ronit came on the line cheerful as ever. The conversation skipped along lightly until Britt asked her about work.

"Oh, nothing ever changes there," she replied grumpily. "Thank God I'm only part time, but it helps pay the bills. I should be thankful. Listen, where have you been? I called you in February and finally gave up trying."

"Oh, away . . . on a trip." Britt was evasive and changed the subject. "Ronit, do you know a good gynecologist?"

"Sure. I know some not so good too. Why? Don't you have one?"

"Of course, but McGuire died as you know, and the guy taking over for him is all right, but . . ."

"You want someone else."

"Yes, someone who's got a bit of pull in town and can get me in to see an endocrinologist. And I want a very good one. Someone who knows what he's doing."

"Well, I go to Halston. She's a OB-GYN and I like her, but Carter's better known and has more clout. Personally, I don't much like the man, but he's good, very thorough, and he usually refers patients who need an endocrine profile to Ashong. She's excellent . . . here some days for clinic and consults but affiliated with either the

General or the Royal Vic. Maybe both."

"Then I'll go to Carter. How booked is he?"

"Very." Ronit thought for a moment. "But I know his nurse. I used to work with her here, and we keep in touch. She'll get you in to see him if at all possible. Do you want me to call her?"

"Would you?"

"Sure. I'll drop by to see her . . . Britt, is something wrong?"

"No, Ronit. Nothing's wrong. I just want some tests done. Maybe specialized tests and you know what it's like."

"Yes, I know. But you're all right?"

"Yes."

"Well then, I'll talk to Sheila. You want the appointment as soon as possible, I suppose."

"Yes . . . please. I don't want to delay this."

Ronit's brow wrinkled. "I'll call you tomorrow evening. I don't suppose you'd want to come to Shabbas on Friday?"

"Sure I would, very much, in fact."

"Fine, and it's all right if you smoke."

"I thought it was against the rules."

"It is," Ronit's voice sounded sour, "but it annoys Rueben, so bring your cigarettes." Then she peeled with laughter and added, "bring that fellow you're seeing . . . Edward what's his name."

"But Edward's never been to a Shabbas meal."

"So? Bring him anyway. If he's as klutzy as Rueben they should get along fine. Then we could have some time to talk."

Britt laughed. "Ronit, your strategy's transparent. I wonder why Rueben puts up with it."

"We love each other. Can't you tell?" The humor in Ronit carried over in her voice. She enjoyed baiting her long-suffering husband.

"As a matter of fact I can." Britt shook her head. "You can't fool me. And I'll see if Edward's free."

"Good, I'll call you back tomorrow. You'll have your appointment. But don't forget about Friday evening."

Unconsciously Britt heard the receiver click, and she sat staring across the room. The day had come to a close, the light having faded entirely from the sky without even a last burst of splendor. No glorious sunset. No bright flame before the light went out. She wondered idly about that and the continuum of gray tedious days that hovered between a wearisome drizzle and a dreary half-hearted sleet. Snow would be better, burying the dirty, grimy streets of the city under a garment all white and glistening; capturing the stark branches of trees in crystal encasements and clearing the low leaden skies. Or even rain. A solid heavy downpour, cleansing and cathartic. But no, just this relentless onslaught of days following in a long and lethargic march of sameness. No change. Spring might never have been at all. There was not a vestige of its approach. No promise of it either. And summer was only a dream.

She got up suddenly and broke the spell. The weather was foul. The winter days dull and dragging on longer than she could remember from past years, and it reflected the way she felt. But she had anchored her thoughts to new resolves, and the day's accomplishments were significant. It was another turning point. She had been living far too long in one or other two false worlds, the fantasyland of hope springing eternal or the pitch black void of not understanding why things were the way they were. It was time for some reality. What she needed now was harder, more demanding work. A new challenge. And she needed answers. No doubt, work would take her mind off the quest and what she might find at the end of it.

It was only a little after seven, and it seemed past midnight. She rang Edward and left a message for him to call her on his answering machine. Then she went upstairs to see her mother.

Ronit phoned the next day and went directly to the point. "Sheila said she could squeeze you in next Tuesday, at 1:30. There was a cancellation. Carter's covering for another doctor and busier than ever. So . . . can you make it?"

"Oh yes, I'll make it. Should I call his office and confirm it."

"Yes, you should. Sheila has your name." Ronit gave her the office number. "Did you speak to Edward? Is he coming Friday evening?"

"Yes, I called him, or rather he returned my call, and yes, he's coming. He's looking forward to it."

"Well, fine. See you at sundown." Ronit went into another fit of laughter, and her mirth was infectious. In no time at all she had Britt laughing too.

-Fourteen-

Terry called from Philadelphia late Wednesday evening, and before they got into any kind of conversation she put Walter on the line. "Hi Britt. How are you doing?"

"Fine, Walter. You sound tired."

"I am. But I'm making a bundle, so what the hell . . . ? Listen, I'm sorry about the kids."

"So am I. Now what do I do?"

"Well, I checked it out. It's unlikely there'll be any kind of problem in the future, but you never know. You didn't get possession, but they could have a claim as your legally adopted sons. You should confirm in writing to Immigration that the adoption was breached. Register the letter. That's required to void it. Stopping the processing of it isn't sufficient. Then put a disclaimer in your will."

"My will? I haven't even got one."

"Well, have one drawn up. You'll need to do that. Kids grow up. Those boys could have a claim. I'm sure you want to leave what you have or will have elsewhere."

"Yes, of course." Britt expelled a long breath. "Thank you, Walter. Anything else?"

"No, that should cover it. It's just a safeguard, you understand? But it's necessary. So when are we going to see you?"

"Maybe sooner than you think."

"Good. I'll put Terry back on." He handed the receiver to his wife and went off into the living room.

"Did that help?" Terry asked.

"Yes, I know what to do now. Listen, Terry, are they offering the Advanced Trauma course down there?"

"I think so. Barbara's still at Graduate Hospital . . . I'm pretty sure they do. She told me some of the courses are horrible. Why, what are you up to?"

"Taking that course. I've got the text from Alberta, but they don't offer it here."

"Well, you don't need it."

"I'm switching to Main E.R."

"If your emergency rooms are anything like ours, I wish you luck." Terry sounded grim. "But I'll find out if you want me to."

"Yes. If they're giving it, I'll come down there to take it."

"I'll call around. Come to think of it, Emergency Psych is no picnic either."

"No, it's hardly that. I'll call you back on the weekend."

"Okay . . . Britt, wait . . . before you hang up . . ."

"Yes?"

"Come down anyway. Bryn Mawr's beautiful. You liked it when you lived here. Remember?

"I remember . . . and I'll be down."

Terry didn't wait for Britt's call on the weekend. She rang the following afternoon to tell her that the trauma course was being offered at Jefferson Hospital the last weekend in March.

"March?" Britt hesitated. "That only gives me nine or ten days."

"Yeah, are you good at cramming?"

"I used to be."

"Then you still are. It's all day Saturday and Sunday morning. Then the testing begins. That takes all afternoon. According to Barbara, it's rough."

"She's right . . ." Britt made a face. "Well, I'll try. How much is it?"

"Two hundred."

"Could you sign me up, and I'll reimburse you when I get there?"

"No problem. When are you coming?"

"Next Friday evening, I suppose."

"Good. So we'll get to see each other at last. Call me when you've booked your flight. I'll pick you up at the airport."

"I'll be bleary-eyed from reading all this bloody material."

"Don't study too much. From what I hear the trick is to stay cool and calm." Terry laughed. "But not too cool or calm, or they'll use you as a trauma victim instead."

"They may do it yet," Britt said gloomily and then added almost cheerfully. "I'll see you soon."

Mary was in the process of getting ready to go out shopping with Nora when Rourke came in unexpectedly Saturday afternoon.

"Well, how is everyone?" He took off his hat and coat and draped them over a chair.

"Everyone's fine" Nora answered him. "Did you come down alone?"

"Nope. I left Claire at her mother's, and the boys are with her."

"Why didn't she come here with you?"

"Because I like some time with my family, and she likes time with hers. So . . . we compromise."

"You call that a compromise?" Nora looked at him moodily.

"I do." Rourke nodded. "And when you get to be as old as me you will too."

"Oh, I don't know . . . seems to me I've already compromised. But only because I had to."

"Exactly." Rourke smiled triumphantly. "They say necessity's the mother of invention, but they're wrong. Invention was swapped for compromise at birth."

"I see," Nora nodded at him. "But it doesn't give mother much of a chance to see Reg and Lee."

"Ach, teenagers are every bit as tiresome as they're reputed to be. Mine are well behaved compared to most, but why shouldn't I take a bit of time for myself?"

"You should," Mary interjected. "And I'm glad you did. So,

why don't we go out for lunch?"

"Yes, why don't we? Where are the kids?"

"They're watching cartoons." Nora got up. "I'll get them."

"Why don't you leave Ruth with Britt?" Mary suggested, "We'll take Aaron with us."

"I'll see if Britt wants to do it. Lately she's been busy."

"She's never too busy for Ruth." Mary turned away from her and Nora left. She didn't see the look on her mother's face, but Mary needn't have worried. Nora was preoccupied with her own problems and plans. She had a large move looming ahead of her, and it was worrying her. But Rourke was watching his mother, and he was very perceptive, more so than usual.

"How's Britt anyway? I haven't seen her for weeks."

"Well, you know she changed her job."

"You told me she just transferred."

"She did, but it's different. Now she's studying all the time, a trauma course or whatever, and then she's taking some course on the heart. It's all advanced stuff, and she's like a dog with a bone."

"So, she won't come up for air," Rourke mumbled and shook his head. "That's just like her . . . stubborn and determined. She's never let go of medicine."

"Well, it's too late for that. Why can't she just enjoy her life?" Mary looked anxious and disconcerted, knowing fully well she couldn't do anything about what was troubling Britt, but a low rippling sound was coming from Rourke. It was the sound of his rare and whimsical laughter.

"Look, Mother," he began philosophically. "The Vikings sacked Dublin, did all kinds of damage, and lost anyway. Then, to even the score, the more hard-headed ones just stayed on and interbred with the Celts. So everybody wins and loses. What's bred in the bone . . ."

"I know. I know," Mary looked at him impatiently. "But what's the point of it all? I think she's still intending to take that job out west. And that would be best. She's an excellent teacher, and it's no effort for her . . . comes naturally. Other people have to struggle in the classroom, but not her. And there's something else. She still wants children. That adoption was a disaster."

"I know," Rourke growled. "Those bastards must be brain dead."

"No, they're cunning, the mother anyway . . . and you should have seen the letter Don whatever his name is, wrote to her."

"What letter?"

"Oh, she didn't tell you?"

"No."

"Virginia has it." She went on to tell him the contents of the letter.

"The damned idiot!" Rourke spat out the words and then sighed heavily. "Well, best to leave it alone. Give fools a wide berth. That's what I do."

"She is leaving it alone, Rourke. But unlike you she's angry and . . ."

"Oh, everyone's angry, Mother," he interrupted her. "How can you live in this world and see what's going on and has always gone on and not get angry. It's a useless emotion, but understandable."

"Yes, so long as it doesn't destroy you." Mary thought about it. "I'm worried about her."

"Don't be." Rourke sat forward. "I rather like her anger."

"Most people don't" Mary reminded him.

"Most people are petulant, petty and pandering. They cave in and go with the flow. But my sister doesn't and never did. That's why I like her."

"Well, you two have had your disagreements. Don't deny it."

Rourke laughed. "Sure we have, lots of them and no doubt there'll be others, but we'll hold. You can depend on that." Mary looked at him, and he went on in an undertone. "You see, Mother, neither of us is so appallingly self-centered we lose sight of the other person. She's not a bitch, and I'm not a bastard. Lots of men and women are . . . despite other very redeeming qualities they undoubtedly have, and they are seldom, if ever, angry."

"Rourke, that's a lousy thing to say."

"But it's true."

"It's a very sorry statement on the human race."

"The human race is and always has been in a sorry state, but don't get me wrong, Mother. There are a lot of good people, not just basically decent, but strong and true. Ideals aren't extinct, and it's people who keep them alive."

"I thought we were talking about anger."

"We are."

"Don't talk in riddles." Mary waved a hand at him. "I'm riddled enough."

Nora came back in dressed for the outdoors, and she had Aaron in tow. Rourke looked over at his nephew and couldn't resist a smile. The small boy was in his best Sunday clothes. The same double-breasted navy blue coat he'd worn at the funeral, Rourke remembered with a pang. Why that image should lodge in his mind, he couldn't think why. He couldn't even recall what he wore himself. What did it matter? Here was young Aaron, with a nature very like his own, his face shining as if it had been scrubbed and his hair carefully parted and combed back from his forehead.

"You look very handsome, Aaron," Mary beamed at him.

"All dressed up."

"And why not?" Nora darted a glance at her brother. "It's a special occasion. We're going out to lunch and Rourke's paying."

"That's right, I'm paying. Hot dogs all round. How'd you like that, Aaron?"

"I like hot dogs."

"Good boy," Rourke got up and struggled into his coat.

"You could use a new coat yourself, Rourke." Mary eyed him critically and then turned to Nora. "Is Britt minding Ruth?"

"Yes, but I doubt if she'll get much studying done."

"I'll go and see her when we get back," Rourke announced.

"Maybe she'll come up to my place next weekend."

"Not next weekend," Mary shook her head. "She's going to Philadelphia to take that course."

"Oh, you didn't tell me that!" He followed them out of the apartment.

Rourke dropped down to see Britt later that afternoon. "I can't stay long," He greeted her. "It's late, and I've got to get back."

"I thought you'd gone. Nora said you had to pick up Claire and the kids."

"I do. But they told me you're studying for some course and going to Philadelphia."

"Well, I've got friends there, and the trauma course will come in handy." Britt rubbed a hand across her eyes. "Do you want something? Tea, coffee . . ."

"Got anything stronger?"

"There's some brandy left over."

"That'll do."

As she hunted through the cupboards for the brandy and found a proper glass, he watched her and frowned. "What's so important about this course? It's not worth getting strung out over."

"I'm not strung out, just tired. And the course isn't so important, but I'm switching to Main E.R., and it might come in handy."

"I thought you liked what you were doing."

"I did. It was interesting."

"So why change?"

"I did it. Now it's time to move on."

"You think you'll like General Emergency?"

"Yes. Do you want the truth? It scares the hell out of me."

Rourke stared at her and then started to laugh. "After working Emergency Psychiatry, that's just not possible." Then he nodded at her solemnly. "I happen to know it's a very hazardous job . . . to your personal safety, I mean."

Britt shrugged. "It can be . . . some people hate it. But psych patients come through the main E.R., and I'll get them too."

"So what frightens you?"

"Oh, it'll be new . . . different. They'll be shouting for Epinephrine or Isoptin, and I won't know exactly where to find it."

"Oh don't be silly. It takes time to get your bearings anywhere. That's not important."

"It is when the patient's coding. And besides, the more you know the better . . . the less chance of missing something. You hear all types of horror stories in a hospital. Some worse than others . . . like the one I just heard."

"There are horror stories everywhere."

"Yeah, I know, but this was pure negligence. Ronit told me about it last night. She has a friend working at one of the emergencies. I won't mention the hospital. That wouldn't be ethical probably. Anyway, this man brings his wife to the E.R. because she's having difficulty breathing. She's just a young woman, pregnant . . . close to delivery time, but not in labor. They do the usual preliminary things and the doctor assesses her and sends her home. He doesn't bother to do an A.B.G."

"What's that?"

"Arterial Blood Gases. One of the reasons for doing it is to see how much oxygen is in the blood. He should have done one."

"You know the doctor?"

"Not personally, no. Never heard of him before" she held up a hand, "But let me finish. Her breathing gets worse, and the husband brings her back to the hospital in the late afternoon. This time, the same doctor does an A.B.G. When the results come back, and that didn't take very long, her PO2 is thirty-five. That's the partial pressure of oxygen in the blood. Far too low, dangerously low, especially in a pregnant woman. So the doctor figures he'd got venous blood. You know, hit the vein instead of the artery, but instead of repeating the test if he wasn't sure and at least putting the woman on oxygen and checking for fetal distress, he sends her home again." Rourke was shaking his head and scowling. "But that's not all. Oh no. That same evening the husband brings the poor woman back to the emergency, and now she's in acute distress, gasping and going into shock, if not already there. She was dying and the baby already dead. To cover the negligence, they rushed her upstairs, did an emergency caesarian, sliced her open, and ran a full code. Ronit's friend was upstairs. The room was a blood bath. She was dead well before they even got started and so was the baby. But the emergency notes gave the full story. It was her third time in emergency that day and a PO2 of thirty-five much earlier on that they didn't take notice of. The poor husband was dazed. He had a healthy young wife and almost a new baby."

"Jesus Christ!" Rourke hissed. "I'd kill the bastard!"

"He doesn't know a thing. The doctors told him they were very sorry. They did everything they could do. And no one said a thing about that jerk in E.R.. Not the other doctors, or the nurses. Nobody said a word. It was hushed up."

"But he must have known something was wrong. He had to bring her back three times."

"People don't know, Rourke. Of course, he can sue, but he doesn't know that. What irks me is everyone shutting up as if they were dummies."

"They're afraid." Rourke looked down at his glass which was empty.

"Well, I'm not afraid of that, but I'd hate like hell to be like that doctor or even the nurses who didn't know enough to at least insist on a repeat A.B.G."

"They probably did know."

"Probably," Britt nodded. "But malpractice isn't always so blatantly obvious."

"No, well I see your point. It's important to be very good at your job, but take it easy. You are going to take that job out west, aren't you?"

"I think so, but I want to get some things done here first."

"Like what?"

Britt stalled, but then went on almost casually.

"Fertility tests. I'm thirty-eight, Rourke, and I've never been able to conceive. I'm going to find out why."

"Can't you just accept it? It happens to lots of people. I'm sorry about the adoption, but . . ."

"No, it's not that. I want to know, and I've waited too long already."

She didn't go into any details with her brother. He knew enough. He raised his shoulders and let them drop in an attitude of frustrated resignation. "Well, if you feel that strongly about it, then find out, but there mightn't be an answer. I've heard there often isn't one."

"I know, but if there is one, I'll find it."

"And so this other stuff is a smoke screen. Right?"

"In a way, yes. It'll take my mind off myself. I don't much like being self absorbed and, when something's hounding you, that's what can happen."

"You're less self absorbed than most, but I see what you mean."

"Good. So how are you?"

"Oh, I'm fine. Everyone's fine. Mother seems to be coping well, don't you think?"

"She seems to be, but I honestly don't know. It's too early to tell. Too early for any of us. Sometimes people don't realize how lonely they really are. It's a very strange thing . . . experiencing something and then realizing it's actually happened."

"I guess so." Looking at him, Britt wondered what dark thoughts he was harboring. Finally he got up. "I've got to go. Call me when you get back from Philadelphia."

"I will. Drive safely."

He nodded absently and left, making his way down the hall with the same steady, unhurried, heavy gait he'd had since boyhood. Britt checked the time. It was almost five o'clock.

Edward had thoroughly enjoyed the evening they spent with Ronit and Rueben. He came away chuckling to himself and once in the car, he turned to Britt.

"Now there are two people who were meant for each other."

"They're always squabbling, or didn't you notice?" Britt said, but she started to laugh with him.

"I noticed, but they have such fun at it. Like us."

"Like us! Are you out of your mind?"

"Not at all." He reached over and drew her close to him. Then he kissed her. "Not ready yet?"

"For what? Marriage, monogamy, or a casual affair?"

"I'm never casual, Britt."

"And the other?"

"Monogamous, yes. You bet I am. I haven't got a death wish. I suppose you'd want blood tests anyway."

"You bet I would, but you're way ahead of me. Right now I'd like to get home."

"Home it is, then." He started up the engine. "Will you be buried in work until after next weekend?"

"Yes. I'm sorry, but . . ."

"It's all right." He took her hand and held it. "But when you get back we'll talk. Yes?"

"Yes."

So Saturday evening she was free to study and recalling their conversation lightened her spirits. The tiredness she'd felt after Rourke's departure lifted too. The material she read through went down smoothly, and it was retained. Everything was coming together, and it was clear and unclouded and restful as her mind started to focus. She felt herself relaxing.

Tuesday morning her thoughts bumped around colliding against past experiences, relationships that had been abortive in their goal to bring about conception and all the senseless agonizing that went with artificial insemination. Well, enough was enough. Rationally she was well planted in the scientific advancements she studied and believe in so adamantly. Emotionally, she was stuck in the mud of the nineteenth century and all its backward, limited, and superstitious traps of moral teachings. It galled her and, despite the fact that she'd proceeded regardless of personal misgivings, everything she'd done had failed utterly, including the latest venture at adoption. What a bloody farce! How was it that some people had less trouble accepting their fate. They settled into the world as if they were always meant to be there. She, on the other hand, was like a person driven. For many years there had been the pursuit of medicine. Most women's first love was a man. And she'd come very close herself a few times. She'd had proposals and turned them down. Medicine and the riveting call of adventure had loomed up before her like the ghosts of Christmas yet to be, and who could resist the urge to follow?

Life had never been boring. It had been an adventure. She threw all of her being into everything she did: teaching, nursing, newspaper reporting, even business. And it had been fun and challenging. Also very draining, but what did that matter? Still, there was the underlying failure to enter the world of medicine. Nursing had helped. She could study pathology and pharmacology to her heart's content, but she felt her own limitations, and that was more frustrating than she cared to think about. Still, it had been advantageous to her, to the patients that she cared for, and to the students that she taught. She was a success in everyone's eyes but her own. The change and upheaval through the years had cast her up on a distant shore where the landmarks were not only unfamiliar to her, but disturbing and inescapable. However, the knowledge was hers alone, and where she found herself, no one could be expected to follow. Not her family, whom she knew now had no notion of her turmoil, or the many and varied friends, that she's made and kept through the years, knew what went on behind the cool exterior. But then how much did she really know about them? Enough to know there was always a mystery to plumb and enough to know that they too, were lonely. She could help keep the darkness they feared at bay. Or so it seemed. But it was never enough, and she knew that too.

Britt sat at the kitchen table drinking coffee and smoking. The text on trauma assessment and treatment lay open before her. Today unfortunately, her mind wasn't focusing and thereby releasing her. In a little over two hours she'd have to leave for Dr. Anthony Carter's office and the story she gave would have to be plausible. That might be somewhat difficult since the truth wasn't very believable at all. Nor was it terribly convincing considering the roller-coaster ride she'd made of her life. So many ventures, departures, and employment changes, including career switches that even she couldn't tally all of them. Her lips compressed into a grim line and her brow creased as she stared down at the words trying to make sense of a straightforward procedure. After a few minutes, she closed the book and leaned over it. It was impossible to concentrate. Between flashes from the past assaulting her with a scourge of unsought for memories and the impending medical appointment, she felt like she was bobbing in a large body of water too far out to get safely back to shore and too close to shore to drown and find oblivion. She tapped her fingers on the table top and brooded over it until she became annoyed with herself. Well enough was enough. A hot bath would help immensely, and then she'd dress carefully and conservatively.

Appearance and presentation could be a deciding factor. At this turn of her thoughts, she started to laugh at herself. When had she ever been flamboyant or even in vogue? Never. She wasn't like her sister--vivacious and alluring. She was cool and reserved. Attractive, yes. At least a number of men thought so, but she seldom, if ever, had to fend off unwelcome overtures. According to Edward, she was maddeningly attractive and charming. It was her cutting sarcasm that most men found difficulty coping with. It intrigued and disconcerted them. Trouble was, a lot of clever men liked insipid women. Failing that, they liked the overtly warm and lively. The fun usually lasted at least until the honeymoon was over. Thank God for small mercies. On the other hand, women were pretty stupid about men too and she, admittedly, was no exception. People were often not what they appeared to be, nor did they know what they wanted. It was just a game, a game called relationships, and everyone was playing it using different rules.

Dr. Carter was not as formidable as Ronit had made him out to be. Perversely, Britt rather liked him. When his nurse had asked her to change and went to one of the examining rooms, she declined, stating that she wanted to speak with him first. An examination mightn't be necessary. A few minutes later, she was ushered into his office. Another patient was just leaving, and he walked out with her down the hall to consult with his nurse for another appointment. That gave Britt time to look around his office which was what she was doing when Carter came back into the room.

"Those are my two daughters." He gave her a short smile and moved around the desk. "Please sit down."

"No grandchildren?" Britt's eyes wandered again to the pictures.

"No, but soon. My daughter is pregnant. That one, the youngest." He pointed to the picture of the young woman on the right. "Now, Miss Erikson? You keep your own name?"

"Yes. My husband's name is Donald Taheny."

"Yes, I see that." Dr. Anthony Carter was looking down at her file that the nurse had given to him at the front desk. He frowned for a moment and then shrugged.

"I've always kept my own name, Dr. Carter."

"A lot of women do." Carter nodded. "I'm just old-fashioned. Also, my father was a minister, so some things just carry over, but not all that much. Now I haven't much information here . . . what exactly is the problem?"

"I don't know exactly what the problem is." Britt expelled a short breath. "That's why I came."

"Well, it states possible infertility." He glanced again at the file before him. "You're what? Thirty-eight, almost thirty-nine."

"Yes. I've been a fool to wait this long. Just a fool. I should have known better." The woman before him looked so furious with herself that the doctor's expression softened.

"How long have you been trying?"

"At least eight . . . nine years. I put it down to stress." Britt shook her head. "I don't know how I could have been so colossally stupid."

Dr. Carter leaned back in his chair and watched her as she looked down at her hands while an expression of self disgust swept over her. "Don't feel bad, Miss Erikson. My wife didn't conceive for seven years after we started trying, and I never thought to have some tests done. And here I am an obstetrician and gynecologist. I just never thought . . ." He brought his arms to rest on the sides of his swivel chair. "Imagine that. It simply never occurred to me . . . finally we had tests done and she conceived. My wife was in her late thirties. I was older. That's why our daughters are so young." He shrugged, "But I have two lovely, healthy daughters. So . . . ?"

"I see . . . well, I do think something might be wrong. Maybe not, but even with artificial insemination . . ."

"Insemination? You went for that?"

"Yes, for almost a year."

"The sperm . . . ? Your husband's?"

"Yes. Most of the time." Britt lied. "He's often out of town. He's a reporter. But what does that matter?"

"It doesn't. I just thought . . ."

"That Donald might mind? He doesn't. Why should he? In any case, it didn't work. A few times I thought I might be pregnant. But I wasn't. Over the last few years, my periods have been erratic. I might have miscarried."

"But you've had no tests?"

"No, he should have tested me. Several times he was certain I was ovulating or starting to. It should have taken, but it didn't. And my periods became more erratic. That's why I thought it was probably stress."

"I see," Carter pursed his lips. "Well, I'll examine you, and then go from there."

Once the examination was completed, Carter asked her to dress and come back into his office. He was scribbling out some notes and a requisition slip when she came back into the room.

"Well, as you probably know, the examination showed nothing. Everything seems fine. But to be on the safe side I'm scheduling you for a hysterosalpingogram next week. My nurse will call you. Are you working now?"

"I'm returning at the beginning of April, but I can always change shifts if necessary."

"Good, and I think you should see an endocrinologist."

"Dr. Ashong?"

"Yes," he gave her a speculative look. "I refer my patients to her if there may be some hormonal problem."

Britt felt relieved. Finally she'd get some endocrine studies done. "Fine, Dr. Carter. When?"

"As soon as possible. She's busy, but I don't think there'll be a problem getting in to see her. My nurse will call her office, and they'll be in contact. Here's the requisition slip."

He handed her a slip for Dr. Julia Ashong indicating an endocrine profile. Tentative diagnosis, partial infertility.

"And I'll see you soon for the salpingogram. You should take some aspirin or Tylenol beforehand. It might help." He held the door for her. "It's too bad you didn't come sooner, Miss Erikson, but it's not too late. Don't look so glum."

"I'm not. But I need some answers. You understand?"

"Yes, I do."

"Good. Because without answers you blame everything else, even God. If there's something I'll understand, but I must know. Otherwise . . ." Britt shook her head.

"We'll find out . . . hopefully. If it can't be fixed, then at least you'll know."

"Yes, it's better to know," and she added softly, "I must know."

Carter nodded. "Yes, of course, it's best to know, I feel the same way."

When she arrived home, Britt thought about the interview. Carter wasn't such a bad fellow. They understood each other very well. He was brusque, but professional, thorough, and honest. She didn't need false hopes or dismissal. She needed the truth. Now if Dr. Ashong was as thorough and forthright, she'd know for a certainty where she stood within the very near future. She'd had to lie about the imaginary husband, an Irishman called Donald Taheny, and frequently absent news correspondent, but the twinge of conscience didn't last long. She thought about Roddy and the truth was just too convoluted to get into. To be honest with herself, she didn't understand it either, so how could she expect some poor doctor to unravel it and grasp the full extent of circumstantial misadventures. The bottom line was that there had been ample opportunity and all attempts had failed. She had tried despite what anyone thought to the contrary. Repeated attempts at adoption had failed too. The fiasco in Nepal was just another failure. Certainly not the first. She wondered what her father must be thinking of all this. Certainly now he would know everything. He felt so close and yet unreachable as if a veil had been drawn. The key had been lost; now he too was only a shade. It had been almost four months, and she still kept waiting for him to walk through the door. Just walk right in as if he'd only been away a short time and now was home again. Home again. The words rang in her ears like a repeated chorus. She too wanted herself to be home again. Once long ago she felt she had been very close to God. But that was when she'd been a child. The intervening years brought a distance that couldn't be bridged. That's what it meant to be an adult, living far away from home. The world was a lonely place. There was beauty all around you. It was also a troubled place inhabited by a dangerous, if often glorious species called man. Well, so much for ruminating, Britt concluded. If she couldn't shake off the sadness or loneliness that had come over her, she didn't have to indulge it either. She decided to study for a few hours. That always restored her equanimity. Then she'd go up and spend some time with her mother. Nora had been very attentive since her return from Toronto. She, on the other hand, felt a growing isolation from her family and that could only be her fault.

The course in Philadelphia turned out to be every bit as taxing as it was rumored to be. She arrived in the city late in the evening because there had been a stopover in Boston, and it was snowing heavily. By the time Terry picked her up at the airport and delivered her back to the home she and Walter had bought just outside the city in Byrn Mawr, it was late and by the look of her old friend Terry decided that a hot bath and bed was the best course by far. A long in-depth chat was definitely out of the question. So the conversation was kept light and both Walter and Terry urged her to go to bed.

Tomorrow would be a long day. And it was.

It was overloaded with information, and clearly it was expected that all those taking the course should be previously well acquainted with the material. The emergency room doctor giving most of the lectures was excellent as were all the paramedics who focused on initial assessment and steps in treatment. At the end of the day, they decided to break into groups and give each course member a run through. It was just a practice try, but true to form, instead of looking nervous which she most certainly was and assessing with paced deliberation and then activating practical measures accordingly, Britt went ahead rapidly and decisively. When she finished, she looked around apprehensively as the other students in the group remained silent and the paramedic shook his head.

"You fail. This is just a practice run, but if you do that tomorrow you'll fail . . . and you have to pass the practical as well as the written."

"But what . . .?" Britt felt her heart starting to pound. "What did I do wrong?"

"You didn't do anything wrong. Your assessments, both the primary and secondary were fine . . . so was the treatment, but you forgot the most important thing--oxygen high flow. That's a given in our situation."

"Of course, didn't I . . . ?"

"You have to say it. Delegate it or do it yourself. That's vital, and failing to mention it means failure." The paramedic looked to be gloating. He's enjoying himself, Britt thought, and she glanced over at the doctor in charge who looked kinder, but was shaking his head.

"He's right. First you check the breathing and even if breathing, you order oxygen high flow regardless of the type of trauma."

"Yes, all right. I just assumed . . ."

" . . . That your assistant clamped on the oxygen? Well, she didn't, and it was your responsibility. I'm sorry."

"Yes, regardless of what you do right, you can't do anything wrong, and," the paramedic added. "You can't omit anything vital. Remember that."

That evening Britt had little to say at supper.

"You look wiped-out" Terry commented.

Walter added, nodding, "Yes, you do. You're not going to study tonight, are you?"

"I have to, Walter. I still have to go over some sample test questions."

Terry frowned but said nothing. She knew from long experience that it was useless trying to reason with her friend when she had that look about her.

"Terry's taking Monday off, and I'll be at work all day." Walter winked at her. "Cheer up, Britt, you'll pass the damn course and then kick yourself for taking all this so seriously."

"Including myself," Britt grumbled and then laughed with them. The meal ended on a cheerful note.

All the same, she sequestered herself up in the guest room for the rest of the evening. When Terry went off to bed at eleven o'clock, she saw the light still on under the door. She tapped lightly and, receiving no answer, she opened the door and looked in. There were papers strewn all over the bed and the book was still clasped in her hands. She was sound asleep.

The following day was difficult, but it seemed the people on the course were learning to pace themselves and discard everything but the essentials, at least for the practical exam. There were five different examiners, and each candidate was called separately. When Britt's name was called she moved down the hall and stopped outside Room five. A different examiner greeted her. Cheryl began, "I'll give you the scenario first, then we'll go into the room. You're tested alone, as you know."

"How many assistants do I have?"

"As many as you want. Just remember, Britt, you must say everything you're doing. I know it's hard. You're used to doing what has to be done, but you must talk through everything you're doing. Okay?"

"Yes," Britt nodded, truly thankful that this examiner was so different and had a gift for putting people at ease.

"All right. Here's the call you receive. Several people have been taken hostages at gun point. They're in a room on the fifth story of a building. One of them is a young man, and he got nervous and jumped out the window. He was shot on the way down, during the fall. Have you got all that?"

Again Britt nodded. Jesus God, why not just call the mortician? She stifled a nervous reaction to laugh and stepped forward to open the door. Cheryl put her hand out, "Remember Britt, just take your time. You have a tendency to . . . to . . ."

"I'll slow down."

"That's it. Just go step by step."

She followed Britt into the room. It was over very quickly, and it went surprisingly well. Eventually she looked up from the multiple trauma victim who was still lying on the floor. A Student from the performing arts.

"That was fine," Cheryl was smiling at her. "I timed you. That was quick . . . into the ambulance, stabilized, and giving report to emergency within three minutes. Your assessment was thorough and your actions appropriate. You just forgot one thing."

"I did?" Britt looked back down at the victim lying so still. "What?"

"If you had asked him, he'd have told you he's a hemophiliac."

"You mean he's conscious!" Britt looked so astounded that Cheryl started to laugh.

"Yes, of course." She looked back down at the victim with the sucking chest wound, fractured radius, compound fracture of the right femur, and already in shock from heavy blood loss even with the two I.V.s running and shook her head, bewildered.

Cheryl laughed again. "Yes, I know . . . hard to believe. Anyway, you pass. You did everything that had to be done. Very good."

And that was that. It was over . . . all over. She felt so relieved, she could have collapsed. But she got up and reached down to pull up the victim who had been made up skillfully to look as if he'd really been through what they said had happened to him.

All the way back to Terry's she felt elated. Tired but triumphant.

"Now we can have some time to chat." Terry looked pleased when she heard the news. "This evening and all day tomorrow. I'm glad you passed it. I don't think you take to failure very well."

"Do you?" Britt asked her.

"No, that's why I seldom risk it."

The following day they went for a long walk. Terry asked about Edward, and Britt told her about the friendship, describing it as if from a distance, almost clinically.

"You know what your problem is," Terry observed. "You think too much."

"Maybe, but I still haven't decided what to do." Britt shrugged. "Right now I'm busy with other things."

"Well, he sounds nice. Why don't you give him a chance? What happened with Roddy, by the way?"

"Nothing really."

"Well, you went with him for quite a while. There must be something."

"Nope. He was and now he isn't. That's all."

"And you don't see him at all anymore?"

"No, but he's all right. Indirectly, I check up on him . . . make sure his health hasn't gotten worse."

"So you don't love him?"

"I thought I might, but he doesn't love me. He loves his family and a few boyhood friends. That's all. That's what he told me."

"Just like that?" Terry was frowning at her.

"Just like that." Britt shrugged. "Actually when I did ask whom he loved because his family, with the possible exception of his father, doesn't seem to give a damn about him, he didn't mention me at all."

"Well, he's been seriously ill for a long time, Britt."

"I know . . . better than anyone, I know. But it's not just the illness. It's Roddy. He simply doesn't love me."

"Well, you're taking it very . . . nonchalantly."

"What would you suggest? Gnashing my teeth?" Britt looked out of sorts and Terry was frankly frustrated with her.

"From you? Hardly. But you're madder than hell . . . about Roddy, about losing the kids . . . everything. And you're hurt. Whey don't you stop acting?"

Britt stopped walking and turned to her. "Because living is acting, and when it's ail over, it's important that you've turned in a good performance."

"Not true, my fiend, and you know it. Besides, I can see through it so . . ."

"So I'll have to clean up my act." Britt laughed.

"Indeed you will." Terry marched on ahead of her, and when Britt caught up with her, she asked hesitantly,

"So what about you and Walter? Don't you want children?"

"I don't mind either way, but Walter's cautious. It doesn't really matter to me. I'm not like you."

"I see."

"No, you don't." Terry shook her head. "I had an abortion years ago. . . before you came to Philadelphia to nurse. You know that. But now I'm married, and everything is reasonably in order. Fact is, I enjoy things as they are now, and a child would ruin that. I don't need or want to change my lifestyle. I'm very content." Britt stared at her, but said nothing. Terry knew she'd struck a nerve, a raw nerve lying dormant in some secret place that her friend would never willingly reveal to anyone.

"Very good, Terry." She said finally. "Ring down the curtain. The farce is over."

"But I'm not acting, Britt."

"Oh yes, you are. Only cows are contented."

Terry started to laugh and Britt joined her. "You're impossible, Britt, and that was insulting."

"I'm sorry."

"You're not a bit sorry, and how are people supposed to understand if you won't say?"

"Oh, it's not so hard. Just listen to what's not being said."

"I might as well try that," Terry shrugged. "What you're saying isn't making much sense . . . do you want some lunch? There's a really nice pub in Chestnut Hill, and it's on the way to the airport."

"Sounds good. I'm packed and ready."

All the way back home Britt thought about Terry and the idyllic life she shared with Walter. That's what it appeared to be. The storm she sensed brewing must be a conjuring trick of her imagination. In any case, Terry would stay married to Walter. Looking for happiness was a hobby with her. She was far too wise to consider pursuing it as a lifetime goal. She had opted for security and got it. And knowing Terry, she'd get much more. It was just a matter of time.

-Fifteen-

On Wednesday Britt returned to work. Her last two weeks in the Emergency Psychiatry Unit went quickly and without a hitch. She started studying for the advanced cardiac life support course that was just as difficult as the advanced trauma. It was being offered at another hospital in mid-May. As long as she kept occupied everything was under control.

Dr. Ashong's secretary called to set up an appointment for Friday morning of the following week, and following that, Dr. Carter's nurse rang to confirm with her Thursday morning at 9:00 a.m. for the salpingogram. To fit in the appointment Britt switched with a part-time nurse who was working the weekend.

Edward rang and she agreed to have dinner with him Friday evening. Halfway through the meal he bent toward her and frowned. "What's the matter with you?"

"Nothing, why?"

"You're so preoccupied and you've hardly eaten anything."

"I'm not very hungry." Britt had been picking at her food, and now she glanced up at him. "But it's very good . . . the food I mean."

"Yes, it is. Look, why don't we drive up to the Laurentians next Sunday?"

"I can't. I'm working."

"How about next Saturday then?"

"I'm working."

"Why is that? I thought you got alternate weekends off. Besides, it's Easter."

"Is it? I'd forgotten about that, but in any case I've got to work. After that, it's back to normal. Alternate weekends."

"In the main E.R.?"

"That's right."

"What days are you getting off?"

"Next Thursday and Friday."

"And of course, you're very busy those days, aren't you?"

"Yes. I'll be busy."

Edward sat back and folded his arms. "Britt, if you don't want to see me, why don't you just say so."

"I do want to see you. But next week is going to be busy. I'm sure you've had weeks like that."

"Well sure, but I get the feeling there's something else."

"Well there might be something else, but there's no one else." Britt smiled at him. "With you it's quite possibly the other way around."

"I've told you that's not true!"

"You know this is the first time I've seen you close to being angry."

"Well, keep watching. It gets better." He paused. "I went for those blood tests."

"Really . . . and?"

"They thought I was crazy."

"Why?"

"Because I haven't been with anyone in well over a year. And I was engaged to the woman. She's the only woman I've been with since my marriage ended."

"What happened?"

"I don't know. She left . . . went her own way."

"Did you love her?"

Edward nodded slowly. "Yes, I think so."

"So what do you want with me?"

His head jerked up. "You haven't given me much chance to find out have you?"

"No, I guess I haven't," Britt thought for a moment and bit at her lower lip. "You see, Edward, I'm tired of men who don't know what they want."

"I may love you, Britt. I'm not sure how I feel." Suddenly he smiled at her. "Besides, you said you wouldn't believe me if I said I loved you. Remember?"

"I remember."

"But I do want to know you better . . . and I don't mean in bed! After all, we're not teenagers with our hormones running amuck. On the other hand, I see no reason to live indefinitely as a monk either."

"No, that wouldn't be fitting would it?" Britt put her head back and laughed with sheer abandon.

Edward started to smile, but said seriously. "You know, that's the first time I've seen you really laugh, and I like the sound of it. I like the look of the woman too."

"Well, I used to laugh a lot more. You just caught me at a bad time. And timing is everything. That's what someone used to tell me when I was very young."

"He was a smart man, your father."

There was a long silence between them and then Britt muttered. "Yes, he was . . . shall we go?"

Edward took her back to his apartment and reassured her. "Don't worry. It's early. Only nine o'clock."

"I'm on the day shift, so . . ."

"I'll have you home by 10:30. You'll be in bed by eleven. How's that?"

"Fine."

And it was fine. By the time he dropped her at her apartment Britt was beginning to think she liked Edward Barrett very much. All the same, as she lay in bed gazing up at the ceiling and waiting for sleep to come, her thoughts were nettled on recent past losses that brought on a frightening feeling of losing her balance and toppling into a dark void. People lost their grip all the time, and she hated the fear she felt that it would happen to her. Wrenching herself away from the foggy landscape of remembering, she clung on to the new resolves she'd made and set into motion: the job change, the additional studying, the medical tests and examinations to be done. And perhaps a relationship with Edward would be fun and warm. She closed her eyes. Maybe it wouldn't sap her energy and give nothing in return. Who ever really knew what they wanted anyway? That special kind of love was rare. As rare as the strength it sprang from. Most people gravitated to love because of need. There just wasn't very much left over to give away freely. That was the truth, the sad and rather ugly truth. Her father used to say that love was nothing more than giving something precious away, and there was always a return, something bountiful and timeless. But he must have been thinking of the loveless and lost. A relationship had to be more than the dangerous and sometimes vicious interplay between the predator and the prey. In the end, Roddy had needed and resented her. It could only end the way it did. She hadn't pitied him as he might have imagined, and he could never believe, nor did he want to believe that someone might love him. Love to him was like being in debt. Well, there'd be no talk of love with Edward. No expectations and no losses on either side. Not this time.

The hysterosalpingogram was done in the X-ray department at the Queen Elizabeth Hospital. For the most part it was uncomfortable, but there were a few moments of deep internal pain as the fallopian tubes were inflated and brought into view on a side screen. Dr. Carter looked at her. "That hurt, I know, but it will be all right now." The radiologist was called in and gave instructions as he watched the monitor. Britt glanced up and saw that the tubes were patent.

"Everything looks in order," said Carter.

The radiologist nodded. "Yes, I'll check the films and send you my report."

Then he was gone. Dr. Carter finished up and then, before hurrying off to another appointment, he addressed Britt. "Everything looks in order. There'll be some bleeding for a few days. Don't worry about it. I'll call you next week when I have the radiologist's report."

When she was helped off the table by one of the nurses and stood up, the blood gushed from her uncontrollably. "Oh God, I'm sorry." Britt looked around, uncertain what to do about the stained floor.

"Don't worry about that. Here." The nurse handed her pads and put another gown around her. "There's a bathroom just over there and your clothes are in the cubicle. It connects. Are you all right? Can you make it?"

"Yes, fine." Britt nodded. "I'll be fine."

The appointment with Dr. Julia Ashong took quite a while. She examined her thoroughly, did a neuro check and ordered a round of blood work, some to be done that same day and the rest the following week early on a morning when she'd fasted. On Monday, she was due to report in Main E.R., but this took priority. When she got home around noon she called Heather Donovan and told her she would be reporting to work late.

Being oriented to the general emergency was a most unpleasant experience. It was a madhouse which Britt had expected, but more to the point, the staff was, for the most part, a nasty lot. From experience, she knew the nursing staff could be irritating, but she hadn't expected to meet up with downright rudeness, impatience, and delusions of superiority. Nothing went right, and nothing she did was fast enough, efficient enough, or close enough to their pattern of behavior. Heather Donovan assigned Mary Lussier to orient her. Mary huffed and puffed and bustled about from the start of a shift to its finish. She always looked busy and harried even when eating her lunch. She also gave orders; half a dozen things to do at one time. There was a large French clique of nurses, and a few of them were difficult, if not impossible, to get along with. In a stubborn refusal to be cowered by them, Britt walked away when they gave report in French and kept herself aloof and dangerously quiet. Several separate incidents brought her temper to boiling point. The first occurred during her second week. With the ever present Mary who watched rather than worked with a nurse she was orienting. Britt was doing a re-assessment of a patient only to find his blood pressure so low he was going into shock. She straightened up and reached over to find a radial pulse. "His B.P. is seventy systolic."

Mary looked down at the patient. "Have you got a pulse?"

"I'm doing it," Britt muttered. "Turn the I.V. up."

"We can't do that. We . . ."

"Yes, do it."

"He's on antibiotics."

"Doesn't matter. Just open the main line. It's beside you."

"I'll ask the doctor." She hurried off to the main desk that was in close enough range to call over. Britt grumbled and looked up to find a doctor craning her neck to see down the row of beds.

"Do you want the I.V. up? He's seventy systolic?"

The doctor nodded. "Yes, open it. I'm coming."

Mary was caught in the middle of the exchange, but Britt was fuming as the doctor came to the bed and looked at her as if she was a moron. Any fool knew enough to turn up an I.V. when a patient was going into shock. Other steps could be taken later.

A second time Britt was ready to choke the ubiquitous Mary was when she interrupted her while she was doing an initial assessment on a patient. She barged into the cubicle and demanded to know if she couldn't hurry it up. They had no time to waste. Britt spun around and glared at her.

"I'm trying to get some information. Do you mind?"

"You can't take so long." Mary complained.

"I've only been in here a few minutes."

"We've got so much to do."

"Then go and do it!" Britt turned back to the patient and Mary left the cubicle. Fortunately she didn't see much of her for the rest of the morning.

The final straw, however, was literally getting pushed out of the way while she was standing at the desk making out some requisition forms. She was in no mood, therefore, for a companionable chat with the Head Nurse and Nurse Clinician near the end of her second week. She sat perfectly still while they pointed out that she had to speed it up, spend less time assessing patients, and do her charting at the main desk where she could keep an eye on things in general -- like the other nurses.

"So you think I'm too slow?" Britt's voice was low and tense, and she never took her eyes off the acting head nurse.

"I didn't say that," Heather balked.

"But that's what you were told. Right?"

"We're just trying to help you." The nurse clinician came in. "You're a good nurse. We can see that."

"But I'm too slow." Britt repeated and felt ready to explode.

"You could be faster. This isn't like . . ."

"And bustle around purportedly getting more done like that lot out there? I don't think so, Heather."

"Well, you've only been here under two weeks, so . . ."

"So, you'd better put me on evenings."

"Yes, that's next and with another nurse, Colleen Hannon."

"Fine. Is that everything?"

"Yes." Heather nodded and was relieved when she left the room. She turned to the clinician. "That one's trouble, Sylvie. I was warned about her."

"Who were you talking to?"

"Sandy Kellermann from Nursing Education. Britt Erikson taught the C.P.R. in her unit last summer. She's clever but can be difficult to handle."

"She'll be fine." Sylvie moved her head from side to side considering it. "Maybe evenings will go better."

"I hope so. That's what she wants . . . permanent evenings. The official head nurse will be coming in Monday. I've got to orient her. Now I'm assistant head nurse."

Sylvie stood up. "She . . . your newest employee, had something to say about that too."

"What?"

"She said it was totally unfair. I guess Tom Flynn told her something about what's going on here. She goes over there on her breaks and uses their lounge. She has friends . . ."

"The natives are friendlier over there . . . at least they think they are."

"Well, we've got a good staff too. Britt keeps away from the staff. I don't see anything they're doing wrong."

"Maybe." Heather thought about it. "Maybe not. We'll have to wait and see."

Evenings did go much better and Colleen Hannon turned out to be a vast improvement over Mary Lussier. There was a little more camaraderie, and the atmosphere was friendlier, at least in part. But a large number of staff rotating from days made working there hellish. Finally someone got around to introducing her to the new head nurse. Britt looked up a little bemused and took the hand extended to her.

"You mean your name is Heather too?"

"Yes, Heather Shaffer."

Britt glanced over the head nurse's shoulder and found Heather Donovan looking on. The expression on her face held everything that needed saying and much more. It was an ironically funny situation, but Britt managed to keep a straight face. Besides, she did feel sorry for Donovan even though she made no attempt whatsoever to make things any easier for her in the unit.

Before too long Britt got tired of the whole sordid affair. She was sitting in Tom Flynn's office and looking thoroughly disgusted with the turn of events.

"They've got me back on days for some kind of extended orientation."

"Why?" Tom was writing and didn't look up. "What's the reason?"

"I don't know. I think patients have to be assessed and sometimes you have to talk to them a little."

Tom stopped writing and glanced up at her. He started to grin. "Now, I warned you about them, didn't I? But would you listen . . . ? No. Besides, I hear the new head nurse isn't too good . . . not too popular either."

"Oh, I don't know," Britt mused. "She seems all right. You can be damn sure they won't make it easy for her. And what's wrong with Donovan anyway? She lets administration walk all over her and then makes it difficult for the one taking over. That's sick."

"I don't know. She should resign, but well . . . call it survival."

"Call it cowardice."

"No, Britt. She's a really nice person."

"I don't know, Tom. Sometimes it's just easier to stay on and bitch about things."

"Like you?" He teased.

Britt scowled at him. "I need more E.R. experience."

"You have enough. The Osler Memorial downtown might take you on. I know Lucy Maxwell. She hires for the specialty areas."

"Really? Well, maybe I will."

"Sure. Why not? I hear they have a nice emergency."

That same afternoon Britt made her decision. Once again they were at her for writing up assessments in the cubicles, spending too much time with patients, avoiding the main desk where the majority of nurses buzzed around.

"We're only trying to help you." Heather Shaffer tried to apply some soothing psychology.

"Help me!" Britt spat out the words and looked so contemptuous of her that Heather became uncomfortable.

"Yes, tell us what we can do to help you." The mild mannered Sylvie urged her.

Britt turned to her and knew for a certainty that she could never trust this woman any more than the humble Heather Donovan who was nowhere to be seen.

"You have done nothing to help me," she said through partially clenched teeth. "Nothing. You made things worse."

She got up and left the office.

The next day, she called Lucy Maxwell at Osler Memorial and sure enough they had openings in Emergency. She set up an appointment to meet with her the following day before reporting for the evening shift. It was all arranged very quickly. She'd give notice at her present employment and start at the Osler E.R. at the beginning of June.

"I don't know," her mother said to her one morning. "What makes you think it'll be any better?"

"Because it couldn't be worse." Britt answered her.

"This is my last shift in that zoo with those orangutans. It's bound to be a pleasant one."

It was anything but pleasant. She was assigned to the observation room with another nurse whom she knew well enough to keep away from. She was sour-faced, officious and offensive. Taking an early break, Britt strolled down the hall to the lounge in Emergency Psychiatry. Jocelyn was there having a cigarette and Daphne came in while they were smoking and chatting. She flopped into a chair and addressed Britt.

"Isn't this your last evening?"

"Yup." Britt expelled a cloud of smoke. "Can't you tell?"

"You do look relaxed." Jocelyn peered at her. "Where are you anyway? Out front?"

"No, in observation, and it's full. I'm working with Marie-Paule."

"Oh that one!" Jocelyn grimaced. "I don't know her well, but . . . "Neither do I." Daphne interrupted. "What's she like?"

"Well, if she lives through the evening, you can add a new chapter to Lamentations."

Jocelyn roared with laughter. "What's she done now?"

"Nothing yet." Britt got up. "I'd better get back."

When she got back, she found Marie-Paule rechecking the orders that she'd already done before leaving.

"What are you doing? Those are my patients. Are you checking up on me?"

"No, of course not!" Marie-Paule looked flushed. "We always go through the orders twice."

"Like hell you do. See to your own lot."

She started to walk away and was across the room at a patient's bed when she heard her co-worker grumbling and muttering.

"I don't know what's wrong with you."

"Wrong with me!" Britt raised her voice and lashed out at her. "You ask what's wrong with me? You've been abominable to me since I came here . . . Yes, you! Just go about your own work and leave mine to me. Stay out of my way!"

All the patients heard the exchange. The man she was standing beside grinned up at her. "Give her hell."

"I've never yelled at another nurse before," Britt muttered.

"Feels good, don't it?" The old man chuckled, "A good fight clears the air."

From that moment on Marie-Paule changed her attitude. She was much more pleasant, even friendly. She requested first supper and got it so she wasn't there when the head nurse came around. Britt was at the desk filling out some requisitions, and she had a paper clip held between her lips. She reached awkwardly for the clip and managed a smile.

"Are you still here? It's after six."

"I know." Heather nodded. "I'm leaving now."

"Well, everything's fine in here."

"I heard you were busy."

"We are, but at the moment, it's quiet."

"So I see." Heather looked around the room. "I wanted to say good-bye." She held out her hand and Britt took it.

"I'm very sorry about all this, Heather."

"No, it's okay." She shook her head and started to walk away. "Good luck."

All at once the woman seemed tired and worried. Her day too had been a struggle and now she knew what she was up against. She wasn't wanted or accepted in her new position as head of emergency. Apparently Heather Donovan had a curious and rather viciously underhanded way of fighting back.

Edward picked her up at the end of her shift which kept her in E.R. past midnight.

"You look tired, Britt."

"I am."

"Then I'll just drop you off."

"No, come in. You can have a drink or some tea?" Britt paused and then added. "I couldn't sleep right away anyhow."

Working at the Osler Memorial E.R. was much better, especially when she started on evenings. They had permanent people on that shift, and once part of the team, she came to know them quickly, and they worked well together. Disputes were settled quickly, and any animosities were lanced like boils before they festered. Just prior to coming on staff, Britt completed the Advanced Cardiac course. It was a chaotic weekend demanding weeks of advance study, but it was worth it, she supposed. By the middle of June, she received a letter in the mail from the endocrinologist's office. On a diagnostic form, Dr. Ashong wrote that her prolactin level was slightly elevated, and she wanted her to go for pituitary function test. Britt stuffed the form back into its envelope and put it in her handbag. She was on her way to work. Thinking about it all the way down to the hospital, no immediate connection came to mind. As for the test itself -- well, she'd never seen it done and had absolutely no idea what went on. Once in the cluttered and claustrophobic lounge area just off the E.R. and where staff members were bustling in and out, she tried to do a bit of investigating. The books were arranged helter-skelter and chained to the wall. She ended up cursing and trying to disengage a large volume on Internal Medicine. She started tracing up elevated levels of prolactin and that led to the pituitary gland. That all important master gland in the brain. Yes, she remembered now. It was just one of the hormones secreted by the anterior pituitary. She kept up the chase for information until they were calling for her in E.R. They were ready to give report.

Report was long and tedious and, much to her later embarrassment, she didn't hear a word of it. Remi, who was usually in charge on evenings, turned around and snapped her fingers.

"What's the matter with you? You look in a daze."

"Nothing." Britt leaned back against the counter. "I wish the day staff would just go home."

"So do I. But you know what it's like."

"Yeah, bedlam."

"They'll soon be gone. Why don't you start the I.V. on that one in cubicle four, and we'll need some blood cultures."

Britt frowned at her. "Where's his chart?"

"You really weren't listening, were you? Here." She handed her the chart. "Nausea and vomiting N.Y.D."

"Oh yes, he's the one with the temperature." Britt rubbed a hand across her eyes. "He'll need vitals done too. Might as well do it all in one shot."

"Right. That'll keep you out of the way for at least twenty minutes. And I'll clean house around here."

"All right." Britt turned away and almost collided into Dr. Nadia Strasberg. Her hands and the large apron she'd thrown over her lab coat were splattered with plaster of paris. "Oh, you're on. Good."

"Yes, but I need Pierre."

"I'm right here." The E.R. nursing assistant came up behind her. "You need some help?"

"Yes, in the cast room." She headed off back down the hall with Pierre.

Well good, Britt thought. She liked Strasberg who appeared arrogant and aloof at times when she was nervous or felt overwhelmed. She could identify with the young doctor's initial reaction to staff. And nurses could be so damnably obnoxious, every bit as bad if not worse than some doctors. A hospital could be a cutthroat, cruel place which seemed odd considering its reason for being. But Britt had few illusions left on that score. From doctors and nurses alike she'd seen fear, resentfulness, back-biting and pettiness. Status was everything and everyone wanted status. Did she? Of course. She had to admit that. But the cost in personal values was just too high. That's why she kept returning to teaching where you worked independently. At least no one had ever bothered her. If other teachers felt intimidated by administration or the board that was their problem. Not hers.

All these stormy thoughts were going through her head while she worked with the patient, smiling at him intermittently and listening to his mangled account of how he came to be in emergency. Finally the I.V. was in, two separate sets of blood cultures done and extra vials of blood drawn for a CBC and Smac just in case.

"Your fever's down a bit," she told the middle-aged man, and he bunched up his lips, taking it all very gamely.

"They think it might be my gall bladder."

"I know."

"So will I have to stay down here?"

"I don't know," Britt told him frankly. "They're not sure what it is. The blood results aren't back yet, and we're still waiting for the X-rays . . . but no supper. Okay?"

"Yes, yes." The fellow nodded grumpily. "Nothing to eat or drink. How long?"

"Not too long. Lay back now and rest."

"Rest . . . !" He smacked his lips. "How can anyone rest in here? Always getting poked at."

"All done." Britt spread out her hands. "And it's quiet now." She looked around the emergency room. True to her word, Remi had cleaned house. There were just as many patients and more waiting, but the place now had some semblance of order.

She found Nadia back at the main desk writing out some notes. Remi had gone off to do something, and there was no one else about. She decided to ask her about a high prolactin level.

"Well, there are a number of possible causes." Dr. Stasberg turned toward her. "You know that. Why?"

"Well, I'm going for some tests . . . possible infertility."

"You want to get pregnant?"

"Yes, and I have an elevated prolactin level. So . . ."

"So you can't get pregnant."

"No, I can't, but high prolactin accounts for failure to conceive."

"Yes, that could do it."

"I need to know possible causes."

Nadia thought about it. "Have you checked the reference books?"

"I started to. The text on Internal Medicine, but it's a bit muddled and all over the place."

"Oh, it's there. Come on." Nadia got up and headed for the lounge just around from the main desk area. She noted the book left on top that had been marked.

"Let's try another text. This one's better."

She pulled out a newer addition on Internal Medicine and found a succinctly written list of causes for elevated prolactin--just a straightforward outline of possible etiologies with pages of information and explanatory passages to follow.

"Here." Nadia pointed along the skeleton outline of causes. "It could be stress. That's usually it."

"That's usually it for everything." Britt grumbled, remembering that she'd put everything down to stress. And why not? The pituitary was connected with the hypothalamus that opened and closed doors to human emotion. The endocrine system, the circulatory system -- all of them.

"And look here, breast stimulation." Nadia was pointing in the book and laughing.

". . . causes increased secretion of prolactin."

"Very funny. They mean breast feeding mothers. Keeps prolactin up. No wonder it's a good old form of birth control. Not fail proof, but . . ."

"Fairly effective." Nadia nodded.

"Weird that I never made the connection before."

Britt was leaning closer, scanning the list, discarding some of the far-flung causes that would most likely have nothing to do with her and stopped at the last on the list--adenoma in the anterior pituitary. "A tumor?" She looked at Nadia who inclined her head.

"Well, it's not all that common, but some women do get these microadenomas."

"Well, how long would it have been there? Wouldn't it grow?"

"It could be there for some time," Nadia shrugged. "There's no telling. But that's probably not the case. It's highly unlikely, probably just stress."

Britt took the book from her and rested it in her lap as they sat on the couch. She leafed through for a fuller explanation and glanced hurriedly through some of the data.

"Headaches . . ." She stared down and read rapidly.

"Do you get headaches?" Nadia asked, glancing at her.

Britt looked up and away from her. "Yes, I get headaches."

Strasberg was silent for a few minutes and then got up. "It's probably stress. If you want a baby take six months off and try to get pregnant."

"Six months! That's not very feasible."

"Well, it'll get you what you want maybe." Nadia put down her coffee cup and headed from the room. "I've got to get back."

"Yeah, so do I." Britt's lips compressed into a straight line.

She found a marker and placed it in the book, resolving to get back to all this material, especially the section on adenoma of the anterior pituitary--what it meant in consequences and treatment. Delightful suppertime reading, Britt mused. But Nadia wasn't telling her everything, and it was senseless to worry over something that might well not be the problem at all. Probably wasn't. After all, she was healthy except . . . except what? She hadn't felt really well or free of headaches for a long time. And there had been weight loss, and she was tired--so tired much of the time. Except, of course, when on the job, but even then she often appeared drained and people were starting to comment. Only lately. Recently it had become more noticeable and detected by very few. But it was all due to stress. She wasn't eating properly or sleeping well. Things hadn't turned out quite the way she wanted. Being a poor loser was very stressful. One had to learn to live with the odd twists of fate. That's what she told herself. You just picked yourself up and kept moving . . . changing. Stagnation terrified her, always had. Well, really sick people were waiting in the emergency. So what the hell was she doing wasting time over turbulent thoughts that wouldn't get anyone very far?

Nevertheless, the data was all there, and slowly over the next few weeks she'd piece it all together. Before she went for the pituitary function test, she'd find everything there was to be found in these reference books about what might well not be.

-Sixteen-

June was a hectic month for everyone. Nora had decided to move up to Ottawa. Mary thought it a wise move too. It was time to get out of Quebec with its oppressive language laws, prohibiting English signs and the usage of anything but French in public places, except when one pointedly opened a conversation in English. Even that was dicey, and certainly no government employee was required to speak anything but French. Many didn't comply, but a number did. Too many, in fact . . . and the Anglo community was divided in the response to open threats of being fired or fined. Most wanted to play it safe. Their protests were sugar-coated and wrapped in attractive silver-tongued whining and wincing. Who could blame them really? They had everything to lose . . . the dwindling numbers still remaining. Problem was--they'd lost already. They were living in Quebec on borrowed time, and they knew it even as they denied it. So Mary was going as well. Nora used a large percentage of the settlement she received and Mary matched it. Together they made a sizeable down payment on a duplex in Ottawa. Nora took the large downstairs flat, and there was a comfortable apartment for Mary upstairs.

"I think it's a good idea," Britt told her mother one morning. "You'll like Ottawa and Rourke's not far away. Besides, you can always come to Montreal for visits. It's close and yet safely over the border."

"You're leaving too aren't you?" Mary looked expectantly at her daughter. Britt hadn't mentioned anything about having more tests done.

"Yes, well . . ."

"You did accept the contract to teach out west?"

"I did, yes. You know that."

"So you're going . . ."

"I suppose so."

Mary gave her a speculative glance. "You do want to go, don't you?"

"I guess so." Britt nodded uncertainly.

"Well, I should think so. What's here for you? You have friends, of course, and Edward What's-his-name . . ."

"Barrett, Mother. Edward Barrett. What's the matter? Don't you like him?"

"I only met him a few times. He seems all right. Do you like him very much?"

"Yes, I like him . . . But I haven't measured it, so . . ."

"You know what I mean. He's divorced, isn't he? Has he proposed anything?"

"Like marriage? No. As for divorced . . . I guess he must be. He's been separated from his wife for years. She lives up in Ontario. They have a teenage daughter, around fourteen."

"Well then, if you like him, and you must because he's around so much, why not marry him?"

"He hasn't asked me. Besides, I'm not sure I want anything permanent right now."

"Yes, you do." Mary looked at her with annoyance. "Why lie to yourself? You've wanted it since this relationship got serious. Serious means marriage."

"Not always, Mother."

"With you . . . always." Mary was shaking her head. "You're fooling yourself. It's just the way you are, and that's not a bad thing."

"Nowadays it is. More marriages are splitting up than staying together."

"Well, marry him anyway."

"Like I said . . . he hasn't asked."

"Then don't stay here on his account. Don't stay on any account. Get out. It's an ugly situation here now and likely to get worse. It grates on the nerves. Almost everyone, the English, I mean, and even some of the smarter French have gone. And why shouldn't they? Who needs this bother on top of everything else?"

"Yes, who needs it?" Britt echoed her mother's words.

"Still, it galls me that we didn't fight back." She added.

"It's not worth fighting for. Nothing is."

"I don't agree. People have to fight back. You don't just let things happen. There's too much of that going on. If you let people step on your rights, pretty soon you won't have any rights."

"Well, there are better things to fight for. It's just not worth it."

"That's what they said about Hitler, not just in Germany but everywhere else too. And look what happened."

"You always go back to that."

"It's true and the same principle applies here. We just move out or pretend if we ignore it long enough, it'll go away. Well, it won't."

"And what would you suggest?"

"Well, we built a lot of this city: major hospitals, universities, schools, homes, and we can take them down."

"That's crazy talk. Doing damage never did any good. And what if someone died or got hurt? What then? Would it still be worth it?"

"No, but no one needs to get hurt. That would be needless."

"It wouldn't solve a thing, Britt, and there's no point in endangering lives. I don't believe it's worth one human life."

"No, I don't either. But if we have to go and we do, we should take what's ours. One way or another. Then if they want what's left all to themselves so badly, they can have it. Mostly rubble." Britt got up and refilled the tea cups. "Now maybe that's insane . . . ludicrous, but there's a very fine line and they crossed it. They're wrong now. Every bit as wrong as they were right to fight for changes years ago. I didn't move here. I was born here. So were you . . . going back generations. And I've a right to use my own language with impunity. As for the government, well it's a disgrace. So is the federal government for that matter. Mental cretins, the lot of them."

"No, they're very clever really." A look of contempt changed Mary's expression from one of sadness to bitterness. "Watch them pull a magic rabbit out of a hat come election time. The economy's in a bad way, and they can't fix it. It's gone on too long."

"That's right," Britt nodded. "It's all gone on too long. And they keep blathering on about reviving it while taxes go up, prices soar and unemployment climbs. Pretty picture, isn't it?"

"That's why you should take that job out west. It's secure, and you'll make double what you're making now."

"I know . . . One thing at a time, Mother."

"There's absolutely nothing to keep you here," Mary concluded and changed the subject. She wanted to fill-in her daughter on her plans for moving around the same time as Nora . . . at the end of the month.

Edward turned up late in the afternoon. It was Sunday, and Britt had spent much of the morning and early afternoon helping her mother pack. Nora had much more to do because she was a collector. Passing up a bargain just wasn't in her nature. As a result her cupboards and every other available space were stocked to overflowing. It would all come in handy someday, she figured, and nothing should go to waste. In the meantime, Aaron and Ruth trotted from one apartment to the next trying to help and managing only to get in the way.

Finally when Britt did glance at her watch she frowned and swore. Mary turned around.

"What's the matter?"

"I've got to go." Her hands were black from wrapping glassware in newspaper, and it was smeared across her cheek. "Edward's due any time now."

"Well, I think we did very well for one day."

"You've got lots of time, Mother. All next weekend."

"You're working next weekend."

"But I'm off on Wednesday and Thursday. Don't worry about it . . . Now I've got to hurry." She looked down at herself. "God, I'm a mess."

"Yes, you are."

Britt shrugged and headed for the door. Ruth trailed after her. She had just got into her apartment when Edward came knocking at the door.

"How'd you get in?"

"One of your neighbors was just going out while I was coming in. What happened to you?"

"Oh, just packing."

"What are you packing . . . stove pipes?" He looked around. "Who's leaving? Not you!"

"No, my mother and sister. I told you that."

"Yes, you did. Well . . ."

"I'll get washed and dressed." Ruth was tugging at her skirt and eyeing the stranger. Britt looked down at her. "And you, my love, are going upstairs so I can get ready."

She scooped the child up in her arms and brought her upstairs. By the time she got back downstairs, Edward was pacing the living room floor. He kissed her lightly on the lips and then started to laugh. "You do look funny, Britt."

"It's that damn newspaper print . . . gets over everything. You're all dressed up. Where are you going?"

"I told you. Dinner and then to a concert . . . It starts at seven. We haven't much time."

"Why not just go to the concert first?"

"Because after the concert I've got other plans." He came closer to her. "And so do you."

"Don't be presumptuous, Edward."

"I'm not, but being clandestine takes some maneuvering. And we don't get much time together. Not enough to suit me anyhow."

"All right. Make yourself a drink. I won't be long."

Edward made himself a cup of tea and picked up the book that Britt was reading. When she reappeared twenty minutes later, showered and dressed in a white linen suit, he looked up a bit dazed and stood up.

"You look lovely."

"Thank you. I guess we'd better go."

He inclined his head slowly, fixing his eyes on her.

"Yes."

All through dinner he seemed preoccupied, and they kept the conversation light. Once at the concert hall near Loyola College, Britt didn't know what to expect. When she'd asked Edward about it, his answers had been vague. The place was swarming with kids and well dressed, eager looking parents. She turned to him as they entered the hall.

"What's all this?"

"It's the annual concert, Britt. Several of my students will be playing as well as those of other music teachers."

"Why didn't you tell me?"

"I thought you wouldn't come. Do you mind coming very much?"

"Not at all . . . are they any good?"

"The ones playing tonight? Yes. You'll see." He took her arm and led to a seat reserved in the front row.

"I have to be backstage, and I'm accompanying a few of the students." He hurried off and a few minutes later the hall was full and the house lights dimmed coinciding with gradual illumination of the stage.

Britt thoroughly enjoyed the concert, and apparently so did the parents. Afterwards, Edward introduced her to the other teachers and several of the students.

"Let's go." He whispered in her ear. "They're talking about going out for a drink, but I'd rather be gone. How about you?"

"Where to?" Britt whispered back.

"My place."

Edward's apartment was dimly lit and cozy. Obviously, he'd gone to great trouble creating just the right atmosphere. Since it was warm, he poured them out gin and tonic, and this time Britt didn't refuse, a good possibility of developing a headache notwithstanding. She had brought along some medication for any such eventuality. They sipped at their drinks, and Edward loosened his tie. He put his feet up on the coffee table and leaned his head against the back of the chesterfield.

"You know I'm always glad when it's over. I worry about the students pulling through, but most of all I worry about getting up there on stage myself."

"I thought you played beautifully . . . not that I'm any connoisseur."

"It's good enough for me. Thank you, dear."

"And you do play with the symphony, don't you?"

"Oh yes. First or second violin. Never solo. I'm buried up there. I just haven't got what it takes."

Britt put her arm around him. "Don't be so hard on yourself."

"I'm not. Just fixing my limitations. It's not lacking talent. It's something else."

"What?"

"Never mind." He took the near empty glass out of her hand and started to caress her. Later lying in bed beside her, he stared up at the ceiling as if it were a curiosity piece and could foretell the future.

"We do have fun together, don't we Britt?"

"Yes, we do."

"I love you. You know that."

"No, I don't, and I warned you about that."

"I'm serious, Britt." He turned her face toward him.

"Don't make fun of it, and don't say you don't believe me either."

"What do you want me to say?"

"Well, how do you feel about me?"

Britt sighed. "I honestly can't say, Edward. I don't know where we're headed."

"Someday we'll be married. I promise. We'll be really together. I want that."

"That's an odd way to put it." She frowned. "If we did want to get married . . . why someday?"

"Well I . . ." he stopped suddenly. "It's just going to take a little time."

"Are you worried about how your daughter might feel?"

"Yes, that's my main worry," Edward nodded, trying to think how he could get what he wanted and yet not jeopardize what he had. "Kids are funny. After all, Sophie is her mother."

"Well yes, but hasn't your wife thought of remarrying? After all, she's free and still quite young."

There was a protracted silence between them and then Edward told her. "She's not free. She doesn't want to be. We're not divorced."

"Not divorced!" Britt sat up and stared down at him. "But you said it was never much of a marriage and she was away . . . living up in Ontario."

"She is away, and it isn't much of a marriage. She's just never wanted out of it." He looked away from her. "I wish she'd meet another man. It would make things so much easier."

"You're not still sleeping with her are you?"

"Not very often."

"Oh God!" This time Britt turned completely away from him and started to get out of bed. He pulled her back.

"Don't, Britt. It doesn't mean anything. It's not like with us."

"But she's your wife, and you're still with her . . . you have been all along, even if it is only sporadic."

"It doesn't mean anything." Edward was looking very upset now. "It's just something she expects."

"And you oblige her!"

"I haven't much choice."

"Of course you have a choice."

"No. Mention divorce to her, and she'll scream bloody murder, and then what'll happen with my daughter? Sophie's her mother."

"This is crazy. I assumed it was over between you two."

"It is over! I keep telling you that. And it's been over for years." Britt shook her head. "But it's not over, and you're not free."

"It will be. I promise it will be, and we'll be together."

As he drove her home through the dark streets with the lamp lights making shadows dance in the swaying foliage on trees in full leaf, Britt wondered at her own stupidity, and small doubts became giant obstacles.

Edward was in a totally different sort of dilemma. He'd been unhappy for many years. Too many, and he craved the happiness he had now. At the same time, he was vulnerable to Sophie. Through her, he could lose his daughter, and his wife could ruin him in other ways too. Her family and the friends they had in common. His position as a reputable music teacher. Britt would never understand what he was up against. She wouldn't wait for him either. Not for very long. They were both very quiet. Just before he parted with her at the front door to her apartment building, he bent toward her urgently.

"You must give me a little time, Britt. I'll straighten it out. Believe me, my marriage is over. It's been over for a long time."

Britt looked up at him. "You're still with her . . . sleeping with her. It doesn't matter how seldom."

"I won't. If it bothers you that much. I won't. Just don't walk out on me. You're the first woman I've ever really wanted."

"You'll have to do something, Edward. This is your decision alone. I didn't create this mess. You told me . . ."

"I told you the truth. There's nothing meaningful between Sophie and me. Just give me a little time. And I need you now . . . Now more than ever. Please, don't back away from me now."

"You have some time Edward, but not a whole lot. Very soon I'm getting on with my life with or without you."

Britt kept her word. They remained intimate, but both knew they were working against time. Although she said little further on the matter, Edward sensed that much was going on with her and plans were being made that would be carried out unless he made a complete break with Sophie. He felt desperate and found himself unable to move decisively in any direction.

In the meantime, June came to a close. Nora and her mother moved up to Ottawa and got settled in. Rourke was on hand to help them when they got to Ottawa. Britt got the day off and helped them pack the truck in Montreal. Nora loaded the car with the most breakable items and followed the truck. In another car, Britt with her mother and Aaron and Ruth in the back seat completed yet another small entourage of Quebec exiles. Late that night only Britt returned to Montreal. She had other matters to settle. On Wednesday morning she was scheduled for the pituitary function test at the Royal Victoria Hospital, and although there was no way of knowing what the reaction would be or how the results would turn out, it was ironically not reassuring to know that a nurse remained with the patient throughout the procedure which took up a full morning. She also knew what they were going to do. She was well informed and that was a help. Yes, it helped considerably.

Nine o'clock Wednesday morning, she presented herself at the hospital, filled in the required forms downstairs, and then went up to the spacious looking lab with several hospital beds in a large room off the main desk. There were no other occupants in the bright room, and the nurse directed her to a bed near the large window. She had everything set up. A hospital gown was not required, but she rolled up the sleeve of her jacket and stretched out on the bed as the second nurse indicated.

"Are you cold?" The nurse was adjusting her arm to insert the butterfly needle and tape it in place.

"Yes, a little."

"So am I. It's always cold in here." She looked up. "Judy, get another blanket, would you?" Then she turned back.

"You haven't eaten, have you?"

Britt shook her head. The I.V. was inserted and connected to a small tubing so that blood samples could be drawn at short intervals. Then the injections through the I.V. began--three separate hormones. Thyroid Releasing Hormone, Luteinizing Releasing Hormone and finally, Insulin measured according to body weight. The hormones, all meant to stimulate the pituitary, were given at intervals and blood samples taken after each. The nurse continued asking, "How do you feel?"

And Britt's reply was the same. "All right."

"You don't feel any reaction?"

"No. I'm just cold."

They piled more blankets on her. When it came to the insulin, she allowed a few moments to elapse and then drew a sample and tested it. "How do you feel?"

"Okay."

She waited a few more minutes, drew another sample, and tested it.

"How about now?" The nurse asked looking down at the result.

"I'm still fine."

The nurse frowned. "You must feel something."

"No." Britt looked at her and then craned her neck to see.

"Lie back. Your blood sugar's dropping."

"I know that. What is it?"

"1.6 and you're still dropping." The nurse looked at her worriedly expecting some kind of reaction.

"Do you feel light-headed? Anything?"

"No, do you want me to sit up?"

"No. Lie still." She took another sample.

"What is it now?" Britt looked over at her curiously.

"1.4." The nurse's mouth compressed in a straight line. "1.2 . . . You must feel something." She was standing right beside the bed.

"No, I just feel a bit warm now . . . these blankets."

Suddenly several of the blankets were removed, and the nurse was holding a plastic container of orange juice before her heavily loaded with sugar.

"Here, drink this if you still can."

"Of course I can." Britt took the cup from her hands and downed it.

"And another one." The nurse handed her another cup which she drank more slowly.

"All right. Just lie back. Stay in bed. Don't get up until I'm back in the room."

Britt nodded and closed her eyes for a few moments. Now she was cold again. The nurse was in and out at short intervals. She wanted to sleep, but couldn't, and that was unfortunate because she had to start her shift at three-thirty.

"Can I get up now?" she asked finally.

"Yes." The nurse came over to Britt's side of the bed, but she was already up and slipping on her shoes.

"Now, can I leave?"

"Oh no." The woman about her age was shaking her head. "Lunch is coming and you must eat before leaving."

"But I'm all right, and I don't live far."

"No. You've got to stay until after lunch."

"I work at 3:30."

"What hospital?"

"Osler Memorial."

"Where?"

"Emergency."

"I see." She turned away. "You'll have to wait. Maybe you can get some sleep before going in."

"That's what I was hoping."

A half hour later they came in with lunch, and Britt set about trying to get it down. She wasn't hungry. When it was over, she waved to the nurse who was now at the main desk and watching her departure. She waved back. Everything had gone very well. It wasn't nearly so bad as she imagined it would be, but she knew from the expression on the nurse's face that all was not well. Her reactions weren't the norm. Whether the blood samples came back satisfactory or not, something wasn't right.

Dr. Ashong rang about two weeks later. She wanted to set up an appointment for Tuesday morning of the following week. It was well into July by now, and the days were hot. Britt had mentioned to Virginia and Ronit who rang quite often that she was going for tests, but few nurses or even general practitioners who didn't work in that specialized area knew much about the procedures or what they were looking for. However, aside from the obvious disadvantage of being the person investigated, Britt found it all very interesting. It was complicated and mind teasing and one thing led to many others. There always seemed something more to learn. On the weekend before seeing Ashong on Tuesday, she found herself working days at the E.R., and as luck would have it, Joe Scallion was working I.C.U. and covering for emergency. Joe was one of her favorite people and, on top of everything else, he was a good doctor. He also liked to talk, and he was effusive in his descriptions. The co-workers around her knew nothing because she told them nothing, but Joe was all right.

He could keep a confidence for all his apparent gift of the gab. He was writing up a consult and chatting away when she asked casually,

"Ever seen a pituitary function test done, Joe?"

"Oh hell, yes. It's not my line. That's endocrinology, but I spent a morning in the lab. Jesus, some of the reactions! I felt sorry for the patients. One guy . . . well, what can you expect when given T.R.H., L.H.R.H. and Insulin?" He waved a hand and looked down to see where he was at with his consult.

"I gathered that." Britt nodded thoughtfully and drummed her fingers on the counter top.

"It's not so bad, Joe. I didn't have much of a reaction."

"You had one?" He looked up and then turned his full attention to her.

"Yes. I have a slightly elevated prolactin level."

"Well, lots of women do. My wife does."

"Really? What's she going to do if she wants children?"

"Right now, that's not a problem but . . . I take it you want to get pregnant?"

"Yes, well, that's the idea."

"It's probably stress. It usually is . . . elevates prolactin, among other things. You know that."

A look of open contempt swept over Britt as she started to turn away from him and his hand came out to arrest her movement. "No, it's true. Stress can do that . . ."

The nurse in charge standing at the other end of the counter interrupted. "Britt, we've got to get ready for report. We have a few patients here to chart on."

"In a minute, Evelyn." She turned back to Joe.

"No now, this is no time for . . ."

"I said in a minute and there's lots of time."

Evelyn moved away thinking if she pressed her point, the unpredictable Erikson might well explode. She didn't trust this fiery woman's cool composure. Joe continued. "Listen, Britt, I can tell just by looking at you . . . your face . . . that you refuse to accept it. Look at you! Anyone would think stress is a dirty word."

"Oh for God's sake, Joe!" Britt felt the tension and her loathing of it mounting. "People are always stressed. In the concentration camps people were really stressed and they didn't have this reaction. Some of the women stopped menstruating but . . ."

"That's stupid thinking. People don't have to be whipped every day to feel stress," Joe said quietly. "You just can't accept that it's human to feel it and have it affect you."

"Well, it mightn't be stress. There is that possibility."

"I know what you're thinking and the likelihood of it being that is . . ." He spread his hands and made a face. Britt got up and reached for a few charts. Several nurses were milling around the desk now, and she decided to check a few patients before signing off their charts. Joe finished up his consult and went back up to I.C.U.

Dr. Ashong was professional and low-key for which Britt was grateful. She was a comfortable looking, wise and knowing middle-aged woman who'd spent a lifetime in medicine and it still intrigued her. Having spent years working with people, her intuitive sense quickened, and she was not prepared to drop the whole matter, but she set the tone at business as usual and she purposely avoided inquiries of a personal nature. She was glancing expressionlessly down at the file as she came into the room and around to her desk.

"Well, the results are all right. Nothing very significant, but I think you should have another test." She sat down and faced Erikson. "It's probably nothing, but I've had bad luck before, missing something."

"The results were normal?"

"Yes, but I'd like you to have an enhanced CT-scan."

"So you suspect an adenoma in the anterior pituitary?"

"Yes, the sella turcica. It'll be an infusion scan, and it's not too comfortable a test, but if you don't mind . . . you see it's turned up before on another patient of mine . . . a nurse like yourself. She ended up with Sheehan's syndrome, poor girl. Quite sick, but she's all right now."

Britt leaned forward. "Did she want to get pregnant too?"

"Yes, she did." Julia Ashong shook her head. "It happens quite frequently . . . women in high stress jobs . . . doctors, nurses. I've been finding more of it in people involved with the medical field. Now as I've said, there's nothing to indicate it in your blood results. Your prolactin's only slightly elevated, prolactinomas usually result in much higher readings, still if you'll go, I'll arrange it."

"I'll go." Britt nodded.

"Fine. I'll leave the request with my receptionist, and she'll call you when it's arranged."

The receptionist called in the early afternoon. "We've got a booking for you in early September." She paused. "Ah, let me see, September tenth at 11:00 a.m. R.V.H."

"But I can't, Marion. I'm leaving town. Can't you book me sooner?"

"It's difficult. They're jammed. Well, let me try. I'll call you back."

She returned the call just before Britt was ready to leave for work. "How about August eighteenth? It's the best I could do."

That took a bit of pull, Britt was thinking, but answered hastily. "That's fine, Marion."

"Okay. It's at the General. Radiology Department. Your appointment's for 10:00 a.m. August eighteenth."

"Thank you, Marion." She put down the receiver and did some quick calculations as she grabbed the lab coat and all the other paraphernalia she carried with her and headed for the front door. The teaching contract out west was effective just before Labor Day. It would be impossible to start on time.

It took ten minutes to drive down to the hospital and twenty minutes to find parking. She was late for report which didn't seem to surprise anyone. Remi turned around and winked at her and then went back to concentrating on the mangled assortment of patients left over from days. It seemed that few were admitted upstairs or sent home on days. They were all waiting for something. There were also a number of people not seen yet.

"Who the hell is the M.D. on today?" Britt whispered to Pierre standing beside her.

Pierre shifted his gaze across the E.R. and nodded almost imperceptibly in that direction.

"Oh Jesus, not him again!"

"Yes, Dr. Tierney himself . . . again." Pierre rolled his eyes and grinned. "He's not so bad."

"No, he's that bad!"

Pierre wanted to laugh, but couldn't. Decorum was important after all. Report was coming to an end. He shrugged. "He's leaving at six. That's not so bad. Then it's Ahmed. He's good."

"Yes, I like him. He makes a point of filling the emergency whether they need it or not, but at least he's pleasant."

Remi turned around. "I suppose you want first supper? Your friend's on."

"Yes, that would suit me just fine."

"I'll see if Sandy's free between six and seven. Richard can go between 5:30 and 6:30. The overlapping will help. It's going to be busy. Let's clear that patient out of the crash room. I.C.U. should be ready to take him."

"I'll call up." Britt was already dialing I.C.U. when Sandy returned her page and was talking to Remi. The work was underway, and it didn't let up until Britt was ready to leave for her break. Pierre went up to the cafeteria. She went into the lounge. Dr. David Tierney hated cigarettes, and he cared even less for people who smoked them.

His nose wrinkled, and he grumbled in an undertone, but he said nothing. Smoking in the lounge had not been banned. Britt was busy reading through more material on prolactinomas. Larger adenomas were removed surgically. There were two well documented avenues of entrance. Both methods disturbed her. The idea of any kind of brain surgery was terrifying. Anything but that, she told herself, although it appeared to be a highly successful operation. There were incidents of recurrence, however. The cells within that lobe of the pituitary were hard to get at. Under 5 mm, they tried to check tumor growth through medication. That too brought fairly good results. Possible complications were rare, but possible: Sheehan's syndrome, continued growth, possible ovarian dysfunction. There were others.

She clapped the heavy volume shut and decided to go out for coffee. She still had lots of time, and getting out of the hospital was an alluring prospect. Besides, she wanted to be alone for a while. Alone to think and try to make plans. Undoubtedly, it was true for most people that the less they knew the better off they were. And for good reason. But that would never do for her. She couldn't and wouldn't leave it alone. No wonder doctors and nurses made the worst patients. They knew too much and had a morbid tendency to anticipate the worst. Still an adenoma after all this time? That was a bit far-fetched even for her vivid and fertile imagination. It was also gruesome to dwell on it and continue hunting up information. But it was hard to let go of a lifelong habit. She had always been a frequent visitor to the haunts of medicine. This particular area was relatively new to her. Common sense told her to let it go for the time being. Another ugly little gnomic creature kept prodding at her and tempting her to muddle through still more information. Well, enough for now, she determined. Time for coffee and a sandwich, then back to work.

Edward was meeting her at her apartment after the shift. He'd spend the night. They had devised a loosely knit routine, meeting several times a week. This night he used the key she'd given him and had made a pot of tea with some biscuits by the time she got home. For himself he poured a drink and was sipping at it. He was in a contemplative mood. It was etched into his expression, his eyes, and body movements; and he was still listening to the selection from Brahms as he reached up, took her hand and drew her down beside him.

"How was your evening?"

"Busy." She looked down her stained lab coat, scrubs and splattered shoes. "I've got to change, and everything's going in the wash. I feel so gritty."

She got up, headed for the bathroom, stripped and took a shower, scrubbing herself and washing her hair. Some evenings in E.R. were messier than others, and this had been one of those nights. She had been standing in the wrong place at the wrong time. Come to think of it, being in the right place at the right time had brought dubious results as well. She thought about Edward in the next room, still pledging his love, promising a future and yet . . . yet he'd done nothing so far to ensure that they might have a life together. Well, so what? Edward was different now because she looked at him differently. He wasn't free, and he could say what he liked. It mattered. But he looked really down tonight and to plague him with questions was unthinkable. Besides, he wouldn't have the answers, and there was a growing awareness at the back of her mind that he never would come up with answers or action. Not Edward Barrett.

"You look better, darling. Not so tired." He glanced up at her as she came back into the living, and then he set about pouring some tea and buttering hot biscuits.

"What are you having?" Britt asked, eyeing his glass. Edward looked into his glass, drained it and got up to get another. "Gin and lemon. Want some?"

"No." She peered at him more closely. "You're drinking too

much."

"No, I'm not and I feel like hell, so . . ."

"Why do you feel like hell? What's wrong?"

"Everything. I can't arrange things before these plans you speak of go into effect."

Britt rubbed a hand across her eyes and wrenched her mind away from the fears and uncertainties that tormented her to ask, "You mean about accepting the teaching contract out west?"

"Well, yes, what else?"

"I can't imagine," she mumbled, and looked away from him.

"No, you can't." Edward got up and started pacing the room.

"Why can't you stay here . . . ? At least for another year?"

"They won't hold the job for another year. You know that. Talk sense."

"I am! I want you here with me."

"As what, Edward? Your mistress?"

"Oh, don't be absurd! I love you. You can't doubt that. I've told you. It's just . . . it's going to take a little time."

"But you've done nothing, Edward. You haven't even told your wife, have you . . . ? No, I didn't think so. Your family knows nothing and mine's wondering what the hell I'm still doing in Quebec."

"But it's very difficult, Britt." Edward leaned toward her.

"She could ruin me. It takes a while to build up a reputation, and there's a chance for me to teach at McGill. Her family is very influential. Even if I don't get it, my hat's in the ring and that's something."

She agreed and was silent for a few moments before adding, "This isn't working, Edward. It's not all your fault. I should have known . . . asked more questions. I just assumed you were no longer married . . ."

"But I'm not!"

"Yes, you are, and you're terrified of what she might do. I don't know what hold she has over you, and . . ." She held up a hand to stop him from interrupting. "And I don't want to know. You're unhappy. I can see that, but there's nothing I can do about it."

"Just being with you is enough." He tried to put his arms around her, and she moved out of his reach.

"Well, it's not enough for me, Edward. You'd better go."

"Go? I thought . . ."

"No, you'd better leave. I'm very tired."

"Are you working tomorrow?"

"No, I'm on the weekend."

"Then I'll see you tomorrow." He snatched up his jacket.

"This whole thing is driving me crazy. We should never have got involved."

He was at the door and upon hearing her words he spun round. "Don't ever say that. Why couldn't I have met you twenty years ago?"

"Twenty years ago I had a lot to do and marriage or a serious relationship wasn't on my mind."

"I'd have changed your mind."

"I don't think anything could have changed my mind. Besides, I've enough to do navigating the present without dredging up the past. And so do you."

She closed the door behind him and locked it. It seemed they'd been through it all before a number of times over the past weeks. Only this time it ended differently. She'd asked him to leave. That was a first since they'd become intimate, and by the look on his face, he didn't like it one bit. He wanted to be soothed and loved. But this time she felt she had nothing to give. Her resources were down, and her thoughts were romping in bedlam fashion. The murky underworld of her fears rose up in shadows without faces. She went to bed exhausted, reminding herself as she drifted into a welcome unconsciousness that tomorrow she must call Mr. Ashcroft out west. It was impossible to make it by the end of August. She could probably be there by mid-September. She'd have to make up some excuse, a plausible one. Certainly she had no intention of giving the truth. Her private affairs were no business of theirs.

That was the night she had another dream. A dream that was to have prophetic value if only she could unravel it. And she could, but decided against it. The bone-chilling truth didn't escape her. It didn't end her quest either.

There was a single image left hanging before her. Few words were spoken, and fewer actions taken. She found herself in a crudely bare room, denuded of all furniture, and she was in the midst of several women: her mother, her sister and one or two others very close to her. But their faces were in profile, vividly outlined and sharply contrasted as if in black and white relief. Like a life-size cameo, and their faces were just as immobile in fixed, unchanging expressions. But she was staring down at the baby she held in her arms. The small child was very ill, and she'd tried everything to restore it, soothe it. All in vain. The child was dying . . . dying in agony. And the women looked on distraught, but disapproving. You can't go on this way, they urged her separately, but agreeing with one another. And the pain . . . their rigid faces spoke the words. You must stop the pain. You must. Yes, I must, she heard her own low voice repeat the words. I must stop the agony. Suddenly there was a needle and syringe with morphine in her hands and, again, no one moved from their fixed position, as she plunged the needle into the child's upper thigh while still holding it in her arms. And the child lay still and dead, cradled against her as the women started to move away. The grief inside her rose up and reared wildly as she clutched the baby to her, and she started to convulse under an emotional anguish she'd never known before or since. I killed it! I killed it! Her mind screamed. But I had to! Had to end its agony. No child can live with such pain.

She was jolted awake by a series of tortured, primitive sounds, atavistic and raw. A piercing pain seared up through her chest and into her throat as the caged-in sobs fought for release. She sat up gasping and struggling for air. Those sounds were coming from her, not some untamed imprisoned animal, but her. Her eyes flashed around the room in the darkness and locked on the open window. She stumbled out of bed and drew back the curtain. The warm night air revealed nothing. The trees swished in a mild breeze, and the street all around her was quiet.

Gradually the heaviness in her chest was a bearable weight and the tears stopped. For a while, it seemed like they'd never end--just a continuous flow of hot salt liquid from some center so hidden within her that she didn't know of its existence. It had never known light, and its darkness and violent grief very nearly overwhelmed her.

Eventually she came away from the window, snapped on a lamp and then went into the living room. She flooded that room with light, and after a time, the constriction in her chest subsided. Her breathing became even again and her reactions controlled. Water. That would be a help. She sat up for some time, drinking several glasses of water and smoking cigarettes. Finally she was calm again. Those horribly frightening sounds couldn't have been coming from her. What she had heard was an exaggeration. It had to be. All the same she felt something go quite dead within her. A hope, a wish, a deep desire. A sadness remained that had no access to words and was beyond reason or understanding. It was just something you lived with and died with.

Britt didn't tell anyone about her dream and knew she probably wouldn't for a long time. But she didn't forget it either. Undoubtedly it would come back to her, unbidden. Inescapable. That cameo-like profile of the women in the room with their dark shawls and large eyes and the dead child in her arms, its torment ended by forfeiting its life, and by her hand.

-Seventeen-

The following week she called Mr. Ashcroft at the board office and caught him just before he was ready to go to a meeting. His voice sounded hearty and welcoming over the line, and Britt wondered idly what kind of reaction she'd get to her request. She fully intended to stay and see through what she'd started whether she lost the job or not.

Marvin Ashcroft could be tyrannical, but he could also be oddly understanding. She told him she'd be delayed until mid to late September, due to matters of a personal nature. Ashcroft's first reaction was right out of the rule book.

"You're under contract, Miss Erikson. We start at the end of August. The week before Labor Day."

"I know, Mr. Ashcroft, but it can't be helped. I could neither prevent nor foresee the problem."

"Of a personal nature, you say?" Ashcroft paused and then added, "Has the adoption held you up? Are you waiting for the children now?"

"The adoption failed, Mr. Ashcroft. They're legally adopted, but not mine."

"I don't understand . . . if it's an immigration problem, perhaps we . . ."

"No, it's not immigration," Britt interrupted him. "It's difficult to explain . . . but I am delayed here."

"For personal reasons . . . yes, I see." However he frowned, not understanding at all. "But you are still coming? You're certain about that?"

"Oh, yes." Britt reassured him. "But not until mid-September. I'm sorry. The delay's unavoidable. If you want to hire somebody else . . ."

"No, I don't . . . All right, we'll find someone to fill in, which isn't going to be easy." he added irascibly, then his voice became unexpectedly warm. "I'm very sorry about the adoption, Miss Erikson."

"So am I, Mr. Ashcroft."

He rang off and Britt put down the receiver. That was one more thing taken care of. She called a few moving companies to get some appraisals. Two representatives would be coming toward the end of the week. The furniture would be sent out at the end of August, and she'd arranged for someone to sublet her apartment. That wasn't difficult. It was cheap, clean, and well-located. She planned to stay with Virginia her last two weeks in Montreal.

Gin was working evenings all week and so she dropped over for coffee around noon mid-week. It was August eleventh.

"You've kept yourself scarce and busy," she looked round the living room before they went into the kitchen. "What are you doing? Packing?"

"Your amateur sleuthing days are over." Britt winked at her in mock admiration. "You're far too observant."

"You're so sarcastic, Britt."

"It's my trademark."

"Well, it's nothing to be proud of . . . So, all the Eriksons will be out of Quebec. Montreal won't be the same without you."

"It wouldn't be the same with me either." Britt laughed and shook her head, remembering the conversation she'd had with her mother. "I've decided we're just too damned complacent."

"So you'd better leave. Nobody wants to fight this out." Virginia's attitude was a reflection of the social barometer, and she was going on. "Coming from Ontario, I find the whole situation ridiculous. But it doesn't bother me. If it did, I'd move. Why should it upset you?"

"You weren't born here, Gin, and it's not your home. That makes a difference. Believe me."

"Well, I've been here eight or nine years."

"That's nothing." Britt turned away and rescued the boiling water before it evaporated into the air. She made tea. "Born and raised in Quebec does make a difference, and we're not all that well received in other provinces. In truth, we really don't have a home. You know the Canadian motto--divided we stand . . . united we stand apart, gamey legged, knock-kneed and all."

"Oh well, never mind." Gin changed the subject. "How's Edward these days? You two aren't nearly so close are you? Or am I imagining things?"

"No, you're right. But I still see him often. Usually at his place. The packing bothers him."

"Why?"

"Why?" Britt's eyebrow lifted and she smiled, but there was little amusement in the look she gave Virginia. "Because it reminds him that time's running out."

"And is it?"

"Of course it is. I'm leaving. But that's not the real reason. I'm beginning to understand, too late as usual, that his time ran out years ago, and I had nothing to do with it. It's an either-or situation. Edward can't manage that, never could. He prefers limbo."

"It's better than hell." Gin was staring at her, and then she looked away abruptly. "Being alone is hell. It's nice to have someone even for a little while."

"You're lonely, Gin."

"I'm bored." Virginia rested her elbows on the table and locked her hands under her chin. "Well, not bored really, but I do need a change. Something different, if not better."

"Well, you've lots of avenues open to you. Make a change."

"That's easier said than done."

"I did it."

"You're not the norm."

"No one's the norm. The norm is a myth. But fear isn't."

"Is that Edward's problem . . . ? Fear?"

"Maybe, but I didn't know we were still discussing him."

"Well, he must have some reason." Virginia mused. "I think he does love you."

"Love's not enough. We've discussed this before, Gin. You know my views."

"Ah yes, I know. So you're just going to fly off into the sunset and leave Edward to his own devices."

"That's right. And don't talk to me of love. For most it's just a game. Very tiresome. And I'm a lousy player. Always have been."

"Seems to me you're doing well enough."

"Things aren't always what they seem."

"It's clear enough to me." Gin got up from the table and put her tea cup in the sink. "Does he know why your leaving is delayed? I mean, about that other test you have to go for?"

"No, he doesn't." And he wouldn't understand anyway, Britt thought. For all the reading she'd done, it was still baffling. She couldn't possibly have anything wrong. There was nothing there. It was just stress as Joe Scallion thought. For that matter, Nadia Strasberg said the same thing. What was it she had suggested? A six month holiday if she wanted to get pregnant. Maybe they were right. Stress could account for everything. The whole damn world was going merrily to hell with itself. Infernal systems within systems were controlling people. The pace was fast, and plans for the future were laughable. Mortal man at war with mortality. You had to look young, feel young and reject maturity. It was an epidemic of psychic turbulence, emotional disturbance and body fitness. In short, chaos, but everyone called it progress.

"Well, I've got to go," Virginia was saying as she headed for the door. "Are you going up to Ottawa the weekend after next?"

"Yes, Saturday morning, the twenty-first . . . want to come?"

"Am I invited?"

"What do you think?"

"Just asking. I'll see you before then."

The CT-scan was done on the eighteenth, and as Dr. Ashong indicated it was uncomfortable. The pituitary on the underside of the brain wasn't the easiest place to film and the dye given I.V. could make one nauseous. However, she'd seen worse tests done on patients. Much worse. Still she was relieved when it was over. Now all she had to do was wait for the results.

Early Saturday morning she drove up to Ottawa with Virginia. Edward elected to remain in Montreal. Over the last week Britt had seen him only once and even then he was moody and seemed more indecisive and desperate than ever. He was, in fact, moving inexorably out of her life. Few things once so sweet smelling and beautiful could give off such a scent of rot as dead roses. That's how it was between Edward and herself.

They stopped at Rourke's first because he was just off the main highway before coming into Ottawa.

"I might as well come in with you," he said once the tea was made, and they were sitting around the living room. "You'll probably be coming back here to sleep anyway."

"Oh, why?" Britt glanced around the comfortable room.

"They've lots of room. You haven't"

"Sure I have. I'm alone for the weekend. Claire and the boys have gone to Montreal, her sister's place. And Gregory's down with Marsha and Jeremy."

"Greg's in Ottawa? I haven't seen them since Christmas."

"Neither have I." Rourke reached for a cookie and dunked it in his tea. "That's why I thought I'd come along. By the way, Marsha's pregnant."

"Is she? Are they sure?"

"Yup . . . three months."

"Well . . . good. That's what they wanted."

"Yup, that's what they wanted." Rourke munched on his cookie. "Isn't it great when people get what they want?" Britt looked at him. Good old Rourke. "Your sarcasm's so subtle it almost escapes me."

That made him laugh, but his eyes coming to rest on his sister were speculative. Virginia, looking from one to the other, wondered at the pair of them.

"Any results yet?" Rourke asked casually.

"Not yet. Next week maybe."

"I'll call you . . . so you'll stay here the night?"

"Sure, but we should go. I expect they're all moved in, and it looks as if they've been living there ten years."

"Of course." Rourke followed them out to the car and he drove. It was a forty-five minute drive into town. Virginia fell asleep in the back seat and the older brother and sister seemed to have any number of things to talk about. Rourke had big dreams that made his thinking tangential much of the time. Britt usually rooted him back into reality discussing some incident or other that happened at the hospital. Both had an endless supply of observations and opinions.

Mary looked around the room filled with people, and for all the loved ones around her, she felt quite alone. She missed Hugh now more than ever and she missed Montreal. She didn't think she'd ever stop missing the man or the place she was born and had raised her children. She remembered the good times and the bad times. Yes, the bad times too. She had a long memory, but somehow it didn't matter. No woman lived with a man for over forty years without sporadic trench warfare. The future still came up changed beyond recognition without him. But Mary was a survivalist with strong instincts for self-preservation and the preservation of her family. Her children were much the same, she suspected, although you'd never guess it to listen to them sometimes the way they went at each other.

Rourke was expounding on yet another plan to make lots of money and retire permanently to country solitude. It was just fanciful thinking but naturally Gregory was arguing with him. The future was in computers. Any fool knew that. He had a nice home in Toronto, but he wanted a bigger and better one. Nora was very pleased with her new purchase. Times were hard all over, but she was getting along all right. She had picked up a job, and she didn't seem to mind the work. Gregory prodded her to find something better, maybe go back to school, but then her younger son didn't know much on the subject of viability especially with regards to the circumstances of others. He was an odd mixture, Gregory. He could be so sensitive at times and he was fun and loving at other times. Mary shook her head. Britt glanced over at her.

"Ready for a bit of peace and quiet, Mother?" Mary nodded, thinking of her pleasant apartment upstairs. "Yes. I think I'll go up."

Nora, who had left the room to refill Gin's glass, returned. "I've got to put the kids down. It's late." She set about herding Ruth and Aaron, and even Jeremy out of the room. Britt darted a glance in her brothers' direction.

"Yes, I'm going too if Rourke's ready."

"You've been very quiet all evening." Mary gave her a thoughtful look and her daughter shrugged. "I've never been very good at family functions."

"No, you avoid them. But you should try not to do that."

"Well, I'm here, aren't I . . .? But then I had no idea it would be a gathering of the clan."

"It isn't. By the way, you went for that last test, didn't you?"

"Yes, on Wednesday."

"What were the results?"

"I don't know. The radiologist has to read them and pass them on to Ashong. I'll call her office next week."

"I thought I might come down for two days next week. Nora's off on Wednesday and Thursday."

"That'll be nice. I'm working evenings but . . ."

"I'll take the bus in the morning. It arrives around noon."

"Fine, I'll meet you at the station Wednesday around noon."

"What about your friend, Edward?"

"I rarely see him."

"Has his wife been around?"

"No, but then I've never known her to be around at all. He's very much married to her, though, and I don't know how I could have been so stupid as to get involved with him at all."

"Well you didn't know."

Britt shook her head. "I should have known, and later I should never have believed him when he said he wanted it over . . . legally over."

"Maybe he does want that, dear. But you know men. They hate anything messy. Oh, it's true," she added when her daughter gave her a doubtful look. "On the whole, men hate domestic upheaval. Happy or not, they'll stick it and take their pleasures elsewhere. They can live like that indefinitely. Just don't rock the boat."

"Well, I'm leaving Montreal anyway. It's over. So, I'll see you Wednesday. You look a little tired now."

"So do you, dear."

Britt got up and called Rourke who was deep in conversation with Virginia and Greg. Nora and Marsha were in the kitchen.

Mary escaped upstairs just as Rourke and Britt were leaving. Virginia followed them out to the car, and Nora, Greg, and Marsha waved from the doorway. All the way back to her brother's place Britt was thinking about the dynamics within a family. The interactions and levels of feeling in tone, and touch, and expression, were multifold. But compared to the cosmic resources and terrifying loneliness within every individual, they didn't amount to very much more than a part of the whole. She had felt isolated in that room all evening. So bloody alone, in fact, that they might as well have been strangers. But her mother had been very quiet too. With everyone gabbling around them, she had said she was coming to Montreal.

Rourke was silent beside her. That wasn't unusual. She and Rourke could go for hours without saying more than half a dozen words to each other.

"You have a gift," her mother told her once. "You can make people feel safe. . . On the other hand, you can make them feel damnedably uncomfortable and they hate that."

-Eighteen-

On Tuesday morning Britt called Dr. Ashong's secretary only to find out that she didn't have the CT-scan results on hand. But the doctor might have the radiologist's report with her, and she'd get back to her.

Wednesday at midday she went down to meet her mother at the bus station, and they drove west along Sherbrooke Street, stopping for lunch along the way. They weren't in the apartment more than ten minutes when the phone rang. It was Dr. Ashong's secretary.

"She can see you tomorrow at 11:00 a.m.. Can you make it?"

Britt thought for a moment. "That's fine, Marion, I'm on evenings; but do you have the results there? What are they?"

"She'll see you tomorrow, Britt."

"All right." She put down the receiver and frowned. Then turning away, she pushed a nagging thought to the back of her mind. The results wouldn't necessarily come through Marion, and in any case, she'd never reveal anything. Certainly not if . . .

"So what did she say?" It was her mother's voice behind her.

"Oh, I've an appointment tomorrow morning. That's all. Are you going to call Aggie now?"

"Yes, I'd better. She knows I'm here, and she'll probably be coming over."

Britt looked around. "Sorry about all the boxes, but I've a lot to pack."

"Don't worry about it. But you'd better hurry. You'll be late." Britt glanced at the time. Yes, she had time for a quick shower and change; then on to work.

The following morning, Dr. Ashong came to get her in the waiting room, and as they entered the office, the doctor closed the door and confirmed without any delay what Britt had to admit came as no real surprise, but in the form of a dull wonder. Yes, there was a small adenoma in the anterior pituitary. The doctor handed her the scan results, walked around the desk, sat down and while waiting, opened the file before her. Britt read the report carefully a second time.

"So, an adenoma 4 mm . . . in the sella."

"Yes, the anterior lobe."

"I know," Britt nodded. "But shouldn't the prolactin levels have been much higher?"

"Usually, but as I've said, it happens, and your prolactin levels aren't greatly elevated, but certainly too high to get pregnant."

"Yes, you did mention that once, and I've been reading too." Dr. Ashong nodded. She seemed to understand everything only too well. "Yes, I see." Britt felt an alien and helpless anger twisting inside her for all the wasted years. "How long has it been there?"

"I don't know," Julia Ashong said flatly. She didn't need to add that it could have been there for some time. Britt already knew that. But then suddenly the anger left her. Other doctors mightn't have the acumen, experience, or instinct, but not the one sitting opposite her.

She sat back in her chair. "So it's only 4 mm, they don't consider surgery until at least 5 mm."

"That's right, I've already been on the phone to Ferrier. They won't go in until it's larger. The cells are just too difficult to get at."

And there have been incidents of recurrence, Britt thought. And radiation was out of the question regardless how large the tumor might get.

"So you'll medicate?"

"Yes, Bromocryptine."

"Right." Britt nodded again. "And that will contain it . . .? On low dosage, I mean?"

"It should and we'll keep an eye on it. It'll bring down the prolactin level too."

"So I can get pregnant?"

"Yes, but of course, pregnancy will enlarge the size of the tumor. Everything enlarges with pregnancy. If you get pregnant come off the Bromocryptine."

"Yes, of course. If it enlarges, well, it's operable."

"That's right. Now, you know there can be other complications?"

"Yes, Sheehan's and . . ."

"And possibly others, but that hasn't happened, and you should be fine. Now I'll write you out a prescription. If you have problems, call me. The medication might cause slight nausea. Take it with some soda crackers before getting out of bed in the morning."

"Right. I will." Then she got up and turned to leave only to look round again. "Yes, thank you . . . about the medications. How long?"

Ashong looked up. "Theoretically, you can stay on it for the rest of your life." And that was it. The answer . . . After all these years.

Once outside, Britt headed up the street to her car. Once behind the wheel, she opened the window and lit a cigarette. Then she stared down at the prescription still clutched in her hand and unfolded it carefully. She didn't mind taking almost any kind of medication, but perversely and without good cause she abhorred this one. It also seemed incredulous now that she should have a small adenoma in her brain . . . in the pituitary and that could lead to many things. Still for some reason she felt very calm. Yes . . . calm. She had her answer at last. Whatever gods might be weren't jesting with her after all. There was a reason, and there had been all along. There was no promise that the headaches would let up and the tumor was most probably stress related, but there was a reason why her efforts had failed. She felt sure it must be terrible for people never to know why things were the way they were. Knowing made a difference. Now all she had to do was figure out the best thing to do.

She thought of Edward . . . Edward whom she thought she loved or could have loved until she learned he belonged to someone else despite all his protests of loving her and his marriage meaning nothing. Eventually she started up the engine and drove home. Her mother was curled up on the chesterfield, reading. She looked up expectantly as her daughter came in.

"So how did it go . . .? Everything's all right, isn't it?"

"Yes, everything's okay." Britt looked at her and knew immediately that it was the answer she had hoped for and expected to hear.

"So what did she say?" Mary was going on. "Is it just early menopause? I know you hate me saying it, but I went into it early and . . ."

"No, it's not menopause, Mother!" Britt suddenly snapped. "And yes, you have been saying it for years!"

"Don't talk to me like that, Britt." Mary looked at her, hurt, stunned. "I'm trying to understand. Did she find something?"

"Yes, she did. A small adenoma. That's what caused the elevated prolactin . . . the inability to conceive."

"An adenoma?" Mary was alarmed, but quiet and thinking furiously.

"Yes, a tumor . . just a small one in the pituitary."

"You've lost me. Where's that?"

"In the brain."

"But where?" Mary sat forward and her eyes searched the young woman's face.

"Can they take it out?"

"The underside, toward the base . . . and yes, it's operable. But it's too small right now. They don't operate unless it's over 5 mm. I'll take medication." And then presumably I can get pregnant if nothing else goes wrong she was thinking. Her mother was very quiet for a few minutes, then she addressed her daughter.

"It's not clear to me, dear, just where in your head this tumor is and using medical terms doesn't help."

Britt rubbed a hand across her eyes. "It's brutal, isn't it? Like another language. But it's nothing to worry about. I promise you."

"Still, you have to take the medication?"

"Oh yes. That's necessary and I'll keep in contact with Dr. Ashong. She also has good connections in town. So . . ."

"What you need is a rest," Mary declared.

"Well, teaching's a rest . . . at least for me, and I'm getting out of nursing for a while. I'll resign this week. I've got to give two weeks notice anyway, and I did promise the board I'd be out mid-September."

"So you'll stay at Virginia's? Aren't the movers coming this Saturday?"

"Yeah, I should pack, but it can wait. I'm off tomorrow."

"Sure, go and lie down for a while. I'll call you in plenty of time."

"Not much of a vacation for you, Mother." She shook her head. "Is Aggie coming later and taking you to the station?"

"Yes, I'll have an early supper with Jim and Aggie and then take the seven o'clock bus. Nora will meet me."

"Good."

"You will be up before you go, won't you?"

"Of course, I will."

"You had better."

Mary looked after her as she headed for the bedroom. When the room was empty she sat back and rested her head on the cushions. The last eight months or so had been hardly bearable. Now this. And she could sense the turbulence and quiet rage in her daughter. It was odd the way Britt could always switch off her personal life the moment she walked into work. And that's what she always did. All the same, she had been so detached the other evening up at Nora's. And they had all felt it. As if she was now closing the door on them too. Nora had even commented on it. She was warm only with Ruth.

The small child had curled up on her lap and remained there most of the evening.

Well, she'd lost Hugh. She had no intention of allowing any kind of rift with her daughter. She'd find a way. Maybe spending a few weeks out west this fall could help. Up to a few years ago nothing could induce her to go anywhere by plane except in an emergency. But all of that had changed. It seemed to Mary that everything living was in flux and dead fears were washed up on empty shores as curiosity pieces. Odd things that made you smile in wonder.

But she wasn't smiling now.

Of course, Britt would be home for Christmas. She was always going away and always coming home. Her older daughter was free and unafraid to try new things. Or so it seemed. In a way she envied her. Closing her eyes, Mary took stock. She had a good deal more than most women, despite everything. She had four children, all in fairly good health and decent enough human beings, several very close friends and enough money to live comfortably, if not in luxury. Thanks to Rourke's none too gentle persuasion. The world news sounded ominous and things could be going better. All very true, but no one knew the future. Despair was something that one lived and struggled with. Hope was something that one followed into the future. Right now, however, the landscape was foggy and frightening. So she prayed for strength. Not being much of a praying woman when in dire need, her thoughts never found words. No matter. God would understand. That's what she believed because that's the only thing that made sense in this mad, half-crazed world where people wanted what they couldn't have, and had what they really didn't need or want. Life was full of ironies. But Britt worried her. She was too thin and persistently tired. It was clear too that she'd rather work than worry. She denied it, naturally. Then again her daughter was no fool, and she noticed things. She'd find it difficult to understand her mother's reasons for not wanting to confront this problem head-on. There were reasons why Mary didn't probe to find the whole truth. She could face her own black night of the soul, if she must and she did, but not the other. Not one of her children. Not Britt. And it wasn't fear that she'd glimpsed in her daughter's eyes. But something more terrible. The lack of it.

Mary got up and made a pot of tea. Then glancing at the time, she decided she'd better call her. A whole hour had slipped by. She realized the shower was running and checking the bedroom she found it empty. There was nothing to worry about. It would be taken care of with medication . . . nothing serious enough to keep her from work. Yes. It wasn't good news, but it could be worse. Everything would be all right. It had to be.

-Nineteen-

The rest of the family took the news much the same way. They were concerned but soon they had it settled in their minds. There was a very small tumor, probably not malignant and, in any case, it was operable if necessary. Nothing life threatening. That was all. Britt said little and didn't seem too concerned. They asked few questions. Possible complications weren't discussed at all. Medical terms sent them reeling into no-man's land and so potential difficulties and dilemmas were left aside. As far as they knew it was a problem that could be handled and that was all that mattered. Only Rourke vaguely guessed his sister's stormy thoughts and worried that the hard-headed, stubborn woman would take unnecessary risks.

Once her resignation was in at the hospital, the days were to become caught up in a whirlwind of activity. One incident, in particular, stood out vividly in her mind, and for some reason, she was sure it would come back to her in the days and years ahead whenever she questioned her reason for being. Her brothers and sister had children of their own, and her mother could say what she liked. It mattered. Having a family of your own mattered very much.

There were many incidents in Britt's life that bolstered her spirits and seemed to make a difference when she remembered them. Like meeting and caring for Joan Enright Adelman. Montreal's own Molly Malone. She felt privileged.

September third there occurred another such incident. It was a particularly trying evening in the emergency and to make matters worse the only person she knew well was Pierre. Two other nurses, Martine and Sergio were filling in for Remi and Allison. Adding to her dismay, Dr. David Tierney took over for Stuart Caplan. She was delighted to get rid of Stuart whose sour disposition set everyone's teeth on edge. He was the glamour boy of the department and took great pleasure in doing such painful procedures as closed reductions without any premedication. He seemed to hate medicine and the people he treated only a little less than the nursing staff. Some people are sadistic by nature--not Stuart. He appeared to cultivate it just to annoy everyone around him. Now, David, on the other hand, seemed on the surface mild-eyed and mild-mannered. But he was clumsy, pompous and disorganized. And for some absurd reason, he had a habit of yelling at drunks. Especially if there was no danger of him getting bloodied in the process.

On this particular evening, he took over as the E.R. doctor while Britt and Martine were still at supper. An alcohol overdose had come in by ambulance and Sergio put him back in the cast room. The doctor was down from I.C.U. Susan Faraday was trying to complete a consult on another patient. Martine was trying to get some paperwork done. People were rushed. The E.R. was filling up, and there was an atmosphere of chaos by the time Britt got back from supper and heard the onslaught of cursing and swearing issuing from the back room.

"Who's that?" She squinted at the chalk board with the list of patients.

"A John Horvath. Hear him? Falling down drunk. And according to Sergio who was here--a nasty character. He's in restraints. The ambulance people were here a while. They helped. He was lashing out. We couldn't get bloods on him or even his vital signs."

"Want me to try? It's busy but, there's nothing very urgent around here."

"No, just that din back there." Susan Faraday didn't look up, but she was frowning. "I can't even think."

"Well, I'll try . . . We should have something on him."

"I'll go with you, Britt." Pierre followed her down the hall. "We told you he was dangerous."

Sure enough, Sergio's handiwork was everywhere. The patient was twisting around in bed with only wrist restraints on. She'd told Sergio how dangerous that could be to the patient and staff. But Sergio knew everything there was to know about psychiatric management. Mr. Horvath was still giving out expletives when Britt came in the room, but he quieted suddenly when he heard her say his name and repeat it adding, "John, how are you feeling now?"

The man, around forty, tossed his head and muttered, but the nasty snarling had stopped.

"John, you've had some alcohol."

"Yeah . . . lots."

"I was afraid of that." Britt paused and Horvath was miraculously silent. "I'd like to do a blood test, John, for alcohol level and others, and you might need a supplement and an I.V. Is that okay? Can I take some blood?"

"Yes, take it." Horvath turned away dismissively. Pierre was watching and moved closer. John glanced at him.

"You remember Pierre, don't you, John?"

"Yeah . . . yeah."

Britt thought about releasing the restraint to take the blood sample, but Pierre shook his head. "Too volatile," he said under his breath.

A lot of good restraints will do the way they're on him, Britt thought, but she went ahead and applied the tourniquet.

"It'll hurt a little, John. I'll be careful."

"All right, do it." John didn't move, and he became momentarily pleasant as Britt kept up a light banter.

"So, what were you drinking?"

"Cognac, and some other stuff."

"Humm. You have expensive tastes."

That made John laugh. "Sure, the best . . . only the best." And his voice slurred.

The blood was taken and vitals done. "How'd you get all that blood in your nose, John?"

"Fight. Got punched."

"When you're a little better we'll get you cleaned up." John nodded and seemed to be drifting into another stupor. The vials of blood were collected and Pierre was stamping labels.

"You got the blood?" David Tierney looked around at the desk.

"Yes. Why not medicate him, David? He's getting loud again . . . can't settle." They could hear John again from the back room.

"No," David wrinkled his nose. "He's just the sort of patient that could have a hematoma."

"He's fairly coherent, oriented in three spheres. He can answer questions. Just a small amount. The way he's thrashing about can hurt him much more."

"No, no." David waved a hand. "He needs an I.V."

Britt looked up and stared at him. "You can't be serious! He's in no condition to keep an I.V. in."

"Well, you got the blood."

"I got lucky and he's really not so bad if not provoked, but the guy can't settle for more than five minutes. He just can't."

"I want him to have an I.V. The usual, with multivites and thiamine."

Britt shook her head, but Sergio went off to prepare it. Once it was ready, Sergio was intent on getting it in and Britt went in to run interference because Sergio could easily provoke even a sober person. He disliked her as much as she had trouble abiding him. For the sake of the patient, however, they worked together. Finally he got the I.V. in and although John was becoming restive Sergio kept fiddling. Now he released the restraint to place John's arm at another angle. That did it. Without even knowing what he was doing, John lashed out, kicked at Britt who moved sideways to avoid the worst of it. But he continued kicking and screaming. Sergio, safe at the head of the bed, eventually grabbed his legs and held them up over his shoulder. The racket alerted them at the front and a code was called.

Within minutes the room was filled with people. The orderlies who responded were excellent and well trained. Especially the one called Sean.

"Put him in right this time, Sean." Britt told him and the orderly nodded, placing the man, flailing his limbs, in the prone position. One arm up, one down. It was all done quickly and efficiently. Sergio was still at the head of the bed, and John continued to curse and swear. By this time, the room was crowded. The supervisor was down, the code team and Martine. Finally Dr. Tierney came in to look on.

"He's spitting." Sergio looked down at the patient in contempt.

"Put extra sheets lengthwise across his back and lower legs," David ordered. That done, the patient, who looked nearly out of his mind, struggled in futile desperation.

"He's spitting." Sergio repeated and roughly shoved the end of the balled up sheet in the patient's mouth.

"Sergio!" It was Britt's voice coming from behind David Tierney.

"No, that's not what we do," David said quietly. He was so calm that everything he did seemed to have a slow motion nightmarish quality to it. "This is what we do in such cases." He took the pillow from the adjacent bed and placed it over the patient's head and held it there. There was a dead silence in the room, a shocked silence with everyone looking on. Britt took one step forward and went to exclaim, "David, don't!" But then her mind spun forward and she thought the bloody bastard would probably push harder, longer. As it was, he was easing up and when John's head reared frantically, David repeated the motion, but for less time. Other than bodily removing the eminent doctor from the room, there wasn't much to be done. But they needn't have worried. Remembering himself, Dr. David Tierney turned on his heel and left the room.

The main desk was thronged with people. The men on the code team were giving their names to Martine who was filling out the required form. In the medication room, Britt was washing her hands and cleaning herself up, but then in a fit of rage that seemed to have been building for some time, she turned on Sergio.

"Who put him in restraints?" Her voice was hard and demanding and could be well overheard at the main desk just beyond the room. Sergio didn't answer her. He worked around the room disposing of the I.V. equipment. "Who did it? Who put him in restraints, wrongly positioned and, with only wrist restraints, wrongly positioned, too . . . Who, Sergio?" This time Britt's voice was loud, and she noticed Dr. Faraday bending her head still more closely to her consult.

"You don't have to shout." Sergio wouldn't look her in the eye, but he knew she was staring at him, and it unnerved him. "And you don't have to point the finger, try to blame someone. You were there. You saw it."

"Yes, I saw it." Britt nodded. "It was duly noted."

"So? Why didn't you do something before . . .?"

"Because, I wasn't the one who received him, and no one can tell you anything."

"Well, if you had done it, it would have been the same."

"No, if I'd have done it, at least it would have been done properly."

"Oh sure . . . You . . ."

But Britt turned and left the room. As she got to the front desk, Susan Faraday was heading back up to I.C.U. where it was blessedly quiet. She had heard the whole exchange. Martine was beside Britt now and asking her to chart on Horvath.

"Get Sergio to do it," she muttered, still angry and mostly with herself for not stopping David, for being afraid if she said anything or moved to stop him, he'd do it harder and it would be worse for the patient. And the whole room had watched, saying nothing, doing nothing. Maybe they were terrified of the same thing. All except Sergio, of course, who appeared to be deriving satisfaction from it.

"He's busy with something else," Martine was saying.

"What?"

"I said he's busy, so would you . . . ?"

"Martine, he put a pillow over that patient's head."

For a moment the charge nurse looked puzzled at the sudden twist in conversation. Then she shrugged. "Well, they do that at the other hospital you worked at . . . in Emergency Psychiatry."

"They did not! I never saw that before. It's illegal, for Christ's sake! Who told you that?" Their voices had dropped to a stage whisper.

"I don't know. I heard it."

"Well, you heard wrong. It mightn't get him a malpractice suit, but certainly misconduct. That patient was terrified . . . simulating smothering. Jesus Christ!"

"Well, there's nothing to be done about it now. Let it go. I wish he'd medicated him. Do you hear him? And the I.V. infiltrated. After all that we had to pull it. This place is a madhouse tonight."

"Is one of those patients in the crash room going up to I.C.U.?"

"Yes, I'll call up. Susan left the consult copy here. Thank God she's moving a couple up. They've a few beds left. Write that note on Horvath, will you?"

At this point, David came by the counter. "Did anyone come with that patient at the back? Anyone call about him?"

Britt looked up. "No, no one's called. Shall I try to contact someone? He probably has family."

"No, no," David tapped his finger on the counter and looked worried. He knows, Britt thought. If anyone finds out . . . family, friends.

"Will you medicate him, David?" Martine asked.

"No" David stubbornly refused and glanced aside. "No sedation . . . Just my luck, he'd have a hematoma." He moved away and Martine sighed. Britt swore. The stupid bastard. Making a patient feel like he's smothering is just the treatment for possible hematoma.

But the evening wasn't over. At least four or five more ambulances came in. They had stopped counting, and then there were those that came on their own or with their families and a few of those were seriously ill. Britt took her break late. When she came back into the E.R. after visiting with a friend up in Hematology, several patients had left and a few new patients were waiting to be assessed and worked-up. Martine turned around and nabbed her before she even got to the desk.

"Go and get some bloods, everything including cardiac and liver enzymes and get an I.V. into that one, will you?"

"What's the problem?"

"Abdominal pain N.Y.D., possible dehydration. He's old. I'll do this one." She pointed to the patient on a stretcher in the corridor. "Sergio's doing an E.K.G. Possible infarct. Crash room."

They saw very little of each other for the next hour. Just getting to all the patients and assessing the new ones took all their concentration. And Martine was intent on keeping the rapid charting up to date because it was already eleven o'clock. And come hell or high water, she was going to leave on time. Pierre was working with amazing speed and Sergio was skulking about, keeping well out of Britt's way.

Just after the witching hour of eleven when the evening staff slowed down to leave in-coming patients for the night staff, another ambulance arrived and a very sick man around fifty-five or sixty. Martine was taking report from the ambulance drivers after she placed the late middle-aged man in the crash room. The ambulance patient was directed to the general area and Pierre set about getting the other poor fellow into a gown and taking his vital signs. Britt was drawing bloods on yet another patient against the far wall.

Pierre stepped outside the curtained-off area and caught Martine as she hurried by. "His temperature's 39.9 C, and he's not very with it."

"Other symptoms?" She pulled the curtain back and, saw a family member beside him as he lay flat out on the stretcher. The history didn't sound any better than the patient looked.

"Get David. He'll have to call Dr. Faraday. But get him now. " She looked up and called across the E.R. "Britt, are you almost through there?"

"Yeah, everything else is done here. I'll only be a minute."

"We need blood cultures over here . . . Now!"

Britt glanced over and frowned. Martine picked up the triage sheet and brought it to her. She pointed at some of the data.

"Look at his temperature."

"And headaches, backaches, sensitivity to light . . ."

Britt scanned the notes. "What do you think?"

"I don't know. Meningitis?"

"Looks like it . . . all right, I'll do him." She glanced across the room. "Pierre's setting up for an E.K.G."

"He's fifty-six. He's having pain all over. So you take care of him. Okay? I'll get the charting up to date. The ambulance case can wait a few minutes. Another alcohol level off the scale. It must be the monthly check day for the indigent." She bustled away.

Shortly afterward, Britt pulled back the curtain that Pierre had drawn around William Weatherspoon, a gray-haired, scraggy-faced man who had piercing blue eyes when they were not rendered soft and rather lost under the frequent waves of wracking pain.

"Have I time to take the first culture before you begin, Pierre?"

"Sure, go ahead. I'll just finish hooking him up while you're doing that."

"Has he had the other bloods taken already?"

"Nope. Might as well do them too. Everything for the I.V. is over here."

"Fine." Britt let down the side of the stretcher and moved closer to the man who gazed up at her with a dazed expression. Unconscious of what she was doing her hand came out and she stroked back his hair. "William?" Her voice was low, almost a whisper. "William? Are you having pain?" He looked at her fully now, but apparently not really seeing her. It was the voice he was responding to. Just a familiar tone in the voice, it seemed.

"I have to do some blood tests, William."

The man nodded, hardly comprehending.

A few minutes later, the bloods were drawn and the first blood culture done. She took everything back to the desk and handed it to Martine who waved her away. She'd take care of the requisition and labeling the vials. Britt headed back to the small cubicle occupying half of the crash room. The E.K.G. machine was making a tracing. Halfway through, Pierre started to disconnect all the leads and Britt was assisting him from her side. At this moment Dr. Faraday arrived on the scene. Pierre handed her the notes and the E.K.G..

Britt looked at her. "I've got to do the second blood culture."

"That's all right. I can examine him while you're doing that."

The second blood culture was more of a struggle. Faraday looked over at her. "Third time in the same arm. The I.V.'s in the other."

"It's coming."

"Yes, but slowly." The syringe was filled and Britt carted away the equipment off to one side to complete the procedure. When she got back to the bed, Susan was trying to see the fundi with the ophthalmoscope.

"Difficult to find?"

"Yeah, it's difficult. He can't focus."

Britt stood at the end of the bed and, raising her hand, called him.

"No, lower. I don't want him to look up."

The head of the bed was raised, and it was difficult to get the right angle.

"William, look at me! Look right at me. Straight ahead." Out of a depth of pain, William stared right into her eyes.

"Got it." Susan nodded, "That's fine."

Then she lowered her voice and moved toward the end of the bed. It was 11:15, and the night staff was beginning to drift in. Martine was bustling around the desk. Sergio and Pierre were ready to leave. Yvette, the night nurse, was looking over the list of patients. Bill, the trained assistant, was standing behind the desk looking bulky and bored. Martine had called the supervisor requesting more help for the night staff, but that would take a little time.

"We'll have to do a lumbar puncture," Faraday said in an undertone and at the look on Britt's face, she added, "It's probably meningitis. It's got to be done."

"I know." Britt mumbled.

She checked the time again. 11:20. If there was one thing in the world she hated, it was a lumbar puncture. She looked up frantically, and her eyes roamed the Emergency room. Martine was starting to give report. The charge nurse glanced over at her, and then threw up her hands. She was busy but Bill was only half listening. Sergio and Pierre had left.

"Bill, can't you come over here?"

"No, I've got to get report!" he frowned and then tossed his head. "But I'll get the tray and extra needles." At these words, Britt started to feel light-headed and was clammy all over. Oh God, don't let me pass out, she prayed.

"Look. I'm going to need someone to hold him," Dr. Faraday was saying.

"He's having total body pain now." Britt muttered, glancing at

William.

"I know. But it's got to be done, and you know I can't sedate him. Not in his condition."

"I know," Britt had been avoiding eye contact with her, but now she took a deep breath and said quickly, "You know how everyone has their nemesis?"

Faraday nodded thoughtfully and then looked at her wonderingly. "Yes."

"Well, lumbar punctures are mine."

"Oh, I see, well . . . there are always small problems. No one likes them."

"The problem's going to be remaining vertical." Britt was ashen and Susan Faraday turned to her quickly, but she was rushing on. "I don't understand it either. I don't mind anything else--fractures, lacerations, suturing . . . all of it, but L.P.'s." She shook her head and Bill returned with the tray. He brought a supply of spinal needles and started voicing various sizes.

"Shush!" The doctor snapped at him and waved him away. Then she turned again to this peculiar nurse whom she didn't know well, but who had stayed behind when the others left. "Now, there's a time factor."

"Right." Britt started to breathe again and her color improved. "I'll start positioning him." Keep busy, she told herself. There was a certain magic in keeping busy. She lowered the head of the bed, carefully got William Weatherspoon turned toward her with his knees bent slightly upward and his body curved.

Faraday was ready. All she had to do was glove, but first she wanted to find just the right entry spot between the third and fourth lumbar vertebrae. Her fingers moved over his lower vertebrae pressing.

"Try to get his lower back a little closer to me." They shifted him on the table. "That's good. It's right there." She looked up at Britt.

"So to . . . Oz?"

"Yes, to Oz."

The antiseptic was liberally added and William's eyes snapped open. "It's a test . . . has to be done, William." She bent her head closer to him and started moving her hand that she'd curled around his head through his hair, gently stroking him, whispering his name and talking to him as one would to a very sick child.

"I'm freezing him now . . . heavily." Faraday assured her.

"The Xylocaine will help." William's eyes opened again staring sightlessly.

"William, I know it hurts, but you mustn't move. Don't move, William." Her voice was so low and the light but continuous stroking seemed to transport the man.

"Mummy," he called her. "Mummy."

"Don't move, William. Please don't move. It hurts, I know, but don't move . . . not a muscle."

Britt's own back was breaking from bending over him with an arm around his lower thighs and knees and keeping her hand at his head and in continuous movement. Susan Faraday tried at least three to four separate consecutive times, and each attempt with all the manipulation going with it took time. Finally she straightened up, looking drained.

"It's right there. I'm in the exact spot, but I'm not getting any C.S.F. return." She glanced at Britt who was flushed and exhausted. "You all right?" Britt nodded.

"I've got to get it," Faraday resolved. "But I'll put in more freezing. Would you . . ."

"Yeah," Britt reached over for the bottle of injectible Xylocaine and held it up inverted. Then she got William back into position and kept up the one-sided repetitive dialogue.

Through it all the man kept moaning. "Mummy . . . mummy." but he never moved. He remained perfectly still, even when it became apparent that the pain was acute, despite the freezing.

"He must be delirious," she commented to Faraday.

"He thinks I'm his mother." And when Susan didn't answer her she thought again. But then they all want their mothers when in pain. That's the one person they want--their mother. William's mother was probably long dead. Right now, however, for him, she lived.

Finally Susan straightened up. Time out. They'd been at it for well over half an hour. As they stood there staring at each other across the bed, the dogged Dr. Tierney, who had just completed another shouting match with a drunken patient on the other side of the E.R., turned up and on his heels the night shift assistants. David had a lot to say about everything as usual.

"Having trouble, Susan?"

"Yeah. I'm right there, but can't get a return. I'll try again."

David stood beside Britt who still had her hand on William's head. "Well, first we've got to position the patient properly." And as he roughly set about directing the assistants, Britt stepped back and away from him.

"He was correctly positioned," Susan growled at him. But she got another needle ready.

Walking away from the bed, Britt saw that they all, with the exception of Susan Faraday, had their hands on the man under Tierney's direction, and she could hear William screaming. He was thrashing about now.

I'll kill him, Britt thought. The stupid, vicious bastard. And I'll get him. By Jesus, I'll get him. . . I'll get the son-of-a-bitch. All the way out of the Emergency, she could hear William's cries. The man who had been so quiet and cooperative and brave, thinking all the while that he was a small boy again, and his mother who must have stroked his hair and talked softly was with him again. The family was outside in the waiting room. They looked anxious, but what was there to say after all?

Her legs felt like lead under her . . . heavy and stiff. Once in the car, she lit a cigarette and leaned her head against the cool steering wheel. Yes. I'll get him. If it's the last thing I do before leaving Montreal. My home, where I'm no longer welcome. I'll make that schmuck's life living hell. Dr. David Bloody Tierney would meet his nemesis.

And by the time she got home, she knew exactly how she was going to do it. It was William's face that haunted her waking and sleeping hours, but it was John Horvath that she intended to use against him. Yes, the fool had made a dangerous error there. The pillow treatment. People thought such actions no longer went on, but they did and more frequently than anyone cared to imagine. She wasn't sure of the severity of the legalities involved, but it was definitely unethical practice. There was nothing she could say or do about William. Loutish behavior was not grounds for complaint . . . Who in the medical field would take it seriously? But the other . . . Yes, the other.

The next few days were like a maelstrom of conflicting ideas, but among friends at the city's largest psychiatric assessment unit where she'd worked there was a consensus of outrage when they heard about the incident. There were no names mentioned for ethical reasons, but they readily agreed that something should be done.

Working Saturday on the day shift, however, she mentioned what happened to two nurses whom she seldom worked with but knew quite well. They were good nurses, knowledgeable, straightforward, concerned, but they didn't in the least like the idea of the occurrence being bruited about when she mentioned the possibility of giving the story to Barbara Sullivan, the Medical Reporter, for the Montreal Tribune. They balked at that.

"But you can't!" Anna Louritis declared. "We're part of this department, and it's a good E.R. It'll give us a bad name."

"But it happened, Anna!" Britt nailed her with a hard look. "The idiot should be brought up for it." She looked so angry and contemptuous that both Anna and the other nurse became uneasy.

"Don't do it." Donna said, using a cautionary note. "You don't even know if the others will corroborate your story."

"Well, they were all in the room."

"So? They might well say nothing or that they didn't see it."

"Then they'll be perjuring themselves. Oh yes." Britt was pacing the tiny lounge area now. "If they lie under oath, it's perjury."

"There's nothing you can do alone," Anna interjected. "It'll come down to your word against his. Don't expect the others to involve themselves. They probably won't."

"No, well nurses are famous for cutting each other up and keeping silent about things like this," Donna added.

"Yeah, they dummy-up." Britt thought for a moment. "Well, I'm not going to anyone in nursing administration.

"Why not?" Anna wanted to know. "Let them handle it."

"That's why," Britt shot back. "They won't handle it. Who's the head of the doctors?"

"Dr. Stevens." And at the expression on the face of this angry woman she added, "You know him. George Stevens. But that won't be much help . . . the old boy network'."

"Still around is it . . . ?"

"Oh yes." Anna nodded. "It thrives, especially here."

"Then who?"

"Well, the Hospital Director would be your best bet. Rejean Gagnon's decent enough. But I don't know . . ."

"And he definitely would not want this to get out." Britt nodded, consolidating her own thoughts. "All right, I'll try him."

Sunday evening late, after she returned from her shift, Britt called Lori Thompson, a good friend and director of nursing out west. They had corresponded by letter, but she hadn't heard from the elusive Erikson in months.

"Where the hell are you?" She demanded to know immediately.

"In Montreal, Lori."

"Well, I tried to reach you, but didn't get an answer."

"I was away for a time . . . and now my number's changed."

"So how are you?"

Britt told her a little about what had been going on. She didn't bother about Nepal or anything of what followed. Then she launched into the main reason for her call. She told her all about the bloody-minded Tierney and culminated with the incident on Thursday evening and what she thought about doing.

"The bloody idiot," Lori responded irritably. "Who the hell does he think he is?"

"God."

"Well, every hospital has quality assurance. In fact, the headquarters is in Quebec. That's where I got most of my correspondence. He could be in deep trouble if you go after him. He's as guilty as hell, and if nothing else you'll rattle his cage more than just a little."

"And will they accept my word? You know the other nurses and staff . . ."

"I know, but they can't ignore a sworn statement, and the others will be questioned. They dare not lie against a deposition if you're willing to make one."

"I'm willing."

"When he finds out it won't be pleasant for you, but what the hell you're leaving anyway. Go for it."

"That's what I'll do," Britt sighed.

"So you're coming out here to Alberta?"

"Yes, very soon."

"Well call me. Damn it Britt! I can't keep track of you."

"I'll call. Everything all right with you?"

"Yup, all quiet on the western front." Lori laughed. "With five kids and a hospital to run I haven't the time to get into trouble. Not like you."

"Trouble follows me, Lori."

"Bullshit! If there's a fight you're in the middle of it. Get yourself out here. We'll get you fixed up."

Britt smiled as she put down the receiver, then she rubbed a hand across her eyes. After all this was worked out she'd have to settle things with Edward. It occurred to her she'd been avoiding him, and now that she was staying with Virginia temporarily that wasn't hard to do. He hadn't been around yesterday when the movers had been in. It took them most of the afternoon, and Virginia had been there until she arrived home from work. When it was all over and the apartment empty, her friend went home and prepared two strong drinks. Britt remained behind for a few moments remembering some of the things that had happened in these rooms, and in the empty flats upstairs. The last few months seemed a wide gap in time, a chasm that eventually one would emotionally and mentally have to leap over. She remembered too the dreams she'd had--one before her father's death and the other during all the tests she was having done for infertility. Loss and knowledge were weighty burdens, and right now that's how she felt. Weary. There were familiar voices and faces everywhere here: little Ruth's eyes lighting up as she ran to her regardless of what she was doing, Aaron talking about his imaginary friends and the way he had looked and acted when he came home for his grandfather's death, her mother; brothers, sister, friends and then, of course, her father. She looked over to the door, still expectant, and then stupidly up at the ceiling. Unconsciously, the tears rolled freely down her face. From an unidentifiable source they seemed unstoppable. There was no logical reason for their being. People died. Many women attempted to have children and failed. Relationships broke up all the time. Human error was as common as the cycling of days. What was there to cry about? Finally it ended very much as it had started--without warning. Checking her face in the mirror on the bathroom cabinet, she noted there was little trace of the recurrent episode. The frightening thing was that it was happening far too often, and the awareness of this was so private that she said not a word to anyone. She knew all about reactive depression. It was like quicksand. One had to be vigilant or one got caught in that dangerous undertow.

Despite the light supper and strong drink that Virginia supplied, Britt slept badly. She tossed and turned for hours before drifting fitfully in the barren landscape of her dreams. At seven in the morning she snapped awake and went into the kitchen to make some coffee. Virginia slept on. At eight o'clock, she brought the telephone with its long cord into the kitchen and closed the door. Then she lit another cigarette and made more coffee. Finally at 8:30, she rang the hospital and asked the switchboard operator to put her through to the director general's office.

"You want Mr. Gagnon's office?" The operator inquired.

"Yes, please."

"Just a moment."

The director's secretary came on the line, and Britt gave her name, position, and where she worked.

"Well you have to go through the nursing department, Miss Erikson."

"No, I don't." Britt came back at her. "It's got nothing to do with them."

"Still, you should talk to the Director of Nursing or her assistant and then . . ."

"No. And I'm not going to Dr. George Stevens either, although it concerns him too. I want to speak to Mr. Gagnon."

"Just a minute." The secretary put down the receiver and went in to speak to the director. When she came back on the line her voice was assertive.

"You must go through nursing, Miss Erikson. That's how it's

done."

"Well, you go back and tell Mr. Gagnon that this matter concerns an incident that happened in the Emergency of the hospital he represents. Not a very nice incident. And tell him I've already contacted Barbara Sullivan, the medical reporter at the Tribune, and she's very interested. I thought it only courteous to give Mr. Gagnon first chance to investigate the matter. He is not going to like his hospital's name smeared all over the pages of the Montreal newspaper. The public isn't going to like what I have to report one damn bit. Go and tell him that."

"Hold the line, Miss Erikson." She was gone for a very short time. "He'll see you in half an hour, Miss Erikson."

"Fine. I'll be there. If you want someone from the nursing department to sit in, I've no objection. And have your representative from risk management there."

"He may be difficult to locate at such short notice."

"Well, try. It concerns him."

Britt put down the receiver and arched her back. She didn't realize she was so tense.

"What was that all about?" Virginia was standing behind her.

"I'm going down now. I've got to dress."

Virginia shook her head. "He must have thought you were calling from the E.R."

"I doubt it, but maybe . . ."

"I heard you just now. Take it easy when you go in to see him, Britt."

"I'll be the soul of complacency."

"God help him then." Virginia frowned as her sometimes curt and cutting friend hurried off to dress. Britt could be formidable and was never easily daunted.

Mr. Gagnon's outer office was empty and when she entered and gave her name, the secretary took her coat and then picked up the receiver to say simply, "two, six."

Within a minute, Lucy Maxwell marched into the office looking annoyed, embarrassed, and worried. Britt hadn't seen her more than half a dozen times since she'd hired her months ago. She had concluded long ago that the decidedly clever woman was systems proofed -- bought and sold. And that was too bad, because underneath it all, Maxwell was a very nice person, but she'd cut her character to fit the presumably faultless patterns imposed on her and there just wasn't enough room left for Lucy Maxwell. Right now, she barely acknowledged Britt, and it was just as well that Gagnon was opening the door to his office and issuing them inside. He shook hands with Erikson and each sized the other up in the momentary eye contact they made. He didn't know quite what to make of this tall, intent and obviously intelligent looking woman and, for her part, Britt concluded that if he wasn't too concerned before their encounter, he was more than ready to listen now and consider very carefully what he was going to do about whatever happened or there would be repercussions.

"So . . ." he began carefully. "What is the problem, Miss Erikson?" Britt fixed her eyes on him. "The problem is an incident that occurred this last Thursday on the evening shift in the Emergency Department."

"An incident?"

"Yes, there were other witnesses, but as you can see, I'm here alone. Still, I'm prepared to testify under oath. The others, if questioned under oath . . ."

Gagnon's eyes flickered and now he did look genuinely concerned. He sat back in his chair. "Tell me exactly what happened."

Britt reported exactly what went on. She talked solely about John Horvath, giving names, times, specific actions. Lucy was writing everything down, especially the personnel involved and she interrupted to ask, "You said the nursing supervisor was Louise?"

"Yes, I don't know her last name."

"That would be Simard. Louise Simard, and Sergio . . . yes, I know him too."

"You can get the last names of the men on the code team from the official report, but I want to emphasize that Sean acted with complete propriety. You know Sean?"

"Yes," Lucy nodded. "Sean O'Hanlon."

"He's a good man. One of the best. He works hard. He's dependable, but . . ." and now she looked across at the director who was listening to this exchange. "You must understand, Mr. Gagnon, that a number of these men have families. Sean has a wife and two children. Jobs are very difficult to come by these days. We're having hard times. It's a matter of survival. Do you understand what I'm trying to say? For some of these people to come forward might jeopardize . . ."

He waved a hand in dismissal and his eyes, still showing worry, had softened, recognizing the unspoken concern. "They have nothing to fear. There is no threat to their job. I'll see to that."

Britt nodded at him. Yes, she supposed he would do that. She had caught the expression of disgust that had swept over his face when she described Tierney's actions and the plight of the patient.

"About Sergio . . ." Lucy cut in. "Shoving the sheet in his mouth and his nostrils blocked . . . he wouldn't be able to breath, but you're not sure . . .? That it was Sergio, I mean."

"No." Britt shook her head. "About that I'm not sure, but he was the one standing there. I'm sure of that. Everything happened so quickly, you see . . . ? And . . . and I feel badly. I should have said something, but I was afraid he'd go at it harder. It would only make matters worse. David would want to prove his point. He's like that. Just like Stuart Caplan, your other director down there, gets his jollies out of doing closed reductions without medicating the patient first."

"What!" Both Gagnon and Maxwell were staring at her.

"It's true. I've seen it on two separate occasions and I know because I had the narcotic keys. I could hear them screaming . . . "

Lucy was shaking her head and the director tapped his hand on the desk.

"All right," he said finally. "It's all important and has to be looked into, but I want you to stick to the events of September third. Would you be willing to give me a written statement of what happened that evening?"

"You want a deposition?" Britt looked right into his eyes, and he observed with uneasy interest that she knew the magnitude of what she was doing and expected results. She also knew the personal risk to herself.

"Yes, a deposition."

"You'll have one by Wednesday. Signed and witnessed."

Maxwell turned to her. "You have resigned already, haven't you?"

"Yes, before this happened. The same day ironically. I gave in my resignation at personnel before going on duty . . . but I've still five or six shifts to complete. I'm on again Wednesday evening and with David Tierney too."

"So you've got to work with him?" Gagnon gave her a reluctant smile. "Well, I think it best we don't release your name until after you leave the hospital, but the investigation, of course, will start immediately."

"So you will investigate?" Britt asked pointedly.

"Yes, definitely." Gagnon nodded. "I do have the reputation of this hospital to protect. I'm not sure just what actions will be taken, but we do have to investigate."

He stood up and Maxwell and Erikson followed suit.

"You may meet with resistance to speak . . . at least initially." Britt reminded him. "But I'm ready to testify under oath." Her look told him that the others had better be ready to do the same. Gagnon held out his hand again and she took it.

"Thank you for coming in, Miss Erikson. And I am glad you came."

Once outside she parted company hurriedly with Lucy Maxwell. She had to admit that the once independent and strong-minded woman was once again, after so long a time, ready to do battle. The secretary looked at them as if to communicate that she hadn't heard a thing and naturally it was all too obvious that she had overheard everything. Everybody knew that in a hospital the walls had ears and yet they perversely kept many deadly secrets to themselves.

Over the next two days Britt drove up to Rourke's and got her sister-in-law to type up the deposition which she had written and Rourke had showed her how to compose the introductory page in the legally binding terms of a sworn statement. Then it was made out in duplicate. She signed it and her brother witnessed it.

"Should I have it notarized?" Britt asked him.

"Not necessary." Rourke shook his head. "It's witnessed and if push comes to shove, Claire will corroborate it and so will Mr. Renaud from next door. He's been here this evening. Neither are blood related."

"I think you've done quite enough." Mary, who was in visiting with Nora and the children, commented. "It's a terrible thing, but I don't know why you must get in the middle of everything."

Rourke turned to her. "Because it's the right and only thing to do, Mother... and you'd do exactly the same. So would Dad. We didn't get to be the way we are from nothing." Then he turned back to his sister. "But, that's it, Britt. Now you must give this Gagnon fellow time to do his job. And it's going to take time. Usually a first offence will just go on his record. It'll be sealed and the Canadian Medical Association usually only acts on a persistent pattern--or something like that. At least, that's what Gabe Nugent tells me. You know he's the only doctor I have for a client. The rest had to go elsewhere. I don't want them. But Gabe's all right. So . . . when do you leave?"

"I work Wednesday evening through to Sunday evening. The plane leaves at 11:00 a.m. on Monday." She smiled briefly. "I've already notified the school. They weren't too pleased but . . ."

"Don't tell me your persona non grata already?" Rourke laughed.

"Not really. The superintendent was understanding. He just dumped the problem of a replacement in the principal's lap. How would you feel?"

"Like strangling you. But, I'll be down to take you to the airport and Nora too. She'll bring your car back here."

"Yeah, I could sure use it." Nora sounded tired.

"I'll sign over the registration to you, Nora, and then you can have it insured in your name."

"Good. And I'll keep up the payments. Never a fear." Britt shrugged. "No worries . . . come here, Ruth."

The small child was racing about and her aunt caught her. "Are you going to come and visit me?"

"She might," Mary put in. "Aaron's in school, but I may well take this one with me. I was talking to Nora about it." At Britt's inquiring look, her mother added, "I hope you're settled by October twenty-seventh. That's when I've booked a flight. I'm coming for just over two weeks. And then, of course, you'll return here for Christmas."

"Yes, I've made the arrangements." Britt looked down and stared fixedly at Ruth's small hand on her arm. "You have to book early during the holiday season."

Her voice was barely audible. It was so difficult to contain the unexpected and unfocused sadness she felt, but when she looked up, her expression showed nothing.

On Wednesday, Britt went into the Director's office and handed a large brown sealed envelope to the secretary. It was addressed specifically to Mr. Rejean Gagnon and marked personal and confidential. At the nursing office she left a similar envelope destined solely for Lucy Maxwell. She could do with it what she liked. Once down in E.R. she assumed a "business as usual" attitude. The day staff was about to start giving report, and Remi and Pierre were standing over near the patient list on the wall. The unit secretary was at the counter and Dr. Stuart Caplan was at his desk on the far side facing the wall. He was writing furiously.

"So, how's everything?" Britt asked casually as she walked by the secretary.

Gina Manetti looked up. "All hell's been breaking loose around here these last few days. Everyone's been through here. I don't know what's going on." She had dropped her voice and leaned toward Erikson. Now she was thumbing back toward Stuart Caplan. "And he's been in one hell of a foul mood. Won't talk to anyone . . . only growls, and he's been acting like a real jerk."

"Maybe it's not an act, Gina."

"I know you always had your reservations, but I thought he was okay. Now, I don't know. The atmosphere around here is charged and no one's saying anything." She threw out her hands. "Something's going on, but I don't know what. Nobody knows."

"I'd better get over to report." Britt looked at the woman's tense face. She liked Gina. "You're here until five. I'll see you later."

"Yeah, maybe we could go in back and have a cigarette. It's quiet and I could sure use one."

"You're on. . . and relax, Gina. Whatever's going on can't have anything to do with you."

David came on at six, and it seemed that he was taking things much more coolly . . . and in his stride as it were. But then Tierney had always been the more deceptive one. He looked kind, even compassionate. Few could have guessed the extent of his clumsiness and the ever diminishing capacity of his concern for others.

It wasn't until much later in the evening that Britt overheard him talking to one of his cronies, saying that it really didn't matter so very much to him that he practice in this city. After all, there were other places in the world besides Montreal. He had a medical license for Switzerland as well . . . So, he's been questioned, Britt thought, and continued writing. She smiled. Probably nothing too cataclysmic would happen this time. No, not this time. It would be sealed and kept on his file. Leverage against future misconduct. But he'd be watched under scrutiny for a time, anyway, and he'd hate that. Yes, the artful dealer in health and illness would loathe and resent the silent threat.

On the Sunday morning before her last shift at the Osler Memorial, Edward came round to take her out to brunch. "You didn't leave an evening open," he accused her, trying to smile and failing. "This was the best I could do."

"It's fine," Britt assured him, "and there were other evenings over the past two months. You've a heavy schedule."

"So do you and don't deny it." He put a hand on her shoulder as they were leaving the apartment building. Once in the car they didn't speak again until they were seated across from one another in a cheerful, widely glassed-in restaurant on Sherbrooke Street. Autumn was splashing its colors everywhere as the leaves were just starting to turn.

"This is nice." Britt looked around. She glanced out at the beginnings of a seasonal orchestration of colors that brought with it a throbbing familiarity and sense of belonging. This is my home . . . my home too, she thought and something twisted deep inside her.

"What are you frowning about?" Edward had picked up the menu and was looking at her over the top of it. She could only see his eyes.

"Frowning? Was I?" Britt shrugged. "Just habit."

"You should break it. Even good-looking women can't afford to frown."

"Pity. When a man frowns occasionally a woman has hopes he might be intelligent."

"And she's usually disappointed, I suppose?"

"Not always."

"Do you think I'm intelligent?"

"Yes."

"And you like intelligent men, but you don't like me well enough to hang around?"

"Edward . . ." She stopped abruptly. The waiter was there with their coffee. When he left she resumed. "That's not the problem and you know it."

"Well, what am I supposed to think? You're leaving just like that." He lifted his shoulders and spread his hands in a gesture of dismissal.

"No. I never start a relationship or end one . . . just like that, as you put it. I thought you were separated, officially, I mean. Actually divorced, but you're not and despite all your talk you haven't made one decisive move in that direction."

"But it's over! I keep telling you . . ."

"It's not over. You have a wife. You belong to someone else."

"It doesn't mean anything, Britt."

"So you've told me over and over again, but it does mean something. Whether you're happy or not isn't the issue. You've done nothing about your discontent."

"Well, there is my daughter," Edward wavered. "I need time."

"Your daughter is a teenager, well able to understand things for what they are. Either your wife has some hold over you, or you are terribly uncertain and confused about how you feel about me."

"I love you."

She leaned forward and lowered her voice into a cold undertone that was just audible. "Love? Well, possibly you do. But it's a meager sort of love, wouldn't you say? No depth. Just yourself and your needs forefront always. If there were some clear dilemma I'd understand. Or even if you weren't married and wanted to remain that way, it wouldn't be so bad, but you're well and truly married."

Edward looked at her and pulled in his lower lip. "My marriage had been hell from the beginning. There was never a reason to go after a divorce before. There is now. Trust me." He put his hand over hers. "We'll be together. I promise you that."

"I'm afraid my trust is at a very low ebb, Edward. Anyway, I'm leaving tomorrow, so . . ."

"Can I see you tonight after work?"

"No. I'm sorry."

"It's been over two months, Britt."

"I know. It surprises me it got started at all. Maybe I didn't want to hear the full truth and only heard what I wanted to hear. That must be it. You've told me there's been no deception."

"There hasn't been. Maybe you heard as you did because you do love me."

"Maybe, but like everything else, it dies, without foundation." She smiled suddenly and the communicating note was one of irony rather than joy. "A professor I had at college used to tell us, "Before you do anything or argue any point, define your premise. I listened, but didn't practice it very well. That's how we ended up playing different games."

"This isn't a game."

"Sure it is. If I took it as anything else I'd be angry and disappointed."

"How do you feel?"

"Feel? Odd question coming from you. I don't know. Weary, I suppose. Yes, just a little weary. Now, can we drop all this and have lunch?"

"Yes." Edward signaled the waiter and they ordered lunch.

"And could we have more coffee please?"

When he was gone Edward gave her an odd look. She was actually leaving and all because . . . but then he thought of his wife. He'd find a way, he told himself. He knew full well that under different circumstances Britt wouldn't be going anywhere at all. Contract or no contract. She'd stay here and marry him. And that's how it would be. Unconsciously he was nodding to himself, and watching him, Britt found it a rather dull ending to what she initially thought an exciting love affair with a future. Now it meant nothing at all. Just like Roddy, a small voice jeered at her. Great expectations and then a deep empty hole. Unexpected. She should be feeling something, but it was like walking on a long, twisting road and the scenery remained the same. In her mind it wasn't autumn anymore with its hard bright morning light softening by degrees until it was a slanting golden illumination preceding twilight. It was a sunless December day, heavy with monotonous drizzle, spiritless and dull.

-Twenty-

The good-byes were said. That was the most difficult part. Leaving was always hard. Odd that it had never become easier through the years. So many departures and the road always looping back to its point of origin. The city built around a mountain. It defeated understanding.

Now everyone in the family was once again over the Quebec border. It had become a pattern and the mark of many an Anglo-Montrealer. Her life, in particular, was a patchwork quilt of comings and goings. This time she remembered the fixed expression in her mother's eyes. Had the woman somehow divined how fragile she was under the silent indifference or the cold anger that sometimes gripped her. She hoped not.

Mary Erikson was not always easy to know either, but she was lonely. Britt could feel it. A palpable essence with a separate heartbeat all its own. It brought to mind the pounding rhythm of waves on a long night's empty shores. When she had moved toward her mother to kiss her good-bye, Mary had suddenly hugged her, and to break the tension, they had both laughed. Laughter was a healing balm that took the sting out of their separate inner rings of fire. Inside the rings, black pits housed loneliness, fear, and pain . . . and a consummate need to understand. But there had been laughter.

As the plane sped forward and westward to her new destination, Britt's mind hurled itself into the past. It swept aside images of Edward and Roddy. It halted momentarily at the promise that her trip to Nepal had held, and later the hollow darkness that followed only six months earlier. Then her thoughts stumbled on her father's death with a flashing vividness that made the persistent sense of loss recede into a safer place to be. Almost a refuge.

But that stark image faded too, and her mind came to rest at an episode that happened close to the end of her childhood. Who was it said the past is prologue? If people could know what lay in wait for them it would be hard to know if they'd let a day, any day just slip from their grasp. It didn't matter how bad things were. They often had a way of getting worse. Or so it seemed. Then again, maybe one just got older, wearier. And things happened to a person, altering perspective. The prospect of that occurring was a disquieting thought. For the time being, anyhow, the excitement had gone out of new ventures. Certainly the great lassitude she felt wouldn't last. It couldn't. Her vitality would return. Once teaching and working again with fresh young minds, things would be different. She'd feel again the future taking shape and, against all odds, finer human beings with bright new visions would emerge. Independent thinkers with brave and challenging ideas. The human spirit had curious ways of acquiring immunity.

"We the people" had undoubtedly been predicated on "I the individual," and that truth had prevailed through the convulsions of war, mass psychoses, and every form of human deception, oppression and entrapment.

For the moment, however, she felt drained. The stewardess came around with drinks and she waved her away, but the young man beside her ordered one and avidly. His eyes twinkled merrily as he grinned at her. He was a pleasant travelling companion and chatted easily, but after a while Britt excused herself and turned away, putting her head back against the high back seat and closing her eyes.

Now what had she been thinking of? Yes, that time so long ago. Almost twenty-five years, but it seemed much longer as if it belonged to another lifetime. She was fourteen.

It comes to everyone, she supposed. Looking back they find separate times rising from a sea of years, like landmarks--lighthouses that point the way to growing up and it can be found in the person the child has become.

Tense evenings in the Erikson home were rare, but they carried a heavy impact for just that reason. Such times had a pattern too. A silence devoid of calm or harmony. Nothing was said and questions had no verbal vehicle. The younger two, Gregory and Nora were already in bed and Rourke was out. So was her father. That was the problem. Hugh Erikson so rarely went out with friends or by himself to have a few drinks after work. He usually worked two or three jobs so there was little time for misadventures. But there were the occasional lapses and Mary's reaction was predictable. She was furious. Hugh simply couldn't drink, and he knew it. More to the point, even a little alcohol affected his coordination. He might well have an accident. That's why he usually returned stone sober. That probably accounted for the delay this night and the lateness of the hour.

It was the expression on her mother's face, a study in worry and anger, that put the finishing touches on the features of turbulence that twisted Britt's mind into knots and hardened her heart. She hated that feeling and was so enraged with her father that the whole episode grew out of proportion. It would take her years to figure out that only a very deep love could cause such confusion and release such anger.

Finally she went off to bed and lay awake thinking, listening. Rourke came in and went to his room. It was late. In the next room she heard her mother pacing up and down. She could almost envision the woman's thoughts. She'd be fuming and listening anxiously for every car that went by. But it was a country road and few people were out at this hour. Sleep wouldn't come and after tossing and turning in bed for what seemed a long time, Britt heard a car turn into the driveway. The motor died and a door slammed. Her mother was standing in the parlor when he came in, quite sober by now.

"Mary," he began.

"Don't give me any of your god-damned excuses." Mary's voice was low, but vehement in the quiet night.

She could hear them quite distinctly. He moved off to the bedroom and started to undress. Mary followed him, snatched up her pillow and a blanket and headed back into the living room. At times like this even the faintest smell of liquor made her sick. It brought back to her, like a recurring nightmare, a whole lifetime of trying to make people stop hurting themselves and hurting her. At times she felt she was being unreasonable, one thought in her mind rebelling against the tide of her emotion. Her Hugh was a fine, solid man, and she'd have no other. Still she wrenched it back and the anger was on her again. Her resolution was firm. No one was going to put her through all that again. First there had been her own father, and her mother had been little help, finally succumbing herself and joining him. Then there had been her brother. So promising a future and look at him now. Well, no more of it. She would have no more of it.

All the same, now she could rest. Still angry, but no longer anxious, she would soon sleep. It seems a blind rage premised on fear and love is soon starved without access to worry, and it dissipates like the early morning dew and the day comes up fine and clear. But how does a child know? A child always knows. Children sense more than any adult would care to imagine. But they seldom understand, and that can make a dangerous difference.

Naturally by the end of the next day it had all blown over. Their home life had always been a happy one except for these brief, but stormy interludes. Living resumed where it had left off. Her mother might never be able to accept things passively. On the other hand, she was a strong, resilient woman. She had, as her father would put it, "come around" and her parents were again as close as they had always been separate and different in natures. And still very much in love.

However in Britt's perception of things, something had gone very wrong. She was still angry with her father and yet felt stupidly unable or unwilling to identify the troublesome feeling for what it was. Instead she felt guilty and that annoyed and frightened her. She loved her mother, but her father had always been the sun in her life. Now that was gone like a light going out and there was no way to escape the dusk to darkness progression. It was inexorable. There was a wall of silence between them that hurt and alarmed Hugh and all but smothered Britt. Still, she wouldn't break it.

Mary noticed it, but refrained from interfering. Whatever it was, they'd work it out. Britt was quiet and somewhat of a dreamer. But she could be stubborn. Besides, although Hugh never said or did anything to indicate it, Mary suspected that of their four children, she was his favorite or rather, the one he felt was more like himself. But Hugh's mother Marlo Erikson was alive at the time. She lived in a small cottage not far from their home. Marlo enjoyed her old age. She claimed it gave her perspective. What she called "a front row seat" and little escaped the keenly observant old lady. She told everyone one of her few regrets was that she hadn't found it earlier. Britt could talk to her without ever really having to tell her anything. She always seemed to know everything anyway.

It was late summer again and it had started to rain. The drops thwacked against the leaves and a fine rustling sounded as they fell to the earth. Her grandmother tugged her thoughts away from the spell of the evening and her eyes bore through her granddaughter. She had a rather disconcerting, direct stare. Everyone said so. There was a long silence before she tossed her head impatiently and demanded, "What's the matter with you, Britt?"

"Nothing. Why?"

"Rubbish. You're not very happy these days, are you?" And when the girl didn't answer she gabbled on. "Of course, you're not . . . can't fool me. Moping about and what's all this new interest in the past? Reading mythologies, are you?"

"I just wanted to understand things better."

"And do you?"

"No, I don't."

"Of course not. Maybe you're expecting too much."

"Maybe we're all expecting too much." Britt frowned and the old woman snorted triumphantly.

"Ah, Ah! Leave it to a child to stumble on a paradox. Do you like riddles, Britt? The Chinese philosopher Chuang Tse liked them, and I like Chuang Tse. Here's a thought from his essay on relativity. "Those who dream of the banquet wake to lamentation and sorrow. Those who dream of lamentation and sorrow wake to join the hunt. Understand that?"

"No." Britt shook her head.

"Neither do I," Marlo smiled and there was a softer look in her eyes. "No one else does either. But it's intriguing, isn't it?"

"Yes." The girl thought about it. "Say it again."

The old woman repeated it and probed deeper. "Now getting back to what you were saying. What's wrong with great expectations?"

Britt shrugged. "Like your friend Chuang Tse says--they make people unhappy. Maybe the disappointment makes them drink."

"What? Since when does someone need a reason for drinking? Never did as far as I know." She was shaking her head vigorously. Nonsense. Explain what you mean."

"Well, people plan their lives with hopes and dreams. Right? Then they become embittered or downhearted when they think they've failed. So they either find new fantasies or drink to make it easier to forget. Problem is they end up hurting people. So where's the justice in that . . . Besides, it's selfish."

It was the longest explanation Britt could ever remember making up to that point, and Marlo sat back to consider it. Then she began slowly: "Well, it might be foolish. Maybe even selfish to go chasing after some damned illusive notion that you're dead certain spells success for you and drinking to drown your sorrows is for fools . . . but not to dream? Living without a dream isn't living. It's a gray, dull existence. That's what I think . . . And Chuang Tse would agree.

I'm sure of it."

"But it is safer," Britt insisted.

"Yes safer, but so drab! No color at all. And," she added emphatically, "without character. One giant step backward for civilization. We can't live without hope, my dear, and hope is built on dreams. Remember that."

"I'll remember. But believing it is something else."

"Well, never mind, remembering's enough for now. So just what are you reading?"

"Oh, about old myths and legends."

"Irish myths . . .? Of course." The old woman laughed.

"Of course . . . like the ones you used to tell us about. And Norse myths too."

"And now you don't believe them?" Marlo eyed her speculatively and sniffed. "You're not on your way to becoming boorish, are you? You know, they put blinkers on horses so they'll never travel 'the road not taken.' Men put up fences in their minds. Silly asses."

Marlo could make just about anything she said sound humorous. Britt wanted to laugh, but didn't. Marlo noticed that too and smacked her lips. "Young people take themselves so seriously."

"No, the problem is--I do believe them. Something in me wants to believe them. Reading them is like magic." And then the girl was moving her head from side to side.

"But there's something wrong in that."

Marlo sighed. "Why must it be wrong?"

"Because the response is real. And so I figure the source of it has truth. It's an actual thing. But it becomes lost in the world . . . and it's dangerous."

"Ah . . . the metamorphosis." Marlo muttered almost inaudibly and her granddaughter frowned, not understanding. "But why dangerous?"

"Because it calls a person to be what he can never become. It's beyond our grasp."

"Oh, I see. I do see. It calls him to see places that he can never go to. To have visions of what is forever lost to him. And then comes the breaking away into the confines of reality. But reality's a mystery too, dear. The greatest mystery of all." She got up and, turning away from the girl, went to the window. She placed her fingertips against the pane and stared out into the black night. Britt loved her more at that moment than at any time she could remember. It was her most vivid memory of the old woman. "The land of far off places." She spoke softly with her back still turned. "The Irish call it Tier Na Nog. A man has a soul, Britt, and it must have some kind of life too . . . Trouble is, people tend to replace the dream with cheap illusion. They are not the true dreamers. They hope to blunt the sharp edges of reality. They can't seem to recognize how reality must become its vehicle. And that failure to see brings about what's troubling you." She turned back to the girl. "I'd hate to think you denied your imagination because you were afraid your dreams would break you."

"But they do break some people, don't they?" It was a challenge and yet Britt wanted her to deny it.

"They do." Marlo nodded. "Dreams and illusions . . . One leads to spiritual life and the other to a distortion of reality and a hatred of life. People often confuse them and get off on the wrong track by letting their dreams rule their lives. Can you figure that out? I'm seventy-six and it's taken me a lifetime. Not to figure it out, but to find the balance. And why? Because our inner voice becomes lost or buried in the clamor of everyday living. The race to get ahead of it. So even when we're quiet, our minds never stop to listen and even if we did, we'd find that we've forgotten the language of this other world." The rain had stopped. It suddenly seemed too quiet in the room.

Britt stared at her. "I've never heard you talk like that."

"No, I seldom bother. But you know, lately . . . sometimes I'm homesick, and it's a heart sickness for more than just going home in the usual sense. Maybe the whole of living is nostalgia. Do you understand?"

"Not all, but some." Britt lied, but couldn't deny her gut reaction as if something said or sensed had touched on a nerve running through the center of her being.

"Good." Marlo's mood changed. "That's a beginning. The rest will come. Now go home. I'm tired . . . and remember, the world needs true dreamers . . . and no one's perfect, dear. I think you understand what I'm saying."

The door closed behind her and looking back at the cottage as she hurried away, Britt saw the lights still dimly glowing. All the way home she resolved to break the silence. Yes, she understood. There were lights in many of the dwellings along the route and Britt felt close to something she couldn't define. She had seen it in Marlo's eyes. The shadow of a forgotten pain. But there were no undercurrents of anger, or tears, or raw emotions. Now everything there was of the earth became linked to the soft lights shining in the windows at spaced intervals. That was the secret link and that was a true dream. Its birth and unending renewal was reflected in Marlo's eyes. The sadness and the ecstasy. Through the years she would again and again come to know and nearly understand the light and the dark bonding humanity in the forms of human suffering, human achievement, human strength, and human weakness. There was a chill in the air now. Early September was whimsical like a wanton woman. She quickened her footsteps. Her mother was waiting up for her.

"You were a long time, Britt. You shouldn't be keeping your grandmother up so late." When the girl didn't answer, she continued. "I've been waiting up for you. Everyone else is in bed."

"That's where I'm going too."

Her daughter had started from the room when Mary stood up and caught her arm. "No, don't. Not yet. Come into the kitchen. I'll make some tea." There was no way around it. Her mother had a way of getting to the heart of a matter you had hoped to avoid. So they sat at the kitchen table where all important conversations took place. Mary looked disturbed and the girl was uneasy, watching her. "Listen, Britt." Her mother leaned toward her. "No one has the right to hurt other people. Sometimes in anger we say things we don't mean. Sometimes we even say things we do mean and regret later on. But to carefully plan out a revenge . . ."

She had a good idea of what her mother was alluding to, but would never admit it. "I don't know what you're talking about."

"Oh yes, you do!" Mary was becoming exasperated with her, but her voice remained a hoarse whisper. "Your father's been very hurt these past weeks. You're upsetting him. He doesn't understand."

"Neither do I." Britt stubbornly denied it, and her mother got up and moved closer to her. "You know, sometimes my children are strangers to me and that's frightening. You know how. You haven't talked to him in over two weeks. You walk away when he comes in the room. You're distant."

"That's not true. I answer him." But it was true and now her mother was annoyed. Her temper was never far from the surface.

"There's a difference between talking to someone and just answering them! You know what I'm talking about. Don't pretend that you don't!"

And this was all very true. It was a comfortable cocoon she had spun for herself and her resolve to break free of it was all well and good, but it would be difficult to find a way out of this maze she'd got herself into. And her mother was trying to pull her out of it in her own inimitable straightforward fashion.

"You know, you worry me." She was going on, "you and your father. All of you. Some families fight and get over it. But not all of them. With some people there's no relenting. Do a wrong thing to them once and you've had it. They break up and grow apart. Not one of them is willing to make the first step. Is that what you want? Is it really?"

"No."

"Well, that's what's going to happen unless this stops now. And you will have lost a lot." Mary added quietly. "Your family is important. And your father loves you. You know that. You've no cause . . ."

"No cause?" Britt's head reared up and she stared at her mother. "How can you say that?"

"What? How can I what?" The older woman stared back at her, puzzled and worried. "What?"

"Nothing . . . nothing."

"Well, go to bed." Mary sighed. Once in bed, Britt wondered if she'd ever understand her mother, or anyone for that matter, even herself. Finally she felt the welcoming descent of sleep while resolving to break the silence with her father in the morning.

Saturday morning everyone was up early. The night had left in its wake the half-light of a new day still struggling in its grip. Hugh was making breakfast, a weekend routine for him. He chatted with his younger daughter.

"Listen to me, Nora," he was saying. "Football isn't necessarily just for boys. Your sister might be too sophisticated for that kind of stuff now. But she used to play."

"Don't encourage her, Hugh," Mary interrupted. "She's too much of a tomboy as it is... And she's accident prone."

They sat down to eat. Hugh smiled tentatively over at his elder daughter and Britt was wondering how to begin and break down the wall and respond when the telephone rang.

"It's for you, dear." Mary held the receiver and handed it to Hugh. " It's the hospital."

She remained standing there and they exchanged looks.

"Something must be wrong."

Rourke started up from the table. "Who is it?"

Mary signaled him to sit down. "We don't know yet."

Their father came back into the room. His face looked gray.

"What is it, Hugh?"

"It's my mother. She died this morning."

"Died!" Gregory gasped and the others stared and were silent.

"But she was all right yesterday."

Hugh turned to him. "It was a heart attack. Very sudden," he said quietly and abruptly left the room. Mary followed him.

They were all stunned and, as with every passing, even of an old one, it took some time before the reality set in. The family gathered: aunts, uncles, cousins. And friends, some close, others they'd known and hadn't seen in years. Rourke was quiet, but polite. A great help to his parents. But Britt noticed him slip away from the crowd after a while and go off by himself.

It wasn't until late that night when she was able to get away. She left the house, closing the door softly behind her and started to run. She ran until her body couldn't carry her further. Out of breath and panting, she slowed her pace and started to walk in the direction of Marlo's cottage. There was a pain in her heart, a mounting constriction in her throat and her chest that made breathing difficult. And finally the tears came, hot and stinging in their release. She started to sob and shuddered with the impact.

The small house had an abandoned air, shrouded in the darkness except for one light which burnt in the front room window. She sensed rather than knew who would be inside and then she saw him. Wood crackled in the fireplace, and he stood staring into the flames. After a time he looked up and around the room. That was when he spotted the ship. It was a handsome, gracefully fashioned vessel. The replica of an old sailing craft. Marlo loved ships, and she prized this perfect reproduction. She also respected the sea.

Britt sat down to wait. It was some time later before her father emerged from the cottage. He carried the ship with him. Shadows obscured his features, and she listened as he drew near.

"Dad?" She called out and he halted, turning toward the sound of her voice.

"What are you doing here, Britt?" He put an arm around her shoulders and clutched the ship with his free arm. Then he held it toward her. "Here. For you. Would you like to have it?"

"It's Marlo's ship," she whispered and her father nodded.

"She was very fond of it. I thought you might want to have it."

"I would, but . . ."

He placed the vessel in her hands and Britt said nothing for a long time. Finally she turned to look up at him.

"Death is very strange, isn't it? Do you think she was scared?"

Hugh thought for a few moments then shook his head. "No, I don't think so. Not my mother."

"I can't say how I feel. Not really."

"Neither can I," Hugh confided and looked down into his daughter's eyes. He was a very perceptive man. "You're very far away. Where are you?"

"Very far away . . . You know, there's an old legend the Claddagh fishermen have off the coast of Galway. Do you know it?" When her father shook his head trying to remember all the tales his mother told, Britt went on.

"Long time ago, when Ireland had kings and chieftains, they would bury them by putting them out to sea in a curragh. The boat was then set on fire, and it was said that their spirits were lifted out of the flames and took the form of swans. Black swans are really the spirits of their dead kings."

Her father's eyes fastened on hers. "Am I hearing you correctly, Britt?" Then he smiled in the darkness.

"Sometimes I can almost believe in old legends. Come on. The river isn't far. We can walk to it."

He looked down at the small craft and ran his fingers across its bow. "This little item won't be missed. Besides, I gave it to her."

There was no one at the river's edge when they got there. It was almost midnight. A brisk wind ruffled the water and tiny whitecaps raced to the shoreline and disappeared. Her father struck a match, and she cupped her hands over it to protect it from being extinguished. They used it to light an old cardboard identification card and placed it in the miniature ship's cabin, away from the wind. The sails were up and they set it into the prevailing wind. The vessel was caught in its grip and lurched forward away from the shore. The surrounding water reflected light from its burning insides.

"Well, it's done," Hugh said. "I'm going to miss her."

"So am I," Britt murmured and leaned against him. He put his arm around her and they both stared out across the water.

The ship rose on a wave, a burning mass of timber still intact and then nosed down. It did not come up again. A smoky haze hung over the spot where it went down. He took her hands in his.

"Do you ever wonder, Britt, about all the loves and wishes and dreams that die when a person dies?"

"But they're not dead, are they Dad?"

"No," he said softly in the night air. "They are free."

The crackling of the plane's intercom system jolted her out of her reverie.

The captain's voice brought her fully alert. They were about to begin their descent into Calgary's international airport. Some would deplane and the others remain aboard for the short flight up to Edmonton. The sign came on to fasten seat belts and people all through the cabin moved restlessly; eager to be out of their cramped spaces and away to their homes or new destinations. And then the lights flicked off throughout the cabin and the voice over the intercom faded. Attendants moved hurriedly up and down the aisles as people all around looked about anxiously in wonder, and then some of their eyes started to roll wildly in naked fear. Passengers twisted frantically as the plane started to plunge, losing altitude rapidly. Like a giant hand reaching out of the clouds and shaking it, the aircraft rocked and spun violently, jarring and battering the people in their seats. And then the screaming and shouting issued from every quarter.

Something had gone wrong, but even after a lengthy investigation, the reasons were vague. The pilot was being directed in from airport control and there had been some confusion. Another plane, having just taken off, was in his line of descent. He dodged it by diving deeper, too quickly. The plane went into a spin and was hurled uncontrollably downward. In a last ditch effort, the pilot tried to right the dangerously failing craft, and it crashed with a deadening thud into a wide open prairie meadow within the boundaries of the airport. Its tail end burst into flames.

Miraculously, of its two hundred and thirty-four passengers and crew, all but seven survived. Some were seriously injured. Still they lived.

Britt's last lucid thought was concise and contained: "I understand. Now I understand . . . it was never meant to be at all." She felt a strange preternatural sort of calm, and she was bathed in warmth. Then someone had taken her hand and gripped it. It was a familiar hand. Her father's. And he was standing right beside her as he always had whether she was home or far away. There was no fear or anguish. Only a perfect peace. It was all over. Britt was among the seven who didn't make it. They flew her body back to be buried in Montreal.

At the grave site, curiously, it was Nora who quoted loosely from her sister's favorite author. They were not the exact words of Thomas Wolfe, but her own adaptation.

". . . A stone, a leaf, an unfound door; of a stone, a leaf, a door. And all the forgotten faces . . ."

The passage continued in a faltering cadence until the last phrase:

". . . lost and by the wind grieved, ghost, come back again."

Rourke had taken his mother's arm and now he was leading her away. The unthinkable had happened and life went on. Mary was devastated, but in her mind, both her husband and daughter had taken on new life forms. She was not alone anymore. She'd never really be alone again. Then she caught sight of Ruth and remembered how Britt had loved the little girl. She was only three and didn't really understand what had happened, but the tears were streaming down her face. On an impulse she reached for the child's hand as she stumbled along beside her mother. Ruth looked up at her and for the first time Mary saw in the child's face what her daughter must have always seen. Yes, she thought, lost and by the wind grieved, ghost, come back to me.

A Sleigh Ride in July

by
Margaret Tedford

Available at your local bookstore or use this page to order.

--1-931633-44-4- A Sleigh Ride in July - $16.50 U.S
Send to: Trident Media Inc.
             801 N. Pitt Street #123
             Alexandria, VA 22314
Toll Free # 1-877-874-6334
Please send me the items I have checked above. I am enclosing
$_____(please add #3.50 per book to cover postage and handling).
Send check, money order, or credit card:

Card #_____ Exp. date _____

Mr./Mrs./Ms._____
Address_____
City/State_____Zip_____

Please allow four to six weeks for delivery.
Prices and availability subject to change without notice.

Printed in the United States
3817